Hot Scheming Mess

Madison Cruz Mystery 1

Lucy Carol

Dedication

To my favorite superhero Irrational Man for your lavish and irrational love. You can leave the cape on.

A humorous mystery laced with romantic comedy!

Chapter One

F OR DESPERATE PEOPLE, a job sometimes can step
up and say "Hello. I'm a bad idea. Do you want
to play with me?" And since Madison Cruz was
desperate, her answer was, "My mother warned me
about ideas like you. But she was just messing with my
head. So yeah. Let's play."

Madison knew that even bad ideas had their merits
if you looked for them. But bad ideas also had
consequences. She covered her face with her hands,
peeking between her fingers. Watching the wrestlers
rehearse, she finally realized what she'd stepped into.

"I'm about to get my ass kicked, aren't I?"

"Don't look at me," said Spenser, "I already told you
this wasn't smart."

They sat at a beat-up old cocktail table in a bar
called Sound Beating, watching the rehearsal for Bruise
Boys, a wrestling show played for laughs. The eager
young men were fun local guys who loved to play rough
with a wink at safety. Their local flavor was part of the

charm, but right now the prospect of being tossed around was not charming Madison.

She lifted her shiny dark hair, fanning the back of her neck with a happy hour menu. The August heat wasn't helping.

"I disagree," said ExBoy, sitting at her left, "Why would anyone want to kick such a fine ass?" He grabbed her backside with a firm squeeze. "High quality."

She slapped his hand away with a loud smack, forcing herself to pay attention to the rehearsal in front of them. But her body responded to his touch, and while she tried to hide that fact, she suspected he knew damn well his effect on her.

Xander Lucious Boyd, nicknamed ExBoy, had the kind of good looks that she took as a warning. His golden hair, blue eyes, and dark honey lashes made her suspect there was Scandinavian blood at work here. Other than stolen kisses, they hadn't yet sealed the deal.

Another wrestler got slammed into the floor, pretending grave injury right on cue.

Madison looked around for the waitress, eager for their drinks to arrive. She'd brought empty beer cans to use as props in the show and had them set out on the table. But it was real drinks with real ice that she waited for.

She'd ordered rum and Cokes, happy to avoid the caustic whiskey Sound Beating had a reputation for.

Maybe they were trying to match their whiskey to their dilapidated décor. Tattered posters on the wall with loose staples sticking out advertised shows that were already over, or bands that had long ago broken up or joined society in nine-to-five jobs somewhere. Pock marks on the walls were big enough to conjure up questions of how they got there, some with old gum shoved inside.

She wrenched her attention back to the rehearsal.

"Okay, I'll rephrase the question. Am I about to get my *fine* ass kicked?"

"Really, Madison," began Spenser, "I wish you hadn't accepted this gig. It makes me nervous." Spenser pushed her blond hair away from her face as she searched in the camera bag in her lap. With an exasperated sigh, she pulled the bag up on the table, looking deeper inside.

"That makes two of us, but I need the rest of my rent." Madison gently knocked her head into Spenser's, peering into the camera bag with her. "And if you happen to find any groceries in there I'd be happy to take them off your hands."

Spenser pulled out her camera, looking through the viewfinder. "When have you not needed groceries?"

"Six years ago."

"High school."

"Pretty much. I can't believe groceries still feel like a luxury. I need higher paying gigs."

"Or a blindfold and a cigarette," said Spenser, giggling. "Isn't that what they give a condemned man in front of the firing squad?"

"But I don't smoke."

"And you're not a man."

"I like that about her," said ExBoy. Damn, the way he gazed in her eyes was too distracting. She caught herself looking at him longer than she should and jerked her face back in the direction of the stage, wondering if her cheeks were pink.

"How do you do that?" he asked.

"Do what?"

"You look at me like your eyes are light green jewels on display."

She blinked. "You love to rattle me, don't you?"

He smiled. "I was just—"

"I need to pay attention to this rehearsal so I don't get killed."

"What are you afraid of?" he said. "They asked you to throw empty beer cans, and a chair."

"They also asked me to improv with them. They said I would be safe," said Madison, "but look at them!"

This kick-ass wrestling show, fueled by soap opera back stories, was unlike anything Madison had ever been involved with. Each guy invented a character for himself complete with stage names such as Dewey Decimator, Sparkle Pecs, Dizorder Lee, and of course Spenser's boyfriend, Atomic Waist.

ExBoy's enthusiasm was shameless as he watched the guys throw punches and slam each other onto the floor. He smirked and nodded, leaning forward to rest his stubbled chin on his fist.

"Don't they seem a little carried away to you?" asked Madison.

A waitress with rainbow hair arrived with a tray of rum and Cokes. Madison pulled her big black tote bag out from under the table to get her purse.

"Don't worry," ExBoy said. "They know what they're doing."

That's when Sparkle Pecs crashed down onto their table like an explosion.

Madison and Exboy sprang from their seats, but Spenser had her face behind her camera and didn't see it coming. ExBoy's wooden chair hit the floor a split second before Madison's chair bounced away. Her purse rocketed across the room. Spenser's whole body jerked to the crashing sound, and she nearly dropped her camera. Nearby chairs mutated into raucous dominos while the empty beer cans popped upward to differing heights before falling to the floor, a hollow metallic chorus in an out-of-sync rhythm.

The table lurched, dumping Sparkle Pecs into Spenser's lap.

The waitress, looking quite bored, still stood there with her tray of drinks, not a drop spilled. Her hands occupied, she blew a stream of air upward to chase a rainbow strand of hair, hot pink, out of her eyes.

"Sparky, you idiot!" Spenser shoved Sparkle Pecs off her lap onto the floor. He sat up rubbing his head but wearing a smug smile. His long, light brown hair was cut like a grown-out mohawk that he didn't bother to gel up anymore, letting it hang limp to one side.

Daniel bounded across the stage over to the chaos, his jeans and baggy t-shirt disguising his physique. One last chair fell over and a can rolled away as Spenser yelled, "Daniel! So help me, if he's broken any of my gear—!"

With medium olive toned skin, Daniel, aka Atomic Waist, had thick Italian hair growing back so fast he already had a shadow on his scalp after having shaved his head that afternoon. He didn't have leading-man good looks, but at six feet six inches tall, with an amazing build, he was hands-down the muscular beefcake of the show.

He grabbed Sparkle Pecs, saying, "That's my woman, moron," as he pulled him up, easily tossing him back onto the stage.

ExBoy nodded his approval. "And it's only rehearsal." Looking over at Madison he said, "I can't believe you get to be in the show."

"Neither can I," she moaned.

Sparky called out, "Sorry, Spenser. But you have to admit, the audience is going to love that move."

"Pick some other table," Daniel growled.

Getting down on the floor, Madison and ExBoy crawled around looking for scattered pieces of Spenser's gear. They found a carrying case and snatched up a few spare camera batteries.

"What's the matter?" ExBoy asked.

"Just fighting my own stereotype is all." Madison lowered her voice, reaching for a small USB cable. "I'm a girly-girl who's scared of all this stuff."

"But you're not in the wrestling part," he smiled.

"Look what just happened with that table. I could get hurt in front of my family." She grabbed a collapsible tripod and a lens cap. They stood up.

ExBoy's smile was gone. "Your family?"

"I invited my grandpa and my mom," she said.

His face seemed frozen.

"What? You already met Grandpa at least, a few weeks ago when I moved into my apartment," she said. Then she added, "You two carried my couch together."

"Yeah. I know," he said, turning his head. His eyes focused in the distance.

The bored waitress said, "Table, please. Someone?"

The wrestlers scrambled, setting the table upright and grabbing all the chairs off the floor, putting them back neatly by each cocktail table. The waitress set the drinks down one by one from the tray, which she then tucked under her tattooed arm. Madison found her purse, dug around, and gave the waitress an extra big tip to help smooth any ruffled feathers.

The waitress leaned into Madison, her smoky eyes taking on a conspiratorial look behind the rainbow hair. "There's a big old guy at the door. Says he's Vincent Cruz, your grandfather. Do you want us to let him in before the doors officially open?"

"Yes, please. Oh, and was my mother with him?" The waitress shook her head and said, "I didn't see anyone with him."

Madison deflated but caught herself, and recovered. "Look, I want him to have a nice time, so could you tell him anything he wants is on the house but charge it to me? It'll be my secret." It was her last few dollars, but she knew she'd be paid after the show tonight.

"Family secrets," the waitress said, nodding as she turned to go. "I like it."

Dewey Decimator, his dark brown hair pulled up in a samurai-style ponytail at the top of his head, said, "That was bullshit, Sparky. I'm supposed to be the one who goes flying into the table."

"You could do your big flying leap and land on top of me," said Sparky.

Dewey Decimator stared for a moment and blinked. "You're right." He rubbed his hands together, thinking. "Then we could pick up Madison's chair while she's still sitting in it. We'll throw her at Atomic Waist!"

"Wait, what?" Madison looked up.

"Dewey, you're an artist," Sparky nodded.

"Well, you taught me, bro," said Dewey.

"Did I just become a crash test dummy?" said Madison.

"No, seriously dude," said Sparky, "your skills are scary."

Dewey beamed. "Thanks."

"Hello?" said Madison.

A deep chuckle erupted from Atomic Waist. "Picking up a girl and throwing her at me might be a bit over the top, don't you think?" he said.

"That's what we're here for, dude," said Sparky. "Over the top entertainment." He grabbed Dewey's samurai ponytail with one hand and pulled back a balled fist with the other, pretending to take aim. Dewey smiled and held up his middle finger at Sparky.

"Don't try to make her wrestle," said Atomic Waist. "She was brought in for a different kind of comedy—as a side character."

"This will be fantastic," said Sparky. "Don't worry about it."

"You guys said this would be improv!" said Madison, looking back and forth from Sparkle Pecs to Dewey Decimator.

"That's right," said Dewey. "We were told you're really good at winging it."

"Sure I can wing it. But getting physical with you animals wasn't part of the deal."

"Yes it was," said Dewey.

"Not like that, it wasn't! I'm supposed to act like a drunk customer out of control, distracting Atomic Waist while you get the drop on him. You said to improvise and try to get you guys some laughs."

"Don't worry," said Dewey. "We do this kind of thing all the time. No one gets very hurt."

"*Very* hurt?" squeaked Madison.

Sparkle Pecs remained excited. "Aw, c'mon, Madison, this will be fantastic! They'll be blogging about it all week."

"Yeah, while I'm in the hospital. Look," she said. "I'm not a sack of potatoes you can throw around. This is not what I thought it would be."

"I'll be a sack of potatoes," said ExBoy. "Fresh potatoes."

"Well what exactly did you think this would be?" asked Dewey, his hands on his hips.

"I was hired to do improv," she said. "I'm supposed to jeer and throw empty beer cans at Atomic Waist so he's distracted with me while he's raging at the audience. From there I improvise to get some laughs. Nothing was ever said about throwing me!"

"It *is* improv. We make up a lot of it on the spot to keep it fresh," said Sparky.

"Oh, please. You're doing fight choreography at best, with improv thrown in. You want improv, I'm your girl. I could be drunk for real and do a better job. But I'm not going to experiment with improvised fighting. Forget it! I'm out!"

"You can't be out!" said Sparkle Pecs. "They're opening the doors."

Madison turned her head quickly. Sure enough, the first few patrons were paying their entrance fees at the door.

Chapter Two

"**I** DON'T CARE if the audience is in their seats. If I can't feel safe, I'm not doing it!" declared Madison, crossing her arms, her face like a rock.

Atomic Waist jerked his head down and back up, mouthing a silent curse. He shook his head as he said, "Didn't I say this would happen if you guys got carried away again?"

Dewey started, "But—"

"Didn't I? And there's no time to fix it now."

Dewey Decimator rolled his eyes as he turned away, pacing the stage, studying the floor with hands on his hips.

ExBoy leaned in, whispering, "You get me hot when you're tough."

She whipped her head toward him with a flinty look.

He flinched. "Or not."

There was a brief silence in the room broken only by the murmurs of people being admitted into the barroom. With a long heavy sigh, Atomic Waist rubbed one hand down his face and turned to Madison.

"I've seen you on stage, Madison. I know this could work. So I'm hoping that if you at least watch the show tonight you might change your mind for next week." He turned, walking backstage, and called, "Come on, we have to get ready."

"I'm sorry," Madison said, wishing there were a way to fix it. She hated leaving them hanging. Her rent would be hanging now, too. Bye-bye immediate paycheck.

"But what are we going to do now?" Sparkle Pecs pushed his limp mohawk back as he called out to Atomic Waist.

Atomic Waist's voice echoed back once more, "Wing it!"

Madison watched them head backstage as Sparkle Pecs and Dewey Decimator kept glancing back at her, then arguing with each other.

"You had to go and land on their table," said Dewey.

"You were the one who said to throw her!"

The summer heat in the barroom added a sense of urgency as the consequences of her lost income sank in on her. So much for the undiscovered merits of a bad idea.

She turned to the cocktail table, dug out her tote bag once again, and put the empty beer can props back into it. No one said a word to her as she packed the props away, throwing the big tote bag back under the table.

Reaching for that icy cocktail, she plopped down in her chair and sipped her cold drink. Rum and Coke was Madison's favorite cocktail and the chilled fluid felt good going down her throat. But it didn't ease the situation.

ExBoy emptied most of his drink in one long draw and looked around the room. Madison could see those blue eyes calculating. He took the last sip then stared at the ice in his empty glass, not moving. The longer he stood there, the more his eyes creased.

"Hey, what's wrong?" she asked.

Shaking it off, he turned his smile back on as if it never had left. He set the glass down.

"I'll have to catch the show some other time. I gotta go." He headed toward the back door. The way he could both show up and disappear without much warning still caught her off guard.

She looked at Spenser, who had her camera all set up on the table, waiting for the show to start, and said, "I guess it's just you and me now."

"What's with him?" Spenser swung her head in the direction ExBoy had left, and added, "And what's with using the back door?"

Madison shrugged. "Wish I knew."

"Are you guys officially a couple yet?"

A rueful chuckle escaped Madison. "No, and I don't think we should be. Forget that he comes and goes like a tormented superhero; he's just too hard to figure out."

"Uh-oh."

"What? I don't like it when you say uh-oh," said Madison.

"He sounds mysterious and brooding. Hard to resist."

"Oh, spare me! He's just...hot as hell, that's all."

Spenser nodded. They clinked their drinks, and each took a swallow.

"I'm glad you quit the gig tonight," Spenser said. "I made Daniel promise me he wouldn't let anything happen to you. I don't worry much about him, though. He's so big, all those guys just bounce off of him."

"Tell the truth," said Madison, curious. "Do you call him Daniel or Atomic Waist when you two are alone?"

Spenser smiled. "Mr. Waist, Atomic Toy—"

"Okay, that's enough—"

"Satin Buns—"

"You can—"

"Tasty Waisty—"

"Stop!" Madison tried slapping her own face, but it was too late. She had a visual. *Tasty Waisty?*

The barroom was getting noisier as people arrived, finding seats and ordering drinks. The crunchy thump of cheap wooden chairs dragging across scuffed wooden floors mixed with bursts of laughter at different tables. The tone of people's voices took on a new quality of bass notes and sharp spots as the size of the audience grew from a gathering of small groups to a crowd.

A local DJ's mix of breakbeat music started in the background.

In Seattle's historical district on the edge of downtown, Sound Beating, like its neighboring bars, was older than its patrons – a proud dive. It got its name from its location near Puget Sound combined with the music that wailed from this place back in its heyday. Its history gave it enough street cred to keep the locals coming, while the occasional novelty show like Bruise Boys brought in new blood.

Madison jerked upright. "I almost forgot my grandpa. He's here somewhere."

She turned in her chair to look for him, leaning to one side, scanning all the patrons gathering around tables and chairs.

"Haven't seen him much this last year. Somehow time gets away." She craned her neck. "And now my mother is back in Seattle."

Turning back around to face Spenser, Madison knew that more than any of her friends, Spenser would understand the significance of what she was about to say. "The FBI finally approved her transfer. So she's working in their Seattle Field Division now."

Spenser looked up in quiet surprise. "Have you seen her yet?"

"No, but we talked on the phone."

Spenser hesitated, then asked, "So how'd that go?"

Madison shrugged her shoulders. "It was nice. But weird."

"Why was it weird?"

"Because it was nice."

Spenser sat quietly, watching Madison. "This is kind of big news. You seem to be taking it all so well."

"You mean like a grown-up? You can say it."

Digging through her camera bag again, Spenser pulled out an elastic hair band. "Well, you actually are a grown-up now." She pulled her blonde hair up into a ponytail. "But you can't beat yourself up for behaving like a kid when you were a kid."

"I invited her and Grandpa to come tonight, but I guess she didn't show."

"You're not surprised, are you?"

Madison sighed. "No." She propped her elbows on the table, bringing a hand up to run fingers through her hair. "What was I thinking? She's never approved of what I do, and she'd hate this place."

"Little Freudian slip on your part?" Spenser pulled her hair through the last twist of her elastic hair band, the ponytail turning out crooked. "You know, like a declaration that you're going to be yourself and all that?"

"No, I wasn't trying to..." She stared at Spenser a moment, the thought sinking in. "Well maybe. So I guess she's being herself, too, and refusing to come." She stood, adding, "Situation normal."

Madison's gaze searched all the way into the back of the barroom until she finally saw her grandfather. Sure enough, he was sitting near the back like a big sentry at the door. "There's Grandpa," she said.

In his late sixties, Vincent Cruz was six feet two inches tall and still robust from the hard toil of his landscaping business. His rolled-up sleeves exposed strong forearms, but his face was leathery and lined like an old treasure map still unsolved. His five o'clock shadow was barely perceptible, but Madison knew it was fierce enough to sand these old tables smooth again. Although he had some hair, he opted to shave off what little he had left, refusing to do a comb-over. He'd finally sold his business and retired last year, but couldn't seem to keep his hands out of the soil.

Madison wished she hadn't forgotten he was here, but she doubted he had noticed. He seemed more interested in everyone who entered, checking out each person as they walked through the door as if they needed to pass his inspection. It wasn't like him.

Madison asked Spenser, "Do people worry more when they get older?"

"I don't know," said Spenser. "Why? Is he worried about something?"

"Hard to say. He won't admit if anything's wrong." She pushed her chair back under the table. "I need to tell him I won't be performing tonight."

Threading her way through the crowd, she squeezed sideways between the backs of old wooden chairs holding excited people, making her way to the more open space where he sat. Through the force field that was his presence, she slipped easily into the space that others seemed too intimidated to occupy.

His face lit up as she approached and he pulled a chair up next to his. They did a well-worn private handshake in which they'd bump fists, press palm to palm, lace their fingers together, and bend their hands downward, pretending to crack their knuckles while they each made a loud cracking sound effect.

Madison said, "How's my hero?"

"Fine. I think that pretty waitress over there likes me," he said, nodding. "Keeps offering me drinks."

"You should take her up on it."

"Nice try," he said. "I already told you not to be spending your money on me. I just wanted to see your show."

"I won't be performing tonight after all."

"Heard that discussion all the way back here." He smiled and knuckled her chin. "My tough little girl."

"Disappointed?" she asked.

"Well, I did want to see you wipe the floor with those young fellas. Show them how it's done." Madison was relieved to see that old twinkle in his eye. "Their loss," he added. "So I think I'll get going." He stood.

"You don't have to go. You just got here."

"Sweetheart, you were the only reason I had any interest in the show. That, and I was hoping to see you and Ann together again. It's been so long I don't even have a photograph of the two of you that isn't old. But she called a little while ago and said she has to work late."

"She probably didn't want to come."

"Well," he looked around the room with a soft chuckle, then back to her face. "This might not have been the best time and place for a reunion."

Madison twisted her lips to the side as if she were giving that some hard thought.

"Don't give me that, you stinker. You did it on purpose," he said.

"Nuh-uh! Spenser says it was Freudian."

"Whatever it was, it was bullshit."

Madison's shoulders dropped. She exhaled.

"Why don't you give Ann a call tomorrow," he asked, "and offer to go meet her for coffee?"

Madison looked across the room. Where was a distraction when she needed one? Spenser? ExBoy? A barroom brawl? "I just want to stay out of trouble," she said.

He laughed. "Since when do you stay out of trouble?"

"You know what I mean. She's never approved of the choices I made even though she was never around."

"She was just a baby herself when she had you. Give her a chance." He took her hand in his, saying, "I raised you both, and I have every confidence that the two of you can pick up the pieces."

Madison sighed. "All right. I'll arrange it."

"It's just coffee, sweetheart. It'll be a good start," he said. "She really misses you."

Madison said, "When I talked to her on the phone, she did say one thing that worried me. She said you may have had some personal information stolen?"

He studied the tabletop. "Ann told you about that?"

"Yeah. She said the University of Washington was hacked. It must have been bad if the UW called the FBI. She said they got into the archives of old employee records. Weren't you one of their gardeners?"

"Ancient history," he insisted.

"She's just trying to warn you, Grandpa. Some people steal social security numbers to open credit cards with."

"Okay. I heard you," he said.

As they hugged, she said, "I promise I'll try to make it work tomorrow." He hugged her even harder after that and left.

Returning to her table, Madison pulled her mobile phone out of her purse and looked through the pictures she kept on it. Grandpa was right. The most recent photo that Madison had of her and her mother together was so old Madison had been in junior high—a painful time of her life. She gazed at the surly image of her young self and wished there were a better picture.

I should hire Spenser to do a portrait of us together. Her heart grew lighter at the thought. *Grandpa would love that!* The more Madison thought about it, the more excited she got at the idea. *Mom would love it, too. In fact, she'd like that it was my idea.*

She knew Spenser would not ask to be paid, so Madison needed to raise the money first, then present it to Spenser and insist that she wouldn't let Spenser do it unless she let Madison pay her. *More money issues but I have to find a way.*

"Are you okay?" Spenser asked.

Madison said, "Other than mommy issues, boyfriend issues, and wondering where I'm going to get the rest of my rent? I'm fantastic."

Spenser stuck her lower lip out. "Can I beat up your mean mommy for you?"

Madison gave a short laugh. "My mom could kick your ass."

Spenser giggled and said, "Special Agent Ann Cruz could kick both our asses at the same time."

"And look good doing it," said Madison.

"While holding a drink and not spilling it," said Spenser.

"Or wrinkling her pantsuit."

"Or smearing her lipstick, or…"

The waitress returned, but this time she brought a tray with four shots of whiskey and a note. Madison picked up the note.

It said: "You said you could do it drunk and still do a better job. So put your money where your mouth is and we'll follow your lead. Double or nothing."

Madison's eyes widened and her heart rate sped up a fraction. Rent and groceries. No, *more* than that. The portrait!

She spotted Dewey off to the side of the stage watching her. He raised his eyebrows and tilted his head, his dark brown samurai ponytail peeking around the side. She stared at the center of the empty stage, calculating the merits of this new bad idea.

She wadded the note, slamming it down onto the table. Snatching one of the shot glasses, she toasted Dewey, making sure he saw it, and raised the shot glass to her lips. When he smiled, she threw it back.

The flood of fire on her throat bent her over, one hand flying up to cover her mouth as she coughed, while the other hand flapped in the air as if she were waving a manicure dry.

Sound Beating's whiskey experience was well earned, with a formula strong enough to melt plastic and bring a corpse back to life. It carved its initials in your throat. This whiskey asked who's your daddy.

She caught a glimpse of Dewey laughing at her.

"What are you doing?" Spenser asked her. Madison didn't want to give her a chance to talk her out of it so she grabbed the next shot and threw that back, too. More burning, and gasping as her eyes watered, her shoulders scrunched up, and her face contorted in sympathy with her stomach. Her pores opened.

"Madison, what the hell?" Spenser grew alarmed, rising from her chair.

Madison couldn't talk, more little coughs escaping her, so she frantically dug around inside her purse. Spenser grabbed the wadded up note, trying to open it.

Madison whipped her car keys out of her purse, thumped them down on the table next to the camera in front of Spenser and grabbed the third shot, throwing it back.

The burning eased up on her throat and her eyes took it better this time, but now her stomach lurched. She felt shaky. She sniffed hard, trying to clear some of the runniness in her nose.

Spenser's lips formed a hard line of annoyance as she read the note. She threw it down and reached for Madison's last shot.

"Nnno!" Madison's raspy voice finally showed up as she dove for the last shot.

"Don't be an idiot—" Spenser said, grabbing the glass at the same moment, launching the girls into a tug of war.

Chapter Three

ADISON KNEW SPENSER'S instinct was to be neat and not spill anything, so she bent over the table trying to sip from the shot glass as Spenser pulled it out from under her.

"Spenser," Madison dropped back into her chair, "they said they'll follow my lead. If they do, everything will be fine. Please understand," she begged, "I can't face my mother with my rent overdue. She has a way of finding these things out!"

"God damn it, Madison! It'll serve you right if you break your neck!"

"I know, but...will you send flowers?"

Spenser covered her face in her hands, expelling her breath. Her voice came out muffled.

"Yes, but only the kind of flowers you hate. Which ones do you hate?" Dropping her hands she fixed her eyes on Madison, her cheeks pink, and Madison knew her dear friend was having a hard time remaining humorous with this one.

"Venus flytraps?"

"Fine! When you break your neck I'm bringing a bouquet of Venus flytraps."

They were silent.

Spenser said, "I'm sending a note ordering Daniel to tell the guys he'll kill them if they don't follow your lead as promised."

In a small voice Madison said, "Thank you."

Feeling her pores opened and the crowd's body heat adding to the heat already in the room, she picked up her rum and Coke and pulled out an ice cube for relief. She crunched on the ice, taking in the room.

It was very carefully painted and arranged to appear indifferent to design. Even the low hanging pipes over the stage, instead of being painted to blend in or disappear, were made into a feature looking like battered industrial chic.

Spenser worked with her camera gear again, giving Madison the impression that she was just trying to look busy. Madison tried to think of something to talk about to ease the situation, at least till the show started.

"You know you've barely come up for air since you met Daniel," Madison said. "You two are pretty mushy."

"Just the way I like it. How's the new apartment?" Spenser said with a smirk. "All settled in?"

"No. Still living out of boxes. And stop mocking me."

"I didn't say a word," said Spenser.

"That wasn't your voice in my head just now?"

"No. You have me mistaken for some other voice."

"Oh. Sorry. I thought that was your voice telling me that I'm a sorry-ass procrastinator."

"How did you find such a nice place for rent that cheap?" Spenser asked.

"ExBoy found it for me. I owe him for that."

The breakbeat music shifted in style and volume, meaning the show would start soon. The anticipation in the room ratcheted higher as conversations and laughter picked up. The increased thumping rhythms added to a growing unease within Madison.

"When are they going to start this stupid show anyway? The sooner the better before all the whiskey really does hit me." She pulled the empty beer cans back onto her table, in preparation for the moment she'd need them.

"I'd better be ready to jump when they do," said Spenser. "I need shots of all the action."

Madison assumed most of the shots would be of Atomic Waist. He'd been wearing normal clothes when Spenser introduced him a few months ago. But tonight, Spenser said he would be wearing ...um... a tight little sparkly, spangly, bathing-suitie kind of thing, denoting his evil character's vanity. It was just so wrong, because

CHEMING MESS (MADISON CRUZ

en   Aisle AZ Bay 07 Item 6682
have some shelf-wear due to normal use. Your
nase funds free job training and education in the
er Seattle area. Thank you for supporting
dwill's nonprofit mission!

canned
OTW006MLU
9673545
30989673549
gasser
4/2022 8:07:07 AM

it was so right. Oh, and wrestling shoes. But she doubted anyone would notice the shoes.

Thinking of how to tell her mother about the portrait idea Madison leaned back, mumbling, "She could've at least shown up." She rubbed her eyes, then looked up at the low hanging pipes over the stage.

Unblinking, Spenser said, "You must have known that someday you were going to have to deal with this."

"With what?"

"Getting to know your own mother. Seeing her through your adult eyes."

Madison blinked, thinking about that idea. "That *would* be different," she said, as a nice little drowsiness came on.

Right then, as if on cue, her cell phone began to play the theme music to the movie *Jaws*, which meant her mother was calling.

Right when the wrestling show started.

Whistles and clapping exploded as the stout and sturdy MC strutted onto the stage holding a microphone with a long cable. Madison looked from the stage to her cell phone.

Now she calls? Now?

She tossed the phone unanswered into her purse under the table and let the show sweep her away.

The gravel-voiced MC yelled, "Oh, yeah! Oh, yeah! You hot writhing hunk of underbelly wetness!"

The crowd catcalled back, drumming their hands on the tabletops, making it sound like thunder in the room. It penetrated, filling her with excitement.

The MC paced back and forth on the stage like an animal searching for a way out of his cage, the microphone cable snaking along with him. "But it's not the rain that's made you wet!"

His voice dropped to a low urgent purr as he pressed the mic to his lips. "It's that fevered anticipation. Your hot breath on our windows." His voice turned to a gravelly whisper. "That bad dream moment when you're scared and tangled in your sweaty sheets."

He returned to yelling. "Scared that you might miss out on BRUISE BOYS!"

The crowd hollered out their enthusiasm, banging on the tables and floor.

Cool but coiled, Madison waited. Determined to win this bet, she listened to every word, watched every move, searching for the right moment to get involved.

Someone threw an empty beer can onto the stage.

She looked around, spotting a guy at a table nearby chucking another beer can. She put her arms protectively around the cans on her table, resisting the urge to start too soon.

The DJ's head bobbed as the throbbing beat of the music picked up a notch, dueling with Madison's heartbeat for dominance.

"I am Dizorder Lee," the MC continued, "your host for this evening! We're so glad you untangled yourselves and got here! All the suits have gone night-night." He made a loud kissy sound into the mic. Almost as one, the audience sent kissy sounds back. "And the real fun can begin! Our first bout has some interesting guys you're going to love, and one conceited asshole you'll love to hate. First up we have Dewwwey Decimator!"

Dewey strode out, waving to the audience. He brandished his fists at every table near him.

"Dewey was fired from the library when he went postal with his fists, punching everyone in sight when all the late book returns hit in one day!" The crowd waved their own fists in the air in salute to Dewey. "He's our kind of guy!"

Dewey, his lanky build belying his serious strength, jogged to the side of the MC, nodding and pointing at random people in the audience.

"Next! We have none other than…Sparkle Pecs!" Sparky danced out in a fighter style, stopping to make muscle poses and show off his strong chest with glitter rubbed all over it.

"Sparkle Pecs spent many bored years as a vampire until he dedicated his undead life to fitness! The result: he has almost cured himself! That's right! But be careful. If he starts to lose a fight, he's tempted to resort to what he knows best." The MC turned to Sparky and said, "Don't make us muzzle you, Sparky. Fight fair."

Sparky reluctantly agreed, nodding his head, and bounced over to stand next to Dewey Decimator.

Dizorder Lee shook his head. "I don't know what to tell you about this next guy. He gives the fine sport of wrestling a bad name. He's disgusting! Coming out here half-naked all the time! He makes me sick! And I think we should all—"

Atomic Waist ran out on the stage in a fury, grabbed the announcer by the neck and punched him full in the face with his huge fist, then repeatedly pounded on the top of his head. If Madison hadn't seen it in rehearsal she would have wondered if it were indeed real.

The crowd gave a loud moan on first impact, shouting and booing as Dizorder Lee collapsed on stage, knocked out. His microphone and long cable draped over his belly.

Dewey Decimator and Sparkle Pecs in the background were too engrossed in a fierce battle of Rock Paper Scissors as they walked off the stage. They didn't notice what Atomic Waist had just done to poor Dizorder Lee.

It was ridiculous fun and Spenser jumped up, booing and laughing with the crowd. Grabbing her camera off the table, she ran off to find better angles to shoot from.

Atomic Waist held his fists up high in the air as he flexed and roared his rage at the crowd. They roared back, begging for more.

Damn! His real name was Daniel, but Madison had to admit the stage name Atomic Waist was a much better fit for him.

Recalling when he and Spenser first met, Madison thought it odd that instead of carrying on about that manly body, Spenser had talked about him having an adorable face, with the way his eyebrows drooped at the outer corners like a hound dog puppy. He always looked like he was happy in an apologetic way. Studying him now, Madison decided his face was as exciting as wilted lettuce. But he was built like a thunder god and when he smiled, Spenser fell apart like she was twelve years old again. *Must be the goofy smile.*

Tonight the storyline that the wrestlers had planned involved Dewey Decimator discovering that his collectible action figure toys were found in Atomic Waist's locker. And Atomic Waist would refuse to give them back—the bitch.

Madison marveled at how much the downtown crowd loved guys coming out on stage in a dive bar and pretending to beat the shit out of each other over imagined offenses. She had the best seat in the house, right next to the stage, and her instincts told her it was time to spring into action.

They want to wing it? They want improv? She started throwing the cans at Atomic Waist.

"Panty Waist! Hey, Panty Waist!" She threw as hard as she could. The empty cans kept flying and bouncing off him. "C'mon! Are you afraid of girls?"

A look of surprise, then fiendish delight, spread across his face, as if he'd just noticed a little bug that needed squashing. He turned his body and his roar of rage in her direction.

Her nerves went on full alert for a second, but all that did was adrenalize her. Adrenaline was good.

She tore off her shoes, her long lean figure climbing up onto her table, pulling her chair up with her. The crowd started hooting and clapping their approval as she stood on top of the table, waved the chair in the air, then threw it at him.

He ducked it easily, crossing his arms as if to say, "Is that all you got?"

Sparkle Pecs snuck back out from the side of the stage while Atomic Waist's attention was on Madison. Cheers grew for Sparkle Pecs as Madison pulled up another chair on top of her table and sat on it, chucking the last of the cans at Atomic Waist's head.

Several people in the audience shouted, "Go! Go! Go! Go!"

He curled his finger at her like, "Come here."

Her answer was to throw the second chair at him, but this time he caught it, held it with both hands, and ran across the stage toward the table she stood on.

Sparkle Pecs lunged at Atomic Waist from behind at the exact instant Madison leaped off her table onto the chair Atomic Waist held in his big hands. She used it as a stepping off platform to plant her foot on his shoulder and spring up into the maze of low hanging pipes over the stage.

The momentum of her spring threw both Atomic Waist and Sparkle Pecs off balance. They crashed together onto the floor of the stage next to the MC. The chair bounced and rattled off the edge of the stage while the audience went crazy with glee.

Madison hung on, feet dangling, and swung her strong legs up to wrap around the pipes, pulling herself up to a sitting position.

The MC returned to consciousness, and began crawling away on hands and knees.

Dewey Decimator chose that moment to burst onto the stage, facing the audience, his face contorted with great drama. "My action figures are missing!" he wailed. "What kind of an insane world do we live in?"

Atomic Waist stood up and grabbed Sparkle Pecs by his grown out floppy mohawk. He dragged him along as he crossed the stage toward Dewey. Sparky desperately scrambled on his knees, trying to wrench the big hand from his hair.

"When the dignity of a man's property is not honored," Dewey pointed a finger in the air, "we have gone down the road of anarchy, of mobocracy, of—"

Atomic Waist grabbed Dewey by his samurai ponytail. Sparky managed to get on his feet, taking a swing at Atomic Waist. He missed, hitting Dewey instead. Atomic Waist then swung his victims roundhouse style into each other. Their faces collided. Their heads bobbed around like Hawaiian hula dolls on a car dashboard.

Madison climbed to a standing position on the pipe as Sparky and Dewey slowly collapsed to the floor. The audience yelled and booed but also pointed at Madison overhead.

Atomic Waist followed the pointing fingers upward. When he spotted her, his eyes flew wide.

Just then Madison yelled, "Potatoes!" and dove out of the overhead piping.

Chapter Four

SHE SAW ATOMIC Waist lunge with his arms outstretched. The crowd screamed their excitement. As the force of her weight fell into his arms, she felt them tense into hard muscle.

Her momentum swung them both around, causing him to stumble across the stage to keep his balance.

She pushed her dark hair out of her eyes as he came to a halt. He studied her face. Her lids felt heavy and she saw him sniffing.

His eyes squinted at her as he whispered, "Holy shit, you're stinking drunk."

"That was the bet," she slurred.

"What bet?" he whispered, "We're supposed to follow your lead."

"Keep moving," she urged. She jumped out of his arms to the floor and slapped at his hands. He slapped her hands back. She slapped again, and wrapped her arms around his six-pack waist. Gritting her teeth, she strained to lift him.

He turned and picked her up easily, holding her away from him by her waist and letting her dangle.

She grabbed both of his ears and pulled his head towards her, as if she were trying to pop his head off, but she leaned in, whispering, "Get mad and spank me."

"*What?*" he whispered.

"You heard me," she whispered. "Do it."

"That's enough!" he roared. He got down on one knee, bent Madison over it, and proceeded to spank her butt, the crowd whooping and screaming with approval.

But without skipping a beat, Madison ("Ow—") grabbed the microphone cable on the ground ("Ow!") and pulled the mic over to her. "Take it easy—*Ow!*" She reached around to his backside as his big hands spanked her bottom. She pulled his tight little sparkly spangly bathing-suitie kind of thing open and shoved the mic down in there, far enough that it came out the leg opening.

With a girly squawk he leaped to his feet.

As Madison fell between his legs, she grabbed the mic that was hanging out of his tight little sparkly spangly bathing-suitie kind of thing.

Then she pulled.

With desperate speed he grabbed his front waistband with both hands. She pulled the cable faster. He instinctively did a little dance trying to get away. But that only made it worse, pulling his tight little sparkly spangly bathing-suitie kind of thing open in the back, exposing a bit of his high and mighty rear end. Madison now had enough slack in the cable, so she stood up and skipped rope with it.

With the audience in hysterics, the MC came over and jumped in with her, both of them keeping the rhythm of the skipping rope. As the cable made each circle, the stretchy waistband on Atomic Waist's backside dipped down and sprang back up. The DJ added classic strip music, and Atomic Waist looked around in a panic, not daring to let go, not able to walk away, not sure what to do.

On the sides of the stage the other wrestlers bent over with the kind of high-pitched laughter that men only produce when they've laughed themselves helpless.

As the crowd cheered, Atomic Waist finally shrugged and took a grand bow. Madison, exhausted, stopped jumping and stood swaying, thinking about vomiting.

One last empty beer can came flying and hit her on her temple. "Oh!" She looked out in the audience, flipping the bird saying, "Show yourself, you mutha—"

That was the moment Madison saw her mother standing in the back of the room. Ann was quite still, looking down at the floor. Then she turned and walked out.

The audience whistled and pounded on their tabletops, as empty beer cans rolled across the floor, aimless.

✦ ✦ ✦

MADISON SAT ON the carpet, leaning against the wall of her living room. A couple of tears from earlier had already dried at the corners of her eyes. A wet sniff lingered.

Spenser had driven Madison home in Madison's car and now rummaged in the refrigerator, packing away leftover tacos they had picked up in a drive-thru on the way home. "Are you sure it was her? The room was dark, and you were pretty hammered."

"Yeah. It was her." With a heavy sigh, Madison rubbed her eyes hard, probably making black smears but she didn't care at the moment. "I think she was trying to call and tell me she was in the audience. But I never answered."

She looked at her bare feet stretched out in front of her and thought how nice it would be to have pretty toes right now. When you can't get yourself a new life, you may as well settle for a pedicure.

Spenser shut the refrigerator door and came over to sit down, searching for a spot. The couch had little room since it was covered in boxes from Madison's recent move, their lids unfolded and hanging open to reveal an assortment of items unrelated to each other. Empty flower vases, books, candle holders, and lots of picture frames shared boxes with sandals, computer cables, and a tire pressure gauge.

Madison jumped up, held the wall a moment to steady herself, and took a few boxes off the couch, leaving a clear spot for Spenser. "Sorry," she said, "Told you I was still living out of boxes."

Spenser sat. "Would it do any good if I asked you never to be that stupid again?"

"Spenser…" She closed her eyes for a moment. She could feel a mild headache starting to come on. "I was sure I'd be all right if they followed my lead."

"You're going to feel like an idiot tomorrow when you've finished sobering up."

Madison already felt stupid but didn't want to admit it. "There was one thing I didn't expect," she grumbled. "The paycheck was double the amount as promised, but they said not to cash it yet. It won't be good for another week."

In the silence that followed they heard a tweeting sound from Madison's cell phone.

She had voicemail from Phil, her agent. As she listened, her face became elated. "Yes! Emergency gig tomorrow. Phil wants my fairy godmother character for a children's birthday party. The usual. Painting faces, balloon animals. He sounds desperate. He already emailed the gig sheet to me in case I say yes. I usually get $200 for birthday parties, plus tips from the parents. I need to call him back right away and say I'll do it."

She punched Phil's number on her cell phone, but a knock on the door made her stop and end the call before it went through. "There's Daniel," she said, standing up. "Thanks for driving me home, Spenser."

She went to look out the peephole, hoping to gauge Daniel's mood before opening the door. But the person she saw standing there was her grandfather. *What the...?*

She was still a little drunk and didn't want him to see her like this. She quickly wiped under her eyes in case her makeup had smeared, gave one more wet sniff, and rushed her hands down her hair to smooth what she could.

She opened the door and put on a cheery voice. "Hi, Grandpa."

Spenser, right behind her but more surprised, said, "Hi, Mr. Cruz."

He walked in, mild surprise on his face. "Well, hey there, you two." He gave Madison a little hug. "I see Spenser is still putting up with you."

"Always," Spenser smiled.

"Well, if anyone can, it'd be you. I'd trust you with anything. You're like family." He looked around asking, "Everything okay here?"

Madison shrugged. "Sure. But did something happen? It's so late."

"Oh." He seemed embarrassed. "I'm sorry, sweetheart; I wasn't paying attention to the time. I, uh, came to get my drill."

"Why didn't you just call me? I could have brought it by in the morning and saved you the trip."

"Well, I wasn't home by the phone and—"

"Use your cell phone."

"I can never get those things to work. I think mine is broken." He took it out of his pocket.

"You have to turn it on," she said, reaching over and turning it on for him.

He looked at it as if the phone had somehow betrayed him. "Oh. I see."

Though his head was inclined toward the small phone in his hands, Madison could see his eyes had already wandered away, lost in thought. "Grandpa, are you all right?"

He looked up. "Hm? Fine. Why do you ask?"

"You seem unhappy. Did Mom call you about me or something?"

His look of distraction melted away as a laser focus replaced it, zeroing in on her.

I had to open my mouth.

"What happened?" he asked. He seemed to be holding his breath. She thought of a few ways to dodge and dazzle and get out from having to admit to the bet she'd won tonight, but he would probably find out tomorrow anyway.

She braced herself and said, "Mom showed up."

"And?"

"I was performing."

"And?"

"I was…" She stopped herself, then said, "Inebriated."

He stared at her. "You were drunk?"

"I said inebriated. You said drunk."

"Just how *inebriated* were you?" He sounded incredulous.

"Honestly?"

"Yeah. Try that."

"Shit-faced."

A freeze frame of confusion. Madison could see the sorting and filing of information going on behind his eyes.

His voice getting louder with each word, he asked, "What were you thinking?"

"Grandpa, it was a bet, I swear! The money—"

"And in front of your mother!"

"I didn't know she would be—"

"How often do you drink like that?"

"I don't! Remember when I got mad and told them I could do it drunk and still do a better job?"

He closed his eyes and sighed. Shaking his head, he said, "Madison." Resigned, he kissed her forehead but his voice was still stern. "We'll talk tomorrow."

He turned and walked out into the enclosed apartment hallway outside her door. Looking up and down the hallway he said, "Lock your door, sweetheart. Don't open it for any strangers no matter what they say."

She felt a tug at her heart and couldn't bring herself to close the door. She stood in the doorway, watching him walk past other apartment doors. Something about his demeanor felt familiar. She wanted to run after him and give him a big hug. But instead she called to him as he reached the stairwell at the end of the hallway, "Goodnight, Grandpa."

He turned around and said, "If Jerry hadn't made her work late—"

Interrupting him, she said, "It was my own fault, Grandpa. You can't blame everything on Jerry."

His grip on the edge of the stairwell railing tightened and his jaw grew hard. "Yes I can," he answered, before heading down the stairwell.

She closed the door and heard Spenser asking, "Who's Jerry?"

"You may have seen him a few times at my house when we were kids," Madison said, walking towards the living room window that overlooked the parking lot below. "He was kind of a mentor to my mother when she was in high school. She met him at a job fair where he was all Mr. FBI talking about law enforcement."

She nudged a few boxes aside with her foot so she could stand closer to the window. "Leave it to my mom to find that sort of thing interesting." She stood at the window waiting for her grandfather to leave the building and head for his car. "So she decided to aim all her college efforts towards applying to work at the FBI. But I never did understand why Grandma and Grandpa didn't like him. I thought he was great."

Her grandfather emerged from the apartment building, heading across the parking lot toward his car. Her inner alarm had been triggered, and she didn't believe his story about coming to get his drill, which he had left without. Grandpa was the one person in the world that she knew loved her beyond a shadow of a doubt. She watched him get into his car and drive away into the dark.

Black silhouettes of trees waved in the breeze outside. She pulled open her living room window, hoping it would help cool off the room and maybe help her to sober up a little faster. Down in the parking lot, she spotted Daniel getting out of his car.

Madison called to him. "Hey you! You're not allowed to kill me, you know. Spenser wouldn't like it."

"I'll make it look like an accident," he called back.

"Story of my life," she called. "I'm just an accident."

From out of nowhere a voice yelled into the night, "Shut up out there!" It sounded uncomfortably near.

Chapter Five

MADISON SLAPPED HER hand over her mouth, sticking her head out the window to look around. She couldn't help herself. She started to giggle. She couldn't tell where the woman's voice had come from and her giggles got louder. She knew that was an inappropriate reaction, but the very fact that it was inappropriate made it feel delicious.

Sure enough, someone else stuck her head out of a window, white puffy hair moving around in the breeze. *She's right next door!* Madison's giggles increased and she started to snort, so she slapped her second hand on top of the first. Inwardly she was mortified at her own behavior.

Behind her, Spenser said, "Madison, seriously?"

The old gal scolded, "What's the matter with you? Decent people are trying to sleep! Knock it off before I call the cops!"

Madison pulled her head back inside. She turned back to Spenser saying, "Should I tell her I know someone in the FBI?"

Spenser rolled her eyes. "So you haven't got in enough trouble for one night?"

"The whole world hates me and I never have any fun."

Daniel knocked on the door at that moment. Spenser let him in while Madison went to the fridge and pulled out the bag of tacos to give them for the ride home.

"I'm sure you guys don't mind if I rush you out the door. I have a lot of self-reproaching to do."

"Well, one thing is for sure," said Daniel. "I'll have to use a different costume now. You gave those guys ideas about how to embarrass me onstage."

"Let's go," said Spenser. "I'll embarrass you at home." He smiled and Spenser turned to Madison saying, "Wink, wink."

Madison used her most bored tone. "In case you hadn't noticed, you just said 'wink wink' out loud."

"Did I?" Spenser smiled as her eyebrows shot up and down.

"Stop already. I get it." She pushed them towards the door and added, "You guys both saved my ass tonight. Let me quickly say... Sorry. Asshole. You rock. I don't."

Spenser said. "Go to bed and sleep it off. You'll rock tomorrow." One last hug and they left.

Madison locked her door and sighed. She didn't have anyone to wink wink about. Not really. ExBoy didn't count. She had to figure out her stupid life.

She decided baby steps were in order. She would start with drilling holes and hanging things up tonight so she could return the drill to Grandpa tomorrow. Then she'd finally finish unpacking. *Tidy up the place. Make it look like home.* She started to get hopeful. *This could work. When I'm no longer in danger of having a condemned sign hung on my door, maybe I'll ask Spenser and Daniel to hook me up with one of his friends. Just no wrestlers.*

Ten minutes later, the high pitched whirring of the drill seared her eardrums. She was drilling the sixth hole and wondering why they called it drywall, when she noticed that the holes seemed awfully big. Crap! She had forgotten to switch out the bit for a tiny one.

Just then she heard and felt a rapid pounding on the wall. Madison heard the old woman's voice drifting through her window. "God damn it, I'm going to come over there and throw you against that wall! Let me sleep!"

Madison sighed, kicking herself. Fine.

✧　✧　✧

SHE DIDN'T REMEMBER waking up exactly. There was just a gradual knowledge of pain, and then the realization that there was too much light in the room. "Oh God," she whimpered. Her head was about to explode. She rolled over. *Ooh, that's worse. Don't move.* But she could tell she had no choice in the matter.

She rolled to the edge of the bed and her frantic fumbling hand located the small trashcan nearby. Just in time. The whiskey and fast food tacos from last night took a curtain call.

I will never, ever, drink again.

She got up and executed a careful ballet across the floor, trying to find a clear path to the bathroom. Reaching the bathroom she hung onto the doorframe, hugging the molding to her cheek.

She remembered something about Phil calling last night. *I think I'm supposed to be a fairy godmother today.* She swallowed some aspirin with a little water, found her phone, and read all the gig details about when and where the children's birthday party would be. Wasn't there something else today? She held her head, wishing her face would fall off.

She peeled off her clothes and for the next twenty minutes, her shower gave her the courage to carry on. The hot water soothed her sore muscles. She hurt in places she didn't know could hurt. Couldn't blame the hangover for that, she knew. The soreness was from her antics with the wrestlers. *I'm lucky I didn't break my head.*

Shampoo and conditioner, the best things ever invented. The warm lathered water rinsed out of her hair and ran down her body into the drain, taking some of the pain with it. The scent of the conditioner made her feel feminine again. *I can do this. I can fix my life,* she thought, as she shaved her legs. *I'll find a better job, I'll fix my apartment, I'll even fix my relationship with Mom. Grandpa will be proud.*

She exfoliated her face with a free sample scrub she had picked up at the store. *No more moping! No more feeling sorry for myself! No more bullshit, Madison. You deserve better, and you can do better.*

She dried her hair and dressed in her fairy godmother costume. She looked like a queen out of King Arthur's court in pastel blue, pink, and gold brocades. The long pink sleeves were tight till they reached the wrist, where they hung open and draped downward in silky pink, making poetic movements whenever she used her arms.

Her big green eyes were a bit bloodshot, so she put in some soothing eye drops. Her skill with makeup had grown over the years to that of a professional. She looked divine. The finishing touch, a square yard of pastel blue silk chiffon, edged with gold thread, draped over her head with two inches of it falling down her forehead like bangs. After pinning it in place, she used a circular tiara to anchor it, with the length of the chiffon going down her back over her dark hair.

She picked up her purse, car keys, cell phone, and put them all in her big black tote bag. Then she added her magic wand—eleven inches of silver with a one-inch rhinestone star at the tip to total twelve inches of make-believe magic. Plus, a small set of gossamer wings that she could attach to her back before walking in to the princess birthday party since she couldn't drive while wearing wings. A set of watercolor face paints, long skinny balloons for making balloon animals, and a small balloon pump completed her party gear.

She checked the time. Perfect. She had enough leisure time to go buy a coffee, head out to Grandpa's place for a visit, then on to the birthday party gig. She knew he would get a kick out of her fairy godmother costume. She'd drop off his drill and ask him point blank what it was he was not telling her. What was he worried about? *I'm a big girl and can handle myself.* After making that clear to him, she'd leave for the party. She could still feel her hangover around the edges, but her spirits were considerably lifted.

Today will be a good day. She picked up her tote bag with all the gear in it and walked out of the bedroom into the living room. She stopped cold.

Oh. My. God. There were six big holes in the living room wall.

She stared. Shaking her head, she added the drill to her tote bag and left.

✧ ✧ ✧

AS SHE HEADED down the hallway toward the stairwell, the next door down from hers opened and out stepped the tallest older woman Madison had ever seen, standing at about six-four or six-five. She wore a pink housecoat, what Grandma used to call a duster, and had puffy white hair skimming the top of the door frame. Her face looked like she was in her 70s, but her body appeared younger somehow. Fit and toned, she was obviously the same older woman Madison had mouthed off to last night. Madison was struck by her height but also by the empty look in her eyes and her slack jaw.

Not wanting a confrontation, Madison decided to keep walking.

Then the old gal swayed and collapsed in her own doorway.

Madison jerked to a stop, her tote bag swinging at her side.

Everything was quiet. Most of the old gal's body had fallen inside the narrow entryway of her own apartment, while her legs from the knees on down were sticking out into the hall. She wore the biggest fuzzy slippers in existence.

Madison looked around, but no one else was in the hallway. It quickly occurred to her that she didn't know anyone else who lived here yet. Who should she tell?

She dropped her tote bag. "Hello? Are you okay?"

The doorway was blocked with the woman's body so Madison bent over and slapped her legs and knees. The huge fuzzy slippers shook with each slap.

"Hey! Are you all right?" She slapped some more, but the older woman wasn't responding enough for Madison's fear to subside. She was barely coherent. *Damn it!*

Madison lifted her long Arthurian gown into the crook of her elbow. Delicately stepping between the old gal and the narrow entryway wall, her Lady Guinevere slippers made not a whisper. Once she was all the way into the apartment she put her hands under the woman's armpits to pull her back inside her home.

Dragging her across the hard flooring of the entryway was not too hard because the old gal's housecoat slid on the slick surface of the floor. But getting her across the carpet proved to be a much bigger challenge. Madison heaved and pulled, her tiara falling off onto the woman's chest.

That got a reaction.

"Errrh…" She was responding.

Madison had her all the way into the living room, the apartment being a mirror duplicate of her own next door. She stopped tugging and shoved her tiara back on. Grabbing a pillow off the sofa, she slid it underneath the old woman's head.

The confused eyes blinked. "What's going on?" Her voice was weak.

"You fainted and collapsed. Just stay still for a moment. I'll get a cold cloth." Madison went into the kitchen, found a small towel, and soaked it in cold water from the faucet.

She noticed trophies and colorful award ribbons all over the place. Autographed black and white glossy headshots of handsome men dotted the walls. There were pictures of old style Vegas showgirls lifting heavy things—barbells, and even Rat Pack era men—into their arms. *Holy crap, is that her in younger days? Wow.*

Madison returned to the older woman whose color was returning.

The older woman said, "It's this damn diet again. It can't be the training." She blinked several times. "Crystal was right. I shouldn't rush it."

Madison said, "Close your eyes a moment."

She complied as Madison used the towel to gently wipe across her upper eyelids and down the sides of her face. She asked, "Who is Crystal?"

With her eyes still closed she said, "My pain in the ass niece." She scrunched up her brows, adding, "I shouldn't say that. She interferes because she cares.

Family is important, but they can be damned inconvenient at times."

Madison refolded the towel to get the cooler side out, and replaced it over the woman's forehead and eyes. "My name is Madison. What's yours?"

"Toonie."

"Toonie? That's...very pretty."

"Bullshit. It's weird. But it's better than Petunia. No one dared call me Petunia except my mother." As if just waking up to the situation, Toonie struggled to get up on her elbows. She pulled the towel off, and squinted at Madison. "Are you that rude girl next door? The one who raises hell into all hours of the night?"

Madison's tiara fell askew down her forehead. She pushed it back with the palm of her hand. "I'm afraid so. I'm that rude girl. Look, I'm really sorry about—"

From the open doorway a voice cried out. "Aunt Toonie! Are you all right?"

Toonie sat straight up and said in a fierce whisper, "Not a word, you hear me?"

A young woman about Madison's age threw down her purse and some grocery bags as she ran in. She had very short light brown hair with pretty brown eyes. She looked high fashion with her short cut and tall, model-like figure.

"Of course I'm all right," Toonie said matter-of-factly. "I was just demonstrating the correct way to do sit-ups to this nice young girl."

Skepticism all over the young woman's face, she placed her hands on her hips. "Uh-huh. Aunt Toonie, really now."

Toonie smiled at Madison. "Now you try it, Madison." She pushed Madison down on her back, the costume riding up to Madison's knees.

"What? Oh! Absolutely." *You've got to be kidding me.*

Madison ignored Crystal's face, as Toonie said, "Just twenty. And let's go for speed this time. Come on!" She clapped her hands.

Madison hung onto her chiffon and tiara and proceeded to do sit-ups as fast as she could. The memory of her sore muscles came rushing back as she groaned, slowed down on the seventh one, and trembled to complete the eighth before collapsing.

Toonie cocked one brow in surprise, mumbling, "Needs some work." Standing, she put her arm around Crystal and said, "This here is my niece Crystal. She came over this morning to make a fuss. A girl can't lose a few pounds without someone making a fuss."

Crystal was quite tall herself at around five feet ten inches tall, but nothing like her aunt.

Lying on her back on the floor, Madison wheezed out, "Nice to meet you, Crystal." She took her time standing up, trying not to show her soreness.

"My aunt shouldn't be pushing herself so hard. I don't know why she's back in training but—"

Toonie interrupted, "Glad you stopped by, Madison. Anytime."

"Actually, I do have some errands to run before going to a birthday party." She straightened out her dress. "That's why I'm dressed this way."

Crystal had the same ability as her aunt to cock one eyebrow to good effect, saying, "You mean that's not the latest fashion to train in?"

"Uh, take care, Toonie. Thanks for the sit-ups. I guess." Madison wondered what training both Toonie and Crystal had referred to, but decided it was more important to get going. She hurried out of the door to get her tote bag that she'd left out in the hallway. If she hurried, there was still time to fit in some coffee before seeing Grandpa.

"Madison?" Toonie stood in the doorway. She looked Madison in the eyes and nodded. "Thanks."

Chapter Six

THE SMELLS THAT filled The Loony Bean cafe were like heaven to Madison as she let the glass door close, little bells jingling near the top of the door. She inhaled the aromas deep into her body, exhaling slowly to the sounds of liquid whooshing as milk was steamed behind the counter. She felt some of her earlier confidence returning.

The soft murmur of people's conversations occasionally caught her ear as someone mentioned her costume with "ooh, look at that" or "now that's just lovely." She looked their way and smiled with a courteous nod.

She stood in line along a glass case that displayed all sorts of tasty treats that were intended to go well with coffee. Rolls, muffins, cookies, and breads competed for her attention. She decided to treat herself to a whole grain raisin roll to go along with her coffee. Anticipating the yummy roll and coffee, she took her money out ahead of time and held it in her hand, waiting for her turn.

She was next in line as the man in front of her searched his palm for exact change to hand to the barista. The barista! *Hello, baby! So cute. Yes, today will be a good day. Be cool, Madison. Think of something clever to say. Quick. It's your turn!*

She stepped up to the cash register with her most beautiful smile, her head tilted ever so slightly to the side, and said, "Hi. I think I'll get—"

"Potatoes!"

Her face froze.

"Hey, that was you, right? In Bruise Boys last night? That was awesome!" He looked over his shoulder at a tall guy steaming the milk. "Hey, Jason. This is that girl we told you about." He looked back at Madison with enthusiasm. "Damn. We all thought for sure you were about to barf at the end there when you stopped jumping. Is that why you left the stage all of a sudden? Were you really that drunk, or was that part of the act? That was so funny," he said, shaking his head. He slapped the counter. "What can I get for you?"

In a hesitant, timid voice, she answered, "Coffee and a whole grain raisin roll."

He slapped the counter again. "Coming right up. But I'll have to go in the back to get some more raisin rolls. Be right with you." He started walking away and called out. "But don't pull Jason's pants down while I'm gone!"

The business lady in line behind her looked away quickly when Madison looked around. Madison felt compelled to say, "I didn't pull anyone's pants, you know, down, or anything." The lady smiled and nodded and began a deep study of the treats in the glass case.

From near the espresso machine she heard a calm, manly voice say, "You don't recognize me, do you?"

She looked over at him. A tall man with curly brown hair wore the solid muscular build that comes naturally when great genes meet hard work. He looked at her and smiled with hazel brown eyes and said, "Jason Clark." Jason's hands were relaxed and steady as he poured a few of the lattes into cups.

He was cute and definitely familiar, but she couldn't remember where she knew him from. "Well," she began, "actually…"

He turned around to set the lattes down on the counter for waiting customers.

Madison dipped her eyes, recognized his awesome backside, and exclaimed, "Oh, my gosh! *That* Jason! You used to work for—"

"Vincent Cruz Landscaping." He turned back around, wiping his hands on a towel. "Yeah. Your grandfather was my boss."

"Yes, I remember now."

"Tough old guy. My dad used to work for him, too. How is he these days?"

"Retired. I'm about to go visit him."

"Well, don't tell him I talked to you," he laughed. "That was a fireable offense when I was working for him. He never let us forget it."

Madison put her face in her hand and laughed. "That's right. None of you guys were allowed to talk to me. And if I ever talked to any of you, I got in *so* much trouble."

"Makes me feel like such a bad boy." He winked at her and said, "This will be our secret. Say hi for me." He resumed working the espresso machine.

"I will."

Such a simple moment felt so calming for Madison as she reflected on how crazily the day had started. But seeing Jason made her feel like things were looking up. Nothing like a good cup of coffee. And Toonie didn't die on her doorstep. And the living room wall was not beyond repair. Life was about to get great.

Toonie seemed older than Grandma ever got to be. Just how old had Grandma been when she died? It was still a hard memory. Ann was such a young mother; she was graduating high school when Madison started preschool, and Grandma had felt much more like her mother. Madison had been only twelve when Grandma died.

The barista returned with her coffee, her roll in a bag, and told her how much she owed. And that was when it hit her. Grandpa's behavior last night. She knew now why it had seemed familiar and had set off some subtle alarm within her. His behavior last night was like when he knew something bad was coming, like when Grandma was going to die, but he hadn't told Madison yet. Her elated mood dissolved, giving way to a new fear.

The barista said, "Hey, it's okay. We have a jar of change right here if you don't have enough." She looked at him without seeing him, tears breaking away from the corners of her eyes. He grew alarmed and said, "Look, I'll pay for it myself. My treat."

She returned to herself and shook her head saying, "No, I'm just an idiot. Really. All my friends say so. I have to go!" She put the money down on the counter and grabbed her coffee and the bag, her fist crumpling the paper loudly.

She ran to her car, threw her purse and paper bag with the roll in it onto the seat next to her, and tried not to slosh the hot coffee as she stuck it in the cup holder.

She headed out to Grandpa's house where she had grown up, realizing she hadn't been there much this last year except to borrow the drill.

✧   ✧   ✧

THE BIG HOUSE had a slightly Victorian look to the architecture and had gone through many shades of paint over the years. Currently it was white, which was always Madison's favorite.

Parking next to Grandpa's car in his driveway, Madison promised herself she would be calm and let him talk. *I'm an adult now. I'm strong and he can count on me. If he's sick like Grandma was, we'll fight it together. Or if it's not illness, like…like…* She couldn't even imagine what else there might be that he would be afraid to tell her.

Carrying the drill, she hurried down the walkway that led to the front door, past the garden. Grandpa always had a fantastic garden designed to have something blooming, or in some way showing color and life, during every month of the year. Whether it was flowers, growing vines, ground covers, autumn leaves, purple kales, or wintered-over tree bark wrapped in tiny white lights during the snows, Grandpa always had a garden to take your breath away. He had been doing that in the same big house for forty-five years.

As she climbed the porch steps she heard a voice from inside yelling what sounded to her like "Ned! Ned!" *That's odd. Who's Ned? Or was it "Annette"?*

At the door, she heard thumps and then a muffled crash coming from inside. She skipped the formality of knocking and grabbed the doorknob, but it was locked.

More thumping hollow sounds, like something heavy hitting the wooden floor.

Grandpa used to leave a key for her in an old wooden cuckoo bird near the door. The key was in its beak if she twisted it the right way. She reached up and twisted. *Yes! It's still here.* She was beginning to feel adrenaline with each sound, and her hands shook as she unlocked the door and rushed in.

A few chairs and a little table were on their sides near the left wall, a vase in pieces in a nearby corner. A throw rug in the center of the floor was rumpled and scrunched up at one end.

Vincent Cruz and another older man about his age and size, a complete stranger to Madison, were slugging it out at a speed that made it hard to track whose fist hit where. Vincent's jowls shook from the blows, but he didn't seem to notice as he hit the stranger just as hard. The stranger's feet tangled in the rumpled throw rug. He fell forward, grabbing at Vincent's arms, turning it into a bizarre dance. They whirled round and round, banging into furniture and walls, knocking down big picture frames.

Then, the stranger's elbow connected in an uppercut to her grandfather's chin, breaking his hold. Vincent hit the stranger's face just as the stranger punched him in the stomach.

For several seconds, Madison was in complete shock like a frightened child. Slowly, she realized that what she was witnessing was real. At last her voice returned to her. She screamed, "STOP!"

But the violent scuffle went to the floor. They rolled, knocking down a lamp that fell against her grandfather's face and tangled his arms in the cord. That gave the stranger a momentary advantage and he sat on top, straddling her grandfather as he put his hands around her grandfather's throat.

Madison didn't remember running across the room to them. But she would never forget the savagery she felt when she walloped the stranger on the side of his head with the wide end of the drill. His hand flew up to his head while he used the other hand to steady himself on the floor. Her grandfather rolled out onto his knees, faced the stranger, and finished him off with a roundhouse punch to his face. The momentum of his own punch threw her grandfather downward, forcing him to catch himself with his hands on the floor.

The stranger fell to his side with a soft plop, rolling onto his back, unconscious. His head flopped to a halt. He had short gray hair with bushy salt and pepper eyebrows that touched in the center, forming a unibrow. His eyes were closed but the features of his face burned into her as she stared down at him.

She heard a small thump when the drill dropped from her hands to the floor. She hadn't noticed the ringing in her ears and her pounding heart till now.

Her grandfather climbed to his feet like a tired rock climber. She moved to help him but he waved her away as he rose to a bending position with his hands on his knees, wheezing, coughing a little, and swallowing. His voice was rough but quiet.

"He called it benevolent deception," he said between whispered laughs. "But the deception…went so much deeper." He scrunched up his face and pounded a frustrated fist on his knee. He gestured to the unconscious man on the floor. "He was used, too. More blackmail."

He gulped more air, straightened up, and shook his head. "You shouldn't be here. If I had lost that fight he would have got you. He doesn't know you exist yet."

She stared at him disbelieving and realized she needed to inhale. Her voice shook as she said, "If I hadn't been here, you might be dead."

"These people are still very dangerous."

"Grandpa?"

His face took on a new note of urgency. "We have to move fast."

"Grandpa!?"

"Now!" He stumbled over to a desk and rummaged around in a drawer.

She blinked a few times and thrust out a shaking finger to point at the unconscious man. Her voice cracked as she fought to control it. "Who is that? What just happened?"

"I need you to do something. I can't stress enough how important it is," he said as he found what he was looking for in the drawer. He turned around holding duct tape.

"Grandpa! What is going on?"

"Run out to the tool shed in the back. Remember all those shelves against the wall? At the very bottom on the concrete floor are a few builders blocks and an old metal box holding up the bottom shelf plank. Tear it all down so you can grab that box! Then leave before anyone else comes!"

Like a deer in headlights, she watched him duct tape the unconscious man's mouth. Her heart pounded.

"This will slow him down," he said. "You need to go!"

"But—"

"Hide that box! Then wait. Go about your normal life. That's the safest thing you can do. I can't tell you more right now. You won't understand till you hear the whole thing, and I don't know how long it will take to get help. Days, probably. Don't call the police. And especially don't tell Ann, promise me. Don't tell Ann."

"This is crazy—"

"There's a very good reason. You've got to trust me, sweetheart!" He pleaded. "I need time! Now hurry!"

Chapter Seven

MADISON FLEW OUT the back door of the house. With her costume dress hiked up to her knees, she ran across the lawn to the tool shed. The shed door was swollen from the frequent Seattle rains. She gave it an extra bump with her hip and it popped open.

The cool damp smells of earth, firewood, and vitamin-rich plant food hit her nose. She'd forgotten how much those smells were a part of her life during her childhood. She used to play in here and sometimes got in trouble for climbing those shelves, accidentally knocking tools down or breaking open a fresh bag of topsoil. That metal box and the large grey builders blocks at the bottom had been supporting those shelves as far back as she could remember. The box had never *not* been there. To her it was just this square thing, and she never knew it was actually a box. She'd never thought about it since it had always blended into the scenery.

In the dim light she could see why he'd said to just knock everything over. There was absolutely no way of getting to the box until all five shelves on top of it were removed. But she couldn't quite reach the first shelf on top.

She hugged her body to the shelves that were covered in dust and old webs, reaching on tiptoe. Using her fingertips, she pushed off old cans of fence paint, metal parts to a mower, and clay pots. They crunched and bounced as they hit the concrete floor. She pulled off the first shelf and flung it. It wasn't attached to the wall and had been supported by big block bricks directly underneath it. Those bricks in turn had been standing on the next shelf down.

Now things were easier to reach, and the process of knocking clutter off the following shelves went faster. Spiders scattered and dust filled the air as she pushed everything as hard and as fast as she could. In her panic a cry escaped her throat once, but she clenched her jaw hard. *No! I have to be strong and find out what's going on.*

Sprinkler heads, curled up hoses, a sack of barbecue charcoals, half empty seed bags, all down, crashing, nipping her toes in close calls. Soon she was able to grab the second shelf and haul one end off of its support bricks and let gravity take over. An avalanche of hand tools danced and flew across the floor; glass jars of nails crashed and shattered. The second shelf took the third shelf with it. She shoved the fourth shelf over, and the fifth, coughing in the dust.

She felt heartsick at the violence she was doing to the tool shed that held so many innocent secrets of her youth. Many childhood fantasies had played out in here. But it seemed this place had been hiding other secrets, too.

Finally, the box was free. It didn't appear to have ever been moved. It buckled inward slightly at the top from the weight of all those years. Madison picked it up and noticed that although its dimensions seemed the same as the grey builders blocks that held up the shelves, it was not as heavy. It had a latch on the side that had been facing the wall.

Holding the box, she had to balance herself as she stepped across the debris toward the door, her long dress snagging and getting caught as she tried to whip it free in her hurry. She ran back to the house. She had been gone maybe five minutes.

She burst back into the house, running into the living room where she had left Grandpa. The stranger now had hands and ankles securely duct taped so that it would be nearly impossible for him to get up or leave without assistance. Grandpa knelt beside him, adding more duct tape around his knees.

Madison was breathing fast. Grandpa looked at her with deep worry. "Why haven't you left?"

"Is this," she gulped for air, "the box?"

"Yes! Madison!" She recognized his impatient tone as he stood up. Wincing, he stooped to rub a knee. "You should be leaving!"

She interrupted him, "I have to know one thing." She tried to steady her breathing. "Are you dying?"

He stared at her, trying to comprehend. "Was my fighting that pathetic?" He drew himself up to his full six-foot-two height.

"What? No!" said Madison. "No, you were amazing!"

"I know I've aged, but—"

"You were kicking ass!" said Madison.

"I thought I held my own pretty good there," he said. "Who knew I could last that long—"

"I mean it was old ass, but that's okay because, you know—"

"—with a trained—" He stopped and looked at her. "What do you mean, 'old ass'?"

"A trained what?" she asked.

Panic returned to his eyes. "Baby girl, you still know how to derail my thoughts."

"You knew something bad was coming, didn't you?"

"What? No. I mean, not till a few weeks ago. They hacked in and found me." His frustration mounted.

"You have to go! You'll be safe if they don't know about you!"

"Who? Hacked? What, that thing with the UW? What's going on?"

She saw fear in his eyes. He seemed about to say something but then shook his head.

She pressed in. "You have to tell me what—"

"I can't! Not yet. But I will."

He put his hands on her shoulders and searched her eyes.

"Baby girl, can you do what I'm asking while I go get help?"

She stared at him, then nodded her head in fast tiny movements, fighting tears. She looked at his scratched face and wondered for the first time who he was. Old folks had an entire past locked away in their heads, and just when you thought you knew them, something new came out and threw you. It might be something funny or a story of some adventure they once had. But sometimes, it could be something dark.

She braced herself for what his answer would be, as she asked, "What were you before you were a gardener?"

Exasperated, he answered, "An unemployed teenager! Please, Madison!"

"Okay, okay! But promise me," she pleaded, "you'll tell me everything?"

"I promise."

A muffled grunt came from the floor. The bound stranger was awake and looking up at them with seething anger. But when his gaze fell on Madison's eyes, he locked on them in seeming shock.

"Get out of here!" Her grandfather pushed her away. She gripped the box and struggled not to stumble on her long dress as she ran across the room and grabbed the doorknob.

She looked back one more time. The stranger's eyes had followed her all the way to the door. His eyes seemed to be creased at the corners. *Is he smiling?*

She ran out.

Dashing to her car in the driveway, she saw nothing but the ground her slippered feet pounded over. She held her long dress up with one hand while holding the metal box under her arm. Fumbling the car door open, she threw the box in. It collided with the paper bag containing the whole grain raisin roll. Jumping behind the steering wheel, she slammed the car door closed on a big fold of her dress. In her panic the coffee in the car's cup holder was bumped and it sloshed on her dress.

She punched the accelerator as she backed out of the driveway, swinging the steering wheel wild, the back end of her car just clipping the edge of another car parked along the curb. A woman behind the steering wheel was opening her door just as her car was jostled. To the sound of tiny broken glass, Madison screeched out of there.

She didn't notice her surroundings for a few blocks. A day that had started out with so much hope and resolve was fast disappearing in her rearview mirror. She stole a glance at the old metal box on the seat next to her. A corner of the smashed raisin roll bag underneath the box stuck out from the side. How could this box not be one ugly piece of bad news, waiting for her to find out? Her attention to traffic was sporadic, and she had to hit the brakes hard at one point, sending the box down with a muffled thud as it hit the carpeted floorboard. She was dying to know what was in it, but also frightened to find out.

Perhaps Grandpa, like many men, had sown some wild oats in his youth? He didn't want the police involved. And come on, no one would want controlling, know-it-all Ann involved.

Obviously, he'd been hiding something in the box from the tool shed. A box that for many years he'd felt no need to get into and no need to get rid of. And she had to face it; it was never a good sign to see someone duct taping an unconscious man, although she had to admit she didn't have any kind thoughts for the man with the salt and pepper unibrow. Seeing him hit her grandfather had brought out a side of her that was new.

It scared her. But uncomfortable or not, she would hit him with a drill again if he tried to hurt her grandfather.

What haunted her was that Grandpa had gestured to the unibrow man saying that he'd been used, too, indicating that they'd both been blackmailed. By whom and for what? Her only knowledge of Grandpa was her ordinary life with him.

He was always willing to listen to her hare-brained ideas, her mad schemes. At the age of thirteen, Madison discovered the joy of the performing arts, throwing her schooling to the wind. Her GPA plummeted. Ann, stationed in Philadelphia at the time, was furious. But Grandpa was there to promise Ann it was temporary. He then made it clear to Madison that taking school seriously was like a voucher she could cash in for his support. He kept tabs on her homework and drove her to auditions and rehearsals. He paid for dance lessons, costumes, acting classes, and most importantly he attended every ridiculous show she had been in.

When she'd gotten older she'd discovered camera work in a few commercials and bit parts, and some real money started to come in. But it wasn't steady work, and Madison hadn't found a way yet where she could relax and enjoy life. Life was a series of small paychecks and the occasional big one. She hadn't been able to admit it to herself until this morning. But turning her life around would have to wait. Grandpa needed her and she wanted to be there for him the way he had always been there for her. Right now, she needed to keep an iron grip on her composure.

She finally started making turns in traffic on purpose, and drove home. She swung into the parking lot of her new apartment complex and wondered when she would stop thinking of it as new. She parked, grabbed the metal box and her purse, and ran into her apartment building. Rushing down the hallway toward the stairwell, images of the fist fight returned to her as she bounded up the stairs to the second floor. She had no idea old men could get so fierce with each other. The desperation and passion with which they fought was truly frightening. She was shocked to see that her grandfather could fight like that. He had a mean right. Who knew? Must be all the landscaping work keeping him strong. But what had made the stakes so high for them both? The mystery of it all drove her nuts, and was really starting to piss her off.

She reached her floor and hurried towards her door. She just might make it inside without having a breakdown out here in the hallway. She dug out her key and jammed it in her doorknob.

That's when Toonie's door opened. Toonie stepped out and said, "Hey, I saw you pull up outside, and I just wanted to say—"

Slam! Madison made it inside. She hurried into the living room, sat down on the floor with the box, and stared at it.

Now what?

It was covered in dust and gave off a mottled rusty mud color, except for the top. The top was a clean dark grey since that was where the shelf had sat for so long, keeping years of dust off of it.

I totally trust Grandpa. Totally. He'll call and explain everything. She pulled her cell phone out of her purse and looked at the time on it. She waited an eternal thirty seconds. Then she set about trying to figure out how to break into the box. She grabbed the latch and tried to force it open. She wiggled it hard and hit it with her fist a few times. *Damned thing is probably rusted shut.*

Just then Toonie pounded on the door and her muffled voice yelled, "I realize that you've returned to being rude again, so it's hard to do you any favors. But you might want to know that someone is breaking into your car right now."

What? Disbelieving, Madison got up and hurried to her window. Down in the sunny parking lot she saw long slender legs attached to a shapely bottom in a black pencil skirt bent over and sticking out from the open door of Madison's car. A woman was rummaging around in the glove compartment.

Madison muttered, "What the hell?"

Chapter Eight

AFTER EVERYTHING THAT had happened in the last few hours, Madison flew into a rage at this final indignity. She went tearing out of her apartment door, and slammed headlong into ExBoy.

"Uuff!" she yelled into his chest, as he stumbled back in surprise, just managing to catch her before she could fall.

"Whoa there, what's going—" he started to ask.

She regained her balance and broke loose. "Not now!" she cried as she ran down the hall.

She hiked her skirt up, her anger propelling her into the stairwell and down each step. The last thing she needed right now was complications. And ExBoy was a complicated part of her life.

She jumped the last few steps to the bottom, then flew out of the building into the parking lot. But by the time she got out there the woman was gone. Madison looked left and right, trying to understand what had just happened. How did the woman disappear so fast?

Her anger had made her willing to face anything. But now that she stood here, alone, her mind filled in the holes that her haste had ignored. The memory came rushing back to her that she had clipped a car in front of Grandpa's house and a woman was behind the wheel.

Madison's indignation melted as fear took its place. The whole time she was driving around, trying to figure out what to do, that woman had been following her. She had this one lousy task of hiding the box and already she was screwing it up.

She checked inside her car to see if anything looked missing. Nope. All the trash was still there. At the very least, the would-be thief could have taken some, just to be polite. She checked in her glove compartment. Everything looked fine. She slammed it shut and saw her tote bag on the floor, with the balloon pump sticking out. Realization sank in on her. *The birthday gig! Oh my God, I no-showed!*

Standing there, a filthy fairy godmother with a supreme case of paranoia, she was at a loss as to how she would explain this to Phil her agent. Some angry mother was probably on the phone chewing him out right now. Jobs were scarce enough without pissing off her agent. And Phil found ways of making you pay for it.

Someone, please just shoot me now.

At the very least, Phil needed a chance to call the client with an apology that things had not worked out in time. Maybe try to save the job with an offer like "The fairy godmother just died, but I have a clown who can be there in an hour." Clients could be pretty understanding if given a little explanation.

She needed to call Phil immediately.

Her cell phone was back in her living room, so she snatched her tote bag and the sad little paper bag with the smashed whole grain raisin roll out of the car and ran across the parking lot back up to her apartment.

She just needed to think of an explanation as she ran. In her mind she offered varying explanations but none of them sounded right.

"Phil, I've been vomiting nonstop since dawn!"

No. I've used that one before.

She reached the stairs and took them two at a time.

"Phil, there were vicious foaming dogs in their driveway, trying to attack me through the car window!"

No. Phil loves dogs.

Reaching the top of the stairs, she ran down the hallway to her door.

"Phil, dude, I don't know what you're talking about. Of course I did the gig. What? They told you I never showed? Why those awful people."

She ran into her apartment and found ExBoy standing in her living room holding the box, shaking it and … *smelling it?* "What are you *doing*?" she screamed.

Startled, he dropped the box with a loud clang and the lid popped open. In a panic, Madison ran and dove on top of it protecting it with her arms, her body splayed out flat on the floor.

"Would you please just go?" she yelled, terrified of what might have fallen out. Body parts? Counterfeit money? Vintage girly magazines? She made sure the lid was closed but not enough to lock.

"After I get my lucky t-shirt back. I need it for the convention. And then we need to talk." He walked off into the bedroom.

Incredulous, she called, "What lucky t-shirt?"

From the bedroom she heard, "The one I left here the day I helped you move?"

Oh. She remembered. She thought of it as the almost-lucky t-shirt. The shirt had a picture of a baby zombie with a little fistful of brains and a caption that said Ready for Solid Food.

"What convention?" she demanded. She needed to wrap this up and make him leave fast.

"Zombie Prom. It's a zombie convention."

"Zombies don't have conventions!"

"In this town they do."

She called, "Damn it, ExBoy, I can return it to you later! You shouldn't have left it here."

Still in her bedroom, he said, "You're in danger, Madison."

"What?" Adrenaline hit her.

"Seriously. This room is going to get fed up with your neglect and attack you in your sleep."

"Get *out!*"

He appeared at the doorway placing his forearm up on the doorframe. "I can't find it." Leaning there he studied her. "You're dressed like a princess but all messed up. Did you get in a princess fight?"

"I'm not a princess," she growled. "I'm a fairy godmother."

"Oh. Magical throwdown. Did you utter incantations then drop your wand like a rap artist?"

Her teeth gritted, she said, "We're about to have a throwdown right now."

He tilted his head with a sly smile on his face. "Very seductive. But it's not going to work. I'm leaving."

"Good."

"What are you hiding? What's in that thing?"

"Go!"

"Fine. But we *have* to talk later." His posture tightened up a bit. "I can't put it off any more." Heading for the door he added, "Oh, your grandpa called. I saw his name on your cell screen. I like that old guy." ExBoy walked out and she heard the door close.

Damn it, I missed his call. She rose to her hands and knees and scrambled over to the spot on the floor where she had left the phone. It said Missed Call on its screen. But it also said Voicemail. *Yes!* She punched in the numbers to retrieve her voicemail and listened as Grandpa's soft mumble mixed with the touch tones.

"Damned thing… *deet, doot* few days *deeeeeeet* but don't *doot, doot…*" There were sporadic words in the background that sounded like overhead public announcements, the word "departure" grabbing her attention. *He's leaving town?* Then one long part got through, "…he'll handle our little friend till we can turn him over. You can trust him, sweetheart. He's known about this *deeeet* him your number in case anything… *dooot…*" and the voicemail cut off.

She clutched the phone tight in her hand as she shut her eyes in frustration. She knew her grandfather was a pretty sharp cookie. So how the hell could an intelligent person screw that up so bad? She pictured him holding the phone out in front of his face while he talked, as if it were a walkie-talkie, his thumb accidentally pressing buttons. She tried calling him right back. He didn't answer, and apparently he hadn't set it up to receive voicemail, so she had no way to leave a message.

Next she called Phil.

She couldn't tell Phil about her grandfather, and she was too exhausted to come up with a convincing story. She was ready to fall on her sword and get it over with. His outgoing message came on and her stomach twisted as she heard the beep.

"Phil? It's Madison. Look, I don't know how to begin." She hesitated. "You've probably been wondering what happened. It's hard to explain, Phil, but you've got to believe me when I say how sorry I am for not showing up for the princess birthday party today, and if you…" *beeep!* "Argh!"

She was about to call him back and finish her message, when her phone rang with Ethel Merman singing, "There's No Business Like Show Business," meaning Phil had called her right back.

She hit the answer button. "Phil?"

In his signature street-tough Boston accent, he said, "Chocolate Mint! How's my gorgeous girl?"

This was a good sign. Phil was calling her by his pet name for her. Chocolate mint referred to her long black lashes surrounding her pale green eyes.

"Phil, you're…you're not mad?"

"Mad about what?"

"The gig. The princess birthday party that I no-showed. I'm sorry, Phil. It's been a hell of a day and—"

"Minty, you didn't no-show. I put that message out to a bunch of you. Jen called back first, so I gave her the gig. Actually, you never called back at all." Madison was confused. *He gave a children's party to Jen? From the stripper unit?* Then she realized that she hadn't completed the phone call to Phil last night because her grandfather had shown up at the door. *But still. Jen? Ew.*

He continued, "But I heard about your wrestling debut last night. I'm dying to meet that Atomic guy. And seriously, girl, you should have let me negotiate that for you. I could have got you more money, even after my cut. And you know that's a fact."

He would have demanded more, all right. He would have priced me right out of the gig.

"Oh, my God, Phil, I don't know whether to laugh or cry. I almost showed up at the birthday party, in my costume and everything. If I hadn't gone to visit my grand—" *Shut up, Madison!*

"Don't worry about it. I made Jen promise no cleavage. I only put that message out because I needed someone fast. You, I prefer to save for the bigger gigs, you know?"

Don't argue. Pretend you believe him.

He continued, "You know I like to keep you busy, girl."

"Thanks, Phil. Have you heard back about the radio spot yet? They loved me at the audition."

"Sorry, kid. They went with someone else."

"Damn. I miss doing voiceover gigs. You used to get me so many."

"I keep telling you, Minty, you've got to get yourself some audio gear. In-studio auditions, like that one, are hard to find now. Most of the auditions are done in the artist's home, and sent as an audio attachment in an email."

"That gear isn't cheap, Phil. I can barely pay my rent. Maybe if you got me more work?"

"Yeah, yeah, I'm looking out for you. You're booked to do the Bumbling Waitress tomorrow at one o'clock, right?"

"Yeah. You already sent the gig sheet. It's at Giovanni's Restaurant."

"Good. So, hey, I have…something…on my desk right now. Big pay. It'll probably be tomorrow. A little unusual. The victim is a whole group of people this time. You'll have to adapt to whatever the reaction is but you're good at improv. If anyone could pull this off…"

She didn't like the sound of this. He was stalling.

"What is it?"

"A singing telegram."

"And?"

"You show up big and pregnant in front of this group. You look low class, dance for the client." She could hear him swallow. "Shimmy at him. And sing, 'You Made Me Love You.'"

"Okay, it's a comedy gig."

He was silent for a moment. "It's in front of the client's family." He was still stalling.

"Phil, you know I don't do stripping. Call Jen if that's what—"

"No, no, Minty, I know that. It's just a little unusual, is all."

"Spit it out."

"The client is dead."

"What?"

"Yeah...uh...he arranged this, just before he croaked."

"Dead?"

"He had a reputation for playing gags. Family always loved it. So he wanted to play a little joke to lighten things up at his funeral."

"You want me to do a comic shimmy to a *dead guy?*"

"He pre-paid!"

She yelled, "Are you out of your mind?"

"Ten minutes and you're out of there, collect five hundred bucks! That's three times the usual cut!"

"You're the king of taste, you know that?"

"C'mon, Minty, you kind of owe me one."

"For *what?* I've been loyal and—"

"You no-showed—"

"I did not!"

"Technically, no. But in spirit?"

"Phil!"

"You no-showed and you need a chance to make it up to me. You know, feel good about yourself again."

"You know I hate you, right? You do know that?"

His Boston street voice softened. "Think of his poor family. He arranged this for them. To give them one last laugh. Help them get through a tough time."

"Damn it, Phil!" she wailed. She felt herself caving in. And she knew that Phil knew. *Watch out.*

"Minty, have a heart."

"One thousand dollars."

"What?!" he screamed.

"Think of his family, Phil."

She heard something slamming down on his desk three times as he sputtered unintelligible words, and then went silent. She added, "The body is not getting any fresher."

After a moment, he snarled, "You won't back out?"

I need the money. "I'll be there."

He grumbled. "Fine. His name was Eddie Willet. I'll send the details as soon as I have them." He hung up on her.

She knew it. She figured the client must have offered to pay a hell of a lot for such an uncomfortable job.

Otherwise, Phil never would have agreed to her demand of one thousand dollars. He would have growled and hung onto his cut like it was the last dog bone on earth. She let her phone drop into her lap and rubbed her temples.

All that was left to do, was to look in the box.

Chapter Nine

S HE GOT UP and went to the window, looking down into the parking lot. Everything looked quiet. A few cars driving normal speed passed by on the street in front of the apartment building. Now that the time had finally come to face whatever was in the box, she delayed. She was afraid that something was about to change forever. She had grown up and stopped playing in the tool shed, but the secrets that were hidden in there were ready to come out.

She closed the window and drew the blinds shut. Tearing off her sad and dirty fairy godmother costume, she threw it over to the couch where it landed on top of unpacked boxes. In bra and panties she went to the kitchen sink and drank water from her faucet. She was dehydrated and starving and the water felt wonderful going down her throat. But food would have to wait. She didn't know how upsetting the contents of the box were going to be, so she'd rather not have food in her stomach.

She sat on the floor next to the box, and opened it. The hinges creaked and complained as she lifted the lid and looked inside.

A big clump of folded papers, fastened together with old rusty paper clips, sat on top of a wad of folded, light colored fabric. The fabric appeared to be padding for the bottom of the box. The papers were yellowed newspaper pages and clippings. With a delicate hand, Madison lifted out the papers, careful not to touch the rusty edges of the paper clips, and briefly wondered how long ago paper clips started being made with plastic. There were also folded pieces of cardboard tucked along the walls within the box. For extra padding on the side? Everything looked dirty or stained.

Okay, so nothing here is obvious. No money, blueprints, or diamonds. Not even one body part. So far, so good. Perhaps the dreaded secret was something in the newspaper stories. She decided she would spread all the papers out on the floor, and one by one, inspect—

She heard steps outside in the hallway. Her heart rate sped up as she stood and looked out the peephole. She saw the backs of people walking past her door at a casual speed, their voices a low murmur with the occasional chuckle echoing in the hall as they continued walking. Sounded like a man and a woman. Just other residents. Everything was okay. Except for her nerves.

She returned to the box and the papers on the floor. Looking down at the seemingly harmless contents, she had to remind herself that her grandfather had fought like a man possessed, and it was somehow related to the contents of this box.

He'd said "These people are still very dangerous." But to whom was he referring? And who the hell was Ned? It hadn't sounded like her grandfather's voice, which meant it had to be the stranger who'd been yelling it. But why would he call her grandfather Ned? His name was Vincent. Vincent Cruz.

And there was another thing that was really bugging her. Grandpa said they hacked in and found him. But who would have the sophistication to hack into the UW archives? And why bother? Her grandfather lived an open life. He wouldn't be hard to find.

A more disturbing memory strong-armed its way to the front of her mind. He had actually been putting duct tape on that man's mouth! She'd never seen that in real life. He probably wanted to keep him quiet so the neighbors didn't alert the police. So if Grandpa needed time to go get help, and he said it would take days, then someone would have to feed and water the duct taped stranger while Grandpa was gone. That must be who he was referring to on the voicemail. But who would that be? Who would Grandpa trust?

Tears flooded her eyes. She was feeling that scared-little-girl moment again. *Damn it, Madison, not now. Fight it.* She roughly wiped away the tears and inhaled through her nose as hard as she could. *My job is to hide the box, but they must know now that I brought it into my apartment.* She had to go somewhere where it would be safe to look over those papers and try to figure out what was happening. And that meant getting dressed because fleeing in your bra and panties was never a good idea.

She hurried into her bedroom and threw on jeans, a tank top, and athletic shoes. She didn't know when she'd be back. She took a quick look around the room. ExBoy was right. The neglect in her bedroom, hell, in her whole apartment, would be turning into mutiny status soon. She had a hard time remembering what was dirty laundry and what was clean. *Laundry. Good thought.*

Maybe she could hang out at Spenser's house and get a load done there. Madison was quite skilled as a seamstress, having learned from her grandmother. The usual deal was Madison would fix hems, tears, buttons; anything Spenser might need in exchange for the use of Spenser's washer, dryer, and laundry soap.

She pulled the pillowcase from her pillow and stuffed it full of dirty laundry and some probably-dirty laundry. She kicked through some of the clothes on the floor. Good thing it was August. It was easy to get by in lightweight clothing in warm weather, making it easier to pack a lot of stuff.

As her toe pushed aside a spare blanket on the floor, a little baby zombie peeked out from underneath: the t-shirt that ExBoy had come looking for. She picked it up and noticed ExBoy's scent still on it. She buried her face in it for a moment. There was something about his natural scent that reminded her of the forest and the deep shadows under heavy tree growth.

Clearly he was attracted to her, too, but his behavior around her was confusing. A friendly smile one minute, lost in some uncomfortable thought the next. Maybe he was as unsure about her as she was about him. Whatever it was, the effect was that she never felt relaxed around him.

He was an artist with a flair for writing. But his art was comic book monsters, and he wrote horror stories. In particular, he loved zombies. He thought zombies were fascinating, scary, cool, and funny all at the same time. And though she didn't have strong feelings one way or the other for the horror genre, it bothered her that he wouldn't talk about it, about something that meant a lot to him. Spenser had called him mysterious and brooding, but to Madison he was more like Dark Peter Pan.

She regretted how hard she had been on him lately. It wasn't his fault that her life was a mess. She looked at the silly t-shirt and remembered him wearing it when his arms were around her, his face seeking hers as she giggled and turned her head side to side, playing hard to kiss. Her giggles turned to giggling screams as he settled for her neck, and her ticklishness took over. Playful wrestling took them down to the bare carpet in her new apartment. Then as stronger urges came on, they had torn off their shirts just as other friends knocked on the door, arriving to help with moving in.

Conflicted, she had pulled her shirt back on, and ran to open the door. But he hadn't put *his* shirt back on. He had finished the move that hot July day with his shirt off, giving her a knowing smile whenever he caught her looking at him.

Maybe she should pick up where they left off that day. Sample the bait. Just a little? She stuffed the baby zombie t-shirt into the pillowcase to wash it with the rest of the laundry.

She went back into the living room and emptied the tote bag. She carefully placed the fabric and the papers from the metal box into the tote, and although it seemed stupid, she added the cardboard tucked along the sides, which remained flat from all the years of being stored that way.

She then put the contents that had been in the tote bag into the metal box. If anyone were to open that metal box now, they would find a watercolor paint set, little paint brushes, a storybook, a balloon pump, a bag of long skinny balloons, her magic wand with the rhinestone star on the end, and fairy wings. The contents from the metal box and the tote bag had officially been switched. Last of all, she closed the lid on the metal box and jammed it back in place. It seemed just as rusted closed as before.

She stacked several of her unpacked moving boxes by the living room window, then put the metal box on top. She pulled the blinds open so that from the parking lot, if anyone were really trying, they would be able to spot the metal box through the window. If anyone had seen her running out of Grandpa's house, they would have seen her clutching the box like her life depended on it. And if they had followed her and were watching, they would likely stick around and wait for her to drive away before entering her apartment to get the box. She hoped.

Carrying the tote, her purse, and the pillowcase of laundry, she left her apartment and headed into the outer hallway.

She stopped at Toonie's door and knocked. After a moment she knew Toonie must be looking at her through the peephole before opening the door. She didn't know how to compose her face for the peephole because she didn't truly understand what it was she needed to say. She heard a few locks turning and the door opened up. Toonie stood there towering, her hands on her hips, her stern face considering Madison.

"Toonie," she began and stopped. "I've been a weird neighbor, and I don't know how to fix it. I suppose my actions have been confusing. Well, nothing is making sense to me right now but I don't want to be that person who doesn't give a shit about her neighbors. I do care. This morning I felt like an ass to realize you were probably sick last night when I was yelling and drilling, and... Are you feeling better?

"Young lady, you have a way of pissing me off and endearing yourself to me at the same time. Kind of like having kids, I guess. Yeah, I'm better. It ain't no virus. I think my new blood pressure medication doesn't like this new diet." She shook her head. "I don't know what's going on with you, running back and forth in the hallway like your hair is on fire." Toonie sighed and said, "Wait here."

She disappeared from the door for a moment and returned with a plastic baggie with some cookies in it. "This is my own recipe. People beg me for it, but I don't give it out." She held the baggie up in the air. "Now if you ever want some of these again, and trust me you will, you will behave yourself around here." She handed the baggie to Madison. "And whatever it is you're going through, don't go making emotional decisions. Make smart ones."

Madison pressed her lips together hard as she smiled and fought new tears. She took the baggie with cookies. "Toonie, I'd kiss you if you weren't so tall."

"Humph. I've heard that from a few men over the years." She looked off in the distance and murmured, "But eventually they couldn't help themselves."

Madison put the baggie into her tote. "I have to go."

Toonie said, "Last night when you were yelling out the window, you said you were an accident. What did you mean by that?"

"I wasn't supposed to be born."

"Aw, now, your mama don't feel that way."

Madison was quiet for a moment. "Honestly? I don't think I was a good idea."

✧　✧　✧

MADISON PULLED UP in front of Spenser's home, a brown two-story house in the suburbs. Before heading to Spenser's front door, she sat in her parked car taking a moment to consider what her next move should be.

She decided to stick with her earlier plan of calling her mother, Ann, about getting together for coffee today. Not only did she need to face her mother about the adventures with the Bruise Boys last night; she needed more information about her grandfather's friends, the ones from his past. There was no way she was going to wait around for him to explain himself. Someone was helping her grandfather at this very moment and she needed to find that friend and make him tell her what the hell was going on.

Her mother was the best chance she had of figuring out where to start, but Madison had to be careful not to tip her off that anything was wrong. Grandpa's mandate to Madison was to hide the box, but he had also said to go about her normal life.

Normal? She wondered for a moment if he'd forgotten who he was talking to.

She called up her mother and held her breath while she heard the phone ringing on the other end. A quick voice, all business answered, "Ann Cruz."

"Mom? Mom, it's Madison. Do you have a minute?"

"Oh." There was a pause. "Well, hello! Uh…" She gave a small laugh. Madison recognized her mother's nervous chuckle. "I'm sorry but you caught me off guard. I had no idea it would be you."

"I'm sorry, Mom. Calling you at work like this."

"No, no. It's okay. I just had to get in a different head space. Believe me, hearing your voice is much better than what I was expecting."

Madison tried chuckling back. "What were you expecting?"

Silence, then, "I'm sorry, honey, you know I'm not allowed to talk about my cases."

"Sorry," said Madison. The silence resumed and Madison heard someone clearing their throat in the background. Maybe that person was waiting for Ann to get off the phone. "I can call another time," Madison said.

"No. I'm sorry, Madness. Please, I'd love to talk to you. Tell me what's going on with you."

Madison smirked. She'd forgotten about the pet name, Madness, that her mother had called her when she was younger.

"I know this is spur of the moment, but I was wondering if you'd be available for coffee today. We can meet at your office, maybe go to a cafe, have a chance to catch up."

Ann's voice came out in a barely audible, "Wow." She resumed normal volume and said, "I would love that, as long as you let me multi-task. I'm supposed to be going over some photos for a retirement party. Remember Jerry Rosser?"

"Of course I do!" The cheer in Madison's voice was real. "I loved Uncle Jerry."

"He's retiring at the end of this week. I have to look at those photos, but I'll have you with me. It'll be fun."

"Okay." Madison hesitated before pushing on. "Also," she took a deep breath and tried to steady her nerves, "I want to explain about last night. What you saw was a performance, not the reality of what I'm like in the everyday kind of way."

After a pause Ann's voice sounded cautious saying, "I'm glad to hear that. I admit I wasn't sure what was going on." Another pause. "So, do you do that sort of thing very often?"

"No, it was a one-time gig to make a little extra money. I know it looked bad but it was just a show."

"I imagine to that crowd it was a wonderful success," said Ann. "You were…very convincing."

Madison could picture her nodding right now, straining to give a compliment. "Thanks. So, I'll stop by your office in a couple hours."

"They'll only allow you to go as far as the reception area. I'll tell them to expect you and they'll call me to come down and meet you there. Try not to wear anything with a lot of metal in it. Bring your ID. I hope you're not ticklish anymore."

"Excuse me?"

"For the pat down. Oh, and you'll need to park out on the street, then enter by walking through the garage. Follow instructions from the guards. Have your ID out and ready. And remember, Jerry is not supposed to know about the party."

As soon as they hung up, Madison knew she had to move quickly in order to go over Grandpa's mysterious papers in Spenser's house, and then get over to the FBI building where Ann worked in downtown Seattle.

Chapter Ten

SPENSER OPENED HER door before Madison even knocked. "All right, what's going on?" she asked.

"Huh?"

"Don't 'huh' me," Spenser said. "Get in here. You hungry?" Spenser headed for the kitchen.

Madison followed with her tote bag and pillowcase of laundry. The savory smells hit her nose. "Oh God that smells good!"

"Daniel will be back soon," said Spenser. "He went to get some artisan bread to go with the stew."

Madison sat at the kitchen table while Spenser stirred a pot on the stove and continued, "You never come over unannounced unless you're worried about something." She squinted at Madison. "I saw you sitting in your car talking on the phone with that anxious look you get. Did you find out ExBoy got a new girlfriend or something?"

"I wish it were that simple," said Madison. "Actually that might solve at least one of my problems. If he got a new girlfriend I could stop trying to figure out how I feel about him."

"Looks pretty straightforward to me. You want him. He wants you. What's there to figure out?"

"Well for starters, how about whether or not it would be a good idea? Everything I know about him I had to find out from other people. He won't talk about himself."

Spenser grabbed a bowl out of her cupboard, ladling stew into it. "Do you like what people say about him?" She placed the bowl of stew with a spoon in front of Madison.

"Well, yeah. But why is he a closed book with me while he's open with everyone else? Feels weird."

"This is kind of odd. But I think it's about sex."

"You think everything is about sex."

"You're driving yourself crazy. Just do him and get it over with."

"Spenser!"

"Do what comes natural."

Madison realized her mouth was hanging open. Spenser had a way of naming problems and solutions in the earthiest manner possible. And although she was often right, she wasn't always right. Madison wasn't even sure what it was she felt about ExBoy, and wanted more time to explore it.

It bugged her that Spenser could reduce it to such a carnal level, so she decided to fix Spenser's perceptions right now. "Well, maybe I already did. Did you ever think about that?"

Spenser looked at her a moment and smirked. "You little slut."

"That's right," Madison said, hoping Spenser wouldn't see through her. Madison was tired of being the one who never got laid.

Spenser giggled. "Now c'mon, eat your stew and tell me what's wrong because I can tell that something is."

Madison picked up the spoon, tasting the stew. "Oh, Spensy!" She gobbled a few bites. "Mmm. That's so…" the spoon clicked against the side of the bowl as she swallowed, "…good." She grabbed one more mouthful as she wondered how much she should say. After feeling so scared and alone today she wanted to tell her everything. Grandpa had specified not to tell Ann. The significance of that still weighed on her. But he hadn't specified not to tell Spenser, and in fact, just last night he had referred to Spenser as family, saying he would trust her with anything. Madison decided that was good enough to be permission. She put the spoon into the bowl and pushed the bowl away.

"Spenser, I don't know how much I can tell you, and frankly, I don't really understand what has happened. But it's serious." Madison wanted to say it before she changed her mind, so she took a deep breath and pushed all her words out extra fast. "I think my grandpa is in trouble and maybe he's been in trouble for a really long time, like longer than me and you have been alive, and he never got caught, only now he is caught, but not really because he's gone. I mean, I think."

"You lost me. You'll have to give me a clue."

"Yeah. Clues." Madison reached down into her tote bag and pulled out the papers, still clipped together. "I'm supposed to protect these papers for Grandpa. You know, hide them? But I don't know why, or what it's about. I might be able to figure out what's going on if I read them. He never said I couldn't, but I haven't had a chance to open this yet. I've been running nonstop since this morning. Meanwhile, Jaws is in her office in the FBI building and I'm supposed to meet her there a few hours from now. Oh, and get this. Grandpa doesn't want me to tell her."

"Tell her what?"

Madison pictured the fight she had witnessed earlier that day between Grandpa and the stranger and realized she was shooting her mouth off a little too much. She said, "I should hold at least something back, Spenser, or I won't be able to look him in the eye."

"Wow. You've outdone yourself on non-clarity."

"Sorry."

"Okay. So far, your grandpa is in mysterious trouble, you're not sure what it is, and he may be gone somewhere."

"Right."

"It may stem from a long time ago."

"Yes."

"He left you papers to guard, and it's the only thing that might give you more information on what his trouble is."

"Check."

"He told you not to tell Jaws, I mean Ann, about any of it, and there's a part that you can't even tell me."

"Damn, you're good."

"And Ann is waiting for you at her office."

"We're meeting for coffee. But I have to take some time to look at these before I go. I could use some moral support."

She pulled the rusty paper clips off the papers and gently unfolded them on the kitchen table. Inside the folded up newspaper pages were more clippings and other papers.

They decided to divide the papers and start reading whatever was in the pile in front of them. Spenser started in on a newspaper clipping, while Madison noticed what appeared to be a crudely scrawled, one-word note. It was written on a corner piece of paper, full of stains, and the one word was not readable. At least, not to Madison. The letters of the word didn't look right. Written with a dull pencil, there was an "a" and an "h" but the next letter was odd looking. It looked like the letter "x" with extra legs on it. It was followed by an "e" and then what looked like a backward square "n" and one more "a." The paper corner appeared to have been torn from stationery. The torn edge was next to what looked like a symbol or logo. The logo looked like the letter "W" with one of its middle strokes reaching up to form the letter "P." The paper had fold marks as if it had once been folded up to be very small.

She put the note aside and started in on a newspaper clipping. As they read and compared notes with each other, what came out was a series of stories about the International Student Exposition held in 1969 in Seattle. There were visiting students from other countries with pictures of the mayor and governor, shaking hands with the winners. Apparently the student exposition was a month-long touring event around the world that had made a final stop in Seattle.

The Seattle locals were quite proud of the new Washington Plaza Hotel, a luxury high rise where the city of Seattle had put up all the student guests, their guardians, and the judges. The University of Washington campus was the site where the science fairs and math contests were held. The campus also played host for some of the spillover from the Washington

Plaza Hotel, putting the university dormitories to good use.

There had been the occasional protest march by people with very long hair. They looked like hippies that Madison had seen in old movies. The newspaper had lots of photographs of various dignitaries posing with teenage students from all over the world who had gathered to compete.

The subject matter was boring to Madison, and her eyes glazed over as she wondered why these stories had captured her grandfather's attention. Each clipping seemed to be more of the same topic, only with different pictures, or an editorial on education in America. There was one story that speculated about whether the contests were rigged or whether judges were biased toward their own countries. Some accused the Soviet Union of sending KGB spies, trying to plant moles since not all of their students were accounted for at the contests. Ruffled feathers were soon smoothed however, with the revelation that one student was homesick and preferred to stay in her room. But most of the stories were upbeat, and the host city of Seattle tried not to let cold war politics override what was supposed to be a celebration of educated youth.

Madison showed Spenser the one-word note. But neither of them could get a hook on what possible secret was hidden in all this paperwork. The only links

Madison could see were that the logo on the note the letters "W" and "P," which she assumed stood for the Washington Plaza Hotel where all the visitors had stayed, the newspaper stories were about international students, and the note was not in English. So what language was it?

Madison shook her head. "The irony here is killing me."

"What?"

"Well, this is one of the few times I could really use the expertise of an FBI agent. My mom might actually know what some of this stuff means."

"Was your grandpa really serious about not telling her anything?"

"He was adamant. And I don't get it. I always thought he was closer to her then he was to me. I think she visits him more often than I do."

Spenser said, "You know, you really should get to know your mom anyway."

"So you keep telling me."

"You're not fooling me. You've wanted your mother all your life."

Madison was quiet for a moment, then said, "She doesn't want *me*, Spenser. She just wants to do the right thing." They both went quiet as they sorted through the clippings.

asked, "You're close with your mom,

guess so."

t picture it. I don't even know what to talk about with her. We have nothing in common."

"Tell her about things in your life. Your friends, your various jobs. Hey, tell her about your boyfriends! That's great 'Mom' material. They always want to know about their daughter's boyfriends."

"That sounds awkward. How do you get started?"

"It practically starts itself. My mom asks all the time. You could tell your mom about ExBoy."

Spenser kept reading a clipping while Madison decided to move on to another paper that looked like a document. Or rather, a copy of a document. It was askew in the center of dark wide borders. As soon as her eyes saw the title of the document, she was immediately confused. It said Certificate of Live Birth at the top of the paper. Her mother's name was there. Anna Lisa Cruz. Female. It gave the usual statistics such as the baby's weight and length. It listed the hospital, physician, father's, and mother's names, which were of course Vincent and Lisa Cruz, and the address where they lived at the time, which was the same house that Grandpa still owned and lived in now.

"I don't get it," said Madison. "This is a copy of my mother's birth certificate. Why would he put it with these papers? There's nothing on this document that is a secret."

"Has he ever mentioned the stories in these clippings?"

"No. But the clippings are all dated the same year she was born. None of this should raise any alarms. Yet he had these things hidden for a long time." Madison felt a small panic trying to get a foothold. "What am I not seeing?"

Spenser looked down at the birth certificate Madison was holding. "I didn't know your mom's middle name was Lisa."

"Yeah, that was my grandmother's name and..." She looked down at the certificate. "That's odd. Her birth date is off. This would make her almost two months older than she is."

"Typos?" Spenser offered.

"If it were just typos, why would he hide it?" She kept staring at the birthdate. *So she might be two months older? Why would that matter?*

Madison's elbow brushed the tabletop causing a few clippings to fall from the table. As they fell, a small but heavy square of paper came loose from the back of one of the clippings, making a beeline for the floor as one lighter paper floated down, taking its time. Madison caught it in the air before it landed and heard a knock on the door.

"That's Daniel. His arms must be full of grocery bags." Spenser shook her head as she got up to go open the door. "He always over-buys."

Madison stared at the little paper she had just caught. It had three capital letters followed by three numbers. It read WWC 989. She turned it over and saw one more thing. It was faint but something was written there. She read, "'Studebaker.' Sounds like a kind of oatmeal."

"It's a car," ExBoy said as he walked into the kitchen. "Collector's item now. They quit making them in the sixties or seventies."

"What are you doing here?" Madison's surprise turned to confusion. She stood up and looked at Spenser as if Spenser might provide an answer.

"Don't look at me. I didn't know he followed you here."

Madison turned to ExBoy. "You followed me?"

"No. I just figured you'd be with Spenser, that's all."

"Why did you think that?"

"Because you were upset earlier. So I drove by and sure enough, I saw your car outside. What's the big deal?"

Madison turned back to Spenser and saw her trying not to smile. Madison knew what she was thinking. To cover her earlier lie, Madison shrugged her shoulders at Spenser and said, "Some guys never get enough."

"Get enough what?" He stood there, his brows creasing.

"Enough attention." Madison knew he was confused and she left him hanging. She needed him not to understand the subtext and hoped he would play along if he did.

"Enough? I couldn't get any. I've been trying to talk to you." With lazy movements he toyed with a few strands of her hair, but his eyes were not happy. "That's why I went to your place earlier, but you were already upset about something. I didn't want to make it worse." He looked at her and asked, "Is it okay if we talk now?"

She answered by snaking her arms around his neck. "You just want your, wink wink, lucky t-shirt. I told you," she looked close into his eyes, "I'll give it to you later." She knew right away that she'd gone too far.

When comprehension hit, ExBoy's face dropped. "What...you want us to be boink buddies now?" He stared at her, while Madison tried to figure out how to get out of this without Spenser knowing she had lied. "Wow," he said, backing away. "Gonna throw me a bone, huh? Little token concession?"

"Wait—"

"I feel so special."

"That's not—"

"If you don't want us to be together, fine. I get it. But I don't need another boink buddy offer." He turned around and headed for the door. Madison hurried after him.

"What do you mean you don't need *another*—"

"But if you don't want to be with me, then at least be a friend." His voice heated up. "I need you to give a shit, Madison."

"Give a shit about what?"

"Who!"

"You?"

"Yes!"

"Mister Boink Buddy Central? Just how many offers have you had?"

"Have. You're not listening!"

"Is one named Jen?"

"I'm trying to make a point here, Madison! With you, I thought..." He shook his head, "Forget it." Walking out, he slammed the door.

Madison, staring at the door, could still feel the sting of the slamming sound in her ears. Her green eyes still wide with shock, her mouth open, she pointed at the door and looked questioningly at Spenser.

"No," Spenser said, "that's not material for conversation with your mom."

Chapter Eleven

MADISON BLINKED. HOW did this get so upside down? ExBoy was now mad at her for implying that they were having casual sex, something that she assumed he wanted. But she was only pretending in front of Spenser and figured he'd tease her about it later when they were alone. Maybe even try to get her to walk the walk if she was going to talk the talk.

"Um," Madison confessed to Spenser, "I lied."

"Yeah. I got that."

"What just happened?" asked Madison.

"You mean besides the lying part?"

"Yeah. Besides that. He's a man. All men want sex."

"How am I supposed to know?" asked Spenser.

"Because you're the know-it-all and you're often right."

"Thanks. I think."

"You're always saying everything is about sex. So how about it? What just happened?"

"I got nothing."

Madison wasn't sure how much time passed in those moments, but in the quiet she heard a clock gently ticking from somewhere in the house and realized that neither she nor Spenser had moved. That's how shocking it was to encounter a man who would turn down meaningless sex.

"What are you going to do?" asked Spenser.

"I don't know. I don't know about anything and I don't have time to deal with it. I should leave for the FBI building downtown."

"Dressed like that?"

There was a thumping at the door. This time it really was Daniel using his foot to knock while he balanced five full grocery bags.

"Good grief," Spenser said, when she opened it. "What have you done?" She grabbed a couple of bags from him, looking inside them. Her eyes got bigger. "Yum."

Madison wanted to be polite so she took a bag from him, too.

Daniel said, "Just saw ExBoy driving away. Did he try to get you to be zombies at his booth?"

"Zombies?" Spenser said, looking down into the bag. Daniel nudged her toward the kitchen. They set the bags down on the kitchen counters as Spenser started pulling out the grocery items from the bags. A package of spaghetti noodles, coffee, a sack of ripe peaches…. As each item came out, Spenser walked back and forth in the kitchen putting things in their right cupboard or into the refrigerator.

"Last night," Daniel said, "he told the guys he needs more zombies to hang around his booth at Zombie Prom."

Madison remembered he had wanted his t-shirt for that convention.

Daniel continued, "Didn't he say anything? He's going to have a booth there to sell his artwork and a book he's written. It's called *Infect Me*."

"Ew," Spenser said. Then to Madison she asked, "Do you think that's what he wanted to talk to you about? Being a zombie at his booth?"

"Who knows?" Madison sighed.

Daniel tilted his chin up at Madison. "Hey, Madison. How was your head this morning?" He smirked.

"Pretty bad, thank you. Then I vomited."

"Good to hear," he said. "Nothing like a bad hangover to teach you a lesson. Makes life more interesting."

"Interesting? You really want to know? I had to drag a giant woman across a carpet and do sit-ups. Then I no-showed for a gig, so now of course I have to look pregnant while I sing to a dead guy."

Daniel and Spenser stood staring at her.

She continued, "But that stuff is not the good parts. I'm not allowed to tell you the good parts."

Spenser picked up Madison's bowl of stew and put it in the microwave. "I'll warm up her stew. Act natural. She'll be okay." To Madison, she said, "Why don't you show Daniel that weird little note?"

Madison snapped to, realizing that she'd left all of Grandpa's paperwork out on the table. With haste she gathered it, replacing the paperclips and sticking it all in her purse instead of the tote bag, leaving out the note.

"Sure," said Madison as she hurried. She felt silly to be in a rush. This stuff could probably hide out in the open and no one would ever guess that it was important enough to hide for years. Decades, actually. Still, it meant a lot to Grandpa.

Her eyes fell on the small heavy paper that had dropped from the table to the floor earlier. Picking it up, she turned it over. On the other side was a black and white photograph. Within a split second she saw it was a man holding something in his arms. Shadows around the borders of the picture looked like black silhouettes of leaves, as if the camera had shot through a bush. Recognition and fear made her shove it deep within her purse to examine later, curiosity burning her heart. Now that Daniel was here she would have to wait until later to get a good look at it.

She picked up the one-word note and handed it to Daniel. May as well make Spenser happy by letting Daniel play along for a minute.

She said, "Do you know what that says?"

"Niet," he said.

Madison froze.

He continued, "I can't read Cyrillic."

Madison hadn't told Spenser anything about the fight that morning, and that she had heard someone yelling what sounded like Ned.

"Are you saying the word on this note is 'net'?"

"Actually I said 'niet.' Niet is Russian for 'no.' I was trying to say 'no' I don't know what the note says because it's in Cyrillic. Cyrillic is Russian."

✧   ✧   ✧

MADISON WAITED IN the lobby of the FBI building. After surrendering her ID, having her purse searched, and walking through the metal detector, she had tried to contain her giggles while a female guard patted her down. Now she had to wait for Ann to come get her. No one was allowed to roam the building without an escort. But even if she had been allowed, she didn't have a clue where her mother's office was located.

Madison sat in business clothes she had borrowed from Spenser, looking very ladylike. A tall suit nearby with dreamy eyes kept looking her way. She had no idea that the FBI hired such hot guys. Yes, there were some fine specimens smiling at her as they passed by, on their way to fighting crime. Maybe she should dress this way more often. It seemed to be giving her some juice with the suit crowd. *Hmm. Suits. Never went for that type before.* She was going to have to rethink that.

Madison was betting that a conservative appearance would give her mother hope that Madison was not beyond saving. Perhaps she could get Ann to trust her a little more. She needed more information about Grandpa's more recent activities, friends, concerns, anything. He had a lot of pals from over the years, but which one would Grandpa trust to handle the stranger with the unibrow, while he went to get help?

She inhaled, deeply and slowly, trying to steady herself. She tilted her head to each side, trying to relax her neck muscles. This was the meeting she had been avoiding for years, fearful that it would only bring pain. But she had a new purpose now. Grandpa needed her. She was ready to act the role of the repentant daughter who was finally interested in her mother's many opinions. But she assumed that she was coming from so far down in Special Agent Ann Cruz's estimation that this might not work at all. Except for a few uncomfortable family gatherings, she had hardly seen her mother since their mutual fiasco in Philadelphia, when Madison was twelve years old.

She closed her eyes against the memory. That was when their relationship really hit the toilet. Right after Grandma died, her mother said it was time for Madison to come and live with her now. Ann believed that daily discipline and routine would help them both heal from their loss. So twelve-year-old Madison was packed up and sent out to Philadelphia, where Ann was stationed.

But Madison wasn't having it. She acted out her pain and anguish at the passing of her grandmother, plus the pain of being taken away from Grandpa, her friends, and everything she had known. She conducted herself like a wild cat, and her mother continually had to pick her up from the police station. Ann finally agreed with Grandpa that Madison needed to go back home to Seattle. Madison realized that might be the daughter that her mother saw in her head. But since her mother believed so strongly in a Boy Scout lifestyle, she might assume that it would be natural for Madison to eventually wake up to it.

She looked down at the expensive-looking high heels on her feet. Good thing Spenser wore the same shoe size. Earlier at Spenser's house, Madison had asked her, "Could I borrow a skirt? A blouse? Something feminine. Do you have any high heeled pumps?"

Spenser had a wicked look in her eye.

Madison said, "Not hooker pumps, you moron. Something conservative."

"You're no fun. But yes, of course."

The heels she loaned Madison were about three inches high. The left heel spike seemed to have a rough edge because Madison could feel it snag the carpet when she walked. Still, she felt like she was on the business crowd's runway of style.

A man's voice said, "Excuse me."

She looked up. Tall, suited, and dreamy was standing right there, talking to her. He looked late twenties with short dark hair, dark brown eyes that were slightly almond shaped, and skin the color of a light and creamy mocha.

"Yes?"

"I think I figured out why you look so familiar. Ann Cruz's daughter?"

"Yes. How did…?"

"Besides the family resemblance, I recognized you from pictures in her office. You're even more striking in person." He smiled and held out his hand. "My name is Aaron Reed."

She reached up, giving him her hand, and he shook it with a gentle squeeze. His hand felt cool from time spent in the air-conditioned offices. She caught herself staring, gave a small smile, and withdrew her hand to reach up to her hair and pretend to straighten something there. She didn't want to show too much enthusiasm in Ann's workplace, but she wouldn't mind if all these hot suits would line up for inspection.

"Thank you. I didn't know she had a picture of me in her office."

"Are you kidding? Dozens. They're all over the place."

Now she really was staring at him. In confusion.

"They are?"

He nodded, still smiling. "From over the years, I guess. Every age."

Madison looked right through him to an imaginary wall of photos of herself in her awkward youth. She felt her eyes starting to tear up. *Get a grip.* She tried to chuckle in a casual manner, looking down at her lap, pretending to pull at the hem and smooth out the skirt while she scolded herself. *Don't fall for it, Madison. You don't really know who this guy is, or if Mom put him up to it. She's never approved of me. It doesn't make sense.*

"How long have you known her?" she asked.

"About five years or so. She's amazing. You must be so proud."

"Oh, absolutely."

"She's always willing to help someone along. It's a hard job, but she acts like she's never forgotten what it was like to be new. Generous with her time, with encouragement."

Madison uttered her most gracious, "Thank you."

"And scary smart! Who-ee! If you inherited that from her, I can't even imagine…. Oh, listen to me," he chuckled. "Sorry, I guess I'm gushing a bit."

In her sweetest voice she said, "A bit. Yeah." She tried not to grimace.

"I guess you can tell how much I admire her."

In a melodious voice she said, "Don't we all?"

The theme music to *Jaws* started playing. Madison jumped to stop the music and slammed the cell phone to the side of her face in a panic. "Hello?"

"I'm sorry to keep you waiting," Ann's voice said. "I need a few more minutes, then I'll come down and take you to this great little place nearby called Choosy Chews."

"No problem. See you then." She hung up and resumed smiling at Aaron.

He said, "I should get going. It was wonderful to meet you. Oh, I didn't catch your first name."

Another man's voice said, "It's Madison." Jerry, smiling, stepped up from out of nowhere and held his arms out to her.

"Uncle Jerry!" She stood and they hugged, patting each other's back. He had aged quite a bit since she had known him in her childhood and preteens. She remembered salt and pepper hair back then. Now there was only salt. It was much thinner now, too, while his body was much thicker.

"How are you?" she exclaimed.

"Forget about me, look at *you*! Little Madness is a grown lady now. I feel so old."

"Oh, you'll never be old," she smiled.

"Flatterer. I thought that was my job." He put his arm around her and faced Aaron. "Would you believe she used to ride on my shoulders? And look at her now."

Aaron seemed pretty impressed, saying, "The daughter of Ann Cruz *and* you know the SAC?" Madison still remembered some of the many acronyms from the bureau. SAC stood for Special Agent in Charge. That meant Jerry was the big boss of the entire Seattle Field Division.

She looked at Jerry. "Wow. You're the SAC now?"

"I'm afraid so, at least till the end of this week. I'm about to retire."

"Well, congratulations."

"Thank you. I'm ready. I'd like to try some new things. I might even relax and see what that feels like."

"Grandpa has loved his retirement."

"How is Vincent these days?"

"He's good." She nodded her head. He looked at her as if he were waiting to hear more about her grandfather. She kept nodding, kicking herself for bringing him up.

"You must be here to see your mother?" He squeezed her hands with a knowing nod. Madison felt sheepish. Jerry probably knew of their troubles, but it would have been from Ann's side of things.

"Yes. She's taking me to Choosy Chews."

His tone remained cheery as he said, "Ah. You'll love it," but his expression had slipped into something a little grim. He reached for the cell phone in her hand, saying, "I want you to have my number." His finger pecked at the tiny keyboard slowly. Then, satisfied, he handed her the phone and said, "Take care now, dear. I'm late for another meeting." He turned to Aaron and said, "Agent Reed, would you follow me on the way please? I have something in mind."

"Yes, sir." Aaron turned to Madison with one last appreciative smile and nodded a good-bye as he hurried to catch up with Jerry.

Her brief reunion with Jerry left a flood of childhood memories to deal with. Spenser's words came back to her, about seeing Ann through her adult eyes, and Toonie's advice not to make emotional decisions, make smart ones. Okay then. As of right now, she was making a non-emotional, smart decision to see Ann through adult eyes. Maybe she would see something she had been too young to understand before. But in the back of her mind she mocked herself. *And just what is it you hope you'll see?*

She spotted her mother walking towards her from across the huge lobby. Ann wore chin length, medium brown hair, not as dark or as silky as Madison's, in a simple and easy care style. Her eyes were big like Madison's, although instead of light green they were dark and fierce. But whenever she smiled, and smile she did upon seeing Madison, her eyes would take on a playful quality. Madison had always marveled that she could look so pretty without makeup. She wore a skirt suit, showing that she had kept her weight down over the years. Her legs were still too skinny, in Madison's opinion. Perhaps a hint of creases at the corners of her eyes, but she looked too youthful for forty.

Madison, who never had stage fright, certainly had it now. She stood up and faced Ann, stunned at how quickly her own heart abandoned any plan of being cool and calculating, all thoughts of trickery fleeing her mind. Ann's firm hands took Madison's hands as they looked at one another, both trying to stay calm and collected at this, their first meeting in many years.

Ann's voice broke just a touch as she said, "You're so beautiful." And in that moment, mixed together with her fear and her hope, Madison's heart was elated that she was dressed all grown-up and ladylike.

Chapter Twelve

THEY STUDIED A few of the old photos laid out in front of them on the large restaurant table: some were in color, some black and white, all of them from an era gone by.

Madison and her mother had walked to the nearby Choosy Chews, a casual dining place where an upscale experience could be had in an unpretentious atmosphere. Nestled among stark downtown concrete, glass, and metal skyscrapers, Choosy Chews was a haven of old woodwork with the eccentric air of a Mad Hatter: the manor born living in a barn.

Fine china sat on old sturdy wooden tables, each crack or divot in the wood accented with rich redwood stains, polished to a high luster. The high end cutlery, completely mismatched, looked as if each fork, spoon, and knife had been picked up in second hand stores or antique shops. Quirky artwork hanging on the walls seemed quite at home with no intention of going anywhere, having already found their perfect placements. The only air conditioning came from burnished wooden ceiling fans moving the air, fresh despite the downtown location. Real plants and small trees were dotted along the walls, their growth healthy and vigorous, delicate leaves quivering or swaying in the moving air.

Madison wondered at the peacefulness of the room. There was no attempt from the patrons to be quiet, yet the room still provided a feeling of lazy respite.

The staff recognized Ann, who specifically asked for the large booth in the back. The lunch rush had been over for a while and the wait staff had a relaxed patrol of a few tables. Sunshine poured in through the big windows in the front. But the large booth in the back was much dimmer and cooler. The light shadow made time feel more like a guessing game, so Madison was guessing that thirty minutes had gone by. They had each ordered only coffee. She pretended not to be hungry, not wanting to eat if her mother wasn't going to.

Madison was surprised at how easy it was to laugh at things that genuinely tickled them both.

"It's the hairstyles that kill me," said Ann with a chuckle. "Look at this one."

Madison shook with quiet laughter as she said, "Can you imagine how long it took every morning before you could leave the house?"

Pointing at a beehive hairdo in a black and white photo, Ann said, "On the other hand, you could probably hide your lunch in it." Simultaneously they said, "Yummy," and laughed at themselves.

A waiter came up with a coffee pot and poured more black coffee for Ann. Madison had hers topped off a bit, adding cream. A waitress seated a young couple at a table nearby, while a woman stepped up to the waiter with the coffee pot and quietly asked about the restroom. He pointed to the back corner, not far from the large table where Madison sat with her mother. The activity in the room was leisurely.

"But I have to say, I love these suits," said Madison. "They're so cool, so retro. Especially this one here." She pointed at a tall skinny man with square glasses in an early 1960's suit.

"That's Jerry, when he first started at the FBI," said Ann, refolding her napkin.

"You're kidding." Madison leaned in closer to study the photo. "Wow. I didn't recognize him. He looks so young here. And skinny. He used to wear glasses?"

"I guess so," said Ann. "By the time I met him, he must have been wearing contact lenses."

"These'll be a big hit at the party. In fact you could present a montage to everyone with all these photos, and start with this one," said Madison, referring to the cool retro suit photo. "You could even add music from each era to go with the photos."

"A montage?" She picked up two photos. "I was going to make lots of little copies for each table," said Ann, staring at one photo in her hand then looking at the second one in her other hand. "Presenting a montage would be so much better." She sighed. "I wish I had more time."

"I could make it for you," Madison volunteered. *What am I saying? She won't like anything I come up with.*

"Really?" Ann turned her head to look at Madison. "You wouldn't mind?" Ann's dark eyes shone with pride. "You were always so good at that sort of thing. You made such interesting collages for your bedroom walls."

Madison, embarrassed at her inner dialogue, smiled. *I'm an idiot.* "This will be fun," she said, "like playing a little trick on him." She was glad to be able to say that with sincerity, then asked, "Where did you get all these photos?"

"Everyone pitched in if they had anything, but most of the old ones came from FBI archives."

"Wow." Madison looked down at the photos with new respect.

Ann said, "Don't worry, they're all copies."

Madison asked, "Do you have any from those lectures he used to give at the high schools?"

"Not really." Ann was gazing down at the stack of photos in front of Madison. She added, "Security has been tightened up since those days, but back then they used to give tours of the FBI building here in Seattle. He took over the tour the day I went. He made it sound so exciting." Reaching for her coffee cup, she said, "I was hooked."

"I'm surprised Grandpa allowed you to go. He couldn't stand Jerry."

Ann looked at her in surprise. "I didn't know you knew that."

"Well, it was the old invisible-kid-in-the-room trick. It's amazing what people will say in front of a child, as long she holds still and lets them forget she's there."

Ann didn't move for a moment, her sad eyes on Madison. She lowered her china cup, clinking it as it hit a little askew in the saucer, spilling a few drops. Ann grabbed her napkin, her lips closed tight as she cleaned the small spill. She stopped wiping, her hand going lax around the napkin. Staring at nothing, she said, "I can only imagine the things you heard." She took a big breath and exhaled saying, "I really made a mess, didn't I? I'm sorry, Madness."

"Hey, I was no picnic back then."

"I'm trying to make up for it," said Ann.

"Me, too." Madison felt it only fair to own up to her share of their problems, specifically her rebellion years. But she was never comfortable with her mother's idea of making up for something and wondered what was coming.

Ann smiled and her enthusiasm returned, saying, "I'm excited about your montage idea. I'm looking forward to seeing the end result."

"I'll scan them in tonight," said Madison. She looked on the back of a photo. "Names and dates," she noted. "That'll help me know what order to put them in." She tucked them all back into the large envelope Ann had brought them in. "You know, Grandpa may not have liked Jerry, but I did. He was cool Uncle Jerry to me. He used to pick me up and throw me in the air, while Grandma got all panicky." Madison laughed as she continued, "She'd pull me away from him as if I were in danger, telling me to go play in my room." She shook her head, smiling at the memory.

Ann was pleasant and quiet. But there was something else there. The lack of anything else to say made it seem as if she were being guarded. Something was not being said. Was her mother uncomfortable about Jerry? *Maybe she and Jerry had a falling out.* Madison decided to ask her about it some other time. She was enjoying a rare and wonderful visit with her mother right now and didn't want to spoil it.

"So," Ann smiled. "Your new apartment. Do you love it?"

"Actually, I do. It's so much nicer than my last place. I'm on the second floor, and the outside hallway is always clean. The toilet never runs, kitchen counters look new, plumbing never drips. It's awesome."

Ann was beaming. She asked, "Is the management treating you well?"

"Yeah, they're really nice! If I need anything they jump on it. It's almost weird."

Ann nodded, seeming very satisfied. She caught the waiter's attention and said, "Check, please?" The waiter came over with the check, passing by the woman who had inquired about the restroom earlier, each of them brushing past the table in opposite directions.

Feeling her confidence build, Madison decided to try Spenser's idea of the mother/daughter talk about boyfriends, though she would have to embellish the truth a little. More than a little. Quite a bit, actually.

She put on a conspiratorial little smile and leaned in saying, "And guess what? I have a boyfriend."

Ann looked up from the check, her eyes soft, and said, "I'm not surprised. You're so pretty. Those sparkly green eyes have always taken my breath away."

Madison thought her heart would burst.

"So tell me," Ann joined in with her own conspiratorial smile, "What's his name? What does he do? Is he really cute?" Madison couldn't believe this moment. This was the best moment ever. *Just like normal people!*

She giggled. "His name is ExBoy, he sells his artwork, and he's beyond cute. He's gorgeous!"

Ann's face didn't move for a second. In a faint tone she said, "ExBoy? Did I hear that right?" The light in her eyes seemed to be having a brown-out, flickering with the strain of staying on.

"Yeah. He's the one who found the apartment and told me about it. I really owe him for that."

"You don't owe him anything," Ann blurted. "Anyone can find an apartment, it doesn't mean anything. With a name like ExBoy he...he's probably a crook. You can't trust people like that, Madison; you don't want to be with a crook. Don't be stupid."

Madison stiffened.

"Why don't you date a nice man?" Ann's tone was pleading. "Someone who would never get in any trouble, or ever give you any reason to worry. Use your head for a change!" Her words came to an abrupt halt. Her hand came up over her mouth.

She lowered her forehead into her hand. "I'm sorry. I promised myself I wouldn't do that to you." She looked back up and said, "Please don't go."

Scattered voices from around the restaurant with their clinking china were all that Madison could hear. A tiny leaf quivered and fell onto their table.

It occurred to her that Ann had just done something that she had never done before. She had stopped herself. So Madison did something that she had never done before, either. She said, "I'm not going anywhere."

✧   ✧   ✧

As THEY WERE leaving, the waiter said, "Please come again, Ms. Cruz."

She answered with a pleasant, "Thank you."

The sun was still coming in through the large front windows, pouring heavy sunbeams into the room. Summer was in its glory. Madison noticed one sunbeam hitting directly on the head of the lady who had brushed past their table earlier. The sunbeam revealed her hair to actually be a stunning dark red color, leaving Madison with the idea of trying that color someday. She admired the hair, but the woman didn't notice, continuing to read her book, sipping coffee.

Stepping outside, they walked in the direction of Madison's car parked down the street. People getting off work caused traffic to slow its pace as more cars appeared, congesting the streets. The occasional honk or street musician added to the sounds of footsteps, car engines, and police whistles. Madison carried the large envelope of old photos under her arm, her high heels clicking on the pavement.

"Madison." Ann exhaled. "Thank you for sticking it out with me back there. I still have a lot to figure out about myself. I've been going through...some changes, lately." She removed her suit jacket, draping it over her left forearm. She rubbed the back of her neck with her other hand as she looked down at the sidewalk.

Madison could see the tension and weariness. She swallowed, searching for the right thing to say, then settled for, "I'm trying to use adult eyes."

"Adult eyes?"

"Yeah. You know. The kid inside me had a head start in forming my opinions, but it's not her turn anymore."

Ann seemed to take this in and nodded her head. "You've come to that conclusion much sooner than I did about myself."

"When did you come to it?" Madison asked.

Ann answered in a rueful tone. "A few weeks ago."

Looking up, Madison saw a tall suit across the street, walking down the sidewalk. Aaron Reed, she smiled to herself. Must be getting off work, too. *He said she has pictures of me in her office. All ages.* She was too embarrassed to ask Ann for confirmation. Not yet, anyway. Aaron made a call on his cell phone but kept walking.

"We had a good start today," Ann said, "but there's going to be a lot to talk about. There's so much to tell you. I decided not to try to fit in too much today."

"Do you want to talk about it tomorrow?"

"I can't. There's a problem." She huffed, "Lots of problems. I need to wait for events to settle down."

Madison stopped walking, letting passersby flow around them. "What are you not telling me? Does it involve Grandpa?" She had tried not to sound too intense.

"No, it's FBI business." Ann looked at her puzzled, then added, "Dad was doing well when I saw him."

Madison said, "I wonder if he's getting out enough. He should see friends. Which ones are his very best friends? The ones he would tell anything to?"

Ann's quizzical look deepened and Madison knew her line of questioning about Grandpa didn't feel natural. But after a pause, Ann answered. "That would be either Ray or Mitch. Those three started out together in gardening jobs at the UW."

"I think I remember those old guys." Madison said. "They would get together once in a while."

Ann said, "I'd say mostly Mitch. When I was a kid, Dad gave his son a job. Then when Mom died, Mitch kept an eye on Dad, cleaned him up when he got too drunk." She looked down, saying, "One of the reasons I took you to Philadelphia so suddenly was because Dad fell apart. The impact of Mom's death almost took him with her. But in an odd way, your rebellion out there in Philadelphia was a blessing. He sobered up fast when he realized how much you needed him. It gave him a purpose." She looked off into the distance. "I couldn't take that away from him." Her fierce eyes glistened, tears refusing to leave their corners.

Traffic continued its pokey downtown pace while the distant roar of an accelerating public bus could be heard. "Anyway, Mitch was the one who held him together at that time. Later still, Dad gave a job to Mitch's grandson. They've always looked out for each other."

"I had no idea." Madison blinked. Had she been that self-absorbed? So much for the old invisible-kid-in-the-room trick. *I guess they could hide things when they really wanted to.*

Ann said, "I'm sure he still sees his friends, but you could ask him." They resumed walking and soon approached Madison's car and the moment for saying goodbye.

Madison chose to offer a light little hand clasp with one hand, while patting Ann on the shoulder with the other hand. She knew it probably looked as awkward as it felt. But her emotions were too raw to trust herself to offer a hug. Not yet. She was walking a tightrope here, navigating between a nervous reunion with her mother and mysterious trouble with her grandfather. Clearly, there were ongoing secrets on both sides. Madison was going to have to do a little secret scheming of her own to get to the truth.

She climbed into her car, feeling the car's interior heat from being parked in the sun, and started the engine. She hit the power button to lower all the car windows and let some of the heat escape. Ann bent down to be seen at the passenger window, saying, "Thanks for offering to meet me where I work. I loved it."

"It was pretty impressive," said Madison. "There are a lot of hot guys working there."

Ann blinked and smiled. "I guess there are."

"I met one named Aaron Reed. I might want to have his baby."

"What?" Ann laughed.

Madison waved at her and pulled into traffic. As much as her mother's reaction to ExBoy annoyed her, she figured there wouldn't be any harm in having an imaginary break-up with her imaginary boyfriend.

Chapter Thirteen

S HE DIDN'T KNOW why she hadn't thought of it sooner. The best place to hide something wasn't a place they would never think of because eventually they'd think of it. It wasn't a place that was guarded because eventually they'd find a way in.

The best place to hide something would be a place that was so chaotic you wouldn't know where to start, and eventually you would talk yourself into thinking that it couldn't possibly be there. The only thing you would find in this place would be something you weren't looking for. Therefore, she should hide the contents of the box in the battered warehouse of Robot Moon Productions. She swung the car around and headed north to Ballard.

Robot Moon Productions was an indoor junkyard to most eyes, but it was prop heaven to stage and local indie film crews on a shoestring budget. Even parades, conventions, exhibitions, and trade shows needing some sort of prop or display eventually found their way to Robot Moon.

And if Robot Moon didn't have it, it could be custom built. The owner was a young woman everyone called Target, and if need be, she knew a lot of talented industrial designers to bring in for the odd job. Need a stuffed crocodile? A dentist's chair? A lifeboat? A coffin? Robot Moon probably had it, somewhere in there. Madison decided that the contents of Grandpa's box needed to sit amongst an acre of theater props until Grandpa got back.

She'd brought all the papers with her, tucked away in her purse, when she'd come to visit Ann. There was a moment at the FBI guard station when her heart went into her throat. She had forgotten about the purse search. But the guard had pushed the folded up paperwork aside as he looked through the purse contents, and had treated the paperwork like everything else in her purse—as insignificant.

Pulling up into the big empty parking lot, she avoided the potholes and larger pieces of concrete rubble scattered around. She picked a parking spot on the edge of the lot where wild blackberry bushes were invading from around the side of the building, thumbing their noses at the old concrete and growing wherever they damned well felt like growing. The tough, thorny, wild blackberry bushes of the Pacific Northwest were the invasive survivors of the plant world. Madison knew they would be here long after humans were gone.

She got out of the car and looked up at the wall of the warehouse. There was the familiar logo of a robot bending over with his pants down, exposing a non-genital but well-rounded shiny metal butt. Heading into the warehouse, she stopped inside the door where old computer gear sat on an even older desk. The gear was so old it should have been part of the props on display. But instead, these old parts were actually in use for the warehouse business.

And there was Target sitting at her desk, her signature brown wavy-haired bangs from the left side of her forehead, curled inward, meeting the hair tips from the bangs on the right side. Thus her bangs formed an open circle on her forehead. The small birthmark on her skin in the center of the circle turned it into a target. She had always laughed it off saying she had a death wish anyway and figured it was appropriate.

She sat at the old wooden desk, reading her computer screen, freckled arms and hands behind her head, elbows calloused and pink. Her boyish skinny frame swam inside one of the many faded t-shirts she found at comics conventions.

"Madison! Look at you, all girly-girl and fancy. Wow!" Her eyes twinkled as she finger combed her bangs up off her forehead.

"Hey, Target. You like?" Madison turned in a circle, her purse swinging from her wrist. "Borrowed it from a friend. Thought I'd come and scare you with it."

"That don't scare me. I know how to fix up and get snazzy, but don't tell anyone. Got a reputation to protect."

"I didn't mean *that*. I meant being all feminine. You told me you've never once worn a skirt." Madison said.

"Well, now, that's true, but it wouldn't scare me. It would just scare the shit out of everyone else, don't you think?"

"No one would be expecting it, that's for sure."

"So what's up?" Target asked. "Are you working props this time? What's the show?"

"There's no show or project. Actually," Madison began, "I have a few small things that need to be hidden for a while."

Target's eyebrows went up, full of question. Madison continued, "It's nothing bad or illegal, just some old newspaper clippings that a friend doesn't want to be caught with."

"Why can't you keep it with you for a while? Or in your house or your car?"

"Because someone might want to take it from me. Look, I know it sounds weird. Okay, it is weird but he seems to think—" *Shut up, Madison.*

"He?" Target started to smile. In spite of all appearances, Target was straight and loved men. She just had to wait till the right type happened along now and then. The type that liked Target. After all, Madison knew not all guys went for girly-girls.

"Yeah. So would it be all right? Look, I'll show it to you." She pulled out the paperwork from her purse and held it out to Target who took it and turned it over a few times while she looked confused. She finally shrugged her shoulders and reached into a drawer, pulling out an envelope, and stuffed the papers into the envelope. Looking up she said, "You want me to keep it in my desk?"

"No, I thought we should keep it in a prop."

Target shook her head, "That wouldn't be very smart in this place. It might get moved around or rented out to someone. Worse, they might purchase the prop so they can destroy it in their film."

Madison looked out into the warehouse, seeking the right way to go about this, when Target said, "I've got an idea." She pulled out a big cardboard tag with thin wires attached. She wrote on the card, "Reserved. Project Title:"—and stopped. She looked up. "What should we call the film this is reserved for?"

"Hot Scheming Mess. That's what this whole stupid thing is turning into."

"Good enough," Target said, and added the rest of the words to the card, then handed it to Madison. "Now you just need to pick the prop it's going to go in. But pick something that is less likely to be rented. I may not act like it, but I really would like to make some money." Everyone knew Target inherited the huge warehouse and only needed to pay property tax. But the money from her prop rentals and designs was enough to support her and keep her happy. For now.

Madison took the cardboard tag and the envelope with Grandpa's paperwork in it and walked deeper into the warehouse, looking around.

There were long rows of shelving along the walls at different heights. Medium sized props such as luggage, vacuum cleaners, and sewing machines were kept on the floor underneath long wooden tables that held table lamps, sets of dishes, and coffee makers. The next level up was shelving that held pillows, carpets, tapestries, and blankets. Overhead were dozens of kitchen chairs in every style and color, attached to large hooks that hung down from the ceiling of the barn. Besides the perimeter, there were rows upon rows of shelves at different heights in the center of the warehouse. The shelving in the warehouse was a mish-mash of different types, from sturdy old dusty wood, to metal grating and brackets that sprang from the walls and ceiling. There was furniture of every kind, car parts, toys, medical gear, kayaks, toilets, and gazebos. There were plenty of things that had no category to live in, but Target had found a place to store them.

Madison made a point of passing by anything that could be used in an office scene, or a kitchen or bedroom scene. She looked for something a little less likely to be needed. Then she saw it.

A huge Victorian grandfather clock was crammed between a few bookcases on one side, and fake trees on the other side, with baskets of fake flowers at the foot of the trees. Madison walked up to the grandfather clock and opened the tall glass door to peer inside. A four foot long pendulum was unattached and leaning into the back corner. Most of the clock guts were missing from inside, making it easier for Madison to reach her hand up into the small square area behind the clock face, and leave the envelope of Grandpa's paperwork that had seemed so important to him. She closed the glass door and wrapped the thin wires of the cardboard tag around the door's handle. Hanging sideways, the tag would tell anyone who was considering the clock that it was already reserved.

Walking back towards Target's desk, she passed a plastic bin with a small assortment of fake handguns. One in particular caught her eye with its matte metal luster. The grip appeared to be walnut wood, smooth and highly polished; its dark golden hue added to the grace of its curves. She picked it up. It was even heavy. But more importantly, it looked real. She took it.

Coming up to the desk, Target sat with her head leaning down on her palm as she sketched on a pad. Madison assumed some new prop design had been ordered.

"I'll take this, too," said Madison, showing her the fake handgun. "What do I owe you?"

Target looked up with a casual air at the gun, her eyes leading up to Madison's face and holding there a moment. "I thought you said there was no project."

"There isn't. I just need to practice in the mirror. Last audition didn't go so well."

Target held her eyes on Madison for another second then said, "Just take it then."

"Thanks, Target. And thanks for letting me leave the paperwork in that clock. As soon as he gets here, he'll take it off your hands. I'll sleep better knowing it's safely stored away."

"No problem." Target's bangs crept back onto her forehead. She pushed them away again. "Now if you'll bring me some new business, I'll sleep better, too. I'm doing props for Zombie Prom in a few days. But after that it'll be getting pretty thin around here." She stood up from the desk, walking with Madison toward the door.

"I'm in the same boat," said Madison. "Phil is so desperate he took a booking for a singing telegram from a dying man that wanted to be sung to at his own funeral. Big money."

"Lots of people sing at funerals."

"Not like this. It's a comedy gig. Stand at the casket, big and pregnant, sing to the body in front of loved ones."

"Seriously?"

"Yeah."

"Not a prop? A real live dead guy?"

"Yeah. A real live, but mostly dead, guy."

"Who would be willing to do that?"

Madison said, "You're looking at her. I'm pretty desperate myself."

Target's laughter bubbled up as she said, "My respect for your nerve grows daily. But, Phil?" She shook her head. "That guy will land on his feet, no matter what it takes."

"Yeah." Madison looked over at the Victorian grandfather clock which now held secrets. "I guess we're all capable of crazy things if we're desperate enough."

She reached for the doorknob, but Target stopped her, putting her hand on Madison's arm.

She said, "Put the gun prop where no one will see it before you go out there. That thing looks too real."

Madison opened her purse and put the fake handgun in, closing it back up.

Target said, "It's dangerous for people to think you're really armed if you're not." She gave Madison a sincere look. "Be careful."

After exchanging goodbyes, Madison stepped out into the parking lot, glad to have the paperwork from the box safely hidden at Robot Moon Productions.

But there were two pieces she had held back: the Cyrillic note, and the black and white photo. Walking toward her car, she looked around, assuring herself that she was alone. Climbing in, she left the windows closed and locked her door. She would have to endure the suffocating heat in the car while she faced the photo. Pulling it out of her purse, she held it down in her lap, away from the windows.

She stared at what her instinct had already told her was bad news. From within a tree or a bush, someone had taken a picture. Leaves forming the frame were giant close-ups out of focus. The light was soft with a sharp bright spot beyond the trees in the distance. Could it be sunset? No. No, it was more likely dawn.

In the background was a door, or porch step. Hard to tell with the leaves in the way. The focus of the camera was centered on the man in the photo who was not coming out of the door; rather, he was facing it. Had her grandfather ever been so young, tall and handsome? His strong arms held a small bundle. A box was at his feet. There was a tender expression on his face mixed with… what? Confusion? Worry? The thing he was holding looked like towels or laundry.

What the hell was going on?

✧   ✧   ✧

SHE STOPPED AT Spenser's house, and after heartfelt thanks for the generous loan of the business outfit, Madison switched back into her tank top and jeans. They made plans for Madison to come over tomorrow morning to do the laundry and catch Spenser up on how the meeting had gone with Ann.

She got back in her car, but before driving off she tried calling her grandfather's cell phone again. Still no answer.

The other heaviness on her heart was ExBoy. She had offended him in a way that she never would have predicted. She called him, but he wasn't answering either. She heard the beep and said in a timid voice, "Hey. Can you call me back? I need to explain. It came off all wrong." She disconnected, leaning back into the seat. Staring up at the ceiling, she wondered if he had intentionally not answered the phone.

The summer sun was bearing down on her windshield as she pulled out the black and white photo again. She hadn't wanted to show it to Spenser. Gazing at the image of her grandfather so much younger, she remembered what her mother had said about his friends Mitch and Ray working with him back in the early days. She said Grandpa had given a job to Mitch's son and later to Mitch's grandson. She jumped to a sitting straight position. *How can I be so slow?*

The car keys rattled a discordant tune as she quickly hooked up her seat belt, shoved the keys into the ignition, and sped off.

She had to find Jason Clark.

Chapter Fourteen

MADISON BURST INTO The Loony Bean, the glass door swinging wildly, little bells jingling in the doorframe. She rushed up to the counter and said, "Where's Jason? Is Jason here? I need to talk to him."

A young woman in a barista apron looked up from cleaning the counter and said, "Sorry. He has the morning shift. He's gone for the day." She wiped some splatters and straightened out a napkin dispenser.

"Could you call him please? It's really important. Tell him Madison is… No, say Madison Cruz…tell him Madison Cruz is here waiting for him."

"I'm sorry but we don't really—"

"Please! Tell him it's an emergency about Vincent. He'll understand."

For a moment, the young woman looked at her without saying anything, then walked over to another employee. They whispered while looking at Madison.

Madison wondered if she looked wild-eyed so she tried to compose herself to look concerned instead of crazy. The other employee shrugged his shoulders and walked into the back room. The young woman came back to Madison and said that it was slow tonight so they would call Jason for her.

Twenty minutes later, Madison was still sitting at a little table inside the cafe, waiting for Jason. She had watched every person who entered or left the cafe. Everyone looked suspicious for no logical reason. She realized in that moment that this was the behavior she had witnessed from her grandfather in Sound Beating.

Just then Jason walked through the door. He looked different without his barista apron. His nice jeans and trendy t-shirt made him look like a customer of the cafe. Madison stood up from the chair in the back corner of the room and waved when he looked in her direction. He walked up, his expression a bit confused.

"Jason," she exhaled. "I didn't know if you would come."

He didn't seem to know if he should smile or not. But his hazel brown eyes looked bright as he searched her face. "I was about to go out anyway, hang with some friends. What's going on?"

Madison took his hands and sat him down next to her at the little square coffee table. "Jason. I'm not going to make much sense right now. But please, please bear with me. I have to ask you a few questions."

"They said it was an emergency with Vincent? Your grandfather?"

"Jason, is your grandfather's name, Mitch?"

"Yeah. So?"

"Do you know where he is right now?"

He leaned back in his chair. "What's going on?"

"I think he's helping my grandfather. Please. Can you tell me how to contact him?"

She watched him stare at her as she tried to gauge how much he needed to know. She hardly knew him, but she was going to have to extend a certain amount of trust in him if she hoped to get to Mitch.

"What's so bad about helping your grandfather? Helping him with what?"

"I need to talk to him, Jason. To Mitch."

He crossed his arms. "Not until you tell me what's happened."

"How about this? We'll leave it up to Mitch to tell you. But I need to see him right away."

"That might be a little tricky right now. He's in the hospital."

Madison caught her breath as her eyes grew bigger.

Jason looked in her eyes and shook his head. In a quiet voice he said, "You have the most beautiful eyes I've ever seen."

"What?"

"Sorry. Little distracted."

"How can you say that when your grandfather has been put in the hospital?"

"Relax. It's routine tests. Guess he needs a tune-up once in a while." He chuckled. "But seriously, I really do think your eyes are…"

Her light green eyes welled up in tears, looking like crystals as her gaze drifted around the room, unsure what to think. Jason grew concerned, uncrossing his arms.

"Hey, hey now." He leaned toward her, putting a hand on her shoulder, his brows knit in confusion. "Madison, you have to tell me what's going on. I can't help if you don't tell me."

"Something terrible happened, something that Mitch probably knows about. My grandfather left town over it, saying he needs to go get help."

He brushed hair away from her face and said, "Start from the beginning."

✧　✧　✧

THEY HAD BEEN sitting in his car for the last half hour, parked under the shade of a few large maple trees behind the cafe. With the windows down, a cooling breeze blew in from Madison's side of the car and out again through Jason's side. The scent of lush maple leaves toasted by a hot summer sun blew through the car, making it tempting to relax. But Madison didn't dare.

She had said she couldn't stand being inside the cafe any longer. Every time the little bells jingled at the top of the door they would stop talking while Madison watched whoever had walked in, trying to convince herself that everything was all right. Everyone looked familiar. Everyone looked suspicious. She felt safer at the idea of spilling the story to Jason inside the privacy of his car. Earlier, with Spenser, she had shared the information from the contents of the box, but nothing about her grandfather's desperate fist fight. Now, with Jason, Madison told him all about the fight and the existence of the box, but nothing about its contents.

"But how did you know that Mitch was my grandfather?"

"You used to work for my grandpa, and you said your dad used to work for him, too. When my mom said that Grandpa had given a job to Mitch's son and later his grandson, I figured it had to be you."

"So if Vincent called my grandpa to handle the guy in duct tape, don't you think it would make sense for Grandpa Mitch to stay at Vincent's house and sort of babysit Mr. Duct Tape?"

Madison thought about this. "Yeah. That would be a lot easier than trying to explain to the neighbors why you're putting Mr. Duct Tape into a car or something."

"All he told you to do was hide a box and carry on like normal, right?"

"Right, and then wait till he contacts me. He said it may take days."

"Did you look in the box?"

She hesitated, then said, "Yes. I didn't understand much of it, but I shouldn't talk about it with you."

"Fair enough. So why not just hide the box and sit tight?"

"That's what I was going to do. But it's a little hard with someone breaking into my car and knowing where I live."

Jason's forehead creased. "Someone broke into your car?"

Madison realized she'd left that out. "Yeah. I think someone followed me home from Grandpa's house. I saw a woman breaking into my car. But she was gone by the time I got out to my parking lot." Madison leaned back, fighting off a sense of defeat. She looked upward through the open car window. A bigger wind blew through the tree tops, causing the rustling sound of the tree leaves to swell.

He exhaled. "Okay. Here's a question for you. Are you willing to risk talking to my Grandpa Mitch? You may be spilling the beans to him because I'm assuming he's not the one your grandfather was talking about in that voicemail. He couldn't be. He went into the hospital this afternoon."

Madison looked at him and could see the same thought was hitting Jason, too. She said, "Just this afternoon? Are you sure it's for routine tests?"

✧   ✧   ✧

THE OLD GUY in the hospital gown growled at Jason. "You say anything to your folks, and I'll kick your punk ass."

Jason nodded at Madison. "Yup. He's going to be fine."

Mitch Clark scrunched up his face, grunting in pain as he tried to recover some dignity, adjusting the gown and the blankets around him. "Bastard caught me off guard. I was bending over him to peel the tape from a corner of his mouth to let him drink some juice through a straw." His voice dropped, and he added, "Idiot."

Madison suspected he meant this insult for himself.

He clutched the edge of his blanket, trapping it in a fist. "His legs may have been taped up, but he could still bend at the waist. Brought both his legs up and kicked me hard in the stomach." He frowned and yanked at the blanket. "Son of a bitch must have hit my gallbladder. Pain was so sharp I could hardly move. I didn't know what else to do, so I called Ray. He came and took over for me. Locked the asshole in a closet, brought me here, then went back. He'll keep an eye on him." Mitch looked past Jason at Madison. "Let me talk to Vincent's baby girl here."

Jason stepped back as Madison stepped up to the side of the bed.

"I'm so sorry this happened to you," she said. "But please, tell me what's going on. I'm going crazy trying to make any sense of it." She remembered him from her childhood and teen hood. Her grandfather had been part of a monthly poker night that involved six or seven guys. They rotated which house they would meet in. On the months that it landed at her grandfather's house, Madison would see Mitch attending with the other guys. She had paid so little attention to her grandfather's social life in those days. She felt embarrassed now that Mitch seemed to be making a fuss over her.

"Madison." He picked up her hand and patted it as if she were the one who needed comforting. "Don't you worry about anything, sweetheart. Your old granddad is out there pulling a fast one on these assholes. They won't know what hit 'em till it's too late."

"But who was that this morning? What's happened?"

In a gentle voice he said, "You have to understand something. Your grandfather is a good man. And like all good men, he does the best he can with what life throws at him. Life threw him a doozy. There are things that are his business and his secret to tell. It's not for me to reveal. His main concern was to keep you out of the way till this all gets worked out."

Madison was torn between hugging him for being such a good friend to her grandfather, and scolding him for keeping secrets from her. *This involves my life, too.*

She was about to say as much when a nurse came in to shoo out the visitors. Madison saw both Mitch and Jason looking from the nurse to her, pleading with Madison with their eyes for her to be quiet. *Shit.* She didn't want the nurse suspecting anything, either. It might bring on the wrong kinds of questions, leading to calling the police. The answers that Madison desired were doomed to be delayed. She couldn't even ask Mitch about the photo, and what it was her grandfather was holding in the picture. Mitch might not want to accept it, but she was involved.

Nodding at Mitch, Jason said, "We'll let you get your rest. I'll check on you tomorrow."

They walked out of the room, and Madison grabbed Jason's arm. She hastened her pace towards the elevator. "Hey, what's the hurry?" he asked.

"As much as I love the air-conditioning in here, we have another stop to make."

"Where?"

"Where do you think?" She fixed him with a look that said she wasn't taking any bullshit.

He shook his head as he walked. "No. You should stay away from the house, Madison. Let it rest till Vincent gets back."

"I can't let it rest! You wouldn't let it rest either if it were *your* grandfather."

In a loud voice he said, "It *is* my grandfather! He got hurt because of this."

In a louder voice, she said, "Mine was about to be killed!" People walking past them in the hallway turned their heads to look at them, then hurried on their way. "Shit!" Madison whispered.

Approaching the elevator, Madison and Jason joined a small group of people already gathered there, waiting. She leaned in close to Jason and said in an agitated whisper, "Whether these old guys like it or not, they need some help. We can't accept a pat on the head and let them risk their lives over some stupid secret!"

A few more people came up to the elevator, holding flowers. A woman with a big sun hat busily looked at her cell phone. A little boy held his mother's hand while he stared at Madison. Soon they were all joined by a man carrying two coffees to deliver.

In a heated whisper, Jason replied, "Our grandfathers insisted we not tell my folks or your mom." He looked her in the eye. "I'm not going to tell. Are you?"

In a breathy explosion, she whispered, "No! Of course not!"

He looked down at her upturned face and whispered, "Well, then we're keeping a secret, too! So, how do you like that?"

She waved an arm in the air as she whispered, "We're keeping the secret to protect our grandfathers!"

"And maybe they're keeping a secret to protect you!" he whispered back. "Who knows who else they're trying to protect?" He leaned over to the wall and punched the elevator button hard.

Madison leaned over with him and angrily whispered, "How are you going to feel if one of them gets killed while we're waiting around?"

After a pause, she heard people behind her whispering, "I think I'd rather take the stairs."

The little boy whispered to his mother, "Is Grandpa going to die?"

To get away from their audience Madison and Jason stepped away a few paces, while the little boy looked around his mother's skirt to watch them go stand to the side.

The elevator dinged and opened. Madison and Jason stayed back while everyone else got on and the door closed. The woman with the sun hat seemed to change her mind and stood off to the side reading the directory on the wall near Jason. He looked around and his eyes landed on the woman, his face knit in concentration.

Madison said, "You don't have to go. I can go to my grandpa's house by myself. I have to talk to Ray. Just take me back to my car." The next elevator opened up, empty. They stepped inside, alone. Jason hit the ground floor button.

"By yourself, my *ass*." He confessed, "I was going to drop you off safe, then go there without you." He kept hitting the button, trying to make the door close.

She smiled, relieved to have someone go with her. But instead of saying thank you, she said, "It's pretty great, actually."

"What is?"

"Your ass."

The elevator door closed, and Jason wore a small smile. But as the elevator descended, Madison felt her heart descending with it…

…wondering if Ann already knew something.

Chapter Fifteen

"**I** HAVE A key. Should we knock or go right in?" Madison asked. She felt her heart start to thump again. Earlier that morning she had witnessed her grandfather's fist fight in his living room. Now, as she stood on his front porch with Jason next to her, twilight was starting to set in.

Jason shook his head. "You have to knock. Ray doesn't know we're coming. He might clobber us if we walk in."

She knocked and rang the bell at the same time. They waited. No answer.

She rang the bell again, hearing its distant hollow sound within the house. All was silent.

Worried, she looked at Jason and knocked again, calling, "Ray? It's Madison. Ray? Mitch's grandson Jason is here with me." She knocked and rang the bell. "Please, Ray, I need to talk to you."

Nothing.

She turned the key, unlocking the knob. Madison started to step in but felt Jason's hands on her waist pulling her back. He placed himself in front of her and slowly stepped inside.

Madison, behind him, called, "Ray?"

They couldn't see very far into the house from the open doorway. The interior of the house was darker than the growing twilight outside. She reached for a lamp that should have been by the front door, but it had crashed on the floor. *Must have happened during Grandpa's fight.* She could see enough, along with furniture silhouettes, to walk to the light switch on the wall.

"Ray?" She called one last time as she turned on the light. Illuminated, everything was the way she last saw it when she had run out that morning. Some chairs and a small table were tipped over. She saw the broken pieces of the vase, picture frames on the floor by the rumpled throw rug, and the overturned lamp that had tangled her grandfather's arms during his fight. She pushed back the fear, remembering Mitch's words "Your old granddad is out there pulling a fast one on these assholes." She wondered what he was out there doing that he couldn't have done sooner.

She was grateful to have Jason with her right now as they went from room to room. They tried to puzzle out what was going on in the kitchen, Grandpa's bedroom, the guest bedroom, and Madison's old bedroom. It felt strange to her to be in the bedroom of her childhood under these circumstances. As a child she jumped on the bed, bounced balls off of the walls, and hit her head pretty hard on the ceiling once when she jumped off her dresser while wearing a towel tied around her neck for a cape. She'd crawled under the bed with a flashlight and read stories to her stuffed animals and dolls. She'd played dress-up with Spenser and an assortment of kittens. She had to acknowledge that although there might be some pretty dysfunctional aspects to her family, at least she had never had to fear for her physical safety. Not like now.

Jason said, "I don't know what feels worse. No Ray, or no Mr. Duct Tape."

"Wait a minute," Madison said. "Mitch said that Ray locked Mr. Duct Tape in a closet. All the closets in this house are sliding door types, except for the den. The closet in the den has the type of door that swings closed and can be locked from the outside."

They went to the den and stood in front of the closet door, which stood ajar. Jason made Madison stand back while he swung the door the rest of the way open, ready to tackle whatever came out.

On the floor at the threshold of the closet was a pair of man's pants with duct tape around the knees and around the ankles. It appeared as if the pants had been unbuttoned, unzipped, pushed down and slid out of, leaving the duct tape in place on the fabric of the pants.

A wadded up ball of used duct tape from the stranger's mouth and hands lay nearby on the floor.

Mr. Duct Tape was no longer duct taped. He had escaped.

"At least it will be easy to spot an old guy with no pants running around Seattle," Madison said.

Jason said, "Well, actually that depends."

Madison nodded, "Yeah. In the right neighborhood, he might blend right in."

"He could have taken a pair of your grandfather's pants."

Madison agreed. "They did seem to be pretty evenly matched in size and strength this morning."

"That's saying a lot. Vincent may be an old guy, but he's no pushover," said Jason as he looked around the room, then asked, "How do you think he got the closet door unlocked?"

Madison pointed to deeper inside the closet. There was an open tool box with an assortment of common household tools. One small screwdriver lay nearby. "Poor Ray," she said. "He didn't know that Grandpa keeps a tool kit in there."

"And we don't know if he escaped before or after Ray got back from the hospital." Jason rubbed the back of his neck, looking around. "Damn it."

In a quiet voice, Madison said, "He's not as big and strong as Grandpa. I hope he's okay."

They stood there in silence. Madison heard creaking sounds. She and Jason jumped as a baseball bat whipped around the corner, pointing up to the ceiling, ready to fly downward. Ray was in battle stance but slackened his posture as soon as he saw Jason and Madison.

"Oh, my God!" The short old man let the bat slump to his side. "Oh, my God, I almost hurt you!" He was breathing as if his heart were racing.

Madison said, "I'm sorry, Ray. But we did try calling your name."

"I was in the backyard checking the bushes." He seemed to be a nervous wreck. He gestured at the empty pants with duct tape still on them. "Did you tell Jason about this?"

In spite of her fright, Madison grabbed Jason's hand and yanked it, making him look at her. She squeezed hard, trying to communicate with her eyes before turning to Ray and saying, "Grandpa called. He said everything went great. Just like he hoped."

Ray blinked and exhaled. "You're kidding." There was a sad hope on his face. "Really?" He kept blinking, confused. "He couldn't have landed in DC more than what, three or four hours ago? And they believed him? Just like that?"

Madison tried a small smile and nodded. *DC? Come on, Ray, keep talking.* When Ray stared at her and didn't say anything, she tried shrugging. Ray looked over at

Jason who was watching Madison with his mouth a little open.

He seemed to snap to, with a jerk of his head, and said, "Yeah. He sure pulled a fast one, didn't he?" He raised his fists to his chin like he was doing a little shadow boxing. Madison tried to copy him, raising her fists to her chin and starting a little boxer two-step dance, shuffling around the floor. She and Jason started trading soft fisticuffs to each other's chins, looking at Ray.

Standing there, Ray closed his eyes and seemed to deflate. "You always were a smart one," he said quietly. "You had me going there."

Madison and Jason stopped, their fists lowering till their hands opened in defeat.

Ray wiped the back of his arm across his forehead. "Neither one of you understand how serious this is." Dragging the baseball bat behind him, he turned to leave the room.

The sight of Ray so dejected broke Madison's heart. "Please, Ray. We weren't trying to make a fool out of you. I've been worried sick and no one will tell me what's going on. Give me something. Throw me a bone."

"You got your bone when you tricked me into saying DC. There! DC! That's more than I should have said. The wrong person could get wind of that, and they'll know exactly what it means. We're trying to keep this quiet till help arrives."

"You, Mitch, and Grandpa?"

He nodded. "Now go home. Jason, get her out of here."

"Did the hacker find you, too?" she asked.

His head jerked up. Madison said, "My mother said she was working on a case involving the UW getting hacked. She was trying to warn Grandpa about identity theft. But this morning Grandpa mentioned a hacker finding him. All three of you used to work at the UW. But this isn't about identity theft, is it? Ann's about to stumble onto something, isn't she?"

His jaw hardened, but it also lifted in pride. "We're trying to fix it before she does. Vincent is the best friend we ever had. He deserves a chance to explain what happened." He pointed a finger at her and said, "You give him a fair chance, you hear me? Ann may not. But you could help her. You're probably the only one who can. You owe him that."

✧   ✧   ✧

AFTER RETURNING TO the The Loony Bean parking lot, Jason waited in his car, engine running, while Madison unlocked her own car and climbed in. Ray had left them little choice but to go home and wait. They each pulled out of the parking lot, heading for Madison's apartment, Jason following her.

She was tired, hot, and hungry, and twilight was giving Seattle its usual spectacular sunset. Lowering the window, she revived herself by letting the evening breezes rush into her car as she drove down the highway. The thunderous wind blowing around her within the little car caused papers and leftover fast food bags to rise up on the air currents, threatening escape. It made her dark silky hair blow like a crazed Medusa, cooling her neck and helping her feel more optimistic. Normally she would always be up for an adventure, but dangerous adventures only sounded exciting when she knew they would never happen. Now that there might be some actual danger around, it didn't sound so cool. She would prefer a safe adventure, and it frightened her to think she'd ever been fool enough to assume there was such a thing as a safe adventure.

Jason drove his car right behind her. He had insisted on following her home and checking her apartment to make sure no one was in there. Besides being a distracting cutie with a bootie, Jason had managed to involve himself in what she considered her family's private problem. She felt a mixture of gratitude at his attentiveness, and annoyance that she had met someone with so much potential when she was at her worst. Her strongest desire right now was for him to see her at her best. Rested, relaxed, looking sexy. No doubt about it. He definitely had to go.

Alone in her car, Madison pondered the odd words that Ray had said. So it turned out Grandpa had flown to DC. Now she needed to find out why.

Meanwhile, she knew she had done what Grandpa had asked. He had asked her to hide the *box*. And she felt she had done even better than that. She had hidden the *contents* of the box. If anyone had been in her apartment today, they would have found a metal box with her fairy godmother tools of the trade.

As she threaded her way down the neighborhood street, she looked at the time on the dashboard and sighed. No wonder she was starving. She'd have to scrounge for something from her cupboards or fridge. And there was still so much that she needed to get done tonight with all the photos that she needed to scan into her computer. She needed to return the photos right away. She had broken so many promises to Ann in the past. She wanted to start keeping a few.

She parked in the apartment lot, grabbed her purse and the large envelope of photos, and got out of her car as Jason pulled up alongside her.

"Jason," she called through his open window, "you really don't have to do any more. I'm fine." He got out of his car, and shut the door as if to make his point.

"As soon as I make sure no one is in your apartment, I'll leave."

Sheesh, he looks good in evening light! The night breeze brought a mild heavenly scent from him. His nice t-shirt was a perfect fit around his broad shoulders, relaxed yet smooth, but the sleeves seemed to strain a bit around his biceps. She wondered if he was hiding a six-pack under there.

He walked over to where she was standing next to her car.

She said, "You should try to salvage what's left of your evening. It's bad enough I ruined the first half."

He shrugged. "I had no idea that kind of thing was going on in the background. Looks like our grandfathers are a couple of wild guys."

That made her laugh. "I guess so. Look, Jason, I'm really sorry I got so mad at the hospital. I've been a little desperate all day. I thought you would come to the cafe, maybe call Mitch for me, or…" He had a crooked little smile. She could tell he wasn't listening. "What?" she asked.

Leaning in dangerously close, his teasing voice said, "I feel like such a bad boy. But I can't be fired."

✧   ✧   ✧

THEY KNOCKED ON Toonie's door. Madison said to Jason in a quiet voice, "If anyone saw or heard anything it would be her."

Locks clicked and turned. Toonie opened the door and looked from one to the other. "Brought it upstairs, did you?"

The surprise on Jason's face when he had to look upward at Toonie made Madison want to giggle.

"I thought you two were going to have 'a moment' down there in the parking lot." Toonie added, "Always best to keep that stuff private."

"Toonie, this is Jason. Jason, this is my neighbor, Toonie."

Jason stared for a second, reached out the wrong hand at first, then quickly switched to the other hand, hitting Madison in the arm as he did so and mumbling, "Sorry." They did a polite handshake.

"You met her mama yet?"

"No."

"Scary woman."

Madison had a wry smile and asked, "How did you guess?"

Toonie answered, "Because she loves you and any mama who loves her child is a scary woman. Now, what's the occasion here?"

"It's complicated," said Madison.

"Seems everything is with you."

"Have you seen or heard anyone entering my apartment since the last time we talked?"

"No. Everything has been quiet. Guess that ends now, huh?"

"I promise to be good tonight."

"When are you going to tell me what's going on? I get a little bored without some juicy story now and then," Toonie said. She looked Jason up and down and asked, "You work out?"

"Not really. No," said Jason.

"You should. Good potential there."

Madison said, "I'll tell you soon, Toonie. I hope."

They left Toonie and went to Madison's door. As she got out her key, Jason said, "Promise me you'll tell the truth. If you see anything at all out of place in your apartment—"

Madison interrupted him and said, "Everything in my apartment was already out of place."

He turned her to face him. He looked earnest. "Promise me," he said.

The truth was, she considered saying whatever she needed to get him to stay. But the way things were going, she would find a way to screw it up with him before she'd had a chance to show him her good side. She should wait until he could see her in a better situation, one in which she wasn't a needy, paranoid, nervous wreck.

She wondered what his kiss would be like. He had full lips. A bit of dark stubble around his mouth made her think he might feel a little rough. She'd like to find out.

"Jason. I'll tell you if anything looks wrong. But you have to promise me that when we get in there, we won't have 'a moment.' That's the last thing I want tonight. There's so much work to do and I really need to concentrate."

He tried not to smile saying, "You were looking at my lips the whole time you said that."

"I was?" Her gaze shot up to his eyes.

"Yeah."

She blinked. "So noted."

As they entered her dark apartment, the street lights from the parking lot flooded in through the living room window that she had left open. The box sat near the window where she had left it, looking pointless and unimportant. She turned on the light and Jason's eyes took in the surroundings. "You don't have to tell me," he said. "I can see this place has been tossed."

"Yes. But has anyone been in here?" she said.

"You mean…? Oh. Sorry."

She walked around. "Everything looks fine so far." She walked into the bedroom, poked her head into the bathroom, then shrugged her shoulders. "It all looks the way it should. I mean, not the way it should, just the way I left it. I left it the way it definitely should not look, but that means it should look the way it shouldn't. Shouldn't it?"

"I'll take your word for it." Jason walked over to the living room window and looked out. "It doesn't look like anyone would be able to enter from this window. There's nothing nearby to climb on."

"Convinced? I'll be fine."

"All right." They typed out each other's phone numbers on their phones. "Let me know if you hear anything from Ray," said Jason.

"Will do. And likewise, if you get anything new out of Grandpa Mitch." She sighed. "And thanks, Jason. It's been good to have someone I can talk to about what happened at Grandpa's house this morning."

"Keep your door locked." He hugged her, saying, "Everything's going to be all right." He left.

Chapter Sixteen

F OR ALL HER bravado with Jason, she was actually nervous about being alone tonight. The stranger that Grandpa duct taped had watched her run to the front door in Grandpa's house. He'd looked like he was smiling. She shuddered. What the hell did he have to smile about?

It was much too hot not to have the window open for breezes, but she didn't want anyone down in the parking lot to be able to see her in her apartment. She turned out the light and threw the window wide open. She sat on the floor where she had set up her computer and scanner next to a wall in her living room. With the glow from her laptop screen she oriented each photo on the scanner bed and began scanning each image into her computer, one by one.

Thinking about how she would present all these photos in a montage gave her a welcome distraction. She decided she should find old music from the sixties to play as background music for the opening. Jerry had begun his career in the sixties so she would find some upbeat music to go with the earliest photos. This would be fun. She liked Jerry. He had been the best part of Ann's visits to the house during Ann's college years. Ann had been the worst part. Ann had criticized everything and had tried to inject her opinions into how Grandma was handling Madison in Ann's absence, from how she dressed, what kind of toothbrush she should be using, to whom she was allowed to play with. Her mom and Grandma would argue. Then all the new instructions would fade away soon after Ann went back to college.

Looking back, Madison realized that her mom's wishes weren't that awful. But her mother couldn't be gone from Madison's day to day life during her childhood, then expect to show up and make decrees, upsetting the accepted order of things. *No wonder I resented her so much.* It's a challenge to be good at mothering when you're that young, much less doing it long distance.

I wish Grandma would have explained that to me. She didn't exactly help us to get along.

This new thought shocked Madison. She had never put it together before. Grandma had always wanted every young child within a mile to be her own, especially Madison. If she were honest, Grandma and Ann had been fighting over her. And Grandma always won. Ann was a teenager looking to her mother for help. Grandma took advantage of that. Then Madison's loyalty to Grandma hit fever pitch when Grandma was dying, and afterwards, Madison couldn't bear to call Ann "Mom" for a long time. But after today's visit with Ann, Madison felt hope in her heart. Maybe they could be a family after all. She couldn't get over how pleasant their meeting had been.

I wonder if she likes rose gardens? There's a really cool one right next to the zoo that I could show her.

She nibbled on an ancient apple that she found in the back of her refrigerator. Yuck. But it was better than that old container of yogurt she tried to eat. She was so hungry, but at this rate she would be found dead from food poisoning. The delicate buzzing sound from her old scanner completed another cycle, and the image showed up on her computer screen. She set up the next photo on the bed of the scanner and pushed the button, the slow buzzing starting up again. Peering at her apple, Madison held it close to the glow of the computer screen, trying to see the next safe place to bite it.

Just then Madison heard the doorknob turn and the door swing open. She jumped up, kicking the scanner and banging her elbow into the wall. *I didn't lock it!* She would have screamed, but she was coughing and trying not to choke on a bit of apple.

A black silhouette stood in the doorway with a large flat box balanced on one hand, the neck of a long bottle in the other.

ExBoy put on a deep announcer-like movie voice to call out, "I come seeking retribuuutionnn! I shall ravage a juicy braaain, and why are the lights ouuut?"

Madison crawled out from behind her couch, saying, "Oh, my *God*, ExBoy! You scared the shit out of me! I swear to God I'll kill you if you ever, *ever* do that—" She stopped. She inhaled through her nose. In the dark her eyes grew wide. The scent of fresh baked crust combined with cheeses, garlic, and oregano. Spices and meats. Fresh hot pizza. The seduction was complete.

"Why are you on the floor, in the dark?" he asked. His foot reached around behind him and kicked the door closed. "On second thought, stay there." His dark shape advanced through the short entryway into the living room where Madison clung to the carpet, her heart still pounding from her fright. With no effort, he balanced the pizza box and the long bottle as he sank down and sat into a cross legged position on the floor. Reaching into his pocket, he pulled out a corkscrew opener and opened the bottle there in the dark on the floor.

Madison, on her hands and knees, sat up into a more dignified position and felt tears trying to burn her eyes. She didn't know if it was from her fright or from the comfort she felt knowing someone who cared about her was here.

She stared at ExBoy's face in the dim light from the window, hearing the small pop as a cork left the bottle. A cool breeze blew in from the window. He reached over and picked up her hand, placing it on the neck of the bottle. It was chilled. From the shape of the bottle she guessed it to be a white wine. In this heat, touching something chilled felt lavish and healing. He pushed it up to her lips. She took a drink from it *(delicious!)* and handed it back.

Reaching to the back of her head, he lifted her hair up and placed the cold bottle on the back of her neck, the length of the bottle going down her back. The sudden chill caused her to arch her back with a shudder and a sharp intake of breath; at the same time she heard the rustle of tree leaves outside the window from the wind picking up. He then gave her the bottle and while she took another drink, he blew a light stream of air on her neck where the chilled bottle had left it wet. He opened the pizza box, the aroma flooding out now, and took out a piece, holding it up to her mouth, feeding her a bite. He sat there quiet, watching her eat in the dim light.

She swallowed and leaned forward to take another bite while asking, "Aren't you going to have any?" He took a drink from the bottle before finally taking a bite for himself. She took the bottle from him. The wine seemed to taste better with each swallow.

He said, "I couldn't stay mad. I tried."

"I'm sorry. I was trying to cover up a stupid lie about you. I'm tired of always being the one who never gets laid, so I let Spenser think that I was getting it from you."

"You're kidding. That's what it was about?" A slow smirk grew on his face. "You're always surprising me. Like now. I thought you'd be mad after all the secrets came out today. I wanted to be the one to tell you."

About other women? His friends with benefits? Huh. She had never kidded herself. He was a flame, and some women were moths. It was his personal business.

This time she fed him the next bite and said, "I understand," then took another bite for herself. Outside the window, the wind was on a busy errand as it rushed past, the rustling leaves picking up in volume and mixing with the sound of tires softly crunching gravel down in the parking lot.

"Really?" he asked, sounding unconvinced.

"Of course," she said. "I'm not saying I like it, but it's not like I can break up with you. We're not even a couple."

He said, "No, but I can never stop thinking about you. I don't know what we are, you and me."

She thought about that for a moment. "Neither do I. That's why I never know how to be around you. But I'm glad you're here."

"Are we okay then?"

"Yeah, we're good."

They took a few turns drinking the wine and ExBoy said, "You realize of course that I'm afraid to put any moves on you now."

"Really?"

"Yeah. Totally paralyzed. Watch."

He leaned in and kissed her mouth, soft at first, but as the pressure of his lips increased, her breathing rate increased with it. With one hand behind her head and the other bracing himself on the floor, his kiss pushed her back and downward. As he gently let go of the kiss, her chin and lips reached upward in protest. Her eyes fluttered open and saw his face in hers, keeping close eye to eye contact as he supported her slow descent, until she felt the floor on her back. Putting his other arm under her, he used his whole body to bury her in the next kiss. Her primal needs kicked into high gear as the material of the t-shirt on his back balled up into her fists. She pushed her fists upward, pulling his shirt off, as his arms came up, taking her tank top with it. Their mutual tangle of arms and clothes cut off the kiss but only for a moment.

Her mind emptied of all the worry and fear from the day. She had delayed this long enough, and it brought to mind her memory of that hot July day, two or three weeks ago, when they had almost taken this next step but were interrupted by friends who had arrived to help with the move into the apartment. Those friends weren't going to interrupt this time.

Because someone else was. The knock on the door made them both jump.

"You've got to be kidding me!" Madison said, jumping up to grope around in the dark for her tank top, plunging her head and arms back into it, tripping on his pants on the floor. Her own pants were still halfway on. She quickly straightened up her clothes to the sound of a second knock on the door. "With the luck I've been having," she grumbled, "that could be my mother right now. She's already decided she doesn't like you."

"She doesn't really know me," said ExBoy. "She just thinks she does."

Madison looked through the peephole in her door.

There stood Jason.

Madison's heart fell and hit the floor. There was no time to argue with the illogical feelings doing battle in her head. She wished it really were her mother instead of Jason. She turned to ExBoy, his naked silhouette near the window, and with her plaintive voice barely audible, said, "Hide."

He expelled a breath, exasperated, saying, "Shit," as he ducked behind the couch.

She opened the door. "Jason, what are you doing here?"

"I couldn't stop thinking about you," said Jason, looking in her eyes from left to right. "You and those gorgeous green eyes, and they reminded me of something I saw before we got into the elevator."

ExBoy stood up from behind the couch, his nudity visible from the hips up, saying, "I may not want your mom to know we're together…"

Madison whipped her head around in panic, seeing ExBoy standing there, his hands on his hips.

"…but I'm not hiding for any dude." He lifted his chin at Jason. "Hey," he greeted, his eyes hard. "This is exactly what it looks like."

Staring wide-eyed at ExBoy, she heard Jason asking, "You're together?"

She turned back to Jason, seeing the hurt and confusion in his eyes. Her mouth hanging open, searching for words, she blurted, "He brought pizza."

She turned back to ExBoy, furious, and said, "You're not afraid of another guy, but you're afraid of my mommy!"

"She's FBI! She could make my life hell with a phone call!

"How did you know that? I never told you that!"

ExBoy's face lost its bravado. "You did see your mom today, right?"

Silence.

Madison heard something and looked back at the door. Jason was gone. She grabbed the sides of the doorframe and thrust her head out into the hallway in time to see him pounding down the stairwell.

THE WHOLE THING came out when she held ExBoy's clothes out of the window, threatening to drop them into the parking lot if he didn't tell her everything he knew. When he said she was being ridiculous, she loosened her grip to drop a few items. Both shoes went down together, and bounced off in different directions when they hit the ground.

He rolled his eyes saying, "I've been trying to tell you about it because I was tired of waiting for your mom to tell you. It started out as a little surprise."

"What surprise?"

He held a hand out and gestured all around her dark living room. "This. The whole scheme to get you into this apartment."

For the next few minutes Madison couldn't believe what she was hearing. Ann had arranged for ExBoy to "find" this apartment for Madison. She paid hefty deposits and made a deal for the landlord to charge Madison cheap rent while Ann paid the difference. ExBoy referred to some tall old lady showing the apartment to Ann while the landlord was on vacation.

"She said she wanted to surprise you," said ExBoy. "I thought that was pretty cool of her until days went by and she still hadn't told you. Then days turned into weeks and I felt kind of weird, so I told her I would tell you about the apartment if she didn't. She said you called her today and were on your way over. She promised she would tell you. Obviously, she didn't. Satisfied?"

"Hell, no!" She dropped his shirt. She still had his pants and underwear and continued to hold them outside the window. "Tell me why she went through all this to get me in here."

"Why do you think? She's trying to help you. Sometimes a mom will do that kind of thing."

"Not this mom."

"What do you mean 'not this mom'? She did it, didn't she?"

Fretful, Madison said, "You don't understand."

"I can see that now. But I swear, I thought I was just being nice to your mom."

He didn't seem as upset as she wanted him to be. He stood there in the buff, acting completely natural. His eyes, still amorous, looked at her as if he were getting back to business. In a conciliatory tone, he said, "This is what I was referring to when I said I wanted to be the one to tell you."

"I thought you were referring to your secrets about other women," Madison said.

He scrunched up his face, "What other women?"

"You said you had boink buddies."

"No, I said I have offers. You're the one who wanted to be my boink buddy."

"I didn't want to be your boink buddy! I wanted to let Spenser think we were having sex."

"Why lie to her? What do you think we were about to do here?"

"Well, keep the first part and take out the buddy part."

"Okay. Let's." He walked toward her, and she flinched.

Finally, he seemed annoyed. "Again, I don't know what we are, Madison. Every time we get to this point, you back out."

"That's not fair. Last time, people were arriving. We *had* to back out." Her arm holding his pants and underwear outside the window was getting heavier.

"What do you want from me, Madison?" He stepped closer and stood in the slanted light flooding in the window from the parking lot lights. She looked from his face, all down his body, and melted.

He must have sensed it because he said, "I want you, too."

He was too gorgeous. She couldn't remember the main point of why they were arguing. Someone should throw a blanket over him and break the spell.

"Was that idiot at the door someone important?"

"He's not an idiot," affirmed Madison.

"Is that what's going on here?" he asked. She tried to look away and he held his palms out, saying, "I'm standing here, asking you an honest question."

"You're standing there with a loaded weapon. It's hard to think right now."

He stepped up close, facing her. In a soft voice he said, "Well, maybe if you gave me my pants back," he put his hands on her rear end, caressing, rekindling her earlier fire, "I could cover up my weapon," he nibbled her ear and whispered, "and you wouldn't have to be so scared of it."

She whipped him back and forth with his underwear, the elastic slapping into his face. He ducked his head with his arms up to protect himself and backed away a little too fast, right into the backside of the couch and went sailing over the top. He then bounced from the cushions to the floor while Madison wadded up his pants and underwear, sending them flying out into the parking lot. Jerking her dirty fairy godmother costume up from the floor nearby, she threw it on top of him saying, "Here. Don't say I sent you out there naked."

Chapter Seventeen

A T TOONIE'S WINDOW, Madison and Toonie were side by side, leaning over with elbows on the windowsill, resting their chins in their palms, watching ExBoy down in the parking lot under the glow of the lights as he continued looking for his shirt and one of his shoes. Madison passed the wine bottle to Toonie, who took a swig. ExBoy was wearing just his pants now, albeit commando. He had found his pants first and had put them on before he located his underwear and the first shoe. The sad fairy godmother costume lay in a heap nearby, having been used like a Turkish towel to get him to the parking lot.

"I never would have pegged him for the tighty whitey type," said Toonie. "It's nice to see those again. Of course, this ain't the circumstance I was hoping for." She eyed the bottle of wine and took another drink. "So your mama never told you?"

"I wouldn't have come pounding on your door if she had."

"And that young man down there, what was that weird name you called him?"

"ExBoy. His real name is Xander Boyd."

"I've seen him around here. Bet the girls are all over him. So how'd he catch the brunt of this?"

"My mother used him to lie to me and get me to move in here."

"Was throwing him out naked a good idea?" asked Toonie.

Madison didn't answer. She looked back down at ExBoy in the parking lot. He was still shirtless and needed to find one more shoe.

Toonie said, "Don't get me wrong. I know you young people have to work out your problems, same as anyone. But did he deserve it? Is he a bad sort of guy?"

Madison hung her head. "No." She rubbed her face and sighed. "I have to get down there and apologize. If he'll let me."

Toonie nodded, saying, "I'll bet it has something to do with that other young man you introduced me to earlier. Jason? Did you two fight about Jason? Handsome brute, that one."

Madison's heart sunk again at the thought of Jason. They were pulled together now through their grandfathers. Like a couple of bad boys, their grandfathers were friends who covered up one another's secrets. She and Jason had promised to check in with each other with any updates from their grandfathers. Only now Jason's opinion of her must be crap. She had chased him away from her place, claiming she had a lot of work to do. Then she let him find her with a naked guy behind her couch. *That takes real talent.*

Madison said, "The whole thing is a mess. I couldn't believe ExBoy would let my mother use him like that. But our argument was winding down, and I was about to let it go. Then he had to go and imply that I was scared of his penis."

Toonie laughed.

Madison said, "It's not funny."

Toonie's laughter increased as Madison tried not to smile, saying, "It's not *funny*. It made me furious." Toonie laughed with her eyes closed, and Madison started to snicker.

Toonie laughed out, "Scary penis, huh?"

Madison's laughter bubbled up. She made her eyes wide and held her hands apart to indicate twenty inches as Toonie covered her face like she was terrified. They fell into helpless laughter as Toonie reached for the bottle in her laughing fit but stopped suddenly. Madison was still laughing with a hand over her face when Toonie said, "What the…" She nudged Madison, and said in a serious tone. "Look." She pointed down into the parking lot.

A car had pulled up. Two men in slacks and button-up shirts had climbed out and were questioning ExBoy, their sleeves rolled up in the summer heat. The taller one had brown hair, while the shorter one had muscular forearms, his hair buzzed extra short. They appeared to be showing ExBoy the IDs in their wallets. Holding his underwear and a shoe in one hand, he started digging around in his pockets with the other. He seemed bewildered, looking around on the ground. He must have been looking for his wallet, which might have fallen out of his pocket when Madison threw the pants.

"Oh, no," said Madison. "One of the neighbors must have called the cops because he was naked." She jumped up, "I've got to get down there and explain!"

But Toonie grabbed her arm and held her still, saying, "Those don't look like cops."

ExBoy pointed up to a window way over on the other end of the building from where she and Toonie were watching at the moment. He then gestured to the ground, seeming to explain about his clothes and missing wallet, but one of the men leaned ExBoy over the car and began frisking him. The other went walking around the cars in the lot and zeroed in on Madison's car, shining flashlights in her car windows.

Toonie asked, "Your mama is FBI, right?"

Madison nodded.

Toonie said, "Do you have anything you don't want found? Because I think your place is about to be searched."

Madison flew out of Toonie's door and heard Toonie say, "I'll try to buy you some time," as Madison went tearing into her own apartment. She jerked open a drawer in her kitchen, the contents of the drawer rattling from rough treatment as she felt with her hands in the dark, till she found the flashlight she was looking for. She kept the light pointed down at the floor as she quickly looked all around the living room for her purse. She would never be able to explain the fake handgun hidden in it. *There it is!* She saw it against the wall, not too far from her laptop on the floor. She remembered stories of the FBI taking people's computers into custody, and though she knew she hadn't done anything wrong, paranoia set in fast.

Throwing her purse straps onto her arm, she slammed her laptop closed, sandwiching the large envelope of pictures inside, held it all pulled in to her chest, and turned for a frantic run out of the apartment door. Out in the hallway she heard Toonie's voice coming from the stairwell. "I'm so sorry. It's heavier than I realized." Madison rushed back to Toonie's door and saw the back of Toonie, standing a few steps down into the stairwell, carrying one of her large stuffed chairs. *Damn, that woman is strong!*

A man's voice said, "Ma'am, if you don't mind, we need to get around you." Toonie said, "Well, I'm a little committed now. If one of you could help on the other end, it'll go faster." Madison slipped into Toonie's apartment and quietly closed the door. She set her things down on the couch.

Then, she couldn't resist, she had to go look out of the peephole in the door. After a moment she saw the two men walking past, heading for her own door. She barely heard the knock on her door down the hall. *At least they had the courtesy to knock.* As she waited and strained to hear something, *anything*, her heart pounded and made her breathing a bit heavier. Standing so close to the inside of Toonie's door, trying to see more through the peephole, her own breath bounced back at her from the door and sounded loud in her ears. Her heart rate accelerated. The heat bore down in the cramped little space at the peephole, making the sweat unbearable. She was wound up like a spring ready to pop. *Stay still. Stay hidden.* After a second knock, she heard the door to her own apartment swing open.

Every second of waiting, knowing that they were in her apartment, added to her growing queasiness. She had never experienced that before. She felt *looked* at, even though she was alone in Toonie's apartment. Just knowing that someone was looking at her stuff, her mess, her home... *What the hell would they want, anyway?* Her time with Ann today showed zero indication that Ann knew anything about what had happened at Grandpa's house earlier. In spite of finding out that Ann had orchestrated Madison's move into this apartment building, the visit from these men didn't feel like Ann's doing. It wouldn't make sense. If nothing else, after her afternoon with Ann, Madison now believed that Ann wanted them to spend time together. She wouldn't want to make Madison pull away.

So what was happening here?

She heard a faint sound. Someone closing a door. The two men walked past the peephole, leaving. The guy with the buzz cut was carrying the metal box.

✧   ✧   ✧

MADISON COULD TELL that Toonie was trying to make herself invisible. That's what people do when they are witnessing a family fight, although Toonie was only witnessing one half of that fight. Madison poured her fury into the phone, with Ann. She wondered if she should put the whole thing on speaker phone so she could have a witness to Ann's words, which Madison assumed were going to be a ridiculous and exaggerated assessment of Madison's life. But that would be cruel to Toonie. Best to let Toonie think that she was invisible.

"He had no right to tell you," said Ann. "This isn't the way I wanted you to find out. It was my gift to you."

"You tricked me into it," said Madison. "Now I'm just supposed to accept it?"

"I knew I shouldn't have trusted Xander," huffed Ann. "He's one of those artistic types. Unpredictable."

Madison's mouth dropped open. The crack about artistic types got to her. But her comeback was, "Can't be trusted to keep up a lie, huh?"

"How many times have you lied to me because you thought I would never understand?" Ann's words were increasing in their heat.

"But this one is huge!" said Madison.

"This one is nothing," said Ann.

That stopped Madison. *Nothing?* Was there something even bigger?

Ann continued, "What did you expect me to do? I didn't know how else to get you out of that dangerous low rent district, and into something nicer. Safer! You cut me off as if you didn't need me, when you obviously did."

"Cut you off?" said Madison. "You've never been supportive of me. You cut me off first! You rejected me *first!*"

"What? You never wanted me in your life! Don't pretend you didn't prefer your grandmother over me," said Ann. "Don't pretend you ever cared if I wasn't there. That was the way you both wanted it! You got your way."

"Well, why didn't you fight harder for me?"

Emotion was creeping into Ann's voice, "I couldn't win. If I wasn't there, I wasn't a good mother. If I *was* there, she would prove that she was better for you. Everyone, except Dad, seemed happier if there was distance between us."

Madison had never heard this from Ann before. Deep down she knew it was probably true. But *damn it*, she didn't want Ann to be right at a time when Ann needed to be busted.

"This fight should have stayed between you and Grandma. I was a child. All I knew was that she loved me, and you didn't even like me."

"Madison, I loved you then, I love you now! I did a lousy job of trying to wrench you back from her. After she died, you hated me even more—"

"I was only twelve—"

"—and Dad needed you in his life."

"—I didn't understand."

"I had to let go again. You were good for each other. Later, you wouldn't even let me send you to college. I offered to pay every cent—"

"I wanted—"

"But you refused to go."

"—to be a theater major! You acted like I wanted to set fire to a pile of money!"

"You could have added all those classes later after getting a real education first."

"Like yours? You want me to be a spy like you, Ann?"

"I'm proud to have served my country!"

"You didn't answer the question. Do you want me to be a spy?"

Ann paused. "What are you getting at?"

"I was wondering what it would take to get your approval."

"Since when do you give a rat's ass about my approval? You only want the fun parts of having a mother. Is this my cue to offer you homemade cookies, call you pumpkin, and tell you how great you are?"

"You're the mother! You're supposed to be encouraging!"

"Encouragement is not the same as approval. You want my approval? Do something constructive with your life, then we'll try this conversation again."

Madison's emotions were hitting a wall. She had little left to care with. "It's *my* life…"

"You're not a real actress, Madison. Playing with wrestlers? Singing telegrams? That isn't what your dream was. You've been making those choices to prove that you can, but not because you actually believe in them. You've been holding your own happiness hostage."

In a quieter voice, Madison said, "It's not my fault you got knocked up. Quit punishing me."

Ann's voice was on the edge of crying, "That's not what happened! I *tried* to get pregnant. I need to explain it to you. There's so much to tell you and—"

"Let's go back," said Madison, "to the way we had it."

"Madison!" Ann was crying.

"You won't have to give a shit about me, and I won't have to worry about your opinion."

"Madison, please! I—"

Madison disconnected.

She stood there, limp, arms hanging loose at her sides. She looked down at the phone she was holding, realizing that she had never told Ann about the men searching her apartment. In those minutes of fighting with her mother, the raw pain from the years of feeling abandoned had stripped everything else from her mind. Saying all those things to her mother, some of them fair shots, some of them cheap, had taken precedence over all other considerations. She felt the grip of her own self-righteousness slowly open its fist from around her heart. She blinked. *What have I done?*

Toonie, who seemed to be weighing whether or not it was safe to stop being invisible, stood in the bedroom doorway.

Madison turned and looked at her, tears running down her cheeks, and said, "I think I broke my life."

Toonie, towering the way she seemed to when she stood in a doorway, said, "It takes a lot to break a life. Believe me, girl, you're just confused about yours. It ain't broken." She came forward and opened her arms. Madison, numb, accepted the offer. But once the old arms enfolded her, it hit, and she finally gave in to a good hard cry.

Chapter Eighteen

TOONIE BUSIED HERSELF in the small kitchen, cleaning up and putting things away. She scrubbed a stubborn stain in a cooking pot. Madison had gone through several tissues to dry her eyes and blow her nose. Her nose always seemed to leak long after a good cry was over. She was doing her best to toughen up and get past her deep disappointment in having the hope of getting her mother back in her life, only to lose her again. Toonie had assured her that Ann wasn't lost, but how could Toonie understand?

Madison gazed at the pictures on Toonie's wall. She said, "I noticed these earlier but I didn't have a chance to ask you about them. You worked in Vegas?"

Toonie seemed to be chuckling to herself before answering, "Yes, a very long time ago."

Madison saw that there were colorful ribbons and trophies, as well as all the black and white glossy eight by ten framed headshots on the walls. Madison said, "That's you lifting barbells, isn't it? And picking up those men?"

Toonie said, "Yup, that was me. Las Vegas isn't as impressed with those kinds of vaudeville acts anymore."

"So you were a weight lifter?" asked Madison.

"Back then we were called Strongwomen. Before my time, you mostly saw Strongmen and Strongwomen in the circus. Later, most of the circus acts modernized and went on vaudeville circuits, or later still, places like Las Vegas. In my day you didn't hear scandals about steroids and overtraining. Strongwomen like myself were natural born, growing up unnaturally strong. That's what made us something of a novelty to pay money to see. My manager loved to dress me up in those showgirl outfits with the huge feather headdresses. Made me even taller. Then I'd go out on stage with some foolish comedian and do skits that always ended with me picking him up and throwing him around. Then I'd pick up men from the audience. The audience ate it up back then."

"You didn't get hurt?"

"Nah. Rarely, anyway. It wasn't hard for me, till after I starting getting older. Then I had to train to keep up. Now it's much harder than when I was young, but I think I'm still stronger than the average woman."

"I'm certain you are. I saw you carrying that stuffed chair into the stairwell earlier." Madison noticed pictures of a whole host of women together. She asked, "Who are all these women with you?"

Toonie was quiet for a moment, then answered, "We were an act. Hit the road together. Had a lot of great times. At one point they were some of the best friends I ever had. Our competition in lifting weights was mild. But our competition for men, well, that got pretty fierce over time. It was stupid. I miss them all. We all let our pride get in the way." She was shaking her head, scrubbing harder at the pot she was cleaning. She stopped, wiped her forearm across her brow, and looked at Madison. "You and your mother remind me of me and the girls. You're letting your pride get in the way."

Madison looked away. Toonie said, "It ain't none of my business. I won't say anymore. And my offer still stands. If you still don't want to go back to your place, you can stay here till you figure out what to do."

For Madison, the idea of going back into her own apartment made her queasy again. It felt dirty somehow. Toonie had offered to let Madison stay there all night if she wanted to. Madison hadn't decided yet, what to do. She sat by Toonie's window staring out into the night trying to make sense of things. It had only been twenty-four hours since Bruise Boys with her dangerous dive from the low hanging pipes and twelve hours since witnessing her grandfather's fist fight.

What the hell is he doing in DC? Him and his lifelong secret. Humph! It erupted in front of her, and then he left with little explanation. He and Ann had secrecy in common. They wouldn't trust her to hear whatever it was that they kept hiding from her. Even hiding secrets from one another, by the looks of it. She was sick of it.

As the day had progressed, she had decided to give ExBoy a chance, then ruined it, given her mother a chance, then ruined it, become drawn to Jason and ruined it. Let's see, there must be something else she had ruined since she was on such a streak. Oh, yes. Her favorite costume. The beautiful fairy godmother costume that she had made herself. Ruined. What else could she add?

Knock it off, Madison. Suck it up and fix it! She gazed out the window. *How?* She didn't know how. She just knew she had to try.

Men in suits had shown up, flashed ID at ExBoy, searched her apartment, and driven off into the night. Her first guess would be that they were FBI, but she didn't believe her mother would be involved. But if Ann wasn't involved, how long would they be able to hide from Ann that they had conducted a search of her daughter's apartment? She saw that ExBoy's car was gone, so she was certain that they hadn't taken him away. There would be no point in that. He hadn't done anything except get mixed up with a girl from a troubled family. She should call him and find out what they said to him, but she knew she'd better let him cool off first.

She put the side of her face down on her arms on the window sill, looking out the window. Even if she didn't need to get information from ExBoy, she still needed to apologize to him. She had acted like an idiot, overreacting to his taunting remarks. She needed some rest. She looked down into the parking lot and saw her fairy godmother costume lying in a rumpled heap on the ground where ExBoy had dropped it to put his pants on.

She sat up suddenly, knowing that she didn't have time to let ExBoy cool off. As soon as those men forced open the metal box, which might be right about now, they would see her fairy godmother items, and know they'd been had. They'd be back. She grabbed her phone and called ExBoy. No surprise, he didn't answer. She would have to go to him.

✧   ✧   ✧

AFTER MAKING A few calls, she located him. Daniel told her ExBoy was back at Sound Beating, watching the Bruise Boys try out some breakable furniture props. Daniel added that ExBoy did not look happy.

Madison hurried over there and parked under a street lamp in their parking lot. She walked inside, feeling the indoor heat left over from a summer day, and saw ExBoy at a table in the middle of the room, talking on his phone. The only staff member on duty was the tattooed waitress with the rainbow hair. She was doing double duty as the bartender, and seemed more than enough to handle the few customers scattered around the mostly empty barroom.

Daniel and Dewey Decimator were on the side of the stage with their new props, taking turns shattering chairs over each other's head, then reassembling them. Madison felt much more comfortable seeing Daniel in normal clothing. The shadow on his scalp had deepened since last night, while Dewey's dark brown hair still sported his samurai style ponytail. Dewey saw her from across the room and raised his eyebrows in salute. Madison stopped at the counter and ordered a few drinks, taking them over to ExBoy's table.

His phone was on the side of his face as he looked up at her, his blue eyes unimpressed, his expression not changing. Madison wondered if he knew how handsome he was. "I'm sorry," she said. "I'm really sorry," as she set the drinks down on the table. She sat down and waited for him to say something.

He looked the other way and continued a conversation he had going on the phone. "I was making sure you'll be open in the morning," he said into his phone. "For the convention. Yeah. I only have a few days left." He rubbed at his temple with his other hand

and exhaled. "You can turn almost anything into a horror backdrop," he continued. "Uh-huh. All you need are some broken things lying around and enough fake blood to make it look like carnage. It just has to be portable and cleanable. Yeah. I'll come by with a truck. Looking forward to it. Thanks." He hung up, and without even looking at Madison, he left the table. Madison watched him walk over to the bar and order his own drink.

Dewey Decimator called over to her from the stage. "Hey, Madison."

She returned the greeting in a gloomy tone. "Hey."

"Did you change your mind about doing next week's show? Everyone's talking about what you did in the show last night."

"That was harebrained of me," she said. "I'm lucky I didn't ruin the show by breaking my head open."

With a small laugh, Dewey said, "Well, that would have been inconvenient."

"Yeah. Blood everywhere," said Madison.

"And brains."

"Actually?" She shook her head. "Not a whole lot of brains. I showed a distinct lack of brains last night." She looked over at ExBoy standing at the bar with his back to her and the stage. She sighed, "And it seems to have continued on into tonight."

"Why?" asked Dewey. "What's the problem?"

Daniel nudged him and pointed over to ExBoy at the bar. Dewey looked from ExBoy to Madison, back to ExBoy and said, "Oh." He nodded and said, "You want a little help with that?" He walked over to Madison and picked her up out of her chair.

"Dewey?" said Madison. "What are you doing? Stop it."

Dewey looked over at ExBoy, but ExBoy's back was still to the stage. Dewey lifted Madison up even higher over his shoulders as she squawked.

"Dewey! Stop it! Put me down!" ExBoy turned around. Madison's legs flailed as her hands searched for something to grab for balance. Her hair hung in Dewey's face. Dewey stepped up on the low stage and hefted Madison up high, getting his arms at full length under her as he held her high overhead. She grabbed for his wrists and elbows, pulling her legs inward to protect herself.

"Stop it, Dewey!" she shouted.

"Come on, Madison," Dewey said. "Show us how you climbed those pipes last night." He motioned his head at Daniel, who nodded, walking toward them without saying a word. Dewey tossed her into the air by just a foot or so, but it was enough to make her squeal.

"No! I don't—" He caught her and tossed her upward again. She screamed, "Stop it! Put me—"

Madison felt a jerk as ExBoy plunged into Dewey, the hollow wooden stage floor giving back sharp bass notes as they went down. Once again, Daniel was there to catch her and set her on her feet as ExBoy reared up, raining punches into Dewey.

"Asshole! How many times does she have to tell you?" Dewey had his arms up to guard himself, deflecting most of the blows but still taking a few.

"Whoa! Whoa! All right! I'm sorry, dude!" He yelled under the punches. "I'm sorry! I didn't mean anything!"

ExBoy angrily pushed him aside as Dewey said, "I'm sorry! Really! I got carried away. I won't do it again." Dewey stood up, taking a couple of slow steps, opening his jaw, moving it side to side as he held his chin, testing for damage. His eyes showed a touch of shock. Madison figured he wasn't used to getting hit for real. But he shot a crooked smile at Daniel, whispering, "That boy can hit," then winked at Madison as he rubbed his sore chin.

Her confusion swept away, she was grateful for the chance he had just given her. ExBoy stood up, straightening his t-shirt, and spit out one last, "Just watch yourself. She's not here for you, anyway. She's here because…" He looked at her and clammed up.

She finished his sentence for him. "Because I owe you an apology."

"It's not that easy," ExBoy huffed.

Daniel and Dewey made eye contact and walked away, leaving Madison and ExBoy standing on the low stage.

"I don't know where else to start," she said.

The two wrestlers sat down at ExBoy's former table.

"Well how about a thank you for helping your mother?" asked ExBoy.

"A thank you? Are you serious?"

"Hell, yes! I was NICE to your mother. I helped her to help you. I'm not supposed to know your history together. I'm just supposed to be NICE."

Daniel and Dewey drank the two drinks Madison had set down at the table.

"Okay Mr. Nice Guy. Do you at least understand how I feel about it?"

"Oh, no. We're not going into your feelings right now. This whole mess has been about your feelings. That's why it's a mess."

"But…I can't stop being upset about it because you say so. She used you to spy on me."

"Not my problem. That's between you and her. With me, you say thank you. You say, 'Gee, I'm sorry she used you, but thank you for being so nice to my mother.'"

Daniel seemed to be nodding at what ExBoy said, while Dewey looked skeptical. They crunched on the ice from the drinks.

"It doesn't upset you that she used you, and then—"

"Madison? Did you come here to lecture me about letting your mother use me?"

Madison ground her teeth, then said in a quiet voice, "No."

"Did you come here to say I deserved being thrown out of your apartment?"

Daniel and Dewey reacted to that by mildly shaking their heads. Then ExBoy added, "Naked?"

Daniel said, "Whoa!" before Dewey slapped the side of Daniel's head.

Madison shrugged her shoulders. "No." *Damn it.* She knew he had a point. "Thank you for being so nice to my mother. And although you really pissed me off, I'm sorry for throwing your clothes out the window. But you weren't naked. I gave you my fairy godmother costume, didn't I?"

Suffocated laugher could be heard from Daniel.

Madison continued with ExBoy, "And let me ask you this. Do I look like the kind of girl who can't get any action?"

ExBoy's face remained stoic, while Daniel and Dewey shook their heads, a hard no.

She continued, "Do I look like I'm afraid of your penis?"

The sound of chairs falling over accompanied the sound of two men giggling like little girls on the floor.

ExBoy leaned into her and said, "I didn't mean that literally. It was just sex talk. I thought you would like it."

Madison blinked. "It was?" He nodded.

"Well," she said, "that was dumb." She crossed her arms and looked at the floor.

"Sex talk usually is," said ExBoy.

Daniel was laughing full out by this point, but Madison remembered what Spenser had told her, so she said, "Keep it up back there, Tasty Waisty!"

Daniel abruptly stopped, cleared his throat, and said, "You two really should take this outside."

Chapter Nineteen

EXBOY WALKED WITH her out to the parking lot. As they approached her car, she noticed the lamppost she parked under had a shoe hanging from it, the shoelace having tangled itself around the pole when someone had thrown it up there. It looked lonely and pointless hanging there all by itself.

The night breeze in the parking lot was gentle but welcome. Temperatures were only a bit cooler now, not providing as much relief as everyone would have liked.

The night air carried music from a nearby club with the bass rhythms easiest to hear. People mixed it up in this part of town. Jocks from the UW, geeks from software or Internet companies, and those in their punk finery mingled as they went in and out of the different colored doors at the various clubs up and down the street.

Most businesses in this district threw the doors open in the hot summertime, and the patrons treated it like one big block party on a busy night. But it was slow tonight. Maybe the heat had taken its toll. Madison suspected the places with air-conditioning were doing unusually brisk business right now. That included movie theaters and grocery stores. Late night grocery shopping was not uncommon in a neighborhood where so many people made their living in the arts. Or maybe the usual crowds were mixing with the hipsters tonight by hitting the air conditioned higher end cocktail bars in heavier numbers than usual, leaving places like Sound Beating a little empty. Even in normal weather, Sound Beating needed occasional shows like Bruise Boys to keep them coming in, keep them packed, and remind the patrons that Sound Beating was still cool, still relevant, even though the grunge music era was far behind in the rearview mirror.

As they walked, Madison said, "My life is a mess right now." Remembering the tag at Robot Moon, she added, "Hot and scheming."

ExBoy said, "Well, just so you know, I'm not running back and forth to give reports on you to your mom. She wanted you to live somewhere safe. That's all it was ever about."

They stopped at Madison's car, as he added, "You're in the apartment so I'm supposed to be done. I was supposed to go away by now. That's why I left Bruise Boys last night. You said your mom was going to be there. I couldn't let her see me with you."

"Oh, boy." She closed her eyes with a pained expression. "I told her I had a boyfriend named ExBoy." Her shoulders dropped. "I thought she'd be happy but she got upset."

ExBoy nodded in an exaggerated fashion. "Great." He turned, looking around the parking lot, then said, "Well, they didn't break my legs. That's something."

"But then," Madison continued, "she apologized. She seemed to accept it even though she didn't like it."

"You lie a lot about your love life, don't you?" He turned, looking at her. "Why don't you just get one?"

"Easy for you to say, you could get a girl anytime you want. I'm picky."

"*Easy*? You think it's easy trying to see you?"

"So why do you bother?" asked Madison.

"I'm picky, too."

Laughter and cigarette smoke caught their attention as a few club patrons walked past, switching from one venue to another.

"For the record? I haven't decided about you yet," said Madison.

ExBoy faced her. "So what about the moony-eyed idiot at your door? Being picky about him, too?"

Madison opened her purse, searching for her car keys. "Leave him out of it."

"Why? What's so special about him?"

She unlocked her car door and opened it. "He got caught up in my problem, is all."

"Is this another lie about your love life?" he asked.

Standing at the open car door, she whirled around and faced him.

He said, "But instead of pretending you have one, now you're pretending you don't?

"No."

"Are you with him?"

"No."

"Do you wish you were?"

Madison took a long time answering. Her voice subdued, she said, "Maybe. I don't know."

"Just do me a favor. Throw him out naked someday, and tell me how he reacts."

"You're not going to get over that, are you?"

He took her arm, gently pulling her toward him as he closed her car door, saying, "It was a first, I'll give you that. You have any idea how much grief I put up with for you? And you still haven't decided about me?"

"Something's still wrong," she said. "You said you were being nice to my mother, and you had me going at first. But you told me about that apartment when I first met you. You had no incentive yet to be nice to my mother."

"Oh, yes I did," he said with a shaky laugh. "I didn't say *why* I was being nice to her."

Madison stared at him. "You were in big trouble, weren't you?" she said. "Something she could fix for you if you did her a favor. Are you going to tell me what she has over you?"

"No. Are you going to tell me what's going on with a metal box and someone breaking into your car?"

"No."

She looked back up at the shoe hanging from the lamppost, tangled and swaying in the breeze. She said, "We never had a chance, did we?"

"We weren't supposed to," he said quietly. "I had strict orders not to get any ideas about you."

"I could have sworn you had an idea or two."

"I had a lot of ideas."

"We both did," she said with a soft smile. "At least now I understand why I could never get to know you."

"We *have* gotten to know each other."

Across the street a small group of lonely revelers tried to outdo each other in making rowdy party screams into the night air.

"No, you got to know *me.* All I know about you is that you're an artist, but I've never seen your work. And you write, but if Daniel hadn't mentioned that you have a book coming out, I never would've known." It was hard to read his expression because he kept looking at the ground.

Madison said, "I don't know where you're from, I don't know about your family, I don't even know where you live. I can't get past the pretty party boy who wants to have a good time."

ExBoy turned his face back to her and studied her for a moment, then stepped closer, making her lean into her car, his face close to hers. The metal touching her backside was still warm from the hot day. His blue eyes with lashes and intense brows the shade of dark honey had always promised pleasure, but those eyes also promised trouble. She was ready for trouble, and overdue for pleasure, but she didn't dare give in to it. Not yet. She needed answers. His face came closer.

"ExBoy, I can't. I have to ask you…"

He looked at her, sheepish. "You think I'm pretty, huh?"

"A little too pretty for your own good, yeah," she said. "Listen, I need to know…"

"Well, how much pretty is good?"

"Put it this way. Most women don't want to have to compete with their boyfriend's good looks."

"That would never be a problem for you," he said.

"Flatterer."

"Did it work?"

"No."

"You don't want to jump in bed with me now?"

"I didn't say that, you big tease."

"Me? I'm the big tease? Who got me naked tonight and threw me out?"

"Who got frisked tonight in the parking lot?"

He stopped. "You saw that?"

She nodded.

He backed up, exasperated, his face taking on a hard look. "This will always be in the way, won't it? Your mom sent a few assholes to give me a hard time, that's all. They didn't even have my name right." He looked up into the night sky over the city. "You know, it's not supposed to be this hard. Either you want to be with me or you don't. It's not up to her, it's up to you."

"Did they show you ID?"

"Of course. FBI. That's how I knew they were from her."

"What exactly did they say?"

"They said they were from headquarters, flashed their badges, and asked me if I knew Madison Cruz. I made up a random name of a resident that I had been visiting and pointed to the wrong window."

"Headquarters." Her breath caught. FBI Headquarters were located in Washington, DC. Grandpa went to DC to talk to FBI Headquarters? *Why?*

ExBoy looked back at her. "I'm wondering if there's any point in continuing here. Whatever the issues are, we can't seem to get our act together."

"I don't know what to tell you. Everything's so…"

The *Jaws* music started playing. Madison shoved her phone further into her purse, trying to muffle it but it could still be heard, coloring her thoughts.

"I'm not going to lie to you," she said. "I don't know what to think. I want you, but I'm not sure how I feel about you. I have other things demanding my attention right now."

"Fine. I'm getting out of the way," he said. "Before I feel any stupider than I already do."

The *Jaws* music stopped playing, meaning Ann's call was going to voicemail.

ExBoy repeated, "It's not supposed to be this hard." He took her head in his hands and kissed her forehead. "I give up," he said. He put his hands in the air and said, "I'm done." He walked backward a few steps before he turned and walked away.

Watching him leave, she heard one last party scream from across the street as the tiny group made their way down the sidewalk. The tangled shoe continued to sway in the breeze, and Madison wondered if it would ever untangle itself and drop.

She stood alone next to her car in a mostly empty parking lot. She felt like crying but there were no tears. One disappointment after another was only serving to make her feel numb. Well, she was learning not to trust her feelings, so being numb came in kind of handy. And since she was numb, now seemed as good a time as any to hear her mother's voicemail. Maybe it wouldn't hurt as much.

She called up her voicemail to hear whatever message Ann had left for her. Ann's voice came on saying, "I owe you an explanation for so much. There's too much that you don't know. It wasn't right for me to hold it back for so long, but I couldn't face it. We will have to disagree with each other about who cut off whom, but you should at least know that you were no accident. I set out to get pregnant. I wanted a baby. I always felt that I didn't belong, and I thought a baby would love me and give me what I thought was missing in my life. I had something to prove." A rueful chuckle escaped Ann. "I was young and stupid and didn't know that babies are the ones who need loving. When you took to your grandmother more than to me..." Her voice stopped for a few seconds as she inhaled and exhaled slow and strong. "I was too young, Madison. I had no idea what I was doing, and my mother was there to salvage my mistake. So I..." *Beeep.* The phone's voicemail time had run out, but Ann hadn't called back to try to continue what she was going to say.

This news hit Madison in an unexpected way. In spite of her sadness, her fatigue, and the emotional numbness, a part of her came alive. She may have issues that needed working out with her mother, but it was worth the fight.

She began to have pleasant thoughts of going home to her pillow when she finally realized a small dark car had been parked across the street this whole time, the nighttime streetlights making hard shadows of its occupants. But based on the silhouettes of their heads they seemed to be looking her way. Feeling stupid for feeling paranoid, she decided to go back inside Sound Beating and wait for that car to be gone. She had big strong friends inside the bar. She would be safe in there.

She walked away from her car, out of the parking lot, and onto the sidewalk as another group of partiers came by. Four guys feeling too much of their drinking were laughing at everything each other said. The door to Sound Beating was a few feet away.

As Madison passed by, their attention to her derriere caused them to turn around with appreciative stares and whoops, just as Daniel was walking out of Sound Beating's door. Relieved, Madison was glad to see him and was about to say as much when a hand came down heavy on her shoulder. She turned around as the drunk young man slurred, "Excuse me, but my friend wants to know your name."

Daniel stepped up, casual, and pushed the hand off of Madison's shoulder, saying, "Move along dude, she's with me right now."

The young man lost his balance, stumbling toward Madison, saying, "Sorry."

Daniel put his hands out to catch the young man and steady him on his feet, but one of his friends, a black gauge in his earlobe, slurred, "Hey! What are you doing?" while another friend threw down the cigarette he'd been smoking.

"Git yer hands off my friend," said the fourth drunk guy in a faded orange t-shirt, taking a swing at Daniel.

Still in good spirits, Daniel easily caught it and used it to turn the guy around, pushing him away from Madison, who was backing up, the heels of her feet bumping into the wall behind her. Cigarette guy and gauge guy ran at Daniel in a tangle of arms, cigarette guy and Daniel going down to the ground. At the same time the faded orange t-shirt guy grabbed Madison's arm, pulling her into his face, his beer breath slurring, "What's wrong with you people?"

Madison's hands came up to push him away but before she had a chance, from nowhere, a figure in black pants and shirt shoved an elbow upward into faded orange t-shirt guy's nose, causing him to let go of Madison's arm. "ARG!" He bent over, both hands covering his nose, blood dripping.

The first guy who had put his hand on Madison's shoulder turned in a circle, trying to see who was attacking whom.

Alarmed by the blood, Madison bent to check on the bloody nose guy who'd slumped to the sidewalk.

The black figure kicked cigarette guy's groin while he tussled with Daniel on the ground, then grabbed the ears of gauge guy, yanking downward while bringing a knee up into his face. He went down.

The black figure spun, her hair flying, dark in the night. *It's a woman!* She stomped the foot of the first drunk guy who started all this. He hit the ground holding his foot.

As the four men rolled and groaned, Daniel tried to sit up from the ground. But she put her foot on his neck, shoving him back down, his head thumping the sidewalk. Madison screamed.

The woman stopped, breathing a little heavy, and asked Madison, "Is he your friend?"

"Yes!" Madison was desperate to make it all stop.

"Do you feel safe now?"

Hell, no! "Yes! Yes, just stop!"

She lifted her foot off Daniel, as Madison dove to the ground where Daniel slowly rolled over, holding his head. "Are you all right?" she asked. Groans sounded all around her.

Trying to sit up, he rubbed his throat, saying, "Who the hell was that?"

Madison looked up, then around, but didn't see her anymore. Across the street, the dark car pulled away, its shadow occupants disappearing past the street revelers, the colorful doors, and the deep bass rhythms.

Chapter Twenty

DIM MORNING LIGHT filled her bedroom, revealing a blanket on the floor, the sheets kicked down to her feet. Sleeping had been difficult on yet another hot summer night. But as temperatures cooled just before dawn, the comfort level went up, allowing Madison's fretful sweaty sleep to turn into a welcome comfortable slumber.

Madison was not quite aware yet, her breathing still rhythmic and even. But the restful silence of the morning was interrupted by a gentle tweedling sound from her cell phone—she had a message. Inhaling deeply, she rolled to reach for the cell phone on her bed stand, and noticed how comfy this new position was with her face down and her arm reaching across the mattress....

A peaceful dream of senseless frolic pulled her down till she was nudged awake again by the soft tweedling.

She lifted her face from the pillow and managed to get propped up on her elbows, head hanging, staring at the pillowcase, her hair making a dark curtain. A long list of things to do came to mind as the sleepy fog gave way to the new day. She had a singing telegram to deliver as the Bumbling Waitress at one o'clock at Giovanni's, a swank restaurant down on the waterfront overlooking Puget Sound.

Last night, after realizing that agents from DC must immediately have jumped a flight for Seattle, Madison thought it best to come back home. Her grandfather must have told them about the metal box and for some reason they had taken it seriously, though she wasn't sure why. She wondered why they hadn't returned yet for the paperwork. Grandpa still wasn't answering the phone. Was he avoiding her?

She needed to get to Robot Moon Productions to retrieve the paperwork from the old Victorian grandfather clock. Having FBI agents show up at Robot Moon Productions might not go over well with Target. Unless they were cute. Then Target would thank her for sending some eye candy her way.

Madison reached for the tweedling cell phone. She had a new gig sheet waiting for her attached in an email, and a voicemail from Phil.

"Hey, Chocolate Mint," his voicemail started, "I'm sorry I got a little carried away yesterday. You surprised me when you upped your fee for this funeral gig. Sometimes I forget who I'm dealing with Minty, and you're no fool. Hell, this is such a weird one, you should get paid more. The gig's in your inbox. It's at noon. That's a tight squeeze with your Bumbling Waitress at one o'clock, but the places are only minutes away from each other, so I okayed it. Leave a message if you have questions. I'll be busy on the phone. I have to find a stripper telegram substitute and fast! Jen pulled a groin muscle yesterday at the princess birthday party. She swears she did it climbing some stairs, but I'll bet she was in a back room again, adding an extra show for the uncles and extra tips, if you know what I mean."

Madison hung up and pulled up the gig sheet on the screen of her phone. Crap. She'd forgotten about the deal with Phil. She was supposed to sing at a funeral today at Holme's Memorial Chapel. Only it wasn't supposed to be dignified. It was a tasteless joke that the deceased had arranged just before he passed away.

For the first time in all the years of working as a singing telegram, Madison considered going against the gig sheet. If the guy was dead, who would be the wiser? Who would know that she had taken the rough edges off of his joke by dressing appropriately for a funeral, and singing a nice song to the audience gathered there, instead of parading around the casket in a pregnant costume, singing about how he made her love him?

A plan formed in her mind. She had to make sure Phil didn't find out. She wasn't sure he would object in this instance, but she didn't want to take the chance. After all, there was one thousand dollars riding on it.

She hopped in and out of the shower, pulled on her last clean pair of jeans, and the last clean tank top. In spite of the world falling apart around her head, there was one fact she could no longer escape. And that was laundry. She would take Spenser up on her offer to do laundry this morning. She'd better hurry.

Her hair dryer was loud but not loud enough to drown out her thoughts. She thought about Spenser and her simple answers to life's problems. *Get to know your own mother, she said. Use adult eyes, she said.* Well, holy crap, what a mixed bag of results. Her mother was more complicated than Madison had remembered. She almost missed those childish eyes that made everything black and white and easy to know what to do.

She tried the fresh perspective that a good night's sleep could bring while her half-wet hair slowly returned to its lustrous state of dark silk. Ann's deception about the apartment was indeed sobering. Madison recognized control issues when she saw them. But she could see that ExBoy had a point. Her mother was trying to help. The hard part now was trying to figure out what to do. Should she move out of this apartment to make a point? Stay on and try to pay all the rent herself? She'd spent most of what she had getting in here. It would take a while to save up for deposits on another place. Her response to her mother on the phone last night may not have been great, but Ann needed to know she had crossed a line.

While packing for her gigs, she pulled out her wigs and makeup kit to take to Spenser's place, and picked out something nice to wear to the funeral. She would get ready at Spenser's house while laundry was in the dryer.

She opened her purse and saw the fake handgun.

She knew Target was right; it was potentially dangerous to let people think she was actually armed with a real gun. But she'd been feeling vulnerable, and the prop looked so real when she'd seen it. Her first thought was that it could be used in an extreme emergency. She'd never held a real gun and wouldn't know what to do with it if she did.

She pulled it out, noticing that it was a perfect fit, or at least it seemed so to her. She didn't know how a gun was supposed to feel, but she liked the smoothness and the way the contours fit her small hand. She wondered if real guns were supposed to fit like this.

Holding the gun, she stood in front of the mirror and struck a sexy pose, her left hand on her hip, the gun near her face but pointed at the ceiling. She watched in the mirror as she moved her left shoulder up and around in a sultry circle. *Hot!* In a slow pull, she took the gun down the side of her face, a delicate sliding touch on her skin. Her eyes heavy lidded, she slowly turned her lips toward the gun and watched the mirror as she blew imaginary smoke from its barrel. *That's right asshole. Don't mess with me.*

She put both hands on the gun, again pointing at the ceiling and suddenly backed up against her bathroom wall, the mirror forgotten. She turned her head quickly to the right and watched the shower nozzle for any sudden move. *You piece of shit!* She whipped the gun around, taking deadly aim at the shampoo bottle. She whipped back around to the other side to aim at her hair dryer and cowed it into submission. *Don't move!* She whipped it dead ahead in the mirror and saw the end of the barrel pointed at herself. *Oh God!*

The effect surprised her. She let her arms drop as she stared at herself, the reality sinking in.

If she couldn't get past the fear of playing bang-bang in the mirror, how could she ever learn to use a real gun? How did her mother do it? She put the prop gun back into her purse.

Her phone tweedled again. She'd missed a call while the hair dryer was on. She was surprised to see Jerry Rosser's name on the caller ID. She called him right back.

"I was wondering how it went yesterday," he said.

She sighed. "I thought it went great, at the restaurant at least. But later on, I don't know, Jerry, I'm so rattled I'm afraid to even talk about it. I'm getting mad all over again."

"My goodness. What happened?"

"She told a friend of mine that she was going to surprise me with a nice apartment. She had him tell me about the place, and she had the landlord lie to me about how cheap the rent was. So I got all excited and moved in here a few weeks ago. Then I find out that she's paying the rent for me!" She paused. She hated the way that had sounded whiney. "Wait," she continued, "I'm not saying it right. She wants reasonable things for my life, but she's willing to be all sneaky and go to unreasonable lengths to accomplish it!" *Argh! I sound like an ass.* Somehow she wasn't capturing the injustice of it all. "The point is she tricked me. I can't trust her."

"Well, actually Madison, I called because I wanted you to know that I'm worried about Ann. Please keep this confidential. I'm hoping that you will help me to help her, before I have to leave my post here as the SAC. Would you meet with me today?"

"Uh, okay." She hadn't expected anything like this. "Where?" she asked.

"I'll meet you at the Seattle Library at 3:00. It's two blocks away from my office, so I won't be gone long enough to be missed. Is that all right?"

"Yeah, that's all right."

After she hung up, she located the envelope of old pictures that Ann had given her to make the montage for Jerry's retirement party. Last night in her anger she'd told her mother that they should go back to the way they had it—in essence, not seeing each other anymore. Now she hated herself for saying that, but she didn't know how to take it back. Maybe she should continue working on the montage while she waited for her mother to apologize.

She looked at the large envelope, wondering what Jerry was worried about regarding her mother. Maybe Ann had come into work with red eyes this morning. The thought that her tough mother, who never cried, had actually cried on the phone last night, left her feeling shook. She'd never realized that she meant that much to her mother.

She added the envelope to the pile of things she was taking to Spenser's house. She missed her big black tote bag, having left it at Spenser's house yesterday.

Minutes later she was in the parking lot packing her things into the car. Her arms were awkward and did a poor job of hanging onto everything while she unlocked her car door.

Nearby, Crystal had just parked and was walking toward her. She waved at Madison, and Madison smiled at her, but then dropped the car keys, a hair brush, and her purse on the ground. Crystal stepped up and helped her with the items that had dropped. "Thanks," said Madison. "Guess I'm starting the day out klutzy."

"No problem," said Crystal. "Actually I wanted to thank you for being so nice to my Aunt Toonie. I knew you were covering up for her yesterday. I was annoyed about it, but then I realized that you were being a friend to her. She's had a tendency to be a loner for too long now, watching life go by through that window."

"I didn't know that," said Madison, looking up at Toonie's window. "She's been really good for me." She remembered Toonie's stories of her time working in Las Vegas and of lost friendships.

Crystal said, "I wish I could find a way to get her out once in a while and do something different."

"I might have something in mind for you," said Madison. "Let me look into it and I'll get back to you."

✧   ✧   ✧

OF COURSE THERE would be a fresh pot of coffee waiting at Spenser's house. But Madison chose to take a detour instead. She couldn't resist. After all, Jason Clark wouldn't be at Spenser's house, he would be here at The Loony Bean on barista duty.

She walked straight up to the counter where customers picked up their latte orders. "Jason?"

He looked up, a light in his hazel brown eyes; then pressed his lips shut, looking back down at his work, ignoring her. His t-shirt was once again a bit snug around his biceps. His strong steady hands set cups of lattes out on the counter.

"Jason, please, can we at least talk later? There's a lot you don't understand."

"That's for sure," he mumbled. He turned around and reached down in a cupboard, searching around for something. Madison tilted her head, watching that fine backside, her fingers coming up to her lips.

An older man said, "Excuse me," reaching over to the counter for his order. Coming back to herself, she quickly stepped out of the way while customers picked up their lattes. Jason started the next cup.

"Well, can—" she started, and accidentally bumped someone trying to get around her, "...can you at least tell me how Mitch is? Is he any better today?"

Jason set down a few more cups. The initial rush subsided as the customers picked up their lattes and walked away. He looked up at her and said, "He's better. I'll be picking him up later today when they release him." He measured out some espresso shots and asked, "How's Pizzaman?"

It took her a second to realize who he meant. She wanted to offer an explanation until he said, "Or should I say how *was* he?" Madison felt heat rise to her cheeks, her eyes taking on that icy green color she had when she was angry. "I'm guessing that he would have been great.

But we were a little interrupted, thank you. Things didn't go so well after that."

He did a poor job of hiding a smile, and said, "Glad to be of service."

She said, "And his name is ExBoy."

Jason actually stopped at that. His hands on the counter, he leaned forward saying, "What kind of a shit ass name is ExBoy?"

"Oh, come on. It's just a nickname," she said.

"So is Pizzaman."

Madison had enough and turned to walk out, but Jason said, "Why didn't you tell me you had a boyfriend?"

She turned around. He was looking at her, his eyes a little hard.

He continued, "You could tell I was interested. You could've saved me feeling like an ass."

"He isn't my boyfriend."

He looked surprised. "Boink buddy?"

"What is it with you guys and boink buddies? No! He's not a boink buddy. Okay?"

Jason appeared to be waiting for more.

She continued, "He literally showed up unannounced with a pizza. We've been dancing all around the edges of trying a relationship, but we never seem to…" She sighed in exasperation. "Look," she said. "If I want to get laid, that is my business." She poked her finger into her chest. "My business. I've made no commitment to anyone, and I don't owe you any explanation!" Whirling around, she headed for the door, carefully stepping around an elderly lady seated at one of the small tables. After another thought, Madison stopped and turned around.

Jason still leaned forward on the counter, his eyes suddenly looking back up. He had been watching her backside, too.

She said, "If you come over unannounced again, you might keep finding naked men in my apartment." As customers lifted heads and looked at her, she added, "So get over it!"

The elderly lady nearby leaned in and said, "You tell him, honey."

Madison resumed walking to the door but stopped and whirled around one last time. Loud enough for Jason to hear across the cafe, she said, "And I am not now, nor ever have been, anyone's boink buddy! Get it?"

Nearby customers nodded at her a bit wide-eyed.

She stormed out the door, the little bells jingling their rage. She crossed the parking lot to her car and proceeded to thump her head on the roof of her car, again and again. *I knew I would ruin it! I knew it, I knew it, I...*

Hurried footsteps. She turned around, and Jason snatched her up, her feet dangling in the air, his full lips locked on hers, her waist pulled in tight, forcing an arch at the small of her back as he bent slightly forward. She was in shock for the few seconds, but her engine revved up fast, putting her arms around him. She knew this was presumptuous on his part, but she didn't care.

He released the kiss suddenly, setting her down fast. His hands held firm on her upper arms. Her breathing was still coming quickly as he said, "If you never got laid last night, you can't blame me. I would have got the job done." With that he stalked off, going back to work.

Madison ran at him, and as he turned around to the sound of her pounding footsteps, she jumped up into his chest.

The momentum threw him back, as she wrapped her legs around his waist. She returned the kiss with her fists in his curly brown hair. He stumbled, his hands under her rump, trying to catch his balance, and wound up with his back against a large bush by the cafe window. His feet slid in a small patch of wet grass at the base of the bush, and they went down in their kiss, with Jason landing on his butt.

Madison's leg muscles pulled him in hard as her fists in his hair pulled him away from her face. "You have no idea what I put him through last night. I may be horny out of my mind, but I'm not easy. Nothing is, anymore."

She stood up to go back to her car but was stopped by a thumping on the window, with a muffled voice coming from behind the glass.

"Dude, Potatoes!" The barista guy from yesterday morning had a manic smile on his face. "Behave yourself, girl!" He stood with some of the customers at the window, watching Madison and Jason. He gave Jason the thumbs up as Madison hurried back to her car.

Chapter Twenty-One

SPENSER WAS NOT pleased. At all.

"She'd better not come near me. I'll kill her!" she said viciously. "Why didn't Daniel tell me about this? I'll kill him, too."

"Spenser, please. It's not like she was kissing him or anything. She was quietly and efficiently kicking everyone's ass. He's probably embarrassed."

Spenser stood, walked over to an end table and grabbed her cell phone. She punched a speed dial button as she muttered angry sounds and put the phone on her ear. The other hand went on her hip.

Madison was glad it wasn't her on Spenser's bad side this morning. Daniel must've known that Madison would talk about last night's street fight with Spenser. He should've told her himself, not that it would make any difference in the outcome, but at least Spenser wouldn't now be feeling like he was hiding anything serious from her. Madison had told her that Daniel had a sizable goose egg on the back of his head when she'd left last night.

Madison now found herself in a place of questioning everything, suspecting everyone, to the point that she didn't know if she was being foolish to think that the woman in black last night was part of this mess or foolish not to. Seattle was, after all, known to have several self-proclaimed defenders of justice, complete with homemade costumes. What a town.

"I think you left something out last night," said Spenser into the phone. As she walked into the other room for privacy, her conversation with Daniel faded into the background and the sounds of the washer and dryer came forward in Madison's hearing.

At the very least, spilling some of last night's experiences to Spenser put a little sanity back into Madison. The act of sharing some of her heart with a friend who understood, who got it, was a luxury that Madison now realized she had been taking for granted. Because now, unlike normal days, she was not at liberty to tell Spenser everything.

The FBI search, the revelation of Grandpa flying to DC, Mitch and Ray, and the escape of Unibrow, formerly known as Mr. Duct Tape, were getting harder and harder to skip over. And now there was Jason! Not being able to share those details made her want to squeeze every moment out of the details that she did feel free to share, such as the street fight from last night, the latest episode of her ridiculous love life, and her painful argument with her mother.

She was trying to figure out how she would describe Toonie to Spenser when she realized that she hadn't eaten Toonie's cookies from yesterday. She poured herself a warm-up of the coffee and pulled out the little baggie from her big tote bag.

Once Spenser returned, Madison offered one of the cookies to her. They each took a bite and chewed as the heavenly flavor came forth. *Oh, my God.* They looked at each other with wide eyes, their jaws working. Their euphoric sounds mingled.

Spenser asked, "Where did you get these?"

Madison swallowed. "My neighbor Toonie made them. She says it's a secret recipe that she doesn't give out."

"That's just wrong," Spenser said. "These could bring about world peace."

Madison added, "Or start a war."

They each had one more with their coffee and sighed at the thought that there were no more cookies.

"Wow," said Madison. "Those were day-old cookies. She gave them to me yesterday."

She heard the ding from the dryer, indicating that the laundry load was finished. Madison took another quick sip of her coffee and hurried to the dryer, sorting her clothes and folding them up. ExBoy's t-shirt was now nicely clean and folded. She kept it separate from the rest of her laundry to return it to him later, and threw the second load from the washing machine into the dryer. She still had some clothes left to wash, but it wasn't enough to make a full load.

"Spenser?" she called out. "Do you have anything you want washed? We can add it to my stuff to make a full load."

Spenser called back, "Let me go check."

Madison came back to the table, reached down into her tote, and pulled out the fabric that had been in the metal box. Grandpa had used it to pad out the metal box and maybe provide a little protection for the paperwork and clippings. She figured she might as well add it to the laundry load.

She opened the first fold of the fabric, and saw that there was a huge stain on it, like brown water. It looked gross, so she put it on the floor and kneeled down next to it, slowly opening up each fold. It was an old linen tablecloth with a towel folded up inside. Madison's heart started to race, as Spenser walked back in.

"I don't really have any clothes to add..." she stopped.

Madison turned her face to her, full of fear.

The towel's stain was heavier and even deeper in color. Old blood made the towel stiff and resistant to being unfolded. The initials WP were monogrammed on the towel.

Madison worked hard to control her voice but it still came out a little shaky as she said, "What am I supposed to make of that? I mean besides the fact that it really resembles a blood stain, and besides the fact that I'm a little lightheaded right now, I'm thinking maybe I better not wash it."

Alarmed, Spenser asked, "Where did that come from?"

"This was in that old metal box. I thought it was in there for padding," said Madison.

"Part of the clues?" asked Spenser.

Madison looked down at the stained fabrics in front of her. She didn't want to say yes. That might make it more real. So she settled for nodding her head.

A thought occurred to her, and she grabbed the tote bag, pulling out the cardboard. "This was in the metal box, too."

She flattened out the pieces of cardboard, and by following the various fold lines, it was easy to return it to its previous state of a small cardboard box. It too had some stains in it, but they were much lighter. The odd shape of the stain at the bottom of the box matched the shape of the stain on the tablecloth. Madison put the tablecloth into the box, lining up the shapes. Whatever had stained the tablecloth had soaked through to the box, leaving the same wet shape.

She looked at the old blood stain on the towel. It was in the center of the towel, darker in color, and had spread further to the sides than it had on the tablecloth. She put the towel on top of the tablecloth and lined up the shapes again. Something watery, combined with some blood, had happened on that towel, then soaked through the tablecloth to the box. She looked at it, perplexed, sick with worry.

She thought of the old newspaper clippings and the odd birth certificate. The point of it was still escaping her. Her grandfather had said, "Especially don't tell Ann. Promise me. Don't tell Ann."

She crawled across the floor to where she had left her purse, digging furiously through it as she kneeled, and pulled out the old black and white photo of a young Vincent Cruz, taken through the leaves of a bush. She didn't care any longer if Spenser saw it or not. She needed her friend near her right now.

The small box in the photo was a match. Her grandfather stood over this same box, holding this tablecloth and towel, with something else inside.

The answer presented itself to her.

In a soft and mournful tone, she said, "Oh." She put her hand at her mouth and said through her fingers, "Poor thing."

"What?" asked Spenser, shaking her hands up and down as if they were burned. "Madison, you're scaring me. What is it?"

"Remember the birth certificate we saw?"

"Yes," said Spenser. "You said your mom's birth date was off by almost two months."

Madison looked at the sad messy fabrics in the box.

"I think that was her real birth date. She was born during the International Student Exposition." Her earlier sense of injustice shifted over and made room for someone else.

She held up the photo for Spenser to see, and Spenser took it, studying it closely.

"I think my grandfather found this box when he was a young gardener at the UW. I think an abandoned baby was in it." She pushed her fingers through her hair as she stared at the box, the far-reaching implications hitting home.

"He took it home to my grandmother." Her mother was adopted. And because there were conflicting birth certificates, it was probably done illegally.

"So who took this picture?" asked Spenser.

"Whoever blackmailed him," she answered.

Why would Grandpa have all this stuff hidden for so long? Why hadn't he thrown it all away when her mother was still a baby? What was he saving it for, and what had he told the FBI in DC? Was he confessing to being a baby stealer?

Spenser was on the floor with her. From her side, she had her arms wrapped around Madison. "You know it doesn't matter, right? You know that. I want to hear you say it before you leave here."

Madison put her hands up on Spenser's forearm.

"Don't worry. Of course I know. Spensy, you're such a good friend; I don't deserve you. But for the first time I wonder if my mom has anyone like you in her life. I mean, who will she have to talk to about this when she finds out?" Anger on behalf of her mother began to ignite in Madison. "Look at how they left her. A baby wrapped in a towel, soaked in her own birthing fluids and blood." Tears burned her eyes. "They didn't even have the decency to clean her up and wrap her in something clean and dry."

Spenser reached out and ran her fingers over the monogrammed initials. "It's that WP logo again, from the hotel we read about in the clippings."

"I saw that."

"She must have been born in there. So odd. An expensive hotel. Then she winds up in a box."

"That's why Grandpa kept all those clippings about the International Student Exposition. All the students, and their guardians, and the judges, were put up in that high rise hotel. I hid all that paperwork at Robot Moon Productions. I was going to go get it today, anyway."

She took a deep breath and exhaled. "I have to get ready for back-to-back singing telegrams today. Then I'll get over there and retrieve the paperwork."

"Remember the one-word note that you showed to Daniel? He said it was in Cyrillic. Russia was still the Soviet Union back then, and one of the articles mentioned a Soviet girl who was homesick and wouldn't leave her room."

"How is it even possible," Madison asked, "for a girl to be that far along in her pregnancy and no one can tell?"

Spenser said, "Remember Elsie in high school?"

Madison blinked. "I forgot about that. She fooled everyone."

"We all just thought she was fat until she went into labor," said Spenser. "Some girls can pull it off."

The implications continued to open to Madison's understanding. "If it was one of the students, then the guardians had to know. That's why they allowed her to skip the Exposition and stay in her room. They probably insisted."

"But why wouldn't they fly her home?" asked Spenser.

Madison stood up from the floor. The sight of the stained fabrics and box made her heartsick. "I don't know. This was a fast and dirty job, to keep it a secret."

The hacking at the UW must have been to find the gardeners on payroll that year. They found her grandfather, who still lived at the address of the first house he'd ever bought. And whatever it was that he said to Unibrow, Unibrow didn't like it. She remembered hearing Unibrow shouting "niet" which she now understood was Russian for "no." It led to their desperate fist fight.

At first she had felt a little sick at the memory of hitting that stranger with a drill. But now…now that she had seen evidence of how callous the treatment of a newborn baby had been, a baby who had grown up to try to be perfect, to the point of driving Madison crazy, but a desire to be good and perfect nonetheless…well, Madison had no regrets about swinging that drill.

I'll do it again if he tries to hurt my grandpa.

She heard the dryer ding. Time to fold up the laundry, yes. But she was also ready to fight.

Chapter Twenty-Two

WEARING HER LITTLE black dress and low heels with her hair neatly tied back into a lovely barrette, Madison entered Holme's Memorial Chapel. She carried her usual tote bag and followed the signs to services for Eddie Willet.

She located the attendant from Holme's Memorial Chapel, introduced herself, and handed him her card from Phil's agency to identify herself as the entertainment hired for the occasion. She made it clear that she would treat this very sober occasion with dignity and respect.

The pudgy attendant peered at her with knit brows. "Are you sure you were hired to do that? I know this crowd. Actually, I knew the deceased. He had a reputation. It's hard to believe that he would want to suddenly be so conservative on the occasion of his own funeral."

Madison asked, "You knew him? You knew Eddie Willet?"

"Well, not personally, but he attended other funerals here. He always put on quite the show."

Other people were starting to arrive and sign the guest book.

Madison asked, "What do you mean by a show? What kind of show?"

"Well, there was the time he showed up dressed as a clown and juggled some urns for the audience."

Madison blinked, "Juggled?"

"I'm afraid so. The urns were empty of course. He also sang 'My Funny Valentine.'" He smiled and nodded at an older lady walking up to the guest book, before continuing. "Then there was the time he arrived very early, dressed as a doctor in surgical scrubs and rubber gloves. He planted dozens of whoopee cushions under the cushions of the pews. Every time someone arrived and sat down, the whoopee cushions would, of course, go off, and people would giggle. But as they kept arriving and sitting, it got to the point that they were laughing in the aisles. Eddie would run up to each person who had set off one of the whoopee sounds and say that he was a proctologist that could help them."

Madison's mouth was hanging open. She could hear a few sniffles behind her. She turned around and saw a man comforting a lady by gently hugging her and patting her back. The lady held a tissue to her eyes. Madison turned back to the attendant.

The attendant said, "He made so many people laugh. It's a large family and he always helped them get through these tough times. Odd sense of humor, I know, but—"

"Are you telling me that all these people that are arriving, are *used* to that sort of thing? At their family *funerals*?"

"Oh, yes," he answered. "It's been a Willet family tradition for years. But now there is no one quite like him to do it for his funeral. That's probably why he called your agency."

"I see," said Madison.

"Once, he came dressed as the grim reaper, dragging a stuffed dog on the end of a leash…"

"I get it already," said Madison. "I need to do a fast change."

As she dashed down the hall, the attendant finished, "The dog had an X sewn over each eye.…"

✧   ✧   ✧

SINCE EDDIE HAD traditionally done his shtick at the start of services, Madison had to move like lightning to change her outfit. Her tote bag provided easy access to a few vitals, and she emerged from her makeshift dressing room barefoot and pregnant, her little black dress mostly covered up with ExBoy's baggy t-shirt that had been folded up in her purse. The fact that it had a baby zombie on the front made it even better. She used a hair ribbon as a belt around her waist to accentuate her big belly, thanks to a small pillow she had grabbed from a chair in the hallway. The effect was perfect.

Her hair was half piled on top of her head with loose hair rollers hanging down, about to escape. She ratted some of the hair that wasn't in the rollers. Mascara that ran under her eyes, smeared lipstick, and a few blacked-out teeth gave her the look she was going for. She found an empty wine bottle in the trash in the hallway.

Phil kept her supplied with all sorts of novelty music for any occasion that might be requested, so from the dozens of CDs that lived in her tote bag, she had what Eddie Willet had requested. After confirming her musical cues with the attendant, she took a deep breath, clutched her wine bottle prop, and staggered into the main room. The music started up for "You Made Me Love You." But this was a raucous, comedic version, complete with bump and grind drum beats at key moments in the song.

She sang and swayed to the music, pretending to lose her balance and almost knock over a chair. She would sing a verse, then hoist the wine bottle up high to take a long swallow, only to lean a little too far backward and stagger over into a spray of flowers. She acted like she'd lost her orientation and spent several seconds singing into the flowers before noticing where the audience really was.

She knew the bump and grind section was coming up. To the audience, she was totally into this and having a great time, as they laughed through their tears, thankful that their tradition had been kept. But on the inside, Madison braced herself and danced over to the casket.

The body of an older man lay there, his blue suit making his final voyage quite dignified, save for the big honk horn in his dead hands. She almost forgot the words of the song when she saw that he was wearing a big red clown nose.

I hate my job, I hate my job.

She paraded back and forth in front of the casket, pushing her belly out on a hard beat to the right, then a hard beat to the left. The music built to the last chorus, and Madison shimmied at the casket with her eyes closed, not wanting to remember Eddie Willet lying there with his red nose.

She shimmied all the way out the door as the music ended. The audience's appreciative laughter, applause, and tears momentarily dried, gave her the sense of a job well done.

But this whole experience brought one point front and center in Madison's mind. She hated to admit it, but in this particular instance, *My mother was right.*

✧ ✧ ✧

IN GIOVANNI'S RESTAURANT, she adjusted her curly blonde wig, fixed her makeup in the restaurant's employee bathroom mirror, and added red lipstick. She made sure her teeth were no longer blacked out from the funeral gig, then added some nerdy glasses. When doing the Bumbling Waitress character, she liked to disguise herself a bit so that there would be less chance that a friend might happen to be in the restaurant and recognize her, ruining the gag for the victim. A gag gone wrong meant there would be no tips, for sure.

Luckily, this restaurant's uniform was a dress for the female servers. That meant Madison could add her big ruffled rumba panties in the bit. Stepping out of her little black dress, and into the spare waitress uniform that management had provided, she locked all sad or anxious thoughts from her mind. The client had paid for an innocent gag to be played on her husband and had every reason to expect some fun and laughter with family or friends. Madison wouldn't disappoint them.

To the side of the busy kitchen, Madison met with the manager who announced the party had arrived and were seated at their table. There were six people in total in the birthday gathering. The main waiter introduced himself to her and said he had delivered the menus and waters to their table.

It was time to introduce Madison to the birthday party as a new waitress in training.

She went through the routine, having done this so many times before. She brought them a basket of bread, then moments later returned to refill their waters, while bringing a second basket of bread to sit next to the first one.

Soon after, she brought the coffees and tea and placed each drink with the wrong person. She then hurried off to bring back a third basket of bread, though the first basket was hardly touched. Returning with the bread, she knocked over someone's water. Apologizing profusely, she proceeded to wipe everything down much too hard, pulling the tablecloth partly off of the table. She said she'd be right back with a water replacement, but instead she brought back two more baskets of bread.

Everyone at the table was in on it, except for the birthday boy. He was starting to act impatient. She made a fuss, apologizing about forgetting the water, hurried off and brought back a pitcher of water, with a sixth basket of bread to add to the bread mountain. Then she refilled each water until it spilled onto the table, and poured ice water into the poor birthday man's coffee.

When he protested loudly, she set the water pitcher down knocking over the salt and pepper shakers and the little vase of flowers. Pretending to stand them all back up, she knocked his silverware off of the table.

He was quite disgusted by this point, but she proclaimed, "Never fear!" and dove under the table pretending to retrieve the silverware. While under the table, she purposely thumped her elbow up into the underside of the table to make a loud bang. She screamed, then stood up holding her head as if she had injured herself.

The man leaned back in his seat and seemed frightened of her. She shoved her hand into his glass of water to grab the ice, put it on top of her head, and ran away. The others at the table were capturing video of the whole fiasco trying not to laugh too hard, too soon, but were red in the face with the effort, their shoulders silently shaking.

The birthday man told the waiter what was happening and with animated gestures, demanded they get rid of her. That's when Madison walked back up to the table carrying a chair.

She ignored everything the poor man was trying to say, and climbed up, standing on the chair, proclaiming that she was the worst waitress in the world because she had missed her calling. Her calling, she said, was to be a singer. She asked, "Would you all like to hear me sing?"

The birthday man's wife nodded a vigorous yes, causing her angry and frustrated husband to slap his hand on the table, begging her not to encourage this.

The entire table joined in, clapping and cheering, saying, "Yes!" Even tables nearby were amused and egging her on.

Still standing on the chair, she bowed to everyone at the table, turned and bowed to the other tables, and made a point of bowing so that her big ruffles on her rumba panties presented themselves quite near the birthday man's face, forcing him to jerk his head back a bit.

She sang Happy Birthday like a diva, turning heads around the restaurant.

As usual, once the birthday victim realized he'd been had, he was flooded with relief that this whole train wreck had been a gag played on him for his birthday. He grabbed his heart saying, "Oh, my God, oh, my God."

When Madison got to "Happy Birth-day, dear…," she stepped down, prancing around the chair as she sang his name, holding it out, modulating upward, her voice demonstrating its strength. In the two seconds between finishing his name and starting the last verse, Madison could hear several people inhale to join in on the last verse.

On the last word "yoooou!" she tore off her nerdy glasses and wound up in his lap, leaving a big red lipstick kiss on his forehead that his friends caught on camera.

Her lips were no sooner releasing that kiss when she saw a familiar woman across the restaurant, sitting alone, and watching Madison with a smile. She had dark red hair. A big sun hat sat on the table.

Patrons around the restaurant contributed to the clapping. Madison, in the man's lap, smiled for the cameras.

But her eyes kept going back to the woman across the restaurant. She wondered if she was not seeing a lot of redheads lately, but rather, she was seeing one particular redhead at various places. It was seeing her face across the room that made Madison realize she hadn't been able to see her face before now. She'd only seen the hair. So how could she be familiar?

She tried to stand up to leave even though the cameras were still going. The man laughed and pulled her back down, saying, "What's your hurry?"

Madison chuckled along with him, her eyes darting over to the woman's table. She was already gone. The birthday man was laughing in relief, swearing revenge on his wife by not letting this pretty girl go, but of course it was a brief jest and he let Madison stand up.

She wished them all a wonderful day, while the wife smiled and slipped her an envelope.

Yes. The tip.

She made her exit from the birthday table, looking all around the room. *How did she disappear so fast?* Her heart dropped as she remembered the last time she had that exact thought. It was last night in the parking lot, about the figure in black.

Madison hurried down the restaurant aisle. She had a close call with a waiter carrying a large tray of lovely dinners. *The redhead at Choosy Chews.*

She worked her way back to the kitchen. The memory of the sun hat returned to her. *The hospital. I was with Jason at the elevator.*

The restaurant manager stepped up, saying, "Great job." He was chuckling and offered to shake her hand. She smiled, shook his hand fast and fretfully, saying she couldn't have done it without his help. She asked if there were a back door. She returned to the employee's restroom and changed back into her little black dress, tearing off the wig, her dark hair spilling out. She stuffed everything into her tote bag, and grabbing her car keys, hurried out.

Her heart rate increased as she made her way toward the back door, smiling at some of the wait staff that passed by. She came up to the door and stopped.

What if she's out there with Unibrow? What if they're waiting at my car? I'm sure he's pissed about that drill.

Then she remembered the fake handgun in her purse. She adjusted everything in her purse so that it would be easy to access if she reached in. She hoped pointing the prop would be a good enough threat. But she *really* hoped she wouldn't need it at all.

She opened the door and looked around. No one in sight. As she trotted toward her car, the meaning of the articles, the references to KGB, and Grandpa's comments about dangerous people came back to her mind. She regretted not paying more attention in school when they'd taught world history. Didn't Russian spies used to be referred to as the KGB? If these really were old KGB agents, she knew she was hopelessly outclassed in the sneaking around department.

She unlocked her car door without watching her own hands. Her eyes kept vigil on the parking lot, looking for any movement. Cars were pulling in, and what appeared to be normal people were climbing out and heading into the restaurant. A family with children were leaving the restaurant and getting back into their car, the parents fussing over seat belts. Madison ducked into her car and locked it. Her hands shook as she tried to stick the key into the ignition.

Calm down, idiot. The back door was a smart idea. Just drive away calmly, and try not to kill anyone.

She clicked her seat belt, and looked up into the rearview mirror. An old man with a salt and pepper unibrow was behind her car, rushing up to her side. She jumped, threw her car into gear and tried to go forward over the parking lot concrete brick in front of her car. The car felt like it was pausing, as the tires spun on the brick, squealing out their protest, trying to find traction.

Unibrow stepped up to her driver's side window and knocked, saying something she couldn't hear. Her shaking hands grabbed the prop gun out of her purse and she raised it to the window so fast, it clicked hard against the glass.

She held a shaky but determined aim at him to show she meant business, and shouted, "Back off! I have a sexy gun!"

Whatever he was saying, he shut up hard when he saw that gun. He put his hands up and stepped backward. Madison noticed a bruise on the side of his head just as her tires caught traction. Her car leapt forward with a jerk, throwing Madison backward, causing her finger to pulse on the trigger. Huge relief hit her that it wasn't a real gun, or she would have a hole in the roof of her car.

The back tires made a big thump-bump going over the concrete brick.

In her rearview mirror she saw the redheaded woman run up to Unibrow. They seemed to be arguing, each with their hands in the air.

She screeched out of the parking lot.

Chapter Twenty-Three

KNOWING THAT SHE left them on foot helped her to relax in the thought that they couldn't be following her. She tore down the street and hopped onto the freeway down by the stadium. She needed to get to Robot Moon Productions in Ballard, so she headed North into the U-District, got off the freeway at 45th, and headed west.

This was nuts. The thought that bad guys might hurt someone she loved gave her the heart of a lion. But the truth was she was a singing telegram, for crap's sake, going up against cold war spies. Could this get any stupider?

Where were the damn FBI guys from headquarters? They were supposed to be the rescuers, weren't they? Is Grandpa at least on a flight heading home yet? Wait a minute. Would he be in more danger if he got back? Why did she have to figure everything out from scratch?

The big sign on the warehouse of Robot Moon Productions greeted her as she pulled in, her tires grinding little gravel pebbles around. The robot with his pants pulled down, exposing his shiny metal butt, used to lift Madison's spirits with a smile or a giggle whenever she saw it. But right now the gloom over her head colored everything. She needed to figure out the rest of what was happening before either Grandpa or her mother, or someone else she loved, got hurt.

That's right. She sighed. *I love my mother.*

She'd always known she did. She'd never denied it. She just hadn't let herself say it or even think about it. Funny how something that she had tried to keep dormant, tried to keep asleep, could come roaring back under the right conditions. She may not get along with her mother, but she'd be damned if she let anyone hurt her.

She parked the car, pulled the key from the ignition, and the rest of her movements came to an abrupt halt. Her earlier thought about who her mother would have in her life to talk to upon hearing the news of having likely been an abandoned baby, made a full circle of logic. It would have to be Madison. This is what Ray meant when he said that Ann may not give Grandpa a fair chance to explain, but that Madison could help her.

Grandpa could tell Ann of course. But how could her mom say how she really felt about it in front of him? She would be thinking that if he and Grandma had come forward, maybe she would have been reunited with her mother.

Perfect Ann. She would also want to say all the right things to him about what a great father he was, and so on. Things that were true, but still not what Ann probably needed to face. She would need to face her anger at being abandoned. She would wonder why they didn't want her. She would wonder what her life would have been like if they had kept her. She would be disappointed in her parents, wondering why Grandpa and Grandma chose to do it illegally.

I'm no shrink. I'm not prepared for any of this. What am I going to say to her?

For that matter, Madison had to admit to her own uncomfortable feelings toward her grandfather now. He and Grandma had kept someone else's baby. How could they live with themselves knowing that they hadn't turned the baby in and let the authorities at least try to put the baby with extended relatives of the mother? And how did they get their hands on a fake birth certificate? Ann, the FBI agent, would have a field day with that one.

She got out of the car and went inside the warehouse. Target was not at her desk.

"Hello?" Madison called out. "Target?" She could hear some hammering going on down at the other end of the giant barn.

Target's voice called out, "Just a minute. Be right with you."

Madison headed in the direction of the voice. Target was working on a broken table, hammering some extra support braces underneath it.

"Hey, Target."

"Hey," Target said, looking back at Madison in her little black dress. "Dressing up is getting to be a habit with you. You're starting to class up the joint. To what do I owe the pleasure?"

"I thought I'd come pick up that envelope. The one that I left in the old Victorian grandfather clock yesterday."

Target looked up at her and said, "Your boyfriend already came and got it. And let me tell you, he is one hot aebleskiver!"

"What?"

"Aebleskiver. It's this awesome Danish pastry that my grandmother used to make for—"

"What do you mean you gave it to my boyfriend? Who was he?"

"Xander Boyd. He said he was the one you were reserving it for."

"ExBoy?" she exclaimed. She stared at Target, trying to comprehend what had happened.

Target stared back. "Uh…I take it he's not your boyfriend, then?"

"Not exactly. No," said Madison.

Target shook her head. "This is terrible. Oh, my gosh. You mean to tell me that you're not getting a piece of that? That guy is so hot that—"

"Target! He took it? Really?"

"Well, yeah. When you put the envelope in the clock, you said, 'as soon as he gets here he'll take it off your hands.' Then Xander said you were holding that prop for him."

"He's not the one I was referring to. And I don't know how he even knew about that paperwork."

"Well actually…" Target pushed her bangs back off of her forehead. "Now that I think about it, he never said anything about the paperwork. It was the tag hanging off of the clock that grabbed him."

Madison held her head as it dawned on her. "Last night I told him my life was a mess," she groaned. "Hot and scheming." She grimaced and pounded her fists off the top of her head a few times.

Target added, "It was this morning. He was looking for more props for the zombie convention tomorrow. He said that was the main piece he had come to collect, and that he was your boyfriend."

"Oh, really." Madison nodded her head. "I'm going to kill him."

"Well, yeah, you should," said Target. "If he's going to go making claims like that and isn't putting out, I mean that's just not right."

"Where did he take it? Did he tell you?"

"He loaded it onto a small truck. He was heading straight to the hotel. He has a room and everything. Guy has money, you know. Probably going to throw a big zombie party or something."

"No, I didn't know."

"Oh, yeah. His whole family is old money."

"What hotel is it?" said Madison.

"Hilton," said Target. "Hope they're ready for the mess because every costume store in the area has had a run on fake blood in their makeup departments. Those zombie fans love to pour it on."

"If he doesn't give me that paperwork, his blood won't be fake."

✧   ✧   ✧

THE SEATTLE LIBRARY was flooded with diffused light. She was too early and sat playing with her car keys. A few people looked her way at the sound of her keys jangling together so she put them away. Everyone looked so smart. Her mother would fit right in here. It was odd knowing that her mother was just two blocks away in the FBI building, probably working in her office.

She looked around the room, searching for red hair or old men. How long would she have to live like this? The woman that had been following her was scary enough, but Unibrow McBruise-Head terrified her. She liked him better when he was Mr. Duct Tape because he couldn't hurt anyone. In addition to being a threat to her grandfather, he might be wanting a little payback for hitting him with the drill. If she were smart she would find a good place to hide till the damn cavalry did their job. Why wouldn't the DC guys at least call her? For that matter, why didn't Grandpa?

She thumped the table leg with her foot, and found a good rhythm. This was a first. Madison had never met with Jerry before. In her childhood, he was the very image of an important adult. At first he was Mommy's nice friend, then Madison came to understand that he was what other adults referred to as a white collar worker, whereas her grandfather was blue collar.

Jerry was always dressed in suits and ties and had an air of class, albeit in a law enforcement sort of way. Most people had a tendency to speak in either harsh terms or hushed excitement when referring to the police or FBI agents. But Jerry's occasional presence in her childhood home usually meant the grownups were going to have to talk about boring things. Things like how smart and exceptional her mother was. As time went by and Madison's relationship with Ann became more strained, Jerry's conversation became harder to take. But oddly, her grandparents never complained about his conversation after he left. No, they would complain about how nosey he was. And Grandpa would instruct her about what not to say when Jerry was around.

Sitting here in the huge, light-filled room of the Seattle Library, she wondered what on earth Jerry was referring to when he said he was worried about Ann. He said he wanted to help her before he left his post as the SAC. As the Special Agent in Charge, he was the head of the entire Seattle Field Division of the FBI. *So help her already. I have enough worries about how to help my mother cope with the hard news she'll be getting, without getting involved in her job performance issues.*

She saw Jerry approaching with his amiable smile. Oddly, Aaron Reed was not too far behind him and took up a post about halfway across the large room. His expression when he looked at Madison was nothing like the warmth and friendliness of yesterday. It was not unfriendly, exactly, but there was a sober quality to his face, maybe a touch of sadness. But his eyes were all business. He looked away and seemed to be standing guard.

"Madison, my dear."

Madison stood up, and Jerry took both her hands into his, holding them in a princely way. "Thank you for agreeing to meet with me. Agent Reed will make sure no one overhears our conversation."

Madison tried to smile back. "You're welcome. But," she looked over at Aaron, "what's the big deal?"

Jerry seated them both at a table. He took Madison's hands again from across the table, looking down. A few seconds went by. Madison slowly pulled her hands away and folded her arms.

"Jerry, you're scaring me. What's going on?"

"There's no easy way to put this. I believe your mother is being compromised. In an effort to protect the people she loves, she is, well...I know she is a quality person, a quality agent but...." He paused. "I believe she is confused about her loyalties, and I want to help her before it gets out."

Madison blinked and repeated after him, "Her loyalties." She waited for further explanation, then said, "I don't get it."

She looked back at Aaron, but he avoided her eyes.

She started, "My mother has always been perfect. What do you mean 'confused about her loyalties'?"

Jerry pulled out a cell phone and punched some buttons. He set it down on the tabletop between them and turned it to face Madison. It showed a picture of Ann with Unibrow on a crowded street.

"I kept this to myself," he said, "till I could find out who this man is. I believe this is Vladik Sakharovsky, a former KGB agent, although the word 'former' is pointless. They've continued to operate, just under different names, different loyalties."

From the angle of the shot, Vladik's prominent eyebrows were plain to see, but she also knew it was him because of the bruise on the side of his head. Vladik appeared to be showing papers to Ann. The papers looked like they might be small pictures. Ann had her suit jacket draped over her left forearm and was rubbing the back of her neck with her other hand as she looked down at the sidewalk.

Jerry said, "I think she's being blackmailed for something your grandfather did."

As an actress, Madison believed that shock was the most difficult emotion to disguise. Even when the face and body language are perfectly composed to show some other emotion, body systems betray you. With a touch of adrenaline, the heart rate increases. Lungs demand more air. The voice might shake, and some people will sweat. But the first tell is the brief enlargement of the eyes. For that first split second, the eyes get wider, betraying the shock that you would like to hide. The voice doesn't have to shake—the eyes have already given you away. A professional like Jerry would spot it. So Madison did what any good improv actress would do. She threw out a red herring and pretended her shock was about something else entirely.

"Oh, my God!" She put a hand over her mouth and stared at the little picture on the cell phone. "It's all my fault! I have to tell her not to pay him one damn dime for those pictures! I'm not famous. No one will care."

"I'm not following." said Jerry.

"Oh God, I'm so embarrassed." She put a hand over her forehead and looked down at the table. "I posed nude for some stupid pictures. I needed the money." She looked up. His expression was starting to change. She hoped it was confusion. She said, "It involved sex toys and a swing. There were monks; lots of monks wearing blindfolds, and I would swing into them, knocking them over like bowling pins—"

"Madison."

"That must be why my mom tricked me into that apartment. She knew all along how desperate I've been. Pretending to cry, she added, "That's why she's been paying my rent. So I wouldn't cheapen myself!"

"Madison, this is a KGB agent from the Soviet Union era. The old guard of the Communist Party."

"I know, right? Those guys must be *so hard up* for work!"

"Where is Vincent?" he asked.

Madison blinked and swallowed. She said, "I don't know. Home, I guess. Why do you ask?"

Jerry rubbed his temples. "You love him. I understand. But I'm going to tell you more because I need you to help me help your mother."

Putting his cell phone back in his pocket, he sighed and looked at her. "I need to know where your grandfather is. You say you don't know, but I don't believe you. This may come as a surprise, but I've always known that he wasn't exactly crazy about me. I think he was a little jealous that Ann had another father figure in her life. I understand. But I know he's a good man, and I assumed in time he would see that I wasn't any threat. I'm not his rival. But you need to know that I've noticed some worrisome activity from your grandfather. I didn't want to get Ann upset about it."

Madison squirmed in her chair. Jerry continued, "He's not returning my calls. I think he's left his cell phone off so I can't track him. But I believe he would stay in touch with you. I want you to locate your grandfather and set up a lunch date with him for tomorrow. I just need to ask him some questions."

He leaned in, his voice quiet, almost a whisper, "And if he's in trouble, I can clean it up for him and make it go away. I'm the SAC, Madison. I can make things go away. But I'm running out of time." He sat back and said, "Think of it as a gift to your mother."

✧　✧　✧

THE SOUNDS OF a computer keyboard, that hollow plastic striking rhythm, held Madison spellbound. The pretty librarian's fingers flew over the keyboard, then stopped. Madison could see her blue eyes scanning left to right as she read the screen. Madison looked around, making sure there was no Jerry, no Aaron, no redheads, and no ... Vladik? Was that what his name was?

The keyboard rhythm resumed for a few strokes, then stopped again. The librarian said, "Anzhela. Russian. It's a girl's name. The English version for it would be Angela. The Latin root means Angel." The librarian looked up from her computer screen, blinked, and asked, "Are you sure that's all you needed?"

Madison's face held both surprise and sadness in it. She hadn't expected this kind of an answer. She didn't know what she had expected, really. But the news that the little one-word note was Anzhela, a Russian name for a girl, hit her harder than any of the other guesses she had braced herself for.

It was heartbreaking to think of a young girl trying to name her baby in haste. A baby that she was about to be parted with. From the condition of the note, she must have folded it into a tiny size and tucked it underneath the baby. Perhaps they had given her a moment to say goodbye.

"I couldn't make out some of those letters," said Madison. "At first I didn't know they were Cyrillic. But if someone were to try to pronounce the letters that look similar to English…" she grew a sad little smile, "it would be pronounced Anna."

"It would not have been correct. But," the librarian squinted at the little note, then handed it back to Madison. "Yes, I suppose you're right. It would sound like Anna."

Chapter Twenty-Four

S HE HAD INTENDED to go straight to the hotel, find ExBoy, rough him up, and get the paperwork back. But events were giving her a different perspective on her priorities. Her former opinions on what was wrong with her family were caving in on her. She went instead to her grandfather's house, changed out of her little black dress into clean shorts and a tank top from her freshly washed laundry, and cleaned Grandpa's house.

The broken pieces were swept up, the tables and chairs set right. The rumpled throw rug was vacuumed and smoothed out. The stupid remnants of duct tape all wadded up into a ball were tossed, and picture frames were stood up, or straightened out on the wall. She even washed some dirty dishes she found in the kitchen. Her grandfather usually kept a pretty decent house, for a bachelor, so most of the cleanup involved fixing the mess from his fight with Vladik.

She missed her grandfather. He wasn't here, so she found comfort in caring for his home. This was the closest she could come to giving him a hug, and she wanted it so much she was willing to take the risk of being here.

Besides, she couldn't think of any reason why Vladik would return. It looked like all he really wanted was to find her mother. He had done that. Her grandfather flew to FBI Headquarters in DC, and they had sent agents out here to investigate. So if Grandpa confessed, and Vladik told her mother, the secret was out. All that was left was the cleanup.

As she rinsed a used coffee cup, she pictured her mother outraged at Vladik, not believing him. But she'd have to believe it when Grandpa got back and told her. Ann might be trying to call her father to confirm it, and he wasn't answering. Jerry's guess was that Grandpa's phone was turned off. And Grandpa wouldn't know that Vladik had escaped and probably had looked at public records to see if Vincent Cruz had any children. Simple. He found Anna Lisa Cruz.

She had no fear of her mother getting in trouble for meeting with Vladik. As soon as Jerry knew the real reason, he could relax. She just had to wait a little longer for her grandfather to return. She wanted to keep her promise to him so he could come and tell his story his own way. She would make sure he knew that he would never lose her love or her support. True, she had to face up to his failings. It was wrong for him to keep the baby like that. Of course if he hadn't, life would have taken a different course for Ann, and Madison might not exist. Strange how events can change so many lives.

Her hands on her hips, she looked around the living room. It was nice. Grandpa could come home to a nice clean house. Now if only the heat would let up. It felt unnatural for the weather to be so hot. She missed the cooler temperatures. She missed the crisp clean air right after a rain. She missed feeling normal.

Her cell phone rang in her pocket. Pulling it out, she saw that the caller ID on the screen said Jason Clark. She was still kicking herself for how badly that conversation had gone this morning. She wished she could have a do-over. Except for the kissing. She had no regrets there.

She sank down to sit on the floor, watching the phone ring in her hand, not wanting another argument with him. But even at the risk of a fight, she couldn't resist. She answered quickly before it went to voicemail. She had to hear his voice.

She answered, "Jason?"

"Yeah. Hi." His voice was quiet.

"Hi," she said softly.

"I don't mean to bother you…"

"You're not bothering me."

"…but I promised you I'd call if there was any news about my grandfather."

"Oh," she kept her voice even to hide her disappointment. "Is he home, safe and sound now?"

"Yeah, he's home. But when I went to pick him up from the hospital, there were two men in his room asking him questions."

"What men?"

"Official government agents. One of them stopped me at the door and asked me to wait outside of the room. Remember when Ray mentioned DC? That's where these guys were from."

"Yeah, I kind of figured out what the DC reference meant. I was going to tell you this morning, but…"

They were both quiet for a moment.

"There was something else," he said. "I couldn't hear much, but I heard my grandfather say that Vincent told him it started out civil."

"What did?"

"I'm not sure, but I think he was talking about that fight you witnessed your grandfather having. Their talk started out civil, then they hit a big disagreement on how to proceed, I think that's how he said it. They gave him a number to call if he thinks of anything else."

"How to proceed?" Madison asked, trying to understand. "Like, they had something they were going to do, then butted heads on how to go about it?"

"That's what I got out of it," he said.

"Well, that was one hell of a disagreement. They were fighting like lives depended on it." Madison looked up at the newly cleaned living room, remembering their fierce encounter.

After a moment, Jason said, "I'm worried about you."

"Don't be. Everything is fine."

"Fine? My grandfather won't tell me what Vincent did, you won't tell me what was in the box, Ray was ready to do battle with a baseball bat, and now federal agents from DC are asking questions. Everything is not fine."

"Oh, Jason, geez, I'm so sorry. This must be driving you nuts, too." She took a breath. "I can say this much. I believe the worst is over. It's all going to wrap up soon and I'll be able to tell you everything. I'm still missing a few details myself.

"The devil is known to be in the details."

"I don't have much choice. I have to give Grandpa a chance to return and do this his way."

There was a pause. Then he said, "I don't like it, but I do understand. I just don't want to let anything happen to you."

"And while I'm at it," said Madison, "I'm sorry about this morning. I..."

"No, you were right, you don't owe me any explanations. I got carried away," he said. "Pretty girls do that to me. I'm over it now."

"Over it?"

"Well, yeah, till the next pretty girl comes along."

"I see."

"We're good. We're friends. I promise I won't forget that."

"Well…" Disappointed, she figured she'd better take the hint. "Okay, then."

They hung up.

Sitting there on the living room floor, Madison hugged her legs into herself, propping up her chin on her knees. Having Jason let her go by declaring they were friends felt different than ExBoy. She hadn't known Jason as long, but the draw was just as strong. They each hurt in their own way. She wished there was a way to merge them into one person. Of course, if she did that the third new person that they would become would be too smart to get involved with Madison in the first place.

She stood up. She needed to get over herself and get out of here. She still had to retrieve the paperwork from ExBoy so that when the DC guys called, she could hand it over quickly.

What bothered her was this new information. If Grandpa and Vladik had disagreed on how to proceed, than Grandpa's idea must have been to go to DC. So what was Vladik's idea? Maybe his idea was to do exactly what he had done after he'd escaped, find Ann and tell her everything. Madison had to admit, if that had been Vladik's idea, it seemed a lot smarter than involving the Feds. So why did Grandpa fight so hard to do it a different way? Jason might have a point about the devil being in the details.

The last thing she did to clean up was to make sure Grandpa's tool kit had all the tools put back in it. As she tucked it back into the closet, her eyes fell on an old photo album. It was Ann's baby pictures. Family photo albums and plenty of pictures and memorabilia of Madison sat on top. She pulled out her mother's album and looked through it. A younger Vincent and Lisa held their baby and smiled. Anna Lisa Cruz's first solid food, first steps, first birthday cake, all recorded, all treasured by her parents.

Madison took the album with her and left.

✧   ✧   ✧

SHE TRIED TO get ExBoy's room number at the front desk, but they said they couldn't give it out. She chose not to call him. Not yet. If she could find the grandfather clock, the paperwork might still be tucked up in there, behind the face of the clock where she had left it. She doubted ExBoy knew anything about the paperwork or would care. He had taken the clock to irk her. He saw the title tag and had known it was reserved for her. Humph. She hadn't seen him as the payback type.

She wandered the huge hotel and found the area where Zombie Prom would be held tomorrow. She preferred to ask forgiveness rather than permission so she went right in. A hotel security person stopped her and asked which exhibitor's booth she was there for. Without missing a beat, she said Xander Boyd, but the guard couldn't find that name on his list. Madison looked over his shoulder and saw various booths in different stages of being assembled for tomorrow morning.

"I'm sorry I don't see it." He kept turning pages over on his clipboard, searching. "Xander Boyd, you say? And he's expecting you?"

"Yes. I'm going to be a bikini zombie babe at his booth tomorrow, but he needs to see if I can fit inside a grandfather clock that he wants me to pop out of." The guard looked at her.

She shrugged and said, "He found that clock at the last minute, and I told him I have a bikini that would be perfect for this. It's all tattered and ripped."

She had his attention. She looked down at herself, describing the lines of the bikini and where the rips would be, and added, "I want to help him sell more of his art and his books."

From behind, she heard, "Did you bring the bikini?"

She whipped around and saw ExBoy standing there. She pressed her lips together hard.

The guard mumbled, "ExBoy," like he should have known. "His booth is called Infect Me." He offered ExBoy a conspiratorial fist, exchanged a quick fist tap, and walked away.

"Where is it?" she demanded.

"The bikini? Do I have to think of everything?" he said.

"ExBoy…"

"Come on," he said, putting his arm around her and leading her into the maze of partially finished booths. "It's over here. No harm."

"No harm? You don't know what you did."

"I got you to come here, didn't I?"

They walked down an aisle, passing ordinary-looking tables typical at conventions, only most didn't have tablecloths yet. Various vendors had rented spaces to sell their wares at tomorrow's event. Most of the spaces were already separated by black curtains hanging from PVC piping. The tablecloths being thrown on the tables were also black. A few work crews labored on backdrops, setting up elaborate displays to delight and entice fans of the undead. Some spaces didn't have tables so as to invite zombie fans to walk in, perhaps to examine a hanging t-shirt, a clothing article of metal studded couture, or maybe take a seat and pay a professional makeup artist to turn them out in excellent zombie style.

Cardboard boxes littered the place with ghoulish body parts sticking out at all angles. It was an adolescent boy's idea of heaven. But there would be plenty of adult men and women who delighted in the chill of a good horror movie, and their appetite for scary thrills would find the menu here to be worth the drive, worth the time, worth the money. In this hotel tomorrow morning, everyone could be a fan of anything zombie, and know that he or she was amongst their tribe. They were going to have a blast.

"Why would you want me to come here? You broke up with me, remember?"

"I didn't break up, I gave up. We weren't a couple, remember?"

"So why?" she asked.

"Because you wanted to see my work. You made me think. I hate that." He nodded at another vendor setting up styrofoam tombstones as they passed by. "I'm warning you, you may have started something."

They came to ExBoy's space, and there was the Victorian grandfather clock standing in the corner. Its door hung open and askew. Blood ran down the glass door. A crumpled figure, a dummy of a man wearing a white doctor's coat, lay at the base of the clock. The dummy appeared to have succumbed to his death. The blood smears running down the sides of the clock made it look as though he had held onto the clock with both bloodied hands as he slid down the sides to the floor. There was blood on the clock, the dummy, and on some of the medical examination instruments, left unattended. A doctor's private office, left abandoned, was the scene of medical intervention that hadn't worked. Madison was impressed but returned her attention to the matter at hand.

"But why didn't you just invite me like a normal person?"

"I didn't think you would come if I merely invited you," he said. "You've been a little preoccupied lately."

She knew he was right.

His space looked well thought out. Besides the grandfather clock, he had a medical exam table with patient charts on clipboards. In the opposite corner from the clock there was a room divider made of an aluminum frame with fabric panels where a patient could disrobe behind a privacy screen. The cloth of the screen had long skinny tears as if claws had taken a swipe, leaving goo and blood in their wake. Signs on the back wall announced the release of a new novella, *Infect Me*.

Besides the posters about his book and some smaller artwork on display, the space seemed a tad empty. Madison didn't want to criticize, but he must have sensed her thoughts.

"Most of my artwork and the shipment of books are in my room. I'll be setting the rest out in the morning."

She nodded, looking around. Overhead, she noticed the huge lighting fixtures of the hotel. Large and round, they had beautiful cut glass domes. It was odd to see something so nice. They seemed out of place for Zombie Prom.

"It looks great," she said. "And I don't mean to mess up your work here," she looked down at the crumpled dummy on the ground holding his death pose, "but I need to retrieve some paperwork that I left inside that grandfather clock."

"What about the bikini?"

"Yeah, right."

"It actually would attract a lot of customers."

"Aw, come on. Don't hold that over my head."

"It really was a good idea," he sighed. "But I'm just glad you came. I figured we'd probably still be friends, but now you get to see something besides the party boy."

She tried not to look sad, forcing a smile.

"Yeah," she said. "Friends."

Looking at the few pieces he had out in his display, she said, "You really are good. I heard you were, but it's nice to see some evidence."

"You mean this stuff?" he asked. "This just happened to be the right size for the space, that's all. My good stuff is in the room. And so is an envelope that fell out of the clock when I was setting it up. There were a bunch of old newspaper articles in it. Is that what you're looking for?"

"Yes! Did it get damaged?"

"No, it's fine," he said.

She put a hand on her heart. ExBoy watched her for a moment.

"You didn't really need the clock, did you? Are those papers part of your ongoing drama?"

"I can't…"

"Just tell me if you're in trouble. Maybe I can help."

"There is trouble, yes. But it's not about me. I'm just caught up in it."

He dug around in his pocket. "Here," he handed her a hotel key card. "It's on the desk in my room. You'll see it. I have to stay here and finish up."

Chapter Twenty-Five

S HE SAT ON the bed, leaning against the headboard with her phone against her face, talking to Spenser. She had the envelope of Grandpa's paperwork on the bed next to her. ExBoy's artwork was all over the room. Most of it was the exact size of a comic book. He used comic book storage methods, tucking each piece inside clear plastic bags with a cardboard insert intended to give it stiffness and protection from being bent. But other pieces were larger and framed. They certainly weren't all about zombies.

In one piece, dragon creatures of wild fantasy swarmed in the sky, their wing spans obscuring the sun, casting deep shadows of certain doom upon the ground.

In another piece, sweet little fairies charmed a maiden to keep her busy, while their fairy kin bared their long sharp fangs behind her back.

One depicted demons from hell contemplating the workings of an elliptical exercise machine, looking at once terrifying yet perplexed at modern life.

Some of his work was dark and moody, or frightening, while some of it was more whimsical. All of it was amazing. It revealed a side of him that she hadn't seen before. Some people can speak of darker things only through their art.

Next, she needed to call her agent. Being followed to her singing telegram gigs was pretty unnerving. The pieces were coming together, but she still wasn't certain whom she could trust. She needed to lie low for a while, so she hoped Phil would understand why she had to cancel a few gigs coming up.

"Holy cow, Minty," his Boston street tough accent boomed, "I can't believe how many calls I got about you today. What'd you do, rob a bank?"

"What are you talking about?"

"I keep getting asked where you are, but they don't want to identify themselves. They all say they're friends, or friends of the family. About five calls in all. All different people, by the sound of their voices."

Madison fought down a sense of dread. She was right about her instinct to lie low. "What did you tell them?"

"Not a damned thing. I protect my people, you know that. But it's making me wonder what's going on."

"Me, too. I thought I had this all figured out, but now I'm not so sure. I haven't done anything wrong,

Phil, but I should keep my head down for a while. I
need to cancel some gigs."

"Ah, Chocolate Mint, don't do this to me, girl. I got
all kinds of trouble right now."

"Trouble?"

"Jen was all excited about trying this new dance she
does with a candle, so she tried to rally from that groin
problem. She's doing the dance, goes upside down with
the candle, and her hair caught on fire. The guys in the
bachelor party all rushed to her aid at once. Turns into a
big fistfight."

"That's terrible!"

"Tell me about it. I gotta pay for her new hair
extensions."

Madison hung up as fast as she could.

She set her phone aside and picked up her big tote
bag. She wondered what life would be like without
always having to bring this thing along. It held
everything and she took it everywhere. She never knew
when Phil might call with an emergency gig, and she
might need to drop everything and get ready to go. Now
here she was, canceling gigs. She dug around in the tote
and pulled out the large envelope of old pictures. Maybe
she could use the old photos as an excuse to see her
mom. She'd pretend she was just returning them, then
ask her in a casual way how she was doing. *That's not
nearly clever enough.*

Madison gazed at the big pile of photos. They were still pretty damned cool, like something out of a black and white movie. There were so many, she hadn't even seen them all yet. She sorted through them in a lazy fashion.

Maybe she should come right out and tell her mom that she had forgiven her, and that she wanted to try again. *But, damn it, I don't want her to think that it would be okay to do that sneaky shit again.* It wasn't okay, but Madison was not convinced that her mother understood that.

She pulled her small mirror from the tote bag, checked her makeup, and reapplied her lipstick.

I could always try the truth. I could say I found out about the adoption and ask her if she would like to talk about it. Madison rubbed her lips together to smooth out the color, and a thought occurred to her. What if she said no? What would Madison do then? It hadn't occurred to her until this moment that her mother might say no. Holy shit. She can't let her say no. Her mom had to face this. This might be the biggest thing to ever happen to her and her mother, and they needed to face it together. Ann strived to be perfect, but Ann wasn't perfect. She still needed someone.

Madison made a quiet little discovery and blinked. She had been sitting here trying to figure out how to help her mother instead of trying to figure out how to trick her mother. Madison was so tired of her own shit; she wanted to rise above it. She inhaled deeply. This felt good. *But how will I know if I'm doing it right?*

She stood up from the bed and sorted through the things in her tote. She made a conscious decision not to hide her love. The fear of that notion was still there, but at least it felt more like a spider you could walk around, rather than pick up. Hiding her love had never worked anyway. It had been a stupid way to protect herself.

There was a knock on the door, and Madison dropped the tote bag. She went stiff. *Who followed me?* With a tiny adrenaline shot to her system, her heart started beating faster. She took a deep breath, more to brace herself than to relax, and tiptoed into the short narrow hallway to the door, looking out the peephole.

It was ExBoy.

Exhaling, she pulled it open fast, once again thankful that it was him at the door and not someone creepy.

"I'm so glad it's you," she said as her shoulders went back down, deflating in front of him.

"Uh…surprise, it's me?" he said.

Fumbling for words, she said, "Well, sure. Who else would it be? Right?"

After a few seconds of standing out in the hallway, he leaned forward and whispered, "Can I come in?"

Madison blinked. "Oh! Of course." She shook her head. "It's not like this is *my* room," she laughed, "this is *your* room." She backed up, holding the door wide open for him.

He stepped in and stopped just inside the door. "Are you okay?" he asked. They were standing inches apart in the short narrow hallway.

His willingness to show her a little more of himself made him seem more sincere, made him that much more attractive to her. She let go of the doorknob, still looking him in the eyes. The door closed with a firm thump.

"Yeah," she said. "I'm good."

"When you didn't bring back the key card," he said, "I wondered if maybe you had decided to stay."

He looked suspiciously casual. Madison took the cue and acted as if she were completely relaxed.

"I got a little caught up on a few phone calls. It was nice to have a quiet place to collect my thoughts." She looked around the room. She had left some clutter. "How's the, uh, booth thing? I mean, is it all done being set up?"

"It's good enough for now," he said.

She saw him looking around the room. He walked over to the desk and set down his pack, straightened out his pens, picking up some papers without really looking at them and setting them back down.

Madison walked over to the bed, removing her phone and paperwork, putting them back into her tote bag on the floor.

"Sorry," she said, "I guess I wasn't thinking. I started to make myself at home." She nudged her tote bag with her foot, scooting it away from the bed.

"Oh, that's all right," said ExBoy, but he sounded uncertain. He added, "You've probably had a long day."

She saw his gaze go to the bed and hold. She noticed the envelope of pictures was still sitting by the pillows. Sauntering over, she picked it up, placing it on the bed stand, next to the lamp.

He watched her.

"I helped myself to a water bottle," she said. "I didn't think you'd mind."

He kept watching her and sighed.

She wondered if he were just tired. "The hotel had two water bottles on the nightstand," she continued as she brought the other water bottle to his desk where he stood and set it down. "Like they knew there would be two people—"

"I can't do this," he said.

"Do what?" she asked.

"I can't give up on you and then have you around. I shouldn't have taken the clock. I'm really sorry. But you have your envelope now, right?"

Madison didn't say anything.

He continued, "You should probably go."

It hung in the air as she watched his eyes, and she saw that his eyes matched the words. She waited to see if he would say more. He didn't.

She broke the silence and asked, "Are you sure?"

"You're a sweet vanilla cake with chocolate icing, and if I'm going to stick to my diet, I should stop looking at the cake."

She got closer, and where he would normally have reached out and pulled her to him, he just stood there.

"You can't have the cake…" she slid her hands under his t-shirt, up the front of his chest. "But a little cupcake is something else."

"You don't mean it," he said simply.

"Well, if you started talking about making a commitment, yeah, that would scare me off," said Madison. She pulled her hands out from under his t-shirt, smoothing it out to leave it the way she found it. "I can't know what I'm looking for, if I don't know what I want."

"That makes two of us."

"And neither of us wants to be boink buddies," she added. "That's not the same as romance."

"Agreed," he said. "Those terms are fine. But the problem—"

"You agree?"

"Yes. But the problem is that although you think you mean it, you'll back out. You'll find some reason to... What are you doing?"

Madison had kicked off her shoes and stepped away, undoing her shorts. She let them fall to the floor as she walked, stepping out of them as she crossed the room, then pulled her tank top over her head, throwing it down.

"Madison. This isn't fair. Of course I want you; you don't have to prove it."

She stepped into the bathroom where he couldn't see her, then let him see her sizable bra go flying out the bathroom door into the room. She heard it hit the carpeted floor. Then she threw out her panties and heard him chuckle.

"You little bitch," he said. "You little teasing bitch. I should throw you out naked and let you see how it feels."

She stepped out of the bathroom with a towel wrapped around her from her bust down to her upper thighs. "You read my mind," she said, and headed for the front door.

"What are you doing?" he asked.

"Penance."

"What? Penance?"

"Yup. You're never going to get over it until I do this."

She looked out the peephole and saw no one. She opened the door, and stuck her head out, looking up and down the hallway. All clear.

ExBoy called out, "You are not! You crazy idiot, you are not!"

She turned around to face him with the door open behind her. He was still standing there at the back of the room with his mouth hanging open but a thrill in his eyes.

She announced, "Room service. There's a cupcake out here. You'd better get it before someone reports it."

She opened her towel to flash him, closed it, and stepped to the edge of the doorway, looking down at the way the pattern on the carpet changed crossing the threshold into the hallway. She took a deep breath. Her hands became a vice on her towel. She crossed, letting the door close behind her. The metallic click and thud announced there was no way back in.

She knew she was in for a wait. She had seen in ExBoy's eyes that he was excited with mischief. He would not break quickly. He was going to make her sweat. She should have checked her sanity before trying this stunt.

Now that she was out here in the hallway, one extra detail came up. It was cold. The heat in the hallway was not at the same comfort level as in the room. In the hot summer months, the air-conditioning blew extra cold, and drafts blew down the hallway sending a chill up her towel. She hoped he would open up soon.

The hallway was still clear. Most of the hotel guests were probably already out to dinner. She leaned against the wall opposite ExBoy's door, putting a foot up on the wall behind her, her knee sticking forward, waiting to see when he would open the door. Now would be a good time to come up with the right kind of story about why she was out here in the hallway wearing nothing but a towel.

She realized he must be watching her through the peephole, so she opened and closed the towel just in the direction of his door. She looked up at the peephole, hoping that he really was there. She wagged her eyebrows up and down, and mouthed the word "cupcake."

The door didn't move.

Uh-oh. She kept her eyes on that doorknob, willing it to turn, but keeping her ears open for the sound of anyone in the hallway. Whole minutes were ticking by and she was getting cold, damn it. She reminded herself of why she was doing this. She wanted him to know that she was sorry for the way she had treated him the other night, and was now trying to back up her apology with this gesture of risk.

Maybe I should turn up the heat a little. She opened the towel again, tilted her head way back against the wall, her face toward the ceiling, and inhaled deeply, letting her breasts rise and fall a few times. But the cold made her nipples into hard and tight little points. This was taking much longer than she had anticipated. Looking at the peephole, she closed the towel and said in a loud voice, "Show's over."

The door didn't move. *Damn it!*

Ding! She heard an elevator. *Shit.* She went rigid, looking down the hallway in the direction of the sound. She waited, and sure enough, the elevator door opened and a waiter with a room service cart wheeled out. She looked frantically at the peephole, eyes wide and pointing in the direction of the elevator, but the door didn't open. She knew damned well he was watching!

The waiter was bent over, hands on the push bar, pushing the cart down the hallway, coming closer, in no hurry. The glassware and china on the cart clinked a delicate rhythm while the metal trays under the cart snapped in time. Madison turned around, pretending to gaze at an abstract painting on the wall, her face getting hot.

This is not happening.

She hoped that the waiter would assume that she was returning from the pool. Then she wondered if the hotel even had a pool. As she faced the wall, obsessed with the painting, the cart drew closer till she thought it would pass.

But it stopped.

She kept staring at the painting. If he doesn't open that door right now, his death will be slow.

She heard, "Ma'am?"

She turned slowly wearing a lovely smile, her fingers drained of any blood from clutching the towel so hard.

"This is for you. Will you sign here, please?"

The smile on her face went rigid when she looked down. There sat a cocktail. A rum and Coke. The bill was charged to ExBoy's room number.

She looked up at the peephole sending death rays through it, then signed, adding a little gigantic something to tip the waiter.

His eyes went huge and he said, "Thank you! Thank you, ma'am! Have a wonderful night!"

Pushing the cart in the opposite direction, he returned to the elevator with a big grin, looking back over his shoulder at Madison. She smiled, hanging onto her towel with one hand, and lifted her drink to him in a toast with the other as he wheeled into the elevator, happy. The elevator door closed.

ExBoy opened his door, unencumbered by clothing, and leaned casually against the side of the doorframe. There was that loaded weapon again.

"You never told me you were kinky," he said.

She stepped closer, relieved he finally opened the door. "You call this kinky? Please. I have the same agent as Jen. I could tell you some stories."

"No need. You proved your point." He took her drink away while his other arm encircled her waist, pulling her into the doorway and lifting her off her feet.

He murmured, "Now it's my turn to prove a few things."

He turned them toward the interior of the room as he kissed her, her feet never touching the ground. The door closed, the towel fell, and seconds later he threw her down on the bed.

The bounce was delightful.

Chapter Twenty-Six

S HE AWOKE FROM the after-sex nap to find ExBoy sitting up in bed, talking on the hotel phone. His golden colored hair hung near his eyes. Reviving from the short sleep, she heard the words "room service" as she slid across the luscious sheets to reach him, laying her head on his pillow and tickling his side. He gave a mild jerk, twisting around to grab her hand as it turned into a silent arm wrestle while he ordered the food.

"Also, add the dessert sampler of... Hold on." He looked at Madison and asked, "Chocolate or citrus?"

"Are you sure you want to do that? That's going to be expensive."

Holding the phone away, he bent down, his blue eyes directly in her face, and gave her a quick kiss. He repeated his question. "Chocolate or citrus?"

"Chocolate."

As she rolled over and sat up, the swoosh and whisper of crisp bed linens spoke of a luxury she was not accustomed to. Cheap sheets didn't make sounds like soft rustling leaves. She could get used to this. She dared not.

Although she still had her problems to contend with, she was sure the worst was over. When Grandpa got back, their little family would pick up the pieces and start over.

For now, she accepted ExBoy's invitation to stay the night. Her affection for him elevated; she had a million questions about his past, his dreams, his goals.

Later, room service indeed arrived with a full spread, and after all the exertion, desperate clutching, and overdue orgasms, Madison was starved. The table being wheeled in brought its own excitement, and Madison was amazed at the luxurious feeling from the simple act of being fed.

The part that seemed to confuse ExBoy was the eagerness of the two waiters that brought the cart. They were all smiles and nods with him. They would have rubbed his feet if he had asked. She realized it was probably because of the giant tip she signed for earlier when ExBoy had a drink sent to her out in the hallway. Word must have spread among the staff. A little payback seemed appropriate at the time, but now she bit her lip wondering what mischief ExBoy would arrange when he found out.

They sat around in leisure, enjoying hors d'oeuvres and wine, tender steaks, potatoes, and buttered zucchini. Madison took note of his appetite. Impressive. She knew she wouldn't be able to eat everything on her plate, the serving sizes being so huge, but she was going to have fun trying.

She listened while he talked about the convention tomorrow. Normally, all this zombie silliness was not something she would have sought out on her own. But seeing it through his eyes, she began to appreciate the fun in it and listening to him in his excitement charmed her. He was animated and happy.

But when she tried to ask about his family, he clammed up.

After a moment he asked, "Why do you want to know?"

"I don't know. Because it's normal to ask, I guess." She was getting full and decided to save room for the chocolate dessert sampler. But one more bite of buttered zucchini first.

"I don't think it should matter," he said. "It's not important." He put his fork down.

"Well, true, it has nothing to do with how I feel about you, but you can't say it's not important." She was surprised by his response, but decided there were still plenty of other things to talk about. "Okay. Well, what about your art? Tell me about that."

"What about it?"

"Well, it's amazing! I had no idea you were that good. Did you study in art school or something?"

"No."

She waited for him to expound but he didn't, and he seemed content to let the silence sit there.

"Where do you come up with all those ideas?" she asked. "How do you…"

"I don't know," he said quickly. "I just do." Then in a lighter tone, he said, "Hey." With some of his animation returning, he asked, "Do you mind if I get to work? I have some signs for the booth I want to make."

Taken aback, she said, "Did I say something wrong?"

Picking up his fork again, he used the flat side to pat a piece of chocolate cheesecake on his plate, making tiny grooves with the prongs of the fork. He exhaled. "No."

She stayed quiet hoping he would talk. ExBoy had been something of an enigma to her since the beginning.

"I don't like talking about my family," he said. "And I don't like analyzing my art. I'd rather keep enjoying it without thinking about why or how. They don't approve of it, and I don't care." He took a bite of the chocolate cheesecake. "Good enough?" he asked.

"Wow. That's it, huh? That's all you're going to tell me?"

He watched her as he ate the chocolate cheesecake, his face a stubborn mask.

She knew she wouldn't get any more out of him. She said. "I was just trying to get to know you more."

"I know. That's what gets to me about you. You want to see more." He used the fork to skim off just the top layer of chocolate icing. "It freaks me out," he said, aiming the icing at her lips. She opened her mouth and accepted the icing as he pulled out the fork, "And draws me in."

She licked her bottom lip. "I know about family trouble."

"I guess you do," he said, and left it at that.

Later at his desk, ExBoy worked on one last sign for the booth. Madison watched him, warning herself he might be sexy as hell, but she'd probably never get much more than that. He talked like she was the one who kept putting the brakes on any relationship between them, but she didn't buy that.

Meanwhile, she really did want to help him at his booth tomorrow. She had a few surprises lined up for him and one more phone call, this one to Sound Beating, should do it. She didn't want him to hear her on the phone so she said, "I'm going downstairs to buy a few sundries. I'll be right back."

He looked up with a devilish gleam in his eye and said, "If you forget the key card, just take your clothes off. I promise I'll get you in here fast this time."

"That'll never happen again."

"Why not?"

"Because I'll never owe you penance like that again."

He looked back down at his work and said, "I'll think of something."

She grabbed the key card and left the room.

✧ ✧ ✧

EARLY IN THE morning, hours before the doors opened for the convention, they set out the rest of ExBoy's artwork at the booth. He used the larger works to fill up some of the empty-looking spots within his space. The boxes of books went under the table, well hidden by the black, floor length tablecloth. Books sat in neat piles on the tabletop. Alongside the books sat long narrow comic book boxes the exact height and width of standard comic books, made to accommodate comics standing upright. That would allow ExBoy's customers to flip through the various plastic bags of his artwork. He had a nice open spot on the table where he could autograph his book for a potential buyer.

The cover of his book puzzled Madison. Besides the title, *Infect Me*, and the author's name, Xander Boyd, it showed three zombies trying to get away from a normal looking young woman. She had her forearm around the throat of one zombie, while she desperately grabbed for the second zombie that was slipping out of her reach. The third zombie was running away.

"I don't get it," said Madison. "The cover shows the zombies trying to get away from her, instead of the other way around."

He said, "It's a comedy horror. She wants to be a zombie, but finds that she can't get bit to save her life."

Madison thought about that for a minute. "You are a strange man. But I mean that in a good way."

She looked up, seeing the surprise that she had arranged for him walking down the aisle toward his booth. With a little prodding, Spenser and Target had agreed to be zombies hanging around ExBoy's booth. Target in particular was quite eager. But best of all, Crystal had agreed to try to get Toonie out of the house by bringing her to the convention, and Madison could see now that they were doing more than just attending. They, too, were walking toward them, made up as zombies.

Crystal, her beautiful complexion drained to a deathly pallor, was dressed like a cheerleader with her little pleated skirt and sleeveless shell top in bloody tatters, carrying what Madison had thought was a dirtied pom-pom but now realized was a head with long bloody hair.

Spenser wore a nurse's old fashioned white uniform, with a little white hat attached to her blonde hair pinned up like Tippy Hedren's in an Alfred Hitchcock movie. Choosing to keep her face its prettiest, she sported a bloody gouge on her left forearm. Instead of sensible nurse's shoes, she wore high heels. The blood on her uniform appeared to have been sprayed and splotched, as if she'd been too near someone who had burst an artery.

Target wore jeans and a faded Robot Moon Productions t-shirt with a few blood streaks running down the front, and carried a dark blue backpack. A big rubber dagger appeared to be embedded in Target's forehead, blood running down her face. A fresh kill.

Toonie wore an old, dirty white chef's jacket and pants, complete with tall chef's hat. The jacket was torn and bloodied with a big gash on the side. Something that passed for guts and sinew hung out from the hole in the jacket. She carried a rubber meat cleaver and looked like she really wanted to use it right now.

ExBoy was looking down at the table, arranging and rearranging the pile of books, his concentration on overdrive for such a small task.

"I have a surprise for you," said Madison. "It might not involve a bikini, but I think you'll like it." Spenser,

Target, Crystal, and Toonie stepped up in all their zombie glory.

"Xander!" cried Target. "Madison said you could use a little help. Zombie cavalry to the rescue."

ExBoy looked up, confused at first, then said, "Target? Spenser?" He looked them all up and down, their undead appeal sinking in while a big smile slowly grew on his face.

Introductions were quickly made for Crystal and Toonie, and the four zombie women made nice with proper "hello, good to meet you, hello…" as bloody handshakes were exchanged, along with a little nervous laughter.

To Madison, Crystal said, "I was shocked Aunt Toonie agreed. She wants to help, although she's not really happy about her costume."

"Oh for God's sake," Toonie fumed. "Just say it. I look like an ass!"

Before she could assure Toonie that she looked fantastic, ExBoy grabbed Madison up and planted a big kiss on her, saying, "Thank you! It's awesome."

"Damn it," said Target. "I didn't have my camera ready."

Having just shook hands with Toonie, Spenser said, "You're the one who made the cookies. The oh-my-God cookies!"

Toonie warmed up at that and smiled. Admiring the Tippy Hedren hairstyle, she told Spenser, "I love your hair. I wore mine like that in high school. Years ago, of course."

"Thank you," said Spenser.

"But why are you wearing high heels if you're supposed to be a nurse?"

"High heels give me a different perspective," said Spenser. "I always seem to be cuter up here."

Toonie considered that and mumbled, "Then I must be just adorable."

Madison said, "Target, I have to get my own costume ready now. Spenser brought me some old clothes she was going to get rid of. Did you bring the liquid latex?"

"Everything's in my pack here. I brought some prosthetic wounds, too, and white contact lenses."

Madison was delighted. "I've always wanted to try white contacts. You can see out through them, right?"

"Oh, yeah. Things will look a bit cloudy to you, but they'll make your eyes look so creepy," said Target. "And I can help you with the prosthetic wounds. I brought the spirit gum to apply them."

ExBoy finished a conversation with Toonie, and walked over to Madison. When she asked him for the key card, he handed it to her, saying, "Your neighbor

Toonie looks fantastic. But for some reason she keeps calling me Tighty Whitey."

It was difficult for Madison to keep her face blank as she shrugged her shoulders and took the key card.

✧　✧　✧

UPSTAIRS IN THE room, Madison and Target hurried to pull Madison's costume together. The hotel would be opening the doors to the convention very soon now.

Together they slashed, tore, and dirtied up an old worn out one-piece bathing suit with matching poolside cover-up that Spenser had donated. With added sunglasses, floppy hat, and sandals, Madison intended to act as if *Infect Me* were her summer reading. She pinned her hair up so that when she added the floppy hat, it would be able to cover all her hair.

Then she added the white contact lenses. *Whoa.* They did have a mild cloudy effect on her vision. She shouldn't drive a car with them, but she could see just fine to see how freaking cool the effect was! *I'm undead royalty, bitches! That's right.* She always felt this sense of silly glee whenever she got a new costume.

Madison had her usual small theater makeup kit from her tote bag, but the supplies that Target brought blew her away. In the bright light of the bathroom, Target spread out her supplies on the counter. She brought out the spirit gum and used it to apply a small rubber prosthetic that looked like a fake wound in the form of a skinny slash on Madison's cheek. Then she painted a few patches of liquid latex on Madison's arms and legs. While the liquid latex was still wet, Target opened a small plastic container full of fresh coffee grounds, mixed with uncooked oatmeal. She pressed that mixture onto the sticky surface of the still wet liquid latex.

Once the liquid latex was dry, she brushed off the excess coffee grounds and oatmeal mixture, then painted the fake blood on top. Madison now appeared to have open wounds that had been dragged through dirt or had skidded through gravel. By now the spirit gum holding the prosthetic wound on Madison's cheek was dry. Unlike Crystal, who had done her costume and makeup to look all the way to decaying, or Spenser who insisted on looking alive and pretty, Madison decided to go partway, looking dead, without decay. So Target added a touch of greenish grey color to give a deathly pallor, hiding the healthy tone of Madison's skin, plus a little more makeup to blend in the edges of the prosthetic wound. Madison thought half of the enjoyment of the entertainment arts was the creation of an illusion. It was plain damn fun.

"Oh, the creepy goodness of it," said Madison. "I don't normally go for this kind of thing. But look at me!" she laughed. "Great job."

"Thanks," said Target. "I like special effects makeup."

"You're good at it."

"I have makeup artist friends that were hired at the last minute this morning. Two guys want a professional job on their costumes. The pictures from today are going to be fantastic."

"These contact lenses rock. I've got to get some just to have them on hand."

"You should try the red lenses sometime. Vampire chic."

"I want to take a picture of this. Let me get my phone."

The doors to the convention were open by now and Zombie Prom would be in bloom. She hurried into the other room to the nightstand where she had left her phone on the envelope of old pictures. Her tote bag sat on the floor next to the nightstand. She grabbed the phone with one hand while she tried to put the envelope back into her tote bag with the other, but the envelope slipped, spilling dozens of old pictures, fanning out on the floor. She plunged into a squat, balancing on her toes to save the photos, picking up each one with quick hands.

In that instant, one photo on the floor caught her eye as well as her breath. Her hand stopped in mid-air as she reached for a picture of a young Jerry with a young Vladik, standing together in front of a large banner that said International Student Exposition. They were shaking hands and smiling for the camera. The old photo lay askew on top of the rest of the evidence of Jerry's long career.

Jerry knew damned well who Vladik was.

She teetered, her balance pulling her backward to slump to her butt. She sat like a child with the photos, like toys on the floor, between her knees. Breathing through her mouth, she blinked at the truth in front of her. The mild cloudy effect of the white contact lenses in her eyes did nothing to soften the blow.

*Wait, wait, wait—why would—*She tried to calm down and put the pieces together.

At Choosy Chews, her mother told her that these older photos of Jerry were from the FBI archives. If Vladik Sakharovsky was KGB, that would make him and Jerry counterparts of one another. This photo implied they worked the student expo together, celebrating some kind of cooperation. Years later, Jerry's long involvement with local high schools brought him to her mother's high school, courting her to choosing a career with the FBI.

Grandpa always had a deep hatred for Jerry but never had said why. Yet he never stopped Jerry from coming to their house or taking young Ann Cruz on field trips. Jerry was even present during Ann's visits from college. Madison always wondered why Grandpa had allowed it.

Maybe her grandfather never stopped it because he couldn't.

The only person who could blackmail Vincent Cruz would be the one who knew he had kept the baby. The one who took that photo from the bushes. The one who waited in those bushes to see who found the baby, because he was the one who left the box there to begin with.

Chapter Twenty-Seven

S HE PULLED OUT her phone, trying to hit the right buttons and pull up Jerry's number. Her tears stopped as her anger grew, her hands shaking. She didn't know why she was bothering to give him a chance to explain, a chance to deny it.

This was why Grandpa needed to get out to FBI Headquarters in DC. Grandpa wasn't just confessing, he was ratting out Jerry in a place where Jerry had no authority to stop him. Uncle Jerry was the enemy.

She stopped, her hands dropping. What was she *doing* calling him like this? The reason Grandpa had said not to tell Ann was probably because he was afraid it would get back to Jerry! He knew Ann would go to Jerry for help, or if she knew more of the circumstances, might go to Jerry to confront him just like Madison had been about to do.

A small, faraway voice said, "Hello? Madison?"

The small voice was coming from the phone in her hand, which had lowered into her lap. She looked down at her phone, a viper in her hand. She needed to proceed carefully. Jerry had been ratted out by now, but if he didn't know that, how far would he go to keep this secret? If he did know, how far would he go to silence the witnesses? She raised the phone to her ear and said, "Yeah, it's me."

"Did you locate your grandfather?"

In a snippy tone she said, "Sorry, Jerry. Things don't always work out the way we want." She made a pained expression at her own lack of self-control. Her attitude was showing and she needed to dial it back fast.

Jerry's voice was low key and deliberate. "You do want me to help Vincent, don't you?"

She picked up the photo of Jerry and Vladik, bringing it closer to her dead white eyes as she stared at it. It mocked her. Her voice came out much more compliant. "Of course, Jerry. I would love that."

"I was hoping you could help me handle this privately. It would be kinder to Ann never to have to know. A benevolent deception."

God, she wanted to throw the phone. Grandpa recalled those very words right after his fight with Vladik. If there were any doubt left in her, Jerry had just killed it.

He said, "I'm out of time, Madison. Where is he?"

She looked down at the liquid latex wounds on her arms and legs. "I don't know, Jerry. He's not answering his phone." She wondered what a real wound like that would feel like. She wondered how to deliver a wound like that. She already knew she could swing a drill if she had to.

"I see that you cleaned up the mess in his living room."

The son of a bitch was keeping tabs on her.

"Well, you know the old saying," said Madison. "A woman's work is never done."

"You don't sound surprised that I knew," said Jerry.

"I'm getting used to surprises lately."

"You did a nice job. You'd never know those old boys had a knockdown, drag out fight. Even the duct tape was neatly wadded up and thrown in the trash. But did Vladik Sakharovsky ever see you? That's what I want to know."

A nasty edge slipped into her voice. "What does it matter?"

His voice, on the other hand, became very warm and full of concern. "Madison, honey, I know you don't understand yet, but it's very important that you tell me this one small thing. Did Vladik see you?"

She looked down at the picture of Jerry and Vladik in younger days. Vladik's smiling eyes in the picture were a younger version of the eyes that had smiled at her from the floor as she had run out of Grandpa's front door.

"No," she said.

"But you know he went to see your grandfather, right?"

Obviously he's already figured that out. "Yes."

"And you must have seen Vladik because you seemed to recognize him when I showed you that picture."

"Vladik was unconscious when I got there," said Madison. "He had duct tape on him, but Grandpa made me leave right away. It was mostly the way his eyebrows touch in the center that I recognized in the picture." *And the bruise that I gave him.*

"How much did Vincent tell you about him?"

"It's your turn," she said. "You tell me what this is about."

There was a long pause. Jerry said, "Vincent should never have pulled you into this. It's irresponsible of him to put you in danger. But I have big shoulders, and I can still keep your family safe. But not if we don't hurry. We can still keep your mother's heart from being broken, and we can still keep your grandfather out of prison. Madison, I can protect you and your family, but only if you tell me where your grandfather is."

"What's the point?" Madison was sick of the games. "Vladik already found my mother. Isn't that all he wanted? You showed me the picture. It's over. Why would you...."

Then it hit her.

In the picture he had showed her, her mother's suit jacket had been draped over her left forearm. She had been rubbing the back of her neck and looking down at the sidewalk. It was just like the moment when she'd been trying to control her tears over the memory of Grandpa falling apart after the funeral. Someone had taken a picture of them at that moment. *Aaron Reed was across the street about then.* When Jerry showed her that picture, she was actually looking at that same moment from a different angle. The photo had been manipulated to make it look like Vladik had been there with Ann, instead of Madison.

Exasperated, Madison expelled her breath and said, "It wasn't real, was it?"

She heard a soft chuckle. "No, actually. I needed to confirm that you recognized him. This can still be contained. But I don't understand why you're playing little zombie games when your mother's happiness and your family's safety are at stake."

"You know a lot of things, don't you, Jerry? You know they had a big fight in Grandpa's house. You know that I cleaned it up later. You know about my little zombie games. Yet you can't find my grandfather. Is it possible he's pulling a fast one on you?"

Another long pause, then the gentle beep she always heard when a caller hung up.

She was furious with herself. She had to go and open her mouth and be snippy, showing attitude, practically boasting that her grandfather was up to something. Jerry might not know how much she had found out, but he sure as hell suspected. With a dark secret to protect, he needed to secure silence from her grandfather. Maybe he would try to use her to secure that silence.

She had to get out of here. If she stayed, it was just a matter of time for him to find her.

She looked up and saw Target standing nearby, watching her with eyes of concern, the ludicrous rubber dagger sticking out of her forehead.

Madison said, "If you were trying to be a unicorn I think you did it wrong."

But Target wouldn't laugh. "Madison, what's the matter?"

Standing up, Madison grabbed the tote bag and snatched out the blonde wig she had stuffed in there right after the Bumbling Waitress gig.

"I have to get out of here fast. I'll explain as I go, Target, but first, can I borrow your clothes?

✧   ✧   ✧

MADISON WATCHED AS Target opened the door and stuck her daggered head around the edge of the doorframe, looking up and down the hallway. Target whispered over her shoulder.

"It's empty except for one lonely zombie down the hall near the elevator."

Madison said, "Let's go."

They slipped out of ExBoy's room, both of them still wearing all the zombie makeup and special effects. But Target was now wearing Madison's shorts and tank top from yesterday, and carried Madison's tote bag. Madison wore Target's jeans and the faded Robot Moon Productions t-shirt, while carrying Target's dark blue backpack. Her dark hair was completely covered underneath the blonde curly wig that now had fake blood smeared down a few strands.

They hurried down the hall in the direction of the elevator. The zombie standing there had a drink in one hand while holding up his cell phone with the other. He appeared to be drunk, and the smell of whiskey seemed to confirm it. In a deep voice he spoke into his cell phone.

"Get off my ass. I told you I'm on my way." He hung up, as Target hit the elevator button.

Surprised that anyone would already be drunk this early in the day, Madison was nonetheless impressed by his elaborate costume and makeup. He was dressed as a zombie fairy with pointy ears, soft leather woodland tunic and belt, and a pointy little hat. He had iridescent skin although the skin around his eyes was dark and dead looking. He wore striped tights on his legs, but the iridescent skin on his muscular arms was smooth, making Madison think he must have had all the hair on his arms waxed off. Blood appeared to have run from a large throat gash and dried down the front of his weathered leather tunic.

He stepped past Madison, impatiently hitting the elevator button again, and Madison noticed little gossamer fairy wings on his back. They looked just like the pair she used in her fairy godmother gigs. She couldn't suppress a heavy sigh as she thought about how easy life was a few days ago compared to now.

The elevator ding announced the door was opening. Coming from within the elevator Madison heard a woman's sharp intake of breath while another woman whispered, "Oh, my God," upon seeing the bloody undead in front of them. Three young women in long matching strapless gowns made of sapphire blue satin and two men in tuxes appeared to be members of a wedding party. Madison, Target, and the zombie fairy stepped into the elevator, causing the women to quietly back all the way up to the wall, their manicured hands pressing their lovely dresses inward, away from the new occupants. Madison did her best to act casual and fought the urge to apologize for existing.

One of the men's hands hovered near the buttons as he asked, "Ground floor?"

"Yes," said Madison. "Thank you."

Target could not take her eyes off of him. His light brown, short faux hawk stood crisply on top of his head. Neatly groomed in his tux, he had tattoos peeking from under his collar. Target smiled at him as the elevator door finally closed, the fake blood streaks on her face crinkling a little from her smile.

The elevator began its descent while Target pointed at the little boutonniere in his lapel, saying, "Nice."

He pointed at the dagger coming out of her forehead and said, "Cool."

They stood there looking at each other as Target's smile grew coy. Madison rolled her dead white eyes and felt like she should look away since they seemed to be having a moment. To look away, she turned to the nearest woman and said, "I love your dress."

The woman blinked. "Thank you," she said, and looked away.

Everyone stared straight ahead, except for Target and her man. The sound of ice tinkling was heard as the zombie fairy tilted his glass upward, draining the last drops. The elevator stopped at the second floor for the wedding party. The women held their dresses as close to their bodies as possible, their shoulders pulled high and elbows tightly inward as they stepped past and out of the elevator. The tuxedoed men stepped out after them, but Target's man looked back with a smile as the door closed.

As the elevator door opened on the ground floor, the zombie fairy bowed to Madison, his deep voice saying, "After you."

Stepping out, Madison and Target quickly navigated their way across the lobby, following signs to the convention ballroom. They could already hear the sound of hundreds of human voices in a cavernous space with high ceilings.

Passing through the main doors, they followed the crowd into the giant room where all the vendors' booths were lined up side by side. Their black curtains and black tablecloths lent some dignity to the event as well as defining boundary lines between the booths. A carnival of the undead and the living crowded the aisles and jostled in lines.

Madison was surprised to see so many different age groups represented. She also saw that half of the people had skipped the costume and makeup option. They'd shown up mostly to see their favorite horror movie actors or graphic novel artists. Perhaps they were hoping for an autograph or a photo opportunity. Madison tried to imagine Jerry Rosser being in this crowd, and couldn't picture it.

She pulled up the backpack's straps, getting the pack into a comfortable position on her shoulder rather than on her back. She and Target parted without saying a word to each other, pretending not to know each other anymore. Target turned left heading deeper towards the center of the ballroom, while Madison continued walking straight ahead.

She had had no choice but to quickly brief Target on the serious situation she was in. She had asked Target to go back to ExBoy's booth and tell everyone not to acknowledge Madison if they happened to run into her anywhere in the convention. She decided the best way to hide was to stay where so many people would be in costume. She would be able to blend in by not looking like her normal self. She'd pinned up her dark hair under a bloody blond wig, and her green eyes were whited out. Her arms were covered in bloody wounds, and even her face sported a fake open gash on her cheek. She felt she had a real shot of hiding out in the open while keeping an eye out for Jerry.

The convention was in full swing. All of the partially decorated booths Madison saw last night were now fully outfitted in scary glamour and fully stocked with whatever the owner was selling.

Posters, t-shirts, comic books, and action figures were just the start of what awaited the fans here today. There was creepy jewelry, home decorations with a dead gothic bent, tattoo artists, and actors with toothy smiles. Zombies poked around the booths looking for exact change in their bloody palms as they purchased a souvenir or a snack.

She tried to stay near a small excited group of zombie fans. They happened to be walking in the same direction, and she hoped she would appear to be one of them. She kept her stride casual, stayed in the back, making a point of looking around to admire the festivities the way she supposed a zombie fan would do. But as she turned her head, she caught sight of Aaron Reed, dead ahead. Her little group was walking right toward him, as she was tagging along behind.

He walked toward the small group but didn't notice her as he spoke into a cell phone, his eyes scanning the crowd. He was actually wearing a suit, of all things, not exactly blending in. A few days ago, his tall good looks and dreamy eyes had turned her head. Today, he symbolized a power and authority that she feared. She kept behind the people of the little group as they passed, not daring to let herself look back at him in case he turned around, too.

To her relief, the little group turned right, heading to the peripheral wall of the ballroom. There, connecting doorways lead out into hallways with a maze of banquet rooms where special events were being held. In one room, fans could see trailers of upcoming movies, while in another banquet room panel discussions were being held to give "experts" a chance to argue the merits of zombie autopsies.

Madison saw that the small group she'd been tagging along with was getting in line to see one of the movie trailers. She chose to keep walking, keeping to herself for now. The further down the hallway that she walked, the slower the pace became and the closer she was to other people. She'd never liked being in a crowd, but right now she had to appreciate the cover they were providing.

The walking slowed to a standstill while a small family in front of her stopped to negotiate who had to go into the nearby ladies' restroom. As the crowd slowly went around them, a hand shot out and grabbed Madison's arm.

Chapter Twenty-Eight

S HE LET OUT a brief but loud yelp as she whirled around and found an eager-faced young girl who said, "Sorry! Didn't mean to scare you, but your eyes are so cool! Did you buy those contacts here? Where can I find them?" Madison put a hand over her mouth. Several people had looked her way with curious faces but already had lost interest. Except the zombie fairy.

Madison's nerves went on full alert realizing that he might have been following her since she and Target left ExBoy's room, even riding the elevator with them.

Right now he was across the hallway scrutinizing the young girl with hard eyes. There was a cool stoic quality to his gaze and a sharpness in his eyes that she hadn't seen earlier. He looked in another direction, shaking his head a small no. Madison followed his eyes for a spilt second to see who he was shaking his head to. She saw *another* zombie fairy with a cell phone in one hand. His zombie fairy costume and iridescent skin were almost identical, but instead of a woodland tunic, he wore an Edwardian tailcoat.

She threw her arms around the young girl in a jovial hug, laughing.

"Don't be sorry! C'mon, let's find a big mirror and I'll show you how easy they are to put in."

The surprised young girl let Madison lead her into the nearby ladies' restroom.

Once inside, Madison moved like lightning tearing off the blond wig, the t-shirt, shoes, and the jeans, revealing the one-piece bathing suit she had kept on underneath Target's clothes.

She looked at the startled girl and kept her voice low.

"I'm going to give you my business card. Call me later, and I swear to you I'll send you a new pair of these contacts, but you've got to promise you'll stay in here for five extra minutes after I leave. I'm being followed and I need to blend into the crowd for now."

She pulled out her card from the pack and gave it to the girl.

The girl stared at the card. "Okay."

Madison flew through her quick-change as she threw on sandals from the backpack, the long-sleeved poolside cover-up, and pulled out the sunglasses, fabric beach bag, and big floppy hat that had been folded up inside the backpack. Her hair was still pinned up so the big floppy hat covered all her hair. She was now a zombie beachcomber.

The young girl said, "Um…be careful."

Target's clothes were quickly crammed into the backpack, then the backpack got shoved inside the fabric beach bag. Madison was transformed in under a minute. She took a quick look in the mirror, made sure everything was in place, and turned to leave.

She looked over her shoulder at the bewildered girl and said, "I promise."

Last, she put on the sunglasses and put her cell phone to her ear as if she were in a conversation. Walking out the door, she pretended to be chewing gum.

She hoped it would be enough to buy her a few moments. She knew they would figure it out fast but at least she might have a chance to get away and hide. It appeared that Jerry had agents both in street clothes and in costume, planted all around the convention. She hadn't expected that. *Stay sharp!*

Her right hand shook as she kept the phone to her ear, having a quiet, fake conversation, her left hand holding the fabric beach bag ties. Seeing through both the white contact lenses and sunglasses at the same time was a unique challenge. It was like looking through a foggy night.

She was dying to know if the zombie fairies were watching her, maybe coming after her, but she knew she shouldn't turn around to see.

The hallway was nearing an end, leading around a corner. As she approached the end of the hallway, she took the chance and looked over her shoulder as she was going around the corner and saw the zombie fairy with the woodland tunic from the elevator staring at her.

The cell phone whipped up to his face as he started walking in her direction. She ran around the corner, seeing a line of people going into one of the banquet rooms, and barged her way past the door attendants.

"Hey!" called one of the attendants. "Miss? Miss! You have to get in line."

He remained where he was stationed at the door, his arm outstretched across the fans pressing inward at the door. The fans hooted at her and called her rude names.

She hurried across the room trying to move around several tight clusters of people, each group seeking enough empty seats to enable their friends to sit together.

She ducked and dodged as she ran across the floor to the door on the other side of the room, where the last crowd had exited. Bursting through those doors, she ran down the hall, approaching a corner, and looked over her shoulder.

Bad move. She crashed into a big zombie hunter.

Most of the fans who chose to wear costumes to today's convention dressed up as zombies. But there was a small percentage who chose to dress up as zombie hunters, prowling the crowded hallways trying to stay in character.

They were in their glory, having more zombies to fake shoot than they'd ever dreamed of. It gave many zombies a chance to act out their death scenes, creating little moments of applause from these spontaneous, playful encounters. Madison knew thespians were harder to kill than zombies and suspected the boredom of standing in all these lines fueled it.

This particular zombie hunter was big and tall. He wore platform boots accentuating his height, and a long dark canvas coat with attached capelet. He had five days beard growth, scraggly dark hair, and a wide brim hat. An escapee from apocalypse school.

"What have we here?" he said as he caught Madison's arms, most likely to catch her from falling over from their impact, as she dropped the fabric beach bag that held Target's backpack. He seemed to be having fun with the moment.

Madison got into the moment with him.

"Thank God, I found you!" she said, straightening her floppy hat and picking up her fabric beach bag. "He's coming after me. Save me, please!"

Taking his cue like a pro, the big zombie hunter grabbed his plastic futuristic rifle from a huge leather holster on his back. "Today he infects his last. Show me this vile transmutation!"

Madison pointed behind her, "He's a zombie fairy." She leaned in, breaking character in a half-whisper so only he could hear. "And frankly the guy's an asshole," she said, rubbing her shoulder and wincing. "He's way too rough on the girls."

The zombie hunter nodded, whispering, "There's one in every crowd. I'll keep him away from you."

With a thousand-yard stare, he stood up to his full height, the business end of his plastic futuristic rifle pointed high in the sky, his mission clear. He bellowed, "To cleanse the earth!" and dove forward with his rifle just as the zombie fairy rounded the corner.

Madison fled. The double doors leading back to the main convention ballroom were in her line of sight.

The short burst of manly screaming behind her made her feel guilty, oh yes, but it made her run faster, too. No doubt it came from the zombie hunter, not from the zombie fairy. She also noted the following applause was louder than usual.

Rushing through the double doors, she ran down the aisle of black tablecloths, her eyes mapping out the open curves between the crowds where she could run.

A sharp turn down an opening between booths put her in another aisle where fans stood at the table fronts examining t-shirts, rubber brains, and lawn ornaments. She ran all the way down to the other end of the aisle before she ducked under the black skirt of the long table that held down the corner where two aisles intersected. She heard a female voice saying, "Did you see that? Some girl just went under the table."

The space under the first table was clear, allowing her to crawl on her hands and knees, dragging her bag behind her, barely able to see inside the darkened tunnel combined with her sunglasses and white contact lenses. But the next table had cross beams that supported the weight of the table. She crawled out to the side of the table where the vendors stood completing purchases with customers. If anyone saw her, she didn't know because she didn't stop to look. She kept crawling.

She saw the black curtain separating the space from the next vendor over. She stayed down on her hands and knees, speed crawling toward the curtain, lifting it with her hand and diving through.

She heard a buzzing sound.

She came out into a vendor booth where a red bearded tattoo artist sat with a customer, his tattoo gun putting the black outline of a new tattoo on his customer's arm. Madison was wedged between the black curtain and several boxes piled high enough to hide someone sitting on the floor, a temporary place to stay out of sight.

She needed help and she needed it now. She pulled out her phone to call for help, then stopped. If the tattoo artist heard her above the buzzing noise, she would be kicked out. Aaron Reed or the zombie fairies might see her. But a text message on her phone could be done silently. She hoped the message would be noticed soon enough to get help. She pulled off her sunglasses and looked up Jason's number.

Once again, she dearly wished she could hear his voice. He had a comforting presence that she'd barely gotten to know, and she wished she hadn't screwed it up with him in the many ways that she had. ExBoy might make her feel adventurous, but Jason made her feel safe. They both pulled at her primal drives, and even now she didn't know why her heart was so divided.

Text message: Jason, call DC agents. I need them fast! Hilton Hotel, Zombie Prom convention. You were right about the devil in the details.

The buzzing stopped.

She finished the text: And he's here at the convention.

She pressed Send.

"What the hell are you doing?"

She looked up, seeing the man with the red beard. The tattoo artist's face didn't look angry so much as perplexed as he looked down at her from over the tops of the boxes she was hiding behind.

"There's nothing back there of value," he said. "Be cool about it and go, or I'll call security."

"It's all right," she said. "I'll go."

She stood up, putting her sunglasses back on, and checking to see that her floppy hat was still secure. Most of the people in the aisle were in normal zombie fan activity mode. But a few were watching her. She heard that same female voice say, "That's her," but she wasn't sure who'd said it.

The urge to hide from Jerry's men and the urge to get away from this embarrassing situation were both strong motivators. Walking out of the booth, she realized the zombie fairies knew what her costume looked like now, so she needed to find somewhere she could hide.

She walked quickly, hoping to blend in with the crowd, but she kept running into people because she was looking behind herself so often. Just the act of bumping into so many people would bring unwanted attention after a while.

Looking down the aisle, she saw three welcome figures, but she didn't dare signal them. Atomic Waist, Dewey Decimator, and Sparkle Pecs were all in their wrestling costumes but with added zombie features on top of them. It was the rest of her surprise for ExBoy.

They were heading across the end of the aisle toward his booth on the other side of the convention. She dearly wished her life were normal right now so that she could join her friends in a relaxed afternoon of zombie silliness. She never cared for this stuff before, but right now it felt so childlike, so innocent and carefree compared to what she was dealing with.

She had to face the fact that the convention was no longer providing much cover for her and it was probably best if she got out of here. There must be a hundred places in this hotel that she could duck into while she waited for the DC agents to arrive.

Why hadn't they at least tried to call her after taking the metal box out of her apartment? Did her fairy godmother props being in the box make them think her grandfather was lying about evidence being in that box?

Surely not. They interviewed Mitch the next day, didn't they? So why hadn't they bothered with her?

She took a decisive turn at the end of the aisle, heading for the main entrance, watching over her shoulder. She couldn't wait to get these contact lenses out. Not only did they cloud her vision, her eyes were becoming uncomfortably dry.

As she neared the main entrance, she saw Aaron Reed. He was standing at the entrance talking on his cell phone, when he looked up and saw her. She had faith in her disguise and kept walking toward the entrance door, toward him.

He squinted at her and said, "Madison?"

She bolted in the opposite direction, and heard him call, "Madison, wait! You don't understand!"

She turned her head frantically from side to side, looking for a new door she hadn't tried. Seeing one in the back corner, she ran for it. She caused a stir in her wake, as well as in front of her. People stared wide-eyed at her as she ran towards them, commenting to one another. They pulled in their kids, getting out of the way.

With her feet pounding on the floor and her bag flying at her side, she arrived at the door. She stopped herself just in time not to crash. Her frantic hands plunged down on the push-bar in a fantastic metallic clap.

It was locked.

She plunged down again and again in a rapid rattle but it wouldn't budge.

She whirled around in a panic. Yanking off her sunglasses she saw the zombie fairies down at the other end of an aisle on her left. They spotted her and ran her way.

Way down the aisle on her right, she saw an arm waving at her, waving towards her as if to say, "get over here."

It was the red-haired woman, standing near an open door. In that split second, Madison knew she could no longer delay this meeting. She could no longer shove the question to the back of her mind and put off dealing with the possibility of who this woman was.

She ran full out toward the oddly familiar woman with the dark red hair, and as she came closer, she saw the woman's light green eyes.

Chapter Twenty-Nine

THEY RAN TOGETHER through the service entrance door, Madison following the quick figure in blue jeans and black t-shirt. The woman's body seemed strong and fit, though the quick glance at her face said she was older. Older certainly than what Madison had expected from the way this woman decisively dealt with those drunks the other night.

Though the hall was long and inviting to run down, the woman made a fast turn to the right into a much narrower hallway. With Madison in hot pursuit, she bounded up a small staircase, up to another level. They stopped on the landing to go through another door. All decorative wallpaper and carpeting was gone as they ran across a hard concrete floor. The walls were painted an old dirty white with black scratches where large bins or cleaning carts had scraped by many times.

Just as Madison thought her heart would pound through her chest with her lungs begging for more air, they ducked into a large closet. It was about five feet wide and ten feet deep, full of mops and vacuums. The redhead hit a light switch on the wall and slammed the door shut.

Sudden stillness, her breathing loud, her eyes slightly burning. She blinked, trying to moisten her dry eyes, vaguely wondering where she had dropped her sunglasses. All she could hear was their combined heavy breathing not quite in sync, and the occasional swallow.

Her brows knit in fear, not knowing how she should ask the question. She stared at the older woman, seeing a smile not quite there, an uncertainty in her expression. Madison didn't know how she would feel whether the answer were yes or no. She felt stupid that she had to ask. Just looking in the woman's eyes told her everything. Her eyes were like looking in the mirror thirty years from now.

Still breathing hard but more slowly, neither one of them spoke, each of them watching the other. Madison couldn't stand the burning dryness in her eyes any longer and wanted to get rid of the cloudy effect so she could see this woman better. She tilted her head down, using her fingers to gently pull off each contact lens. Relief flooded her eye sockets as she lifted her head, blinking furiously to moisten her eyes.

She resumed looking at the red haired woman and watched as the woman looked into Madison's eyes, back and forth, taking in both.

The woman's own light green eyes filled with tears, great pain in her expression. Her hand came up to her mouth. Then a little laugh escaped her. Joy seemed mingled with her pain. She said, "Malien 'kaia vnuchka."

Madison kept staring at her. "I'm sorry," she said between breaths. "I don't speak...whatever that was."

With a mild Russian accent, the woman said, "Forgive me, I am carried away. I said 'little granddaughter.'"

Madison stared at her. She started to nod, kept nodding, and started to cry.

The woman took a tentative step toward her, but Madison took an equal step back, stifling her tears. She didn't want anyone to take the place of Grandma, who had loved her—maybe a little too much—but nevertheless, loved and raised her.

But she saw instant hurt and embarrassment on the face of the woman, who backed up immediately, smoothing back her dark red hair, ducking her head and apologizing, saying, "I am sorry. I don't know how...to be."

Their breathing was coming a little easier. But Madison's heart was beating quickly for other reasons now. She didn't know this stranger and didn't know the ramifications for herself or for her mother. Would this woman's presence, her existence, make life even harder for Madison's family?

The only thing Madison could think to say was, "Please don't hurt my grandpa."

"Hurt him?" the woman said, her features taking on confusion at the request. "I would never hurt him," she said with conviction. "I would sooner kiss his feet."

"Wow," said Madison, shocked. Tears and a short laugh burst from her. "You shouldn't say that. You've haven't seen Grandpa's feet."

❖   ❖   ❖

ON A SMALL sofa in a hotel room, Madison sat up straight, her floppy hat sitting next to her on the sofa along with her fabric beach bag. She kept her elbows tight at her waist, her hands folded neatly in her lap. She tried to be the most prim and proper zombie she could possibly be. She questioned her own sanity. It was one thing to consent to come along with her newly introduced biological grandmother, Veronica Fedora. But it was quite another thing to be introduced to Vladik Sakharovsky.

His Russian accent was much heavier than the woman's accent.

"And her eyes. Did not I tell you?" He looked at Madison as if marveling. "The moment I saw them, I knew." He turned to a wall mirror, looking at the bruise on the side of his face, saying, "You should have seen her, Nika, fierce look on her face." He turned away from the mirror. "You would have been proud."

Veronica Fedora, nicknamed Nika, sat on the opposite side of the room from Madison, in a chair by the desk. "I am already proud. She makes people smile, for her living. Few are so gifted."

He laughed. "All I know is she has passion of mama bear protecting those she loves, just like her grandmother." He delicately touched the bruise on the side of his head, the discoloration having spread into his short grey hair.

Madison was not used to feeling self-conscious. But these two really knew how to bring it out in her. She cleared her throat. "Yeah, about that." She could hardly bring herself to look in Vladik's face. "I don't normally go around hitting people with a drill like that." She could see him start to smile again. "But you looked like you were trying to kill my grandfather. That's not cool."

"No," he said, "It was not...cool. I would not have killed him, but my temper did escape me. I am sorry for that. I think now that he was right, your grandfather, but in moment of fight, I feared he would get us all killed."

"How so?" asked Madison.

"Because I did not think he understood how powerful Jerry Rosser is. I feared for his life, thinking

Vincent Cruz would not arrive in Washington DC. If Jerry found cause to take one of us out, it could go like domino." Vladik pointed his finger as if his hand were a gun shooting each of them, one at a time, including himself. "As it is, your grandfather is lucky that Jerry did not figure out what he was doing."

Hearing Jerry referred to in such a super villain way was terrifying to Madison. He had come and gone at will in her family's home over the years. To think of him as being that cold-blooded, with the power to back it up, was hard to fathom. But she was getting to the point where she felt it would be too dangerous not to take this seriously.

"Vladik, do not frighten her," said Nika.

"She should know," he said flatly. "She has proven she will fight back if needed. She would want to know."

Madison had to admit, yes, she did want to know.

From the desk, Vladik picked up the key card that went to the door to the room. "I should hurry," he said, and headed for the door.

"Wait," said Madison. "If you believed Jerry would never let Grandpa make it to DC, then what was your solution? How did you want to handle Jerry?

Vladik shrugged his shoulders. He said, "Kill him." He looked over at Nika. "Like I should have done many years ago." He walked out, letting the door close with a heavy thump.

The shock of what Vladik said was still sinking in when Madison looked at Nika.

"I am sorry you are hearing these rough words. Vladik is good man."

Again Madison questioned her own sanity about the company she was keeping right now. "But he also said that now he thinks my grandfather was right. Didn't he?"

"Yes. I, too, have great hopes that it will finally be over. I am anxious to meet my daughter."

Your daughter? Strange to hear someone refer to her mother in such a personal way.

"Why did you break into my car?"

"I was seeking your name on registration in glove compartment. That is how I knew you were somehow related to Vincent Cruz. Then when Vladik told me color of your eyes...well, it was shock."

Madison hesitated to speak while her thoughts were still warring within her. She fought the urge to hug, to accuse, to demand answers, to comfort, all of it spiced with burning curiosity about this new person. There was so much as yet unexplained. She took a deep breath, and started with the thing that bothered her the most.

"Why did you leave without your baby?"

Nika leaned forward in her chair, seeming to search the floor for the answers she needed, her elbows on the knees of her designer jeans, her hands clasped.

Madison vaguely wondered if her clothes came from Russia or the United States. They seemed so fashionable, not like the stereotype that Madison had in her mind of Russian life. Yet this modern woman, so beautiful, strong, and capable, seemed reduced somehow, drawn inward as if better answers might be found inside, if only she would look one more time.

"This is hard to..." Nika searched for words, "...to succeed in understanding, but Vladik had to do all he could to protect us. Our group at exposition, his own family back home... We were all so vulnerable. If word got out that Soviet student gave birth while on tour, it would have humiliated our country for all world to see, sabotaging image we were there to portray. We were supposed to be shining example of proud Soviet dream."

Nika's face had an urgent tension that Madison couldn't look away from.

"This was no small thing in days of Soviet Union. Power struggles never cease. An embarrassment of that magnitude could be used to topple careers in high places, followed by revenge for those who caused it, or failed to prevent it."

Madison tried to recall everything she'd read in the old newspaper articles. "But the tour was only two months long. Why would you go, knowing you were pregnant?"

"This is part of what is hard to see. I was fourteen, in love with boy back home, and so naive I didn't know I was pregnant until I went into labor. I was embarrassed, thinking I was getting fat, so I dressed to hide it." She looked around the room, sighing like it all sounded so pointless now.

She continued, "Jerry Rosser was assigned as our Seattle docent, but we assumed he was actually FBI, just as they probably knew that Vladik was KGB. The night I went into labor, he was out in hotel hallway watching everyone panic as they ran in and out of my room. He knew we were in trouble. He told Vladik he would hold off reporting it if Vladik told him what was happening. Vladik thought we were doomed anyway, so he told him. Then Jerry offered to take baby in exchange for great deal of money. Vladik agreed, and I hated him for many years. But after working in KGB myself, watching struggle within politburo, I finally understood danger he was trying to save us from."

"So how did the baby wind up on the grounds of the University of Washington?"

"Jerry said it was more believable if newborn was found at girl's dormitories. He was supposed to wait and see who found my baby so we could track her, to smuggle her out later."

Nika lapsed into silence for a while, then stood up, walking over to the long curtains on the wall. She pushed them open, revealing sliding glass doors overlooking a balcony. She said, "He lied. Or perhaps he changed his mind, but he withheld secret."

The hot Seattle sun reflected off the metal railing surrounding the balcony, an unforgiving light, harsh on the window panes. Restless, Nika turned to walk back across the room, nowhere to go.

Madison hated herself for pushing on, making this stranger relive and regret. "What happened after that?"

"Jerry had taste of money. He demanded more. But only way Vladik could get his hands on that kind of money was if he could convince KGB that Jerry was valuable informant. Jerry agreed and became double agent."

Madison's eyes went wide. A double agent? And all while being promoted through the ranks of the FBI.

"Vladik was his handler, but no one truly understood that it was Jerry who was handling Vladik. Even after KGB was disbanded and FSB took over, he and Vladik each had secrets against each other. They used those secrets to keep each other in line all these years. To keep *me* in line." She turned around, facing Madison. "But I am not going to stay in line any longer."

Comprehension hit.

"It's Jerry's retirement, isn't it?" Madison asked. She brought a hand to her stomach. "That's what made you guys start searching," she said. "He's going to retire and no longer have access to the information. No more information, no more money, no more protection. All he has is my mother. And she doesn't know."

She stood up from the sofa with an anxious reach for the fabric beach bag that held her cell phone. Her frantic hands dug through it. "That's why Vladik was going to kill him. Once you two located my mother and told her the truth, you knew she would have to turn him in. But not if he killed her first!"

Her hand wrapped around her cell phone as Nika came over and grabbed Madison's wrists, bringing them upward out of the bag.

"Madison, no—"

Madison flinched at this sudden physical intervention, her face a foot away from Nika's face, eyes so much like Madison's own but with many years on them, pain within them, but coolly determined nonetheless.

Madison froze, uncertain of what was at play. She pleaded, "I have to warn my mother. Please! You can't just—"

The door opened, and Madison's head turned sharply to plead with Vladik as well. But although Vladik was indeed walking in, he had company.

In walked the two zombie fairies.

Chapter Thirty

MADISON THRUST BOTH of her elbows upward, slamming Nika's chin as her wrists yanked free of Nika's half-hearted grip.

"*Uhh!*" Nika's breath cut off as her teeth clicked. She doubled over, holding her chin.

Madison ran for the balcony and tore the sliding glass door open.

A big hand from the shorter zombie fairy came down on her shoulder. He was the first one she had seen in the elevator. "I'm Special Agent Riley—"

With a flood of adrenaline, she shoved her elbow backward and made contact with something hard that produced a growl. She tried to run out onto the balcony but felt arms go around her waist. She pulled at his iridescent hands, trying to pry his fingers open, seeing an FBI badge in his hand fall to the floor while she bucked and rocked.

"Stop it!" his deep voice ordered, as he pulled her back in. Holding her so her feet couldn't touch the ground, he turned around, facing Madison into the room. "You need to listen, young—"

She reached behind her head trying to scratch his face. He whipped his head back and forth avoiding her fingernails.

As the second zombie fairy in the Edwardian tailcoat approached the scuffle, she lifted her feet in the air and kicked, grazing his groin.

Vladik laughed in the corner as the second zombie fairy dropped his badge, too, and a wand, and held his groin for a second. His face reddened and he snatched for her feet. She screamed.

Nika grabbed Agent Riley's arms, releasing Madison, yelling, "Get away from her! You have no finesse!"

Madison couldn't see what Nika did behind her to produce a shout of pain from him, but he let go.

Nika yelled, "Vnuchka! It's all right! Do not be afraid!"

Vladik's laughter got louder as the second zombie fairy put his arms up to fend off a flurry of slaps from Madison. He managed to pin her arms to her sides as she tried stomping on his feet. He lifted her off the ground as he grunted out, "I'm Special Agent Cole. Jesus!"

"You don't have to get rough!" said Agent Riley, turning to face Nika as he pulled his leather tunic back down, the redness in his face coming through the iridescent makeup. "We're being gentle with her. Let us handle—" His back was to Madison as she kicked out again, making contact with the gossamer wings on his back.

"Hey!" he said turning around, his deep voice saying, "Don't hurt my little wings." He winked. "I'm sure you don't want them broken when I give them back to you."

She came to a dead stop, breathing heavily. She looked down at the wand on the floor that Agent Cole had dropped along with his badge. It had a rhinestone star at the tip just like hers. Agent Cole released her.

She knew it was no coincidence. She'd put her fairy godmother props in the metal box, and now two grown men with sparkly skin and pointy ears were using identical props at Zombie Prom. They had to be the FBI Special Agents from headquarters in DC.

Shaking from her fright, her mouth hanging open, she looked back and forth at the undead fairies in their professional quality costumes and zombie makeup. Her voice came out in a high pitch as she said, "*Seriously?*"

Not holding back his laughter, with a hand on his red face Vladik said, "What did I tell you? Fierce little bear!"

Agent Riley shrugged as he and Agent Cole looked at each other. "We thought you'd pick up on it right away," said Agent Riley. "We were trying to give you signals."

"You couldn't *call* me?"

"No."

"Why not?"

Nika said, "For same reason I couldn't let you call your mother. They believe Jerry Rosser has tapped your phone."

It took a moment for this news to sink in. She was worn out from all the fright, the running, the incomprehensible stories of human foibles and suffering. And now the local super villain was listening in on her phone calls. *Well, that's just…peachy.*

"Wait," said Madison, "wait." The situation in front of her finally registered in her brain. She stared around at the four people occupying the same room. "You're working together?" She turned to Agent Riley. "And why didn't you tell me who you were when we got in the elevator?"

"We didn't know for certain what kind of surveillance he had," said Agent Riley, "or if he was using any agents from the Seattle Field Division. We needed a safe moment to present ourselves to you but had to stay nearby, just in case."

"I saw Aaron Reed out there," said Madison. "I think he's working with Jerry."

"No," said Agent Cole. "Agent Reed is here with your mother."

"My mother is here?"

"Well, down in the convention, yes. Looks like she's searching for you. From the way she's looking at people, she doesn't seem too happy."

"Yeah, I don't think she likes zombies," said Agent Riley.

Agent Cole's cell phone rang. He pulled it out of a pocket from inside his Edwardian tailcoat, and stepping away he talked quietly into it.

"Why is she searching for me?" Madison asked Agent Riley. "How'd she even know I was here?"

"Unclear. It wasn't part of her orders, so we're still trying to confirm all this."

After hanging up, Agent Cole came back, speaking to Agent Riley. "We take Agents Cruz and Reed to the other room. Headquarters says to go ahead and brief them." He paused for a second and said, "And that other thing. That's a go, too."

"Other room?" Madison asked, "Is that where my grandfather is?"

Agent Cole said, "Yes. We'll be taking your mother to him soon."

Madison was quiet. Her grandfather was going to sit Ann down and try to explain his part in all this. She tried to imagine how he would say it, the look on her mother's face. "I have to go, too," said Madison. "I want to be with them."

"Actually, we'd like to get you back out on the convention floor," said Agent Riley.

Madison studied him. "Why don't you save me the trouble of figuring out what I don't know? I've been trying to play along. I've been a good girl—"

"Hah!" said Agent Cole.

"…mostly."

The zombie fairies looked at each other. Agent Riley said, "I think we've covered it, wouldn't you say?"

"No. There's that…thing."

"Oh, yeah."

"What thing?" asked Madison.

"You tell her. I think she likes you more," said Agent Riley.

"Are you kidding?" said Agent Cole. "She tried to kick me in the nuts."

"What thing!"

Exasperated, Nika interrupted. "What is matter with you Americans? She has no training, no experience. You think you are all cowboy? You will ride in and save her?"

Vladik stepped up. "I also do not like this thing."

Agent Cole said, "It's not up to me. And Madison gets final decision, anyway."

"What. Thing?"

"They want to use you as bait," said Nika.

Surprised, Madison said, "Why?"

"Two things," said Agent Riley. "We were already investigating Jerry Rosser for double agent activity. Your mother is part of our team. We even suspected a connection to Vladik Sakharovsky, but we've been looking for proof. The second thing is that even if your grandfather's story turns out to be true, his story is about an illegal adoption and blackmail. Not for money in this case but for silence and occasional access to the home to monitor the childhood and early adulthood of the child in question. The connecting factor for us was Vladik showing up to discuss how to end the blackmail for both of them."

"Sorry for getting impatient," said Madison, "but what does that have to do with me?"

Agent Riley said, "For their final exchange, Jerry offered you to Vladik."

Madison stared at him for a second, her face crinkled up. "That doesn't make sense. Even if he could catch me, I'm the least important person in this whole mess." She looked around at the dubious faces. "Think about it. I wasn't there when my mother was born. I'm not a witness. I can't testify—"

Agent Cole's quiet voice broke in. "Agent Cruz would do anything to keep you safe."

Madison turned and studied him.

He added, "Once she found out about it, she would say or do anything Jerry wanted to back up any alibi he came up with. So would your grandfather. They would both be quiet and uncooperative if they thought talking would bring you harm. We'd never get testimony out of your grandfather, or..." he looked over at Nika, "or your grandmother, I imagine."

Nika agreed, "No, you would not."

Madison went still. She'd never thought of any of this before. She'd never want her family to fear for her safety.

"To me," said Vladik, growling in his heavy Russian accent, "this is disgusting thought. He thinks I am that kind of man. He sees only his own motives."

Agent Riley said, "But that's why this will work, Vladik, because he thinks you're just like him. We'll honor our agreement with you, if you continue to help us with this."

"I have already said I would. I did not come all this way to wish Jerry happy retirement. I did grave injustice to Veronica Fedora." He put his arm around Nika. "We have tried many times over years to find her little Anzhela, but this time it worked. I will see this through."

Madison walked over to Nika and took her hand, saying, "I don't know much about you, but I'd like to.

When this is all over, let's get to know each other. All right?"

Nika nodded but stood still. Remembering her own reaction to Nika in the hotel broom closet, Madison realized that it was up to her to break the ice now. She opened her arms to Nika, who smiled, coming forward, and Madison enjoyed the most heartfelt hug she'd had in a while.

"I'm sorry I hit your chin with my elbows. I got so scared; I didn't understand what was going on."

Nika chuckled, wiping tears from her eyes. "You completely surprised me. It was good move."

"So," said Madison, turning to Agent Riley, "how would this work?"

"Vladik will bring him the money, they'll have a chummy drink together like they usually do, then Jerry will call you to come meet him, somewhere here in the hotel. We don't know how he intends to convince you, but he told Vladik he can guarantee you'll show up. I'll be nearby the whole time. He'll hand you over to Vladik and you'll go with him. Vladik will be wired, so we'll hear the whole conversation." He added, "Then I'll take you to see your grandfather. He'll be with Agent Cole."

"So I'm supposed to go back down to the convention floor and wait for Jerry's call?"

"That's right," he said. "But one last thing, we still need the contents of that metal box. Your grandfather listed a lot of things that were supposed to be in there. A couple of them could be helpful."

"Oh. Well, it's downstairs in the convention. When I switched clothes with Target, I gave her my tote bag to take with her."

Agent Cole said, "We'll take it all off your hands as soon as we can."

✧   ✧   ✧

NO WHITE CONTACT lenses or sunglasses, and her dark hair was no longer pinned up. She had it hanging down underneath her big floppy hat. She carried her phone in one hand, the fabric beach bag in the other. She wished she could change out of her zombie bathing suit and the poolside cover-up. She was tired of her zombie costume and the liquid latex wounds had started to itch.

Agent Cole had taken her mother and Aaron to meet with Grandpa and Nika. Maybe Aaron would give the other three a little privacy. They were going to need it.

With Agent Riley down the aisle from her, she had to force herself not to look in his direction. As she wandered the convention, undead life having gone on without her presence, she wondered what she should say to her friends. She longed for normal life, surprised to realize it had only been a few days since everything had turned upside down.

Maybe she shouldn't go to ExBoy's booth. There would be uncomfortable questions and even more uncomfortable answers. No, as it was, they were probably having a great time. She wanted to keep it that way for them.

Stepping around a stroller containing a rosy-cheeked cherub of a baby boy, she exchanged a quick smile with the mother. The little guy was somewhere in that in-between age, not quite an infant but barely a toddler. He was passed out cold, his head tilted to the side, pink little heart-shaped lips in a wet pucker. His small hand clutched a soggy cookie while a favored toy lay forgotten in his lap. Something about his peaceful oblivion brought tears to Madison's eyes. She wanted to feel like that, perhaps watching a field of flowers bending in the breeze or a litter of puppies at play. But no, instead of puppies, she got Uncle Enemy.

She had to get a grip. Her part in all this was not done.

Trying to appear as if everything were normal, she stopped at a table, feigning interest in baking molds in the shapes of brains, skulls, and single bones. Picking one up, she turned it over, pretending to examine it while she wondered when Jerry would call. Did he know where she was right now?

Feeling impatient to get the meeting over, Madison exhaled loudly. *If he doesn't call soon, I'm going to go out of my—*

A gentle voice said, "Madison."

Toonie stepped up, her chef's costume still in perfect zombie condition. "Your mother's been worried." She looked around the nearby area, adding, "Did she find you yet?"

"Not exactly," said Madison, feeling self-conscious again, taking off her hat.

"We all split up," said Toonie. "Everyone is looking."

"Who's everyone?" asked Madison.

"Your mother and a nice young fella named Aaron something and all your friends." She gave her a wry smile. "You sure have some interesting friends."

"Why is my mom looking for me?"

"She got a call from ExBoy. He told her about Target coming back to tell us you had to hide from someone, that you were so scared you had to disguise yourself. She heard you talk to him on the phone, calling him Jerry." She looked at Madison for a second, thoughts going by unspoken. She added, "We were all under strict orders not to call your cell phone. What's that about?"

Looking around, Madison said, "This isn't a good place to talk about it." She started them walking, saying, "Come on. Let's start by meeting up at the booth."

Still down the aisle a way from ExBoy's *Infect Me* booth, she could see Target and Crystal in conversation, worried looks on their faces. Target looked up and saw Madison. Madison could make out the words on Target's lips saying, "Oh, thank God." Target looked over her shoulder at ExBoy, saying something to him. Madison girded herself, seeking access to her most confident face. Time to look strong.

ExBoy turned his head for a moment from customers browsing his artwork in the long comic book boxes on the table. He saw Madison approaching before he bent to sign the inside cover of a copy of *Infect Me*. Target said something to him, gesturing towards Madison with her hand, and he nodded. It looked as if Target was taking over the money exchange to free him up for a minute.

But he stood there instead next to the Victorian grandfather clock, a slight smirk on his face, looking sexy as ever as he watched Madison approach. Madison wondered what he had to smirk about.

Then, from around the grandfather clock, out stepped Jason, his expression deeply worried till he saw her and his eyes locked with hers. Relief flooded his face.

Her pace went into slow motion with her shock, losing all the girded up strength she had summoned. The bag dropped.

He caught her as she ran into his arms, tears and zombie makeup smearing the t-shirt on his chest. She looked up at him, her green eyes wet, trying to understand what he was doing here. "I thought you'd be all wrapped up in the next pretty girl," she said.

"You *are* the next pretty girl," he said. "And the next." Turning his face away, his soft expression went hard and smug as he looked over at ExBoy saying, "This is exactly what it looks like."

"Just because she ran to you?" said ExBoy. "Want to use my room? Her things are already in there."

"Stop it!" said Madison. "There's no time. Something serious is…" Then realization grew, her blunder becoming clear. She looked at Jason. "You're here because I sent you that text." *Jerry would have seen it.* She looked around in a panic. Where was Agent Riley? He should be told.

"I couldn't get here fast enough," said Jason. "My grandfather couldn't remember where he'd put the phone number those federal agents gave him. He was still looking for it when I left. I saw your mom when I got here and joined the search, then she asked me to wait here at the booth."

Target stepped up, giving Madison a hug while Madison said, "I'm sorry to put you all through this."

"You'd do it for us in a heartbeat," said Target, "and we all know that."

Madison craned her neck over the crowds. Agent Riley was on his cell phone, storming up the aisle towards her, his expression furious.

He arrived in a huff, saying, "I just got a call from Mitch Clark. You sent a text? You mentioned DC?" He yelled, "What the hell were you thinking?"

ExBoy inserted himself between them. "Hey, fairy ass, back off!"

"I'm sorry!" said Madison over ExBoy's shoulder to Agent Riley. "I sent it before you told me about the phone tapping."

"Why didn't you tell us?" he yelled.

Without saying a word, Jason shoved him hard, and Agent Riley almost came at him, but controlled himself at the last second. With one hand on his hip, and the other rubbing his forehead, he said, "We were thinking of calling if off anyway. Your little family reunion went badly, with your mother storming out. She could ruin this if she's seen. Your grandfather went after her, we don't know where Veronica went, and Vladik is already with Jerry." He tossed his hands in the air as he groused, "They only sent two of us, and we can't babysit everyone!"

He pointed at her, his voice still angry. "So you stay here while we sort out this mess." He stormed off.

Just then, the phone in Madison's hand started ringing with the theme music to *Jaws*. Embarrassed that she still hadn't changed the ringtone to something nicer for her mother, she confessed, "That's my mom calling. Oh God what am I going to say to her?"

She looked up at her perplexed friends, knowing there would be a lot of explaining to do, but right now, her mother was more important.

She took a deep breath, calming herself as much as was possible, and answered. She was not prepared for what she heard.

From her cell phone, Jerry's voice said, "Listen and don't react. We wouldn't want your new little fairy friends to get too excited."

Chapter Thirty-One

"WE'LL KEEP IT simple. Vladik tells me there was an interesting box that you rushed out of Vincent's house with," said Jerry. "I'm very curious about it. Now nod your head and say I understand, Mom."

Madison nodded her head, her voice coming out small, "I understand, Mom."

"Very good," he said. "You know, she tried her best for you, but you were an ungrateful little shit. I almost felt sorry for her. There she was, brilliant like her mother, but stuck with you. I'll bet you never apologized to her. Why don't you do so now? Say, I'm sorry, Mom."

Fear was making her voice shake. "I'm sorry, Mom."

"Well," he said, "I guess some of it is the influence of this generation. They don't grow them like they used to. Even this newer generation of agents is a joke. It's been so easy to play these guys." He sighed. "Ah, well. Fun's almost over. Now ask your mom when you can see her."

"Mom?" Madison's voice shook, "When can I see you?"

"Well now that depends. Would you like to see some blue satin gowns?"

"What?" Like a bad dream where unrelated things added to the confusion, Madison tried to grasp his meaning. "Blue satin gowns?" Target stepped closer.

"Yes, they're quite lovely. Bring the contents of that box, and you'll get to see them."

Madison looked up at Target, worry reflected in her eyes. She looked around inside ExBoy's booth, and spotted her tote bag that Target had taken with her when they'd switched clothes and bags that morning. "Okay," said Madison, trying to smooth the expression on her face while she picked up the tote bag, putting the straps over her shoulder.

"Wonderful. Say, I'll rush right over."

She couldn't look any of her friends in the eyes as they watched her, confused. She said, "I'll rush right over."

"There's a lovely wedding reception going on right now," said Jerry. "It's up on the second floor. You should sit with your Uncle Jerry for a spell. Say, that sounds great, Mom, just the two of us."

Madison cleared her throat, trying to regain control. "That sounds great, Mom. Just the two of us."

"And so we understand each other; if you really do want to see your mother again, you'll get your little ass up here, alone, in less than three minutes. I suggest the stairs. The elevators are prone to having fairies in them." He hung up.

She sprang down the aisle not seeing or caring about the destruction she left behind her. People were pushed aside, packages dropped, drinks splashed, and brain-shaped gelatin treats smashed to the floor. Holding her right arm down tight on the tote bag at her side, she ignored the numerous bruises being born on her legs and hips as she rounded corners a little too tight. Painful table edges left marks.

Like a bad dream in her peripheral vision, the chaos in her wake held no urgency compared to the greater nightmare waiting at the finish line. She flew out of the main convention doors, back out into the main lobby of the hotel. *How much time? How much time has passed?*

She came to a stop that wasn't really a stop since she was hopping up and down, shifting her weight left to right to left again, as she whipped her head around, searching the periphery of the lobby, seeking the stairs. An agonized cry broke from her throat when she couldn't see stairs anywhere.

"No!" She spun around in time to see a young woman wearing a long strapless gown in sapphire blue satin, just like the ones in the elevator that morning.

The young woman had entered the main lobby from a hallway. Madison bolted for that hallway, racing so closely past the woman that a stroke of her leg slapped the edge of the satin gown, causing it to snap like a flag in fierce wind.

Running down the hallway, her hope elevated as she saw that although this direction had more people and was harder to navigate, many of them were well-dressed as if they might be attending a wedding reception.

She dodged and pivoted around the wedding guests, looking frantically for the stairs, finally spotting them. They were wide and carpeted with an elegant balustrade of dark wood, the type of staircase intended for making a grand entrance. Madison tried to fly up the stairs, attempting to take two steps at a time, but the steps were simply too deep for her stride. She ran one step at a time keeping away from the inner balustrade where most of the people ascending or descending had chosen to cluster.

Gasping for air, her burst of speed spent, Madison pushed onward as fast as she could, arriving at the mid-level landing. Easier running across the long flat landing allowed her a moment to look upward to see the well-dressed population thicken at the next level. Music floated down to her.

As she arrived at the top of the stairs, a few heads turned her way, with a smile or a confused look. But some seemed to be making a statement by ignoring her so pointedly. No doubt the word had spread by now that there was a zombie convention going on downstairs, and one stray zombie wouldn't ruin their fun. The tinkling of ice could be heard from the varying cocktails being held by the guests in the hallway, an open bar somewhere on this floor doing a brisk business.

Madison felt a new terror growing as she suddenly realized she didn't know where to go from here. She had arrived at the open doors of the wedding reception. But now what?

Breathing heavily, her legs weak from the run, she stepped past the doors into the party. A male singer with too much reverb in the mix was crooning an old lounge jazz standard accompanied by a keyboardist, light on his fingers. The beat of the drummer's brushes lent an attitude of old time cool.

A small dance floor in front of the band held guests in fine attire, pulling out their best moves and grooves. A few of those sapphire blue gowns tried to shake what was covered by all that satin.

On the edges of the dance floor were dozens of large round tables. Each table seated eight to ten, small islands of crisp white linen with flowered centerpieces. Clear plastic forks, leftover cake and drinks, or a jeweled evening handbag here and there were on the tabletops.

A mirror ball at the ceiling spun, throwing little lights over the tables, dancers, and band.

Laughter, music, and the occasional pop of yet another bottle of champagne, blended with the singer's voice. And someone, somewhere in the crowd, sang along off-key while others begged him to stop.

A woman slapped a man not too far from where Madison stood, angry accusations drowned out by the man's voice claiming the lady in his arms was the one kissing him.

Madison cried out a quick burst when Jerry suddenly stepped up alongside her, putting his arms around her with jovial laughter as if he'd just understood her joke. Guests nearby gave polite chuckles as if they'd heard the joke and understood it, too. He then led her to one of the round tables in the corner of the room.

Sitting on the white tablecloth beside the flowered centerpiece were a few small plates with the remnants of wedding cake. The icing was left with crumbles on the plates. There were a few glasses with a bit of amber colored drink left at the bottom. Jerry appeared to have the table all to himself at the moment.

Incredulous at his gall and feeling angry with herself for letting her fear show, she raised her chin and said, "How did you manage to get yourself invited here?"

He smiled, then shook with quiet laughter. "I'm not invited. I'm a dignified old man in an expensive suit, who acts hard of hearing. They probably think I'm someone's great-uncle."

"Where's my mother?"

"Don't you mean where's Vladik? I'm supposed to give you to him, you know."

"I'm more interested in where my mother is."

"We'll get to that. First, I'm going to introduce you to Vladik Sakharovsky," he said, his expression cold and indifferent. "Oh, wait, I forgot. You already met, then lied to me about it."

Madison had never seen this side of Jerry before, and it frightened her to see a childhood assumption so thoroughly wrong. "You wanted what was in that box. Well, here it is." She slammed the tote bag down on the table. "I want my mom."

The band changed to another song with a harder rock beat. Guests were switching out on the dance floor, some sitting back down while others sprang up.

"That's not how you're supposed to play this," he said with a mock disapproving tone. "I'm afraid you wouldn't have made a very good spy. Not like your mother, or your grandmother, for that matter. Those two are naturals. Must have skipped a generation."

A small scuffle broke out on the dance floor; the need for some of the guests to blow off some steam had other guests running up trying to stop the fight, and barely succeeding.

Standing up, Jerry said, "Very well, then. Come on."

Putting the tote bag back on her shoulder, she followed him along the edge of the room, heading in the direction of the band as the dance floor got crowded, then past the band, down a short empty hall to a closed door. He unlocked the door, holding it open so Madison could pass through.

Out of habit when a man held a door open for her, she walked through, cursing herself for not being more careful. But the room looked harmless enough. There were chairs stacked on top of each other in the far corner on one side of the room. This seemed to be the room where the hotel stored the chairs being used at the reception party.

On the other side of the room was a long flat push cart used to transport the heavy stacks of chairs to other banquet rooms. Currently there were linens and tablecloths haphazardly thrown on the floor in the corner by the cart.

She heard the door close and click, as if it locked. She turned around, seeing Jerry smiling, walking towards her. She tensed up, ready to fight, but he walked right past her.

"You should take some time to get to know Vladik. You'll like him. He's a lot of laughs when he's feeling up to it, but he drank something that didn't agree with him."

He walked over to the pile of linens in the back and pulled up a corner of one of the tablecloths.

There was Vladik's body.

"Hmm," said Jerry. "I guess he's not feeling up to it anymore."

Shock and nausea hit Madison, seeing him on the floor again like when he'd been unconscious in her grandfather's house. But this time he wasn't unconscious. He was dead.

She put her hand over her mouth, backing up into the wall. She heard a blend of ringing in her ears and rowdy party outside as the band's driving beat came through the walls.

Jerry observed her coolly. "Do you understand now? Vladik outlived his usefulness because he wouldn't do as he was told anymore. But you're going to be smart and do everything I say, aren't you?" From his front coat pocket, he pulled out a small revolver. "You don't want to wind up dead."

Madison yelled in her fright, "What have you done with my mom? Where is she?"

"I don't know. I don't have her. I don't need her, if I have you."

Madison blinked. "What do you mean you don't have her? How'd you get her phone?"

"I didn't. I made the wrong caller ID show up on your phone when I called you," he said, then shrugged. "I used a phone app."

Madison shook her head no. She couldn't believe it was that simple.

"Yes," he said. "And tracking you was just as easy. There's a GPS built into your phone. All I needed was the device ID."

She remembered when he had her phone at the FBI building. He was supposed to be putting in his phone number.

The rowdy party outside was still muffled but getting louder, stronger. The music broke off in an odd staccato way, with each instrument out of sync.

She felt lightheaded.

He said, "Now this is how it's going to go. We're going to leave this room. I'll have the gun in my pocket, like this." He put it away. "You're going to understand that this is very real, and that you might survive this if you're smart and do as you're told. This could go very easy for you," he said, patting his pocket. "But don't get me wrong," he gestured over to Vladik's body, "I didn't mind feeding that drink to old Vladik, but it's inconvenient. It causes other problems. But if blood is called for, then it's all the way. No impressive wounds that heal in time. There won't be any healing from this. You either cooperate and get through it, or you don't and you die." He pulled out the key, unlocking the door. "Pretty straightforward really."

Madison looked down at her tote bag, saying, "So you don't really care about all the evidence that Grandpa saved against you all these years?"

He laughed, "Oh, I can't wait. This should be rich," he said. "Dump it all out."

She pulled the tote bag off her shoulder, bracing herself. With one hand, she turned it over like a teapot spilling its contents to the floor.

In a rush the contents poured out. The large envelope of old pictures from Jerry's past, a small makeup kit, CDs of music for Madison's singing telegram gigs, cell phone, purse, car keys, the sad stained tablecloth and towel, the flattened cardboard box, the paperwork all clipped together, and… the prop handgun tumbled out.

Like lightning, Madison caught it before it hit the ground, aiming at his face, just feet away from him but out of his reach. He had started to reach for his gun but froze.

"Okay, you son of a bitch!" She clutched the fake handgun in both hands, arms straight, feet apart, knees slightly bent, just like she'd practiced in the mirror at home. "You get a chance to run, keeping your little gun in your pocket so no one will notice you. Remember, blood is inconvenient. It causes other problems. You keep it quiet and uneventful, you might get away after all. There's no one here to chase you. You'll be ignored. And I'm not going to chase you because you have a gun."

She aimed the prop gun carefully at his head, keeping distance between them and putting as much intensity into her voice as she could, although it didn't take much pretending. "Otherwise, I shoot you in the head right here and now." Gesturing toward the door with the prop gun, she said, "Do it."

He didn't move. Instead, he stood there studying her, his eyes weighing.

Damn it!

"Move!" she screamed. She tried doing that crazed one-eye twitch she'd seen in so many movies where the bad guy was clearly losing his shit, about to blow his top. "Do it NOW asshole!"

That got some movement. His lips pressed hard together like he was pissed as he put his hand on the doorknob, then he stopped. He looked back at her, seeming to make a choice, and said, "I don't think so."

"Well, you'd better think again!"

She took a risk and tried getting closer to him, letting him see the gun get nearer and nearer, hoping he would try to take it from her.

He went for the bait and lunged for the gun as Madison let it flip into the air, his body weight diving forward with his hands trying to catch the prop gun.

She ducked downward, her hand diving into his pocket grabbing the small revolver as he caught the prop gun. Their feet tangled at that instant.

Jerry almost lost his balance, one leg lurching forward to catch himself.

Madison tripped, her body and the real gun both tumbling to the ground and skidding towards the door.

She scrabbled to her knees, speed crawling to the gun.

From behind her, Jerry yelled, "Freeze!"

She snatched the real gun as she sprang up, grabbing the doorknob, looking over her shoulder at Jerry. The prop gun was expertly aimed at her, but his brows were creased, looking down at the prop in his hands.

The truth, a bitch slap on his face.

His shocked eyes whipped up at her.

She shrugged and said, "Spy blood."

Then she ran out the door as screams from the party room hit her ears.

Chapter Thirty-Two

OUT IN THE party room, there was a different sort of fight going on which accounted for all the screams and muffled chaos she'd heard through the walls. Not having any pockets and not wanting anyone to see the small revolver, she shoved it down the front of her zombie one-piece bathing suit as she ran down the short hallway, pulling her poolside cover-up closed to help hide it.

Almost to the end of the hallway, she slid to a stop as a round table flew in her direction and landed at the entryway to the hall, falling to its side and rolling, blocking her exit. She shoved the table out of her way, seeing a full blown riot of wedding guests and angry zombies playing out in front of her.

Dashing across the hostile room, she dove under one of the other tables, eager to call for help before Jerry got away. But... *No!* She didn't have her cell phone. It had dumped onto the floor when she'd emptied her tote bag. Peeking out from under the tablecloth, she tried to make sense of the pockets of fighting going on everywhere she looked.

Sparkle Pecs (in a confusing blend of his wrestling vampire character turned zombie) held one of the groomsmen over his head. He threw him onto one of the round white tables. The table crashed in on itself, and the tablecloth swallowed the groomsman in a tangle of linen.

Shattering centerpieces mixed tinkling sounds with women's screams and men's roars of rage. Chairs bounced across the dance floor where Daniel stood and fought. In his Atomic Waist attire with zombie blood running from his head, down his face, and across that amazing six-pack, he grabbed a fistful of a man's white shirt. His other fist hit the man's face, as another man in a torn shirt tried to grab Daniel's arms. Spenser grabbed what was left of that torn shirt. She swung the man in a circle trying to keep him away from Daniel, until the man tripped on his own feet, dragging himself and Spenser to the floor. Toonie rushed up and put her hands under Spenser's armpits, picking her up and walking her away while trying to yell some sense into her head.

Men and women yelled, trying to pull friends away from the fight. Two women in blue satin gowns rolled across the floor in a hair pulling match.

Madison turned in time to see Dewey Decimator run and jump on a table and use it for a launch pad. He leaped onto a small group that was beating up Sparkle Pecs. Madison could only see his elbows coming up and his fists going down, but she couldn't see who was on the receiving end.

She was trying to tell the real blood from the fake blood when another chair flew through the air. It landed in a cluster of fighters near where Target, on the floor, held her foot in pain as Crystal tried to examine it. The faux hawk guy from the elevator ran up to Target, scooping her up in his arms. He carried her away from the fighting and out the doors as Crystal hurried after them.

Madison realized her friends must be here because of her, because Target remembered the blue satin gowns from the elevator and knew they were on the second floor.

Across the room Madison saw ExBoy and Jason. They were back to back, punching and swinging, fending off young men who'd removed their suit coats, fighting in their slacks and cummerbunds. A punchbowl skidded across the floor nearby.

Madison didn't know where to look or how to stop the mayhem. She scrambled out from under the table and ran up to Daniel who'd just thrown off an opponent. "Daniel!"

He turned, surprised, yelling, "Madison! Are you okay?"

"I'm all right! Help me get to ExBoy! He has my mom's number in his phone!"

They ran to where ExBoy and Jason were doing their best but were definitely outnumbered. Daniel grabbed the back waistline of a man's pants with his left hand and slung him around backward into a second guy, causing both to go down stunned, while Daniel's right fist plowed into a third, making an opening for Madison to get close to ExBoy.

She yelled, "Your phone! Call Ann!"

ExBoy threw the phone to her. Then Daniel, Jason, and ExBoy surrounded her, forming a protective bubble.

She called her mom. The call connected.

Ann, speaking quickly and panicky, said, "Xander, we're in the lobby. Have you found Madison?"

"Mom!" Madison cried over the din, her mother's voice sounding wonderful to her. "We need help! Second floor, wedding reception. We have Jerry!"

"What?"

"Hurry! And Mom? The zombies are the good guys!"

Just then she saw Jerry at the back of the room, crouched at the end of the hallway. He sprang out to make a run for it. Madison dropped the phone, bursting out from the protective bubble, and tore off after him.

In the three seconds she ran at him, picking up speed, she didn't know what the hell she would do when she caught him. But she'd be damned if she'd let him get away after everything he had done. She was sick of the nightmare he'd created and wanted it over—now.

She leaped in her best imitation of football games she'd seen on TV over the years, her shoulder slamming into the side of his ribcage. With one arm around his back, the other arm around his belly, her arms locked down one of his arms in her clutch as they sprawled to the floor.

She was shocked to find that her tackle was effective. It also hurt like hell.

He rolled across the floor with her, and she didn't know how long she could hang on, since every limb ached. Her skin still hurt from the scraping impact with the floor. Worn out muscles from fighting with the zombie fairies, combined with bruises and cuts from table corners, added to the indignity of wrestling a man on a hard dance floor.

She'd never been trained on how to fight, so this was the best she could do. She thought of poor Vladik, the passionate old Russian warrior lying in the back storage room, having tried to right a wrong. She held on even though Jerry was hitting her with his one arm, trying to stomp down on her legs with his feet, dragging them both halfway up off the floor before falling back again, Madison's body taking the brunt. His savage desperation put real wounds next to the latex wounds. She closed her eyes, and gritted her teeth; her arms like a vice, she held on.

A familiar voice said, "I'll take it from here."

She felt herself being quickly pulled up and away from Jerry as she gladly released her grip. She thought her heart would burst as her big strong grandfather got her out of harm's way.

Then as Jerry tried to scrabble across the floor Vincent grabbed him. He wadded up Jerry's expensive collar in one fist, and with the other he poured his fury into Jerry's face in one spectacular blow, knocking Jerry out as well as some teeth.

The FBI traitor slumped to the floor.

Vincent held his motionless right hand within his left hand, likely having broken it, as he said, "God damn, that felt fantastic!"

"WELL, THE GOOD news," said Daniel through a lower fat lip and swollen jaw, his right leg limping as he walked up, "is no one wants to press charges."

They were all sitting up against a wall just outside the wedding reception room. All the guests from the wedding reception had gone home. Madison's group of friends had stuck around, having been mildly or moderately involved in the events surrounding Madison and the FBI. They each had questions to answer, giving their version of how things went down. Seemingly satisfied for now the authorities said they could go.

"You're kidding!" said Sparkle Pecs. A cut above his left eyebrow counterbalanced one bloody nostril. "I know we won most of those fights. They don't want to get even?"

"We won because half of those guys were drunk, you idiot," said Dewey, his black eye swollen mostly at the bottom half of the eye. He followed up his comment with his usual punch to Sparky's shoulder, but this time it produced pained groans from both of them as Dewey bit his lower lip, shaking his sore hand, while Sparky held his tender shoulder.

"No," said Daniel. "They're not pressing charges because they know we could press charges back. They attacked *us* when we ran in."

Toonie said, "No one wants any trouble that'll last longer than their injuries." She had her tall chef's hat in her lap, her puffy white hair looking none the worse for wear.

"What about the hotel?" asked Spenser. "They're not pressing charges either?"

With a fat lip like Daniel's and a purple bruise blooming on his left cheek, ExBoy said, "They probably don't want word getting out that a murder happened at their hotel."

"Okay, so that's the good news," said Dewey. "What's the bad news?"

"The elevators are out of order."

"No way—"

"Nuh-uh!"

"Yup."

"No way!"

"We have to take the stairs?"

"All the way up?"

A chorus of moans and groans sounded at this news.

"Can't we camp out by the elevator till it's fixed?"

"Or sleep at the booth?

"I'm hungry."

Madison sat against the wall with her friends but leaned into her grandfather, his good arm around her, a temporary sling for his broken hand on the other arm until he could get it x-rayed. He'd been relegated to the wall with everyone else; something about missing teeth.

She loved hearing her friends carry on about normal problems, aches and pains that would heal and go away, complaints that made them all feel like they were in this together. She hadn't been this happy in a while.

Yet she knew that new problems awaited her small family. The Cruz family, population three, had just increased by one, making it four as far as Madison was concerned. But Grandpa warned her that it was going to be a hard sell for Ann. Madison's mother was not upset with her father, Vincent Cruz. Not in the least. She thought him the most decent and wonderful man. But they couldn't get Ann to even talk about Veronica Fedora. Madison knew it wasn't fair if Ann wouldn't at least hear the whole story.

But for now, Madison was going to enjoy the fact that Grandpa was safe and not in trouble with the authorities. They had offered to waive any illegal adoption charges in exchange for his testimony against Jerry Rosser.

Nearby, Madison heard Agent Cole say, "Vladik was still wired, so even though he was dead, we got everything that was said near his body. It's more than enough to convict."

Aaron Reed stepped up to him, offering his hand, saying, "It was a pleasure working with you. I'm sure you'll be glad to get back home."

"We have to figure out how to get this stuff off, first," said Agent Riley. "This damned glitter gets everywhere. You can follow it like breadcrumbs to see where we've been."

Aaron chuckled. "Better you than me."

"You realize we'll never live this down?" said Agent Cole.

"Ah, come on," said Agent Riley. "I had a blast. How many special agents can say they had to dress up as a zombie fairy in order to help catch a double agent?"

"Hopefully, none."

Madison looked around, wondering when her mother would get back. Their initial depressurizing hug had been brief and not nearly enough. Her mother had remained professional, seeking assurance that Madison was all right, then immediately donned her special agent persona and gone to work.

There was a brief moment when her mother had looked down at Madison's stomach. Her face had twisted into confusion upon seeing the outline of the small revolver Madison had hidden in her zombie bathing suit.

Madison said, "No. I'm not pregnant with a gun."

She leaned forward from the wall, looking down the line of her friends to where Toonie and Crystal sat together.

"Toonie?" said Madison. "I'm sorry the day turned into this. I didn't realize—"

"Don't apologize," said Toonie. "I had a wonderful time. I haven't had this kind of fun since Vegas when four showgirls all realized they were dating the same man."

They all turned their heads in Toonie's direction.

"I really enjoyed that fight. I watched them beat the crap out of each other till the fighting got so bad, they'd ripped up their costumes and torn out hair before I tried to stop it."

"Why'd you wait so long?" asked Madison.

"Because I was dating him, too," she smiled.

At about that moment, the faux hawk guy came up to them carrying Target. Her arms were around his neck where a tattoo peeked out from under his collar.

Madison stood on weak legs, and steadied herself by the wall before walking over to them. She gave Target an appreciative hug as Target sat in the arms of the new guy. Madison said, "Thank you, Target. If you hadn't sounded the alarm, I don't know what would have happened."

"If we hadn't come up here to the wedding reception, I may not have seen Wyatt again. Everybody?" Target gestured to the man holding her. "This is Wyatt. Wyatt? This is everybody."

A chorus of "Hi, Wyatt" followed.

Wyatt nodded, seeming a little shy, and only had eyes for Target.

"Let me know what the doctor says about your foot," said Madison. "I can come help out at Robot Moon till you're able to move around again."

"Thanks," said Target. "I'll keep that in mind."

"Well," said ExBoy, "if you all can make it up to my room, I'll feed you and we can clean up our cuts. Room service on me."

Several voices insisted on pitching in on that effort. They all slowly and with great pain, tried to move, find their feet, and help each other up.

"If you guys don't mind," said Madison, "I want to spend some time with my family."

"I think we all understand that," said Spenser, coming over for a goodbye hug. "Call me. I want all the details." She smiled at Madison before going over to put her arm around Daniel, and helping him limp away.

Jason, with chin abrasions on his right side that seemed to match the scratches next to his right eye, also had a big bump on his forehead near the hairline. His knuckles were pretty cut up and swollen but his hands seemed to work well enough. He and ExBoy stood up at about the same moment, looking at each other, poker-faced, each giving a small nod to the other.

Madison figured that was probably as close as they would get to being okay with each other.

Jason turned to Madison and Vincent. "Well, I'm going to get going. My grandfather will want the blow by blow."

"You tell Mitch he can be proud of his grandkid," said Grandpa. "I'll tell him myself tomorrow." He shook Jason's hand, and Jason winced but smiled.

Madison put her hand on top of Jason's in a protective gesture. "Careful," she said.

He touched her hair with his other hand and said, "It's okay. I'm all right. Everything's going to be all right."

She blinked, trying to let his words sink in.

Grandpa said, "I should go see both Mitch and Ray tomorrow. They'll be glad to hear the news."

While they were talking, Madison went up to ExBoy, taking his hands. She said, "I'm sorry you got hurt."

"Hey, you said I was too pretty. Doesn't this make me look all rugged and shit?"

She laughed, "It does." Then sighing, she said, "Leave it to you to look even sexier when you're beat up." He was watching her. She knew he was waiting for more.

She said, "I want to get to know him."

He nodded. "I figured." He held her chin in his hand, lightly brushing her lower lip with his thumb. "But he has *no clue* what he's in for with you. He'll make you feel tied down inside of two months."

She started to protest but he pressed that thumb on her lips as he said, "Just remember, it's not about proving me wrong. It's about you finding your happiness. So take some time. Find yourself and all that." He tilted her chin up to make her look him in the eyes. "I'll be around."

He looked up, and Madison saw him see her mother walking back from an impromptu meeting with the special agents from headquarters.

ExBoy said, "Gotta go." He held her gaze a moment longer, kissed her cheek, and walked away, joining the limping brigade as they headed for the stairs.

Turning her head back toward Ann and seeing that her mother was not in conversation with anyone, Madison took advantage of the moment. She came forward without saying a word and put her arms around her mother. She didn't let go. And somewhere in the next minute, the polite hug turned to holding, though it was unclear who was holding whom. They each had silent tears running down their cheeks, and seemed content to stay that way for a while.

Finally, with much sniffling, they backed away, and Ann reached into her pocket, bringing out tissues for them both.

Madison said "All this time, you knew Jerry was being investigated."

"Yes, for selling secrets, but I never suspected his involvement with Dad all these years. It explains a lot. Wish I could knock out the rest of his teeth."

Madison asked, "Did you see the things on the floor where I dumped out my tote bag?"

Her mother nodded, her dark eyes tearing up afresh. "I found that metal box when I was thirteen. It explained why I never looked like anyone else in the family." She pulled out another tissue, dabbing her eyes. "That's why I went out and got pregnant. So I could keep the baby and prove a point." She sniffed, wiping her nose. "Then I wound up abandoning you anyway."

Madison used to wish that her mother would admit it. But now that she had, it hurt too much to hear, and to see her mother's pain. "Mom, it's okay. We're going to move on now. Right?"

"Right."

"We'll do fun things together."

"Right."

"We'll go out drinking."

"Uh...right."

"We'll go dancing and we'll get you hooked up with a guy."

"Now wait..."

"I'll show you how to get free drinks by dancing sexy on the bar."

"Now wait just a minute young lady!"

Madison winked at her, saying, "See? I still need a mom."

Ruffled but smiling, Ann exhaled. "You certainly do."

Epilogue

MADISON CHECKED HER makeup in Toonie's bathroom mirror one more time. She wanted to look extra pretty today. Everything needed to be perfect. She heard the tinkling of fine china coming from Toonies's kitchen, and wandered back into the living room with its tiny excuse for a dining room off to the side.

"Did I hear china dishes?" asked Madison.

"That you did," said Toonie. "I don't get enough opportunities to use them. It's a shame, too, because I own a nice set."

Madison walked over to the sink where Toonie had set down a few stacks of small dessert plates, with matching teacups and saucers, from a high shelf.

"Ooh," said Madison. "Butterflies. And blossoms." She loved the delicate colors of the butterfly wings on the flowers, with the occasional pop of color. "These are pretty!"

"Thanks. It seems like a good chance to use them," said Toonie.

Madison couldn't help herself. She put her arms around Toonie in a spontaneous hug. "Thank you for doing this. I'm so nervous. I want this to work so bad."

Toonie hugged back, patting her on the back. "Everything will be all right. You just need to give them time. It's not going to come overnight, but I think you're giving them a good start. I'm just flattered that I get to be involved."

"Are you kidding? It's your recipe. Those cookies could go a long way toward making everyone comfortable. And frankly, having you around makes *me* more comfortable. I feel like I'm barely getting to know my mom, and now there's a new grandmother in the mix."

She walked over to the table to check the flowers one more time. "It kind of rattles me, you know?"

"She doesn't look old enough to be a grandmother, your Nika. At least not enough to have a granddaughter your age."

"She said she was fourteen when she had Mom. And I think Mom was about fifteen when she had me, so our ages are a little too close for normal."

"Well, no getting around it kid, your family dynamic is unusual. But that doesn't mean it can't work."

Madison was quiet for a moment. Then she said, "It just seems like they need each other. Mom is fighting it the most, but she needs it the most. She probably wouldn't come if she knew Nika was going to be here."

"Give her time," said Toonie.

The heavenly aroma of Toonie's fresh baked secret recipe cookies filled the air. They would come out of the oven soon.

Madison went to check her laptop, making sure it was powered up. The montage, starring Anna Lisa Cruz, was going to be fun, whether her mother liked it or not.

She smiled to herself. *So this is what it feels like to force some goodwill on someone.*

"Thank goodness the weather has lightened up a little," said Toonie. "Makes it easier to do a little baking."

"I love it. Waking up to the rain this morning was such a relief. It made the air feel clean and fresh again."

She set the laptop on top of a short bookcase near the small dining table. She played with the angle of the screen, making sure it could be seen by all four chairs at the table. She checked the volume, leaving it set at the right amount.

Lastly, she queued up the montage she'd been working on all week. She'd used the old photos from the family album of Ann's baby pictures. Her first steps, her first solid food. Her first little Mary Jane black patent leather shoes. All recorded by her parents. All saved and in the montage for Nika to see and experience.

Her mother needed to forgive Nika for not being there, the way Madison had to forgive Ann. *We both have a second chance to get to know our mothers.*

There was nothing left to do but wait. And hope.

Toonie brought the china dishes over to the table, setting them at each place setting. There was a knock. Madison felt that rare flutter of stage fright, checked her clothes to make sure everything looked right, then went to the door and let Veronica Fedora into Toonie's home. Nika brought a bouquet of multi-colored roses that Madison put in water right away, adding them to the table.

She and Nika looked at each other, their nerves on high alert. And the irony did not escape Madison that here they were, an international spy and a singing telegram, both professions that required staying cool under pressure. Both were accustomed to thinking fast on their feet, improvising, and moving with confidence. Yet Ann had this effect on them. She and her grandmother Nika wanted this so much. They had talked, plotted, and schemed. Now they were nervous to see if it would work.

There was a knock at the door. Madison and Nika flew into a tight hug, and Madison whispered, "Curtain."

The End

The Elite Readers List are the first ones to find out about new releases, sales, or giveaways. Sign up for the Elite Readers List at LucyCarol.com.

Thank you so much for reading Madison's story in HOT SCHEMING MESS. If you thought that was fun, you'll love KILL THE CRAZY. Find out what happens when Madison joins her mother, her new grandmother, and her best friend Spenser for a day in a high-class luxury spa. They want to get to know each other, but leave it to Madison to stumble into trouble. Read on for a preview.

Kill the Crazy

Chapter One

MADISON TRIED TO be a good girl, damn it. She told herself to go along with it: don't complain, don't spoil everyone's fun, don't tell everyone they were all going to die.

As their enclosed gondola rounded to the top of the giant Ferris wheel, she convinced herself that she was pulling it off; that no one knew about her panic. As long as she kept her eyes away from the four glass walls surrounding them, resisting the urge to look down at the ground, she'd be fine. Thank God the floor wasn't glass too.

There was a nice paycheck at the end of this gig, although she'd have to give Phil a piece of her mind when it was over. He knew damn well she had a fear of heights, but he had let her think the photo shoot would take place in the restaurant at the foot of the Ferris wheel. She'd like to think her agent would look out for her sanity as well as her employment, but she wasn't too surprised. Phil would book his own grandmother for a dog fight if the price were right.

The costume she wore was a Blue Heron, Seattle's official bird. It was her job to pose for publicity pictures with Iris Alexander, the wealthy owner of the soon-to-be-built Blue Heron Mall. Iris's sleek brown hair reflected the sunlight as they sat together, glass wall behind them. A sweep of high-rise buildings filled the background. The morning sun ignited the dazzle of the city.

"Hey, bird person," said an irritated voice, breaking Madison's concentration. She looked up at the thin, blond photographer as he lowered his camera. With a big sigh he said, "Would you please stop staring at the floor?"

She took a deep breath and fixed her eyes on him, trying to ignore the glass walls in her peripheral vision.

"That's right. Look at me. Let us see those pretty green eyes." He aimed the camera, his voice taking on a cheerful quality. "You and the client person... celebrating... you're so happy..."

Madison concentrated. *Look at the camera, look at the camera...*

"Okay, now you're a deer in the headlights," he said, rubbing his face.

"I'm sorry," she said, panicking for new reasons. A big paycheck was at stake here, so she had to get a grip. *Think of the money, think of the money.*

"I'm happy now, see?" She put on her most dazzling smile. "Celebrating…" As she turned her head to show the client her gorgeous smile, she smacked Iris's forehead with the long skinny beak. "Oh! Sorry, Iris!"

With a subtle jerk of her head, Iris remained composed, leaning away from Madison to smooth down her hair, its shoulder length cut falling perfectly back into place. She smiled politely and motioned to her nearby assistant. "A little help here?"

The assistant stood up to a partially bent position, her flawless skin and deep ruby lips suggesting her attention to detail. The gondola was not tall enough to stand fully upright in, unless a person was under five foot four, which the assistant clearly was not. She came forward to check Iris's perfect hair, pretending to fix something. With a sharp glance at Madison, the assistant's gray eyes conveyed disapproval. Then stepping back to her seat next to the photographer, she scribbled a note on a clipboard.

Madison wondered if those notes were about her. She felt tattled on.

Dramatic sighs came from the photographer. "We only have a few more minutes before they start to rotate the wheel again," he said, looking at Madison. "Please don't make me lose my shot."

"Troy dear, I'm not worried," said Iris, leaning back in, close to Madison. "You always manage to pull off miracles."

He smiled. "That's why you're my favorite client person. You have faith in me."

"And it helps that she rented the entire wheel," said Madison in a sunny voice, "so our gondola can stay at the top."

All three turned to look at her in silence. She gently flapped her wings on her thighs, noting how difficult it was to maintain credibility when you're dressed like a bird. "I was just saying how lucky we are," she added.

The assistant looked down and scribbled another note.

Madison could feel the headpiece of her costume coming loose, causing the beak to droop. But with feathers for hands she needed help to fix it.

"Okay, let's try this again," said Troy.

"Um, could I get some help from the assistant person?" she asked. "My head piece is getting wobbly."

"Excuse me?" The assistant's face went hard. "I have a name. It's Catherine Gabrielle."

Madison's headpiece continued to fall forward. She pushed it back up with her feathered appendage. "I'm sorry Catherine, I didn't mean—"

"Ca-ther-ine Ga-bri-elle," she said slowly, looking Madison in the eye. There seemed to be an expectation, so Madison repeated the name while the assistant joined in unison.

"Ca-ther-ine Ga-bri-elle," they said.

More sighs from Troy. "Client person, while they're working this out, would you scoot forward in your seat, please?" he asked pleasantly. "That's it. Big pretty smile. When the bird person is ready, we'll have her leaning over right behind you. Those blue feathers will make your eyes pop."

Madison shoved her headpiece back up, harder this time. "Never mind about the head piece," she said in resignation. "This is fine." She leaned behind Iris, trying not to look at the window, not look at the floor, not be a deer in the headlights. Instead she focused on pleasant thoughts. *Plot Phil's demise, plot Phil's demise...*

"Bird person, turn your head to a profile behind Iris's head... no... please don't shut your eyes... come on. That's it. Now tilt your beak upward so that—"

Suddenly the gondola vibrated as the giant Ferris wheel began to turn again. Madison jumped, throwing her winged arms up with a scream, propelling herself away from the glass and into Iris and the photographer.

The assistant took a note.

✧   ✧   ✧

"PHIL, YOU DON'T understand," said Madison into her cell phone. "They'd have nothing to complain about if you hadn't booked me for a photo shoot in a glass cage, 175 feet up in the air!"

She threw her tote bag onto her bed and pulled the hairband from her ponytail. Her shiny dark hair spilled over her shoulders while she tried to rub the tension out of her head with one hand.

"You should be grateful," he said in his Boston street accent. "That was a fantastic gig for you. I'm always looking out for my little Chocolate Mint." Phil often likened her pale green eyes, fringed with black lashes, to chocolate mints.

"Don't 'Chocolate Mint' me," she said. "I was terrified. Afterward, I couldn't stop apologizing to Iris."

"And here I thought the scariest part would be working with Iris Alexander herself," said Phil. "You could get pointers on how to eat your rival for lunch from what I hear."

"At least she was the nicest of the three of them," said Madison. She dug around inside her tote bag looking for the gift envelope that Nika, her new Russian grandmother, had given her.

"Well she plays hardball in all her business interests, I'll tell you that," said Phil. "Having money ain't enough for her. Iris likes to win."

Madison sighed. "I can't imagine what it's like to not worry about money."

"Which is why I get you good gigs."

"And why I do them even if they're up in the air. But have a heart next time, will you, Phil? You know I have a hard time with heights."

"Yeah? Well, how about paychecks? You have a hard time with those too? That's going to be a big one, you know. Jen almost killed me when I gave the job to you instead of her."

"Well maybe you should've given it to her. Then you wouldn't be getting complaints from Ca-ther-ine Ga-bri-elle."

She found the envelope and exhaled in relief. It held the potential to make this all go away. It was a day pass for two people to a luxury spa. She and her girlfriend Spenser had been invited to meet up with Nika and Madison's mother, Ann, for a special afternoon of pampering.

"You kidding?" said Phil. "I can't trust Jen with classy clients, you know that. The complaints would've been about being trapped in that glass cage with a naked maniac."

"You might have a point," said Madison.

"You know Jen. There's no gig that she thinks can't be made better by taking everything off."

"Phil, I'm just saying that I can't do my best work when I'm scared."

"Come on, Minty," his voice softened, "I knew it'd be a little tough for you, but I also knew that you always pull through, girl. And this time is no exception."

"How can you say that? The assistant called you and ratted me out. They may withhold payment over this."

"I say it because Troy called me after I hung up with the assistant, and he's thrilled. They don't dare withhold payment if they want to use that shot."

"I don't get it," said Madison. "What shot? The whole thing was a screw up."

"That last shot was the money shot, Minty. He loves it. Iris Alexander loves it."

"The last... what?" She sat down on the bed.

"He said it was an action shot, that you were freakin' out, throwing your arms up or something. But it looked like the Blue Heron opened its wings like the stupid bird is blessing Iris or some garbage, and they can see the head piece and beak, but your scream was hidden behind Iris's head, her beaming smile, blah blah blah." He took a breath. "Doesn't matter. They're *happy,* you understand? You'll be seeing that shot all over Seattle. They're even buying bus ads. How do you like that, eh? My little Minty on a bus."

"It *worked out?*" She couldn't believe it.

"Sure did. But now I gotta find extra gigs for Jen to make it up to her or she'll make my life hell after what happened at her gig."

"I'm afraid to ask."

"She was hoping you'd chicken out at the last minute on account of the height and all that, so she made changes to her costume to look like a Blue Heron."

"How can a stripper look like a Blue Heron?"

"She put lots of blue feathers in key places, if you know what I mean. Assumed she could rush over to the Blue Heron gig and be a sexy little birdie or something. But she used the wrong glue for that sort of thing and those feathers wouldn't come off during her dance without a lot of yanking and cursing."

After hanging up, Madison got ready for the spa. The morning's gig was behind her now, and she could let herself relax a little, maybe get some of that tension out of her shoulders. She tried to let the good news sink in that the photo shoot wasn't as disastrous as she'd thought. The shot would even be used as a bus ad, although no one would be able to tell it was Madison. She pursed her lips as she gave that some thought.

Looking at the clock she noted it was almost time to make the obligatory scream call. After all, Spenser and she were about to be partaking of the most talked about luxury spa in Seattle, The Lazy Petal. She had to hurry.

She changed her clothes and packed her bag for the spa, hoping she could afford a massage. As she thought about the bus ad, she decided she was glad no one would recognize her since she didn't want to tell her mom about it anyway. They were getting along better than they ever had, and she didn't want to ruin it by reminding her mother of the main thing she still disapproved of: Madison's job.

She was eager to see if her mother and Nika were getting along better than the last time she'd seen them together, which was at a gun range. Her mom had finally come to accept the truth about Nika as her own biological mother, and had invited her to some target practice. This seemed like an odd getting-to-know-you outing, but as uncomfortable as Madison was around guns, she couldn't resist the invitation to come along.

No doubt about it, the shock of how Nika entered their lives had thrown a new light on everything. Watching her mother take tentative steps toward forming a relationship with Nika made Madison proud of her. Ann may have spent her days fighting crime as an FBI Special Agent, but this was the bravest thing Madison had ever seen her do.

Her cell phone doodled a happy tune. Darn it, Spenser beat her to it. She picked up her phone, hit the answer button and put the phone to her ear. Silence. She waited the customary two seconds because she-who-makes-the-call gets to scream first. Spenser screamed into the phone and Madison screamed back and hung up. At twenty-four years old they still hadn't grown tired of this little ritual left over from their high school days.

She was glad that Spenser would be there to share in all the fun. It made Madison happy that Ann was giving Nika a chance, but they needed more time, and the spa was as good a place as any for everyone to continue getting to know each other.

What could possibly go wrong?

Chapter Two

"**O**H MY GOD, Spenser. It's him," Madison whispered. "Stay in line, and don't move." Her breathy whisper had panic in it.

Madison ducked behind Spenser as the spa manager in black uniform passed the line of women at the check-in counter.

"What, the manager?" whispered Spenser. "Why?"

"Act natural," said Madison. "I swear it's him."

"Him who?" whispered Spenser.

"The guy."

"What guy?"

"You're not acting natural."

"Me? What about you?"

"I'm not supposed to be acting natural," said Madison as she hid her face behind Spenser's blond hair. "I'm hiding, for God's sake."

"What guy, damn it?" said Spenser.

"The guy I buried alive."

"Oh." Spenser blinked, as the thought seemed to sink in. "So… you think he's still mad?"

In the posh front lobby, the line moved forward, bringing Madison and Spenser closer to the check-in counter. Black uniformed clerks with pleasant smiles greeted each patron, the plastic clacking of keyboards filling the room as they checked them in.

Stepping behind the counter, the dark haired manager mumbled to a lady in black uniform. Her neat ponytail swept across her shoulder as she turned her head toward him.

"Clare, in case I don't see Lettie," said the manager, "could you remind her I need to leave for a dental appointment this afternoon?" Looking grim, he walked away.

"It's safe," said Spenser. "He's gone. Reminds me of a cute college professor I had."

Madison came out from behind Spenser and snapped her fingers, remembering. "Frank Bergman. That was his name."

"Don't say 'was' as if he died. He's not the dearly departed."

"No. He's the pissed and present."

"It was an accident, Madison. It could happen to anybody."

Madison looked her in the eye, making her point with her silence.

"Okay, you're right," said Spenser. "This stuff only happens to you. But still, it was an accident. The prop malfunctioned."

"The crew tried to explain it to him but he wouldn't listen."

"Kind of hard to listen when you're traumatized. But that was, what… two years ago?"

Madison looked around, her eyes full of concern. "If he sees me, don't say anything about Mom and Nika in front of him. I don't want him to involve them."

"Come on," said Spenser, pushing Madison's dark hair back behind her shoulders. "You're making a big deal out of nothing."

"Well I did, you know, sort of bury him and stuff."

"Well, yeah, there's that."

"Surely he has lots of administrative things to do in his office?" said Madison, trying to encourage herself.

"And while he's in his office we'll all be getting pampered in The Lazy Petal," said Spenser, gently shaking Madison's shoulders.

Madison's smile slowly returned. Coming to the front of the line, she handed the day pass to a clerk whose name badge read Clare. Clare smiled and entered their information in the computer. Looking at her screen, she asked, "Are you Madison Cruz?"

"Yes."

Her brow creased. She typed some more and stared. "I'm sorry. I should probably get the manager to help me."

"I'd rather not bother him," said Madison, trying to think fast. "It's just a day pass from my grandmother. If it's expired I'll pay for it myself." She felt Spenser squeeze her arm. They both knew how expensive that would be.

"Quite the opposite," said Clare. "There's a new account set up for you. All services are available to you every day, and all charges are waived." She put her fingertips to her cheek. "I've never seen one like this." She looked up at Madison. "Please forgive me for not knowing who you are."

Madison's face felt stuck. She finally managed to say, "What?"

"Are you an actress?" said Clare.

"Well, I... was a bird this morning."

An older woman with perfect makeup and gray streaked hair in a stylish bob appeared behind the counter and looked over Clare's shoulder. "Well, what have we here?" Her eyes lit up with interest as she scanned the screen. Her name tag on her black uniform jacket read, Lettie, Assistant Manager.

"Thank goodness you're here," said Clare. "None of the usual codes are working. I've never seen an account like this."

Clare stepped back as Lettie took over. She typed with impeccable nails, her eyes scanning the screen. "Who set this up for you, dear?" She looked at Madison.

"I don't know. There must be some mistake," said Madison. "My grandmother gave me a day pass for two. That's all."

"Your grandmother's name?"

"Veronica Fedora." Lettie typed as Madison spoke. "We call her Nika. She has a permanent day pass and can bring visitors if she likes."

Lettie scanned the screen. "Yes, I see that here. And now it's been extended to you. Curious." She looked at Madison. "Your grandmother has no address."

Madison had no answer for her. What would be safe to say? She wanted to wrap her arms around herself, but resisted.

"Is she friends with the owner?" asked Lettie.

"I don't know," said Madison, her discomfort growing. "She said it was an added thank you for work she did for the owner." She almost wished Frank Bergman would come out and make a fuss. Anything to change this subject.

Lettie held her gaze on Madison for a moment, her expression neither approving nor disapproving. Finally she said, "Such privilege is rare around here."

Lettie turned to Clare. "Frank must have set it up. You'll need to use the VIP code to check them in."

"I thought that code was only reserved for the owner, or her family," said Clare.

"Yes," said Lettie. "It was." She returned her gaze to Madison. "What does your grandmother do?"

Answering Lettie's question made her nervous. Nika was ex-KGB, and Madison wasn't comfortable trying to describe the employment Nika had turned to after the KGB was shut down years ago. It could be called private investigating at best, mercenary spy work at worst. Had Nika and Ann had that talk yet? She'd like to be a fly on the wall for that one.

"Dance teacher," Madison blurted out. "She's a dance teacher." *Oh that's just brilliant Madison. Stupid, stupid...*

"Really?" said Lettie, looking confused.

"Um, yeah, she really knows how to do a good shuffle ball-change."

Lettie and Clare both stared at her. Even Spenser was staring at her. Anxious to get out of there, Madison asked, "So, is everything okay now?"

"Certainly," said Lettie, shaking it off and entering the correct code for a VIP account.

She turned a cool smile their way. "Welcome to The Lazy Petal."

✧   ✧   ✧

"I SHOULD BE thrilled. I should be happy. So why am I nervous instead?" Madison closed the door to her locker, having changed out of her street clothes and into the required spa robe and hair towel. The front check-in lobby led straight into the locker room, so they hadn't actually seen the main spa area yet. Spenser was still neatly folding everything and putting it in her locker, arranging her belongings into some kind of order that to Madison, as usual, seemed like overkill. But she knew Spenser was more peaceful when everything was neat and tidy.

"I think it's because of the way that older lady acted, as if the day pass were suspicious. She should've been happy for you. I don't know. It did feel odd."

"I keep thinking there's some kind of mistake and I'll accidentally run up a bill that's bigger than my rent."

"In this place, that's not hard to imagine, but you should talk to your grandmother. Let her assure you that everything's okay," said Spenser. "Besides, she must have danced pretty hard for this." Her eyes held laughter in them like she could barely contain herself, and in a very unladylike manner, she snorted, falling into giggles.

Madison rolled her eyes. "I had to say *something* about what she does. That was the first thing that entered my head."

"And what are you going to do about Frank?"

"What do you mean?"

"Well she said Frank must have set up your account. If he did, then he knows you're here. If he didn't, then... well..." Spenser trailed off.

"It's all right," said Madison. "You can say it."

"If he didn't, that would only leave Nika, right? And she probably knows how to do stuff like that, right?"

Madison was quiet for a moment. "We don't really know her very well, yet. That's true. But she wouldn't risk causing trouble over something as stupid as a spa pass. So you're probably right about Frank." She didn't know what else she could do but ride out the day. If she ran into Frank, she hoped he would be cordial, and who knows, he might even let her explain that awful day.

Minutes later they left the locker room for the main hallway, stepping out barefooted onto a floor with threads of red embedded in pale marble tiles.

"Holy mackerel," said Madison, coming to a stop in the doorway. The door swung closed, gently hitting her backside like a push of encouragement. "This hallway is wider than my bedroom."

"Everything is wider than your bedroom."

Recessed lighting hidden along the edges of high ceilings threw a soft glow on the walls.

"Look at this place," said Spenser, turning in a circle, her eyes sparkling.

"Take it easy, Spensy. You might hit critical mass and implode."

"I'll die happy."

"But I would miss you," said Madison. "Should I throw down some trash and break the spell?"

"You do, and I'll shoot you."

"No you won't. That would get blood on the pretty floor."

"It's gorgeous." Spenser looked down at the marble tiles. "Looks like streaks of raspberry puree swirled on a frothy cream."

They sighed.

"I feel guilty walking on it," said Spenser.

"I want to eat it," said Madison.

"I think I could still shoot you. Blood coordinates with raspberry. You could get shot in here and match the decor."

"Wow," said Madison. "They thought of everything."

Soft harp music followed them down the hallway, reminding Madison of glass slippers and fairytales. Barefooted ladies passed by in identical robes and hair towels, some of them carrying glasses of wine, some of them with creams or mud on their faces.

On the left side of the hallway was a wall made of rounded gray stones on the bottom half, while the upper half was glass, covered in fluffy white curtains so sheer Madison could see through them to golden points of candlelight that shimmered next to the deep blue of the pools. It was like seeing heaven through a white fog.

In a breathy voice, Spenser said. "It's like a dream. How do you get in there?"

"I'm not sure. I think we're on the south end right now, but this hallway is supposed to run along the south and east sides of the pool room, so I guess we'll come to the entryway if we keep walking."

"But that's huge. Look how far the hallway stretches," said Spenser. "Why would they need a pool that large?"

"It's not one pool, it's four. All free of chemicals, can you believe it? And each pool is a different temperature depending on your preference."

Spenser knit her brows. "But how can that work? The chemicals I mean, how do they keep it clean?"

"The brochure said something about copper and silver ions." Madison shrugged. "I don't understand it, but wouldn't it be cool to go swimming without our eyes getting red?" She looked to the right side of the hallway where all the doors to all the specialty salons were. "There's the nail salon. We're too early for our appointments, but let's go see it."

"You go ahead," said Spenser, "I want to go touch the curtains and see if they're made of polyester."

As Madison approached the nail salon, a pretty young woman in black uniform and honey brown hair changed old flowers for fresh ones on a table near the door. Madison turned to call Spenser when she heard a loud pop of pottery hitting the floor and the clink and clatter of pieces scattering. The young woman who had knocked over the vase stood staring at the flowers and the broken pieces of vase. Some of the shards had skittered across the hallway to where Madison stood.

Madison quickly crouched down to pick up the pieces, moving around the floor to wherever she spied another piece, afraid that someone might come along and step on them. Carefully kneeling, she was filling her palm with several small pieces when Lettie the assistant manager emerged from the nail salon and stood in the doorway. Her icy gaze at the young woman did not look happy.

"Brittany," she said, quiet and exasperated as if in a secret rage. "Now what?"

"Why didn't you tell me he was quitting?" said Brittany, petulant, ignoring the broken vase.

Lettie's voice grew frosty. "Is that what this is about? I've run interference with Frank to clear the way for you, and you're willing to gamble the job for a snit fit?"

"I do want the job, it's just that—"

"If you can't stay off Frank's radar—"

With the pieces of broken pottery in her hand, Madison stepped up, interrupting Lettie. "I'm so clumsy, please forgive me," she said, placing the pieces on the table. "I just wanted to smell the flowers."

"Oh—" said Lettie. She seemed surprised, looking quickly at Brittany and back to Madison. "Please don't worry yourself." She smiled. "Brittany will clean it up. Continue enjoying your stay with us, and don't give it another thought." To Brittany she gave a tight smile. "I'm sorry, dear. I thought you'd broken another one. Resume your duties." She turned to leave, but looked back for a moment, silent. She walked down the hallway, rounded a corner and disappeared.

Brittany looked at Madison with confusion. "Why did you do that?"

"It sounded like you were about to lose your job over a broken vase," said Madison. "I couldn't let that happen."

Expecting a thank-you, she was startled when Brittany spit out, "That was an expensive vase. Maybe I was trying to break it. Maybe I'm tired of the shit I have to put up with around here. Did you ever think of that?"

Not sure how to respond, Madison could only stare in disbelief before answering. "I... no. That thought never crossed my mind."

"I hate this place," said Brittany.

Embarrassed that she'd somehow screwed up, Madison still couldn't understand such a contemptuous response. "I'm sorry I said anything. I was only trying to help."

As Spenser walked up, Brittany said, "Things are not what they seem around here. You should stay out of it." Without another word the girl left through the doorway into the nail salon.

"What the hell was that?" Spenser asked.

"Good question," said Madison, confused.

"Another glorious welcome to The Lazy Petal?"

"More like red flags. Some people leave big hints that you should stay away from them."

Knowing they had manicures and pedicures scheduled for later, Madison couldn't help but hope that Brittany would be gone by then.

"Forget her," said Spenser. "Let's go find the massage rooms. We have appointments."

"Just promise me no more challenging people to deal with," said Madison. "I think I've met my quota for today."

"That's a good way to look at it. You've met your quota. Everything will be smooth going from here on out."

"Oh man. You had to say that."

About the Author

Lucy Carol's top priority is to entertain you, and keep you turning pages. She writes mysteries for those who like it fun, fast, and don't mind losing a little sleep. Living and writing in the Pacific Northwest, she loves martinis, flowers, dancing, a good lipstick, and cake. Her background is in the performing arts, having been an actress, voiceover artist, choreographer, and singing telegram.

Keep in touch by visiting LucyCarol.com.